"There's one thing we haven't yet discussed. How you respond may be the difference between my accepting your offer or respectfully declining it."

Oliver folded his hands, his gaze never wavering from her face. "You have my undivided attention."

"Ever since we've met, I've noticed this crazy kind of electricity between us. That's why I think it's important we agree to keep things strictly platonic. Giving in to the attraction would only complicate the situation."

"Electricity?"

The twinkle in those blue eyes had her jerking to her feet, a hot flush shooting up her neck.

"Forget it. Forget I said anything. This isn't going to work." Shannon whirled toward the door.

She'd taken only a step or two when Oliver grabbed her arm, his expression contrite.

"I didn't mean to wind you up. You have my word as a gentleman that I will never take advantage of you while you're under my roof and in my employ."

He stood an arm's breadth away, near enough for the scent of his cologne to tease her nostrils and make her want to lean close. Instead she tilted her head back and once again found herself drowning in the shockingly blue depths of Oliver's eyes. She reconsidered her hardlin... ago.

One kiss.

What would really be wr...

the stance of only a moment.

Does really be strong with one little kiss?

Rescue on the Ranch

Cindy Kirk & Amanda Renee

Previously published as *Fortune's Little Heartbreaker*
and *Wrangling Cupid's Cowboy*

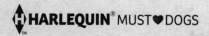

HARLEQUIN® MUST♥DOGS

ISBN-13: 978-1-335-69094-4

Rescue on the Ranch

Copyright © 2019 by Harlequin Books S.A.

First published as Fortune's Little Heartbreaker
by Harlequin Books in 2015
and Wrangling Cupid's Cowboy
by Harlequin Books in 2018.

Recycling programs
for this product may
not exist in your area.

The publisher acknowledges the copyright holder
of the individual works as follows:

Fortune's Little Heartbreaker
Copyright © 2015 by Harlequin Books S.A.

Wrangling Cupid's Cowboy
Copyright © 2018 by Amanda Renee

Special thanks and acknowledgment are given to Cindy Kirk
for her contribution to The Fortunes of Texas: Cowboy Country
miniseries.

For questions and comments about the quality of this book,
please contact us at CustomerService@Harlequin.com.

Printed in U.S.A.

www.Harlequin.com

CONTENTS

FORTUNE'S LITTLE HEARTBREAKER   7
Cindy Kirk

WRANGLING CUPID'S COWBOY   239
Amanda Renee

From the time she was a little girl, **Cindy Kirk** thought everyone made up different endings to books, movies and television shows. Instead of counting sheep at night, she made up stories. She's now had over forty novels published. She enjoys writing emotionally satisfying stories with a little faith and humor tossed in. She encourages readers to connect with her on Facebook and Twitter, @cindykirkauthor, and via her website, cindykirk.com.

Books by Cindy Kirk

Harlequin Special Edition

Rx for Love

The M.D.'s Unexpected Family
Ready, Set, I Do!
The Husband List
One Night with the Doctor
A Jackson Hole Homecoming
The Doctor and Mrs. Right
His Valentine Bride
The Doctor's Not-So-Little Secret
Jackson Hole Valentine

The Fortunes of Texas: Cowboy Country

Fortune's Little Heartbreaker

The Fortunes of Texas: Welcome to Horseback Hollow

A Sweetheart for Jude Fortune

The Fortunes of Texas: Southern Invasion

Expecting Fortune's Heir

Visit the Author Profile page at Harlequin.com for more titles.

FORTUNE'S LITTLE HEARTBREAKER

Cindy Kirk

This book is dedicated to some of my favorite Facebook friends and Fortunes of Texas fans:

Pamela Lowery
Deanna Vrba
Theresa Krupicka
Caro Carson
Nancy Greenfield
Veronica Mower
Mary Spicher
Dyan Carness
Brenda Schultes Bengard
Nancy Callahan Greenfield
Jennifer Faye
Sherri Shackelford
Ann Roth
Holmes Campbell
Michelle Major
Cheri Allan
Susan Meier
Betsy Ehrhardt
Kim Thomas
Laurie Brown
Deborah Farrand
Linda Conrad
Amanda Macfarlane
Lee Ann Kopp-Lopez

Chapter 1

Shannon Singleton took a sip of the Superette's medium roast coffee and exhaled a happy sigh. Since returning to Horseback Hollow several months earlier, she'd come to realize how much she'd missed the town in north Texas where she'd grown up.

The postage-stamp eating area of the Superette consisted of three orange vinyl booths and two tables, each adorned with a bud vase of silk flowers. Nice, but no comparison to the cute little coffee shop Shannon used to frequent when she lived in Lubbock.

Still, the location was bright and cheery. Thanks to a wall of glass windows, Shannon even had a stellar view of the large pothole in the middle of the street.

"I wish they'd choose one of us and get it over with." Rachel Robinson expelled a frustrated sigh and sat back in the booth.

Shannon enjoyed meeting her friend every Tuesday morning for coffee, but frankly was tired of obsessing over—and discussing—the job they both wanted.

It was a bit awkward, being in competition—again—with her friend. The other times Rachel had bested her, it had been over inconsequential things; like the last piece of dessert at the Hollows Cantina or the pair of boots they'd both spotted at that cute little boutique in Vicker's Corners.

This time was different. *This* time the outcome mattered. Professional positions in this small town an hour south of Lubbock were few and far between. And Shannon really wanted the marketing job with the Fortune Foundation.

In the four years since graduation from Texas Tech with a degree in business, all of Shannon's experience had been in marketing. Rachel had readily admitted she didn't have experience in the marketing arena.

But that fact didn't mean squat. Just as with those pretty turquoise boots, it seemed whenever she and Rachel competed for anything, Rachel came out ahead.

"Earth to Shannon."

Shannon brought the cup to her lips and focused on her friend. She and Rachel were both in their midtwenties, had brown hair and similar interests. But that's where the comparison ended. Shannon considered herself slightly above average while Rachel was stunning.

"What? Rewind."

"Wouldn't it be cool if they hired us both?" Rachel smiled at the thought and broke off a piece of scone. The woman's cheerful nature was just one of her many admirable qualities.

"I guess we'll find out…but not until the end of February." Shannon added more cream to her coffee, her tone pensive. "I don't see why it has to take that long. They completed interviews last month."

"It's probably because they're just getting this office location up and running," Rachel said, sounding way too understanding.

Of course her friend could afford to be charitable. She had a job and was earning her way. Shannon was back living with her parents and, other than the chores she performed at the ranch for her mom and dad, had been out of work for over two months. "Just between you and me, I can't believe they're going to open a foundation branch in Horseback Hollow."

"Doesn't surprise me." Rachel laughed. "This town is turning into a Fortune family hot spot."

The Fortunes were a wealthy family with business ventures all over the world. Their largest Texas base of operations was in Red Rock, just outside San Antonio. But there were also Fortunes in Horseback Hollow. Christopher Fortune Jones, who'd grown up in the area, would be heading the foundation branch in town.

"I'm tired of worrying about a job I might not get." To soothe her rising stress level, Shannon bit into the scone. *Oh, yeah, baby—sugar and blueberries, topped with a lemon glaze.* Talk about stress eating. She could almost feel her waistline expand.

"Are you going to the party on Saturday?" Rachel asked, changing the subject.

The "party" was actually a couple's baby shower being thrown by friends. The fact it was a couple's baby shower practically guaranteed there wouldn't be any unattached men attending. After all, what single straight guy would willingly give up his Saturday night to attend such an event?

"I promised Gabi I'd attend." Shannon paused and narrowed her gaze. Outside, a sleek black car she didn't recognize pulled into the lot. "My other choice is playing cards with my parents and their friends."

Rachel gave an exaggerated shudder.

"It's not that bad." Shannon liked her parents and enjoyed the members of their card club. In fact, if she hadn't given Gabi Mendoza her word she'd show, she'd be seriously tempted to skip the shower and play cards instead.

Rachel took a sip of her chai tea. "I'm crossing my fingers there'll be some fresh meat at this little soiree."

"Don't hold your breath." Shannon could have said more but pressed her lips shut. Let the woman have her dreams…

Rachel startled her by emitting a low whistle and pointing to the window. "Get a load of that."

"I saw it." Obligingly, Shannon leaned forward for a better look. Just south of the humongous pothole sat a shiny vehicle that cost more than she used to make in a year. It was rare to see such an expensive car in Horseback Hollow. "Mercedes."

"Forget the car." Though they were alone in the café, Rachel's voice was soft, almost reverent. "Feast your eyes on him."

Shannon swung her gaze from the sleek lines and shiny black finish of the SL250 to focus on the tall, broadshouldered man with dark brown hair exiting the vehicle.

A man obviously on a mission, he rounded the back of the car with decisive steps. When he bent over to retrieve something from the backseat, Shannon's lips curved.

"Ooh la la," Rachel breathed.

For a second Shannon forgot how to breathe as the pristine white shirt stretched tight across the breadth of shoulders, muscular legs encased in dark trousers.

Shannon's heart quivered. "If his face is half as good as his backside, we're in for a treat."

As if in answer to her prayer, the guy straightened and turned. Ooh la la, indeed. He had classically handsome features with a strong jaw, straight nose and cheekbones that looked as if they had been chiseled from granite. She'd wager his stylishly cut dark hair had never seen the insides of a Cut 'N' Curl.

Yes, indeed, the man was an impressive hunk of masculinity even with sunglasses covering his eyes.

While the set of those shoulders and confident stance said "don't mess with me," messing with him was just what Shannon longed to do. Until she saw two little legs dangling from the blanketed bundle he'd pulled from the car.

Rachel expelled a heavy sigh, apparently seeing the evidence of daddy-hood, as well. "He's got a kid."

Her friend sounded as disappointed as Shannon felt.

"Figures he'd be taken." Shannon heaved her own sigh. "The cute ones always are."

"Marriage doesn't stop some of them from sniffing around."

"My old boss Jerry was a perfect example of that." Even as she spoke, Shannon's gaze returned to the dark-haired stranger.

"You taught Jerry the Jerk not to mess with you."

Shannon just smiled and shrugged. Lately she'd begun to wonder if there was a way she could have handled the situation differently and kept her job.

Water under a collapsed bridge.

The man shut the door firmly, then stepped away, giving Shannon a glimpse of a furry head with perked-up ears, little paws braced on the dash. She couldn't stop a smile. She loved animals almost as much as she loved children. "He's got a dog, too."

Rachel looked up from the text she'd glanced down to read. Apparently discovering the stranger had a kid had turned her initial interest to indifference.

"The hot guy has a kid *and* a dog," Shannon told her friend.

"Bet you five he also has a wife with blond hair and a killer figure." Rachel's tone turned philosophical. "That's practically a given with guys like him."

Shannon grinned. "Aren't you the cynical one?"

"Realist." Rachel popped a bite of scone into her mouth. "I should have known he was too good to be single."

Shannon rolled her eyes.

"He's coming inside," Rachel hissed.

Shannon turned in her chair just as the automatic doors of the Superette slid open.

Francine, the store's lone cashier, was in the back of the store stocking shelves. Since they were the only customers, Frannie had told them to holler if someone showed and was ready to check out.

The man paused just inside the entrance and removed his sunglasses. He glanced at the empty checkout counter, impatience wrapped around him like a too-tight jacket. Shannon expected any second he'd start tapping his foot.

Shannon pulled to her feet and crossed to him, wishing she was wearing something—anything—besides jeans and a faded Texas Tech T-shirt. "May I help you?"

The man was silent for a second, staring at her. His eyes were a cool blue with a darker rim. Shannon forced herself to hold that piercing gaze.

"I find myself in need of some assistance," he said after a couple of seconds, his smile surprisingly warm and charming. "My GPS has gone bonkers. I'm looking for a ranch called the Broken R."

In addition to the killer smile, the man had a totally de-lish British accent. Shannon surreptitiously slanted a glance down but his ring finger was hidden beneath the blankets.

"Are you a relative?" Though Shannon didn't like to pry, Rachel would kill her if she didn't get at least one or two deets.

"I'm Jensen's brother." He adjusted his stance as the child beneath the blanket stirred. "Are you familiar with the location?"

Shannon couldn't tell if the toddler was a boy or girl. The shoes were gray leather sneakers that could belong to either sex. The only thing she could see above the blanket was a thatch of slightly wavy brown hair.

"It's super easy to find." Shannon quickly gave him directions. She offered to write them down, but he told her there was no need.

"Thank you." He smiled again and his whole face relaxed. "You've been very kind."

Though she wanted to volunteer to ride with him and show him the way, Shannon resisted the temptation. Married men were not on her radar.

Still, she remained where she was and watched him

stroll to the car. Once he reached the vehicle, she scurried over to where Rachel waited.

"Ohmigod." Rachel's eyes sparkled. "His accent is incredible."

"The rest of him is pretty incredible too." Shannon surreptitiously watched Jensen Fortune Chesterfield's hot brother buckle the child into the seat. The blanket around the toddler fell to the concrete but was quickly scooped up.

"He's definitely a boy," she told her friend.

"You're wrong." Rachel chuckled. "That one is all man."

"Not him. The kid. I couldn't tell initially boy or girl, but he's wearing a Thomas the Tank Engine shirt. Definitely a boy."

"Who cares about the child?" Rachel fluttered her long lashes. "Did you hear that fantabulous British accent?"

"You said that before."

"It bears repeating."

The sleek black sedan backed up and headed out of the lot, careful to avoid the asphalt crater.

"It doesn't matter." Shannon sighed and turned her attention back to her scone. "Like you said, a guy that gorgeous has a beautiful wife somewhere."

Oliver Fortune Hayes once had a beautiful wife. Then he'd had a beautiful ex-wife. Now, the stunningly beautiful blonde was gone.

"Diane was killed in a car accident two months ago," Oliver told his brother Jensen. He kept his tone matter-of-fact, tamping down any emotion. "She was in the car with a man she'd been seeing for quite some time. He also died in the crash."

The two men sat in Jensen's kitchen, having a cup of tea. Thanks to the concise directions from the pretty brunette at the grocery shop, Oliver had easily found the Broken R ranch. Jensen had been surprised to see him a full twenty-four hours earlier than expected and apologetic that Amber was in Lubbock shopping.

Oliver looked forward to meeting his brother's fiancée but appreciated the opportunity to talk privately first.

Jensen hadn't changed much since Oliver had last seen him. His brother's dark hair was perhaps a trifle longer but he was still the very proper British gentleman that Oliver remembered. Though the cowboy boots were a shock, Jensen's gray trousers were perfectly creased, and his white dress shirt startlingly white.

"This is the first I've heard of Diane's death. Why didn't you call?" Jensen was his half brother from the second marriage of Oliver's mother. Though seven years separated them in age, Oliver had always been fond of Jensen.

When Oliver had announced his intention to come to Horseback Hollow after their sister, Amelia, gave birth, Jensen had offered to let him stay at his ranch.

"My life has been topsy-turvy since the moment I found out." He'd discovered Diane had died at a cocktail party when a mutual friend had expressed sympathy.

"I bet."

Oliver continued as if Jensen hadn't spoken. "Diane's parents didn't notify me. They took Ollie into their home even though they knew full custody immediately reverted to me upon her death. They kept my son from me."

Jensen flinched at the underlying anger in his brother's carefully controlled tone. "I'm surprised they didn't put up a fight once you found out and arrived on their doorstep to claim him."

"There would have been no point." Oliver waved a hand. "I'm the child's father."

"Given your lifestyle, taking on a child had to be difficult."

"Once I established a schedule, it went quite well," Oliver said in a clipped tone, irritated his brother could think him incapable of caring for one small boy. "The nanny I hired is excellent and believes as strongly as I do in the importance of a routine. And she fully understood why I needed to make this trip. Unfortunately she refuses to leave the country."

Jensen obviously had nothing to add. He didn't have children. Not even a wife. Not yet anyway.

Oliver glanced down, noting Barnaby had fallen asleep at his feet. He only hoped his son was sleeping as soundly as the dog. The moment he'd arrived at the ranch, Oliver had put Ollie down for a nap. After a sixteen-hour flight from London to Lubbock the day before, even the brief respite in a hotel overnight hadn't been enough sleep for a toddler.

His son had been fussy after the long flight and had kept Oliver up most of the night. Oliver had dreaded the forty-five-minute car ride from Lubbock to Horseback Hollow, but the child had fallen asleep while Oliver was strapping him into his car seat. He'd slept during the entire trip, not waking even when Oliver brought him inside and laid him on Jensen's bed.

Jensen's gaze dropped to the corgi. "What's his name?"

"Barnaby." Oliver wasn't sure who was more surprised at the fondness in his voice, him or his brother.

"You don't like dogs."

"I've never disliked them," Oliver corrected. "I simply never had time for one. Diane purchased Barnaby for Ollie when she left me. He's quite attached to the animal."

"You're going to keep him?"

"Are you referring to Ollie? Or Barnaby?"

"Both." Jensen grinned. "I've never considered you the kid or dog type."

"Ollie is my son. My responsibility. When Diane and I split up, I thought our child's needs would be better served living with her. That's the only reason I didn't fight for custody. I've already explained about the dog."

Jensen stared contemplatively at the animal that had awakened and now sat, brown eyes scanning the room, ears perked up like two radio antennae.

"Corgis are herding animals."

Oliver nodded. "I observed some of that behavior when he first came to live with me. But that's no longer an issue."

"You have the dog on a schedule, too."

"Certainly."

"Is Barnaby a dog that goes in and out?" Jensen asked in a tone that was a little too casual.

Oliver cocked his head.

"Could he be an outside dog?"

Oliver thought for a moment, considered. "He likes being outdoors, but I don't believe he's suited to roughing it."

Jensen rubbed his chin. "That presents a problem."

"How so?"

"Amber is allergic to dogs." His brother grimaced. "Come to think of it, I probably shouldn't have let the animal in the house."

Ah, now Oliver understood. "No worries. I'll stay with Mother."

"You're forgetting something, aren't you?"

"Am I?"

"Mother is also allergic." Jensen's expression was solemn. "Remember the puppy Father brought home? She got congested and broke out in hives."

Bugger. He'd forgotten all about that episode. He'd been older and away at boarding school, so the fact that the dog had to be returned to the breeder hadn't affected him.

"It appears I'll have to rent a suite at a hotel." Oliver gave a shrug. "Is there one you'd recommend?"

Jensen gave a hoot of laughter. "You saw the extent of our business district when you stopped at the Superette."

Was his brother teasing him? The way he used to when he was a bit of a boy? "I assumed the more populated area of the city was elsewhere."

"Horseback Hollow isn't a city, it's a town. There are no hotels, motels or even any B and Bs." Jensen's expression sobered. "Right now there isn't even a hotel in Vicker's Corners. You'll have to go all the way to Lubbock to find one."

Oliver pressed his lips together. There was no way he'd flown across an entire ocean and half a continent to stay an hour away. Especially not with a child. The whole purpose of this trip was to spend time with family.

"There has to be a vacant house in the area," he told

his brother. "Do you have the name of a real estate broker I could contact?"

"Now?"

"Since Ollie and I don't have accommodations for this evening, time is of the essence."

His brother rose and went to a desk where he pulled out a thin phone book. "I suggest starting with Shep Singleton. He's a local rancher and I believe he has an empty house on his property. I'm not sure if it would be satisfactory or what he'll want for rent—"

"Money won't be an issue if the house is clean and nearby."

"It's in a great location." Jensen pulled his brows together as if picturing the place in his mind. "It may even have a fenced yard."

"Do you have Mr. Singleton's mobile number?" Oliver pulled the phone from his jacket, his fingers poised above the keypad. He wanted to inspect this home. One way or the other, he would secure appropriate lodging for him and his son, today.

Because Oliver Fortune Hayes was used to going after—and getting—what he wanted.

Chapter 2

Shannon swore under her breath. She and Rachel had plans to see a movie in Lubbock this evening, then check out a Mexican place that had recently opened in the Depot District. Instead she'd had to call her friend and cancel.

All because her father had gotten a call from someone interested in renting the empty ranch house on the property. Apparently that someone had to see it immediately. There was no telling how long this would take. Or who the impatient person would turn out to be.

Her father only had a name… Oliver. He wasn't certain if that was the man's first or last name, as he'd been distracted during the call. One of his prize mares was foaling.

Shep Singleton might be focused on Sweet Betsy but Shannon was still his little girl. He ordered her to take one of the ranch hands with her for safety. It made sense, but she hated to pry them away from their duties.

The odds of Mr. Oliver being a serial killer or crazed lunatic were next to nil. Besides, she'd had self-defense training and could hold her own.

When she pulled up in front of the home and saw a dusty Mercedes, a prickle of heat traveled up her spine. Surely it couldn't be…

Even as she hopped out of her dad's rusty pickup with the gash in the front end, the man from the Superette stepped from the vehicle. Ooh la la, he looked just as good as he had several hours ago and ready for business in his hand-tailored navy suit.

Smiling, Shannon crossed the gravel drive and extended her hand. "You must be Mr. Oliver?"

"Oliver Fortune Hayes," he corrected, smiling slightly. "And you're the helpful lady from the grocer's."

"Shannon Singleton." She gave his hand a decisive shake. "Shep's daughter. My dad said you wanted to check out the house."

"Indeed." Those amazing blue eyes settled on her, warm and friendly. "I appreciate you showing it on such short notice."

What was left of her irritation vanished. "Happy to do it."

He surprised her by turning back to the car. When he opened the back door and unfastened the boy from his car seat, she realized he hadn't come alone. Once the child's feet were firmly planted on the ground, the toddler looked around, gave an ear-splitting shriek and barreled after the corgi that had just leaped from the vehicle.

"That's Ollie. My son," Oliver told her, pride in his voice.

Oliver let the boy scamper a few yards before scooping him up. Ollie giggled and squirmed but settled when Oliver said something in a low tone.

"Barnaby."

The crisp sound of his name had the corgi turning. Oliver motioned with his hand and the dog moved to his side.

He looked, Shannon thought, like a man totally in control of the situation.

Oliver gazed speculatively at the house. "Since your father knows I'm looking for immediate occupancy, I assume the home is empty."

Shannon smiled. "You assume correctly."

The entire tour of the furnished home took all of five minutes. If Shannon hadn't been looking she might have missed the slight widening of Oliver's eyes when he first stepped inside the three-bedroom, thirteen-hundred-square-foot ranch house Shannon's grandparents had once called home.

Once she'd finished the tour, she rocked back on her boot heels, feeling oddly breathless. "What do you think?"

"I'll take it." Oliver put the boy down, reached into his back pocket and pulled out a wallet. "Sixty days with an option. I'll pay in advance."

"Just like that?" Decisiveness was one thing, but he hadn't asked a single question. "Don't you have any questions?"

"You've explained everything to my satisfaction." He kept one eye on his son, who was hopping like a frog across the living room. "The fact is, I need to secure lodging close to my family."

As Shannon opened her mouth, she wondered if she

might be stepping over some line. But surely the man had other options. From what she'd observed of the Fortunes, they were a tight-knit family. "You're not staying with them?"

"That was the plan. But apparently Amber—my brother's fiancée—is highly allergic to dogs. As is my mother, which I'd very inconveniently forgotten." He gestured with his head toward the corgi, who intently watched the hopping boy. "Ollie is very attached to Barnaby."

"He's a cutie. The boy, I mean. The dog is cute, too." Shannon paused to clear the babble from her throat before continuing. "Will your wife be joining you?"

For just an instant a spark of some emotion flickered in his eyes before the shutter dropped.

"Ollie's mother and I were divorced." His tone was matter-of-fact. "Well, Ms. Singleton?"

"Please call me Shannon."

"Well, *Shannon*. Do we have a deal?" He extended his hand.

When her fingers closed over his and a hot, unfamiliar riff of sensation traveled up her spine, something told Shannon that this deal might be more than she bargained for.

To Oliver's way of thinking, money smoothed most rough patches and made life extremely manageable. Unfortunately, in the past few days he hadn't found that to be as true as in the past. There hadn't been anyone to carry in his bags or help him unpack once he'd closed the deal on the ranch house.

Oliver glanced around the small living room, smiling at the sight of Ollie playing with his A-B-C bricks, the dog supervising from his position under the kitchen table. The place was so small he could see the kitchen from where he stood. Unbelievably, there was only one lavatory in the entire structure.

Since it was just him and Ollie, even when they added a nanny, it would be workable. Not ideal, but they would make do, much the way he had on those school camping trips when he'd been a boy. He decided to view the next two months as an adventure.

Both Ollie and Barnaby seemed to like the small space. Even Oliver had to admit he found his temporary residence comfortable, quiet and surprisingly homey. Still, after two days of settling in, he was ready to get to work. For that to happen, he needed a nanny.

He'd made inquiries, as had various family members. So far, none of the women he'd interviewed had been acceptable. Oliver would also consider a manny, but when he'd mentioned that to the woman at the agency in Lubbock, her eyebrows had shot up. She informed him mannies were scarcer in Texas than rain in August.

Man or woman, Oliver didn't care. He simply needed someone he could trust to tend to his son while he worked. He ran a busy brokerage firm in London. While he trusted and valued his employees, he prided himself on being personally involved with many of the firm's larger clients.

Dealing with time zone issues was frustrating enough, but then to have Ollie call to him or start crying over his bricks tumbling down was totally unacceptable. There had to be someone suitable in the area.

His hopes of finding someone from Horseback Hollow were rapidly fading. Amber had given him a couple of names, neither of whom was willing to live in. What good would they be to him living a half hour away?

With the time differences an issue, if he needed to go out or simply make a phone call, he didn't want to wait.

The head of the placement agency guaranteed she'd find the perfect person, but kept asking him to give her more time. Well, he'd given her over two days. Since she couldn't make it happen, he would take the reins.

He pulled out his wallet and removed the card Miss Shannon Singleton had given him to use in case of emergencies.

Oliver paused, considered. As far as he was concerned, being without a nanny for forty-eight hours qualified as an emergency.

Shannon stared at the phone in her hand for a second before dropping it into her bag.

Rachel slanted a questioning glance at her as they exited the movie theater in Vicker's Corners. "Who was that?"

"Oliver Fortune Hayes."

Shannon had told her friend all about playing rental agent with Mr. Fortune Hayes. Rachel had only one question—was he married?

"Mr. Hottie from the Superette." Rachel's smile broadened. "Tell me he called to ask you out."

"I'm not exactly sure what he did."

Shannon slowed her steps as the two women strolled down the sidewalk of the quaint community with its cute little shops with canopied frontage and large pots of flowers. "He said he had a proposition for me."

A mischievous gleam sparked in Rachel's eyes. "What kind of proposition?"

Shannon swatted her friend's arm and laughed. "Not that kind."

"Don't be so sure." Rachel gave her an admiring glance. "You're a hottie, too. He'd be a fool not to be interested. And that man didn't look like anyone's fool."

"Thanks for that." Still, Shannon held no such illusions. If guys thought of her at all, it was as a buddy. She was twenty-five and had only had two boyfriends. Hardly a guy-magnet. "But remember, his home is in England. I want a nice local guy. Is that too much to ask?"

To Shannon's surprise, Rachel didn't go for the flippant response. Instead Rachel's dark brows pulled together in thought. Her friend was a strikingly pretty woman, tall with big blue eyes and long hair so dark it looked almost black.

Though they were good friends, so much of Rachel was still a mystery. Sometimes when she turned serious and got this faraway look in her eyes, Shannon could only wonder what she was thinking.

"I love it here, too," Rachel admitted. "I can't imagine living anywhere else. So when you find that nice local guy, make sure he has a friend."

"Will do. Just don't hold your breath."

Shannon stopped short of telling Rachel if her friend was back in Austin, she'd have men beating her door down. She still didn't fully understand what had caused Rachel to leave Austin and move to Horseback Hollow. But in the five years that Rachel had been in town, she'd become part of the community.

"I'm not giving up hope. And you shouldn't either. Look at Quinn," Rachel continued. "Amelia shows up in Horseback Hollow and—boom—she and Quinn fall in love."

Amelia Fortune Chesterfield had come to Horseback

Hollow last year for a wedding and had a romantic fling with cowboy Quinn Drummond. Now they were married with a baby girl. It was their baby shower that loomed on the horizon.

"That whole thing was like a made-for-TV movie," Shannon admitted. "But really, how often does that kind of thing happen, especially in a town the size of Horseback Hollow?"

"The fact is, oh ye of little faith, almost anything is possible. Hey, Mr. Oliver Fortune Hayes could fall in love with you, give up his home in London and the two of you could live happily ever after right here."

Shannon paused in front of a bakery, inhaling the scent of freshly baked chocolate chip cookies. "Have you seen a pig fly?"

"Pigs don't fly," Rachel said automatically.

"Exactly right," Shannon agreed. "Until they do, your little scenario isn't going to happen."

Oliver glanced at the Patek Philippe watch on his wrist. His new living room was so small he could cross it in several long strides, which did nothing to dissipate his agitation.

He'd asked Miss Shannon Singleton to come over as soon as possible. That was precisely one hour and forty-five minutes ago. Oliver wasn't used to his requests being ignored.

Of course, as she didn't work for him, Miss Singleton was under no obligation to comply. Still, she'd promised to come as soon as she was able.

Another full hour passed. Ollie was sitting in his high chair, eating a snack of yogurt and apple slices, when Oliver heard the sound of a vehicle coming up the gravel drive.

Barnaby's head jerked up. He let out a surprisingly deep woof, then raced to the front door, tail wagging.

Oliver tousled his son's light brown hair. "Be right back."

His hand was already on the doorknob when the knock sounded.

Looking decidedly windblown, Shannon stood on the porch, holding her flapping purse firmly against her waist as the strong breeze continued to pummel her. Her shoulder-length brown hair whipped around her pretty face and he realized her lips reminded him of plump, ripe strawberries.

He wondered if they'd taste as good as they looked.

She cleared her throat. "May I come in?"

"Of course." Pulling his gaze from her lips, he stepped back and opened the door wider to allow her to pass.

"Whew." She stopped at the edge of the living room to push her hair out of her face. "It's like a hurricane out there."

"Hurricane?" The wind couldn't possibly be over thirty knots.

She laughed. "A figure of speech. If there's a hurricane in the gulf, the only thing we get this far inland is rain. And that's usually in the fall."

Oliver found himself intrigued. Most women of his acquaintance would never think to appear at a requested meeting dressed in blue jeans and a white cotton shirt. Yet, he was oddly drawn to her. It didn't hurt that she smelled terrific, like vanilla.

Yes, the beastly day was definitely on the upswing. "I appreciate you coming on such short notice."

"I'm sorry it took so long." She smiled up at him with such charming sweetness he found himself returning her smile and taking her arm as they strolled to the kitchen.

"You're here now. That's what counts." He resisted the urge to brush back a strand of hair from her face, even as he inhaled the pleasing scent that wafted around her.

"My friend Rachel and I went to a movie in Vicker's Corners. That's where we were when you called. Then we went and got coffee at one of the little specialty shops. This time, we got ice cream, too. I told Rachel we shouldn't. I mean we had a big lunch, but—"

He did his best to process her rapid-fire speech but it was as if she was speaking a foreign language. Apparently cueing in to his glazed look, she broke off and laughed without a hint of self-consciousness.

"I'm babbling." She laughed again. "Which I sometimes do when I'm nervous."

"I make you nervous?"

A bright pink rose up her neck. "A little."

Truly puzzled now, he cocked his head. "Why?"

"You're different from the men I know, the guys in this town."

"My brothers live here. I'm not different from them."

"I'm not well acquainted with your family. At least not with the ones from England."

"Hopefully that will change." Oliver gestured to the refrigerator. "May I get you something to drink?"

"Thanks. I'm fine." She moved to Ollie's side, the dog like a little shadow at her feet. Taking a seat at the table near the child, she smiled and picked up a piece of the apple. "This looks yummy."

The toddler's fingers closed around the apple slice.

Her smile flashed with delight when he put it into his mouth and began to chew.

Oliver considered offering her something to eat, but rations were in short supply at the moment. He really needed to make a trip into town to the grocery shop they called the Superette.

"You said you had a proposition for me, Mr. Fortune Hayes?"

She was direct. Oliver admired that quality. Spared all the posturing.

"I'd like you to help me find a nanny for Ollie."

Shannon leaned back in her chair and studied him for several seconds before speaking. "I thought you hired an agency in Lubbock to do that for you. That's the buzz around town."

Jensen had warned him there were no secrets in Horseback Hollow. "Their efforts so far have been disappointing."

"You've been here two days."

"It's difficult to get work done when you're caring for a child."

Unexpectedly, Shannon laughed; a delightful sound that reminded him of bells ringing. "I don't think any parent would contradict that statement."

"The fact is, Miss Singleton—"

"Shannon," she reminded him.

"Shannon." He found the name pleasant on his tongue. "My business is a demanding one. While I'm happy to come and spend time with my family, I need to stay involved."

"What is it you do?"

"I run a brokerage house." It would be bragging to say more, to tell her that his firm was one of the top ones in London. Besides, it had no relevance to the current conversation.

"Oh."

"The point is I need to find someone immediately. Of course, not just anyone will do. Ollie's happiness and welfare is paramount. The women the agency has sent so far were totally inappropriate. This has caused me to doubt the adequacy of the agency's screening process."

"How were they inappropriate?" Shannon knew he'd acquired the services of the premier placement agency in Lubbock. To hear he was dissatisfied so quickly surprised her.

"The first woman hadn't been informed this was a live-in position." Oliver snatched from the air the piece of apple Ollie had tried to fling to a waiting Barnaby. "Interviewing her was a complete waste of my time."

"Probably an oversight," Shannon said diplomatically. "What else?"

"The next woman found the accommodations—" he hesitated for a second before continuing "—substandard. That didn't concern me because I found her supercilious attitude unacceptable."

"Many live-in nannies—" Shannon chose her words carefully since the lodging they were referring to was owned by her father "—require a private bath."

"I completely understand her concern," Oliver said briskly. "I'm not looking forward to sharing the lavatory either. I'd hoped the salary I was offering and the fact that it wouldn't be a long-term placement would make that fact more palatable."

"It must be difficult living in a home that is so far below your circumstances."

He appeared to ignore her dry tone. "This home and

Horseback Hollow may not be where I'd choose to live forever, but for the short term both are adequate."

Shannon knew he was being kind and exceedingly tactful. But his comment only served to remind her that Oliver Fortune Hayes wouldn't be like his sister, Amelia, or his brother Jensen, who'd come to Horseback Hollow and not only fallen in love with a local but with the town and its people, as well.

She had to keep that in mind. Despite the ooh la la factor, any relationship with Oliver would be a dead-end street.

Chapter 3

Oliver found himself enjoying his conversation with Shannon. She was obviously an intelligent woman who appeared to truly care about his situation.

"I asked Amelia for names since Amber and Jensen were fresh out of ideas." Oliver paused and tilted his head. "Are you certain I can't get you a refreshment?"

Shannon smiled. She had quite a lovely one. While her features were too strong to be considered classically beautiful, there was an arresting nature to her face that made a man—even one who'd sworn off women temporarily to focus on his son—take a second look.

Though he must admit, he couldn't recall the last time he'd seen a woman in denim and cotton. Not to mention cowboy boots. The pants hugged her slender figure like a glove, and the shirt, though not tight, hinted at underlying curves. Yes, she was striking indeed.

"I guess I could take a cup of tea, if it's not too much trouble."

He was so focused on her lips that it took him a second to process. "No trouble at all."

Oliver was putting the kettle on the stove when the doorbell rang.

"Would you like me to get that?" Even as she asked, Shannon was already rising to her feet with a fluid grace comparable to any of the ladies he knew back in London.

"Thank you, yes." Oliver pulled his gaze from her backside and gave Ollie a biscuit. His son squealed with delight.

He heard Shannon speak, then recognized his brother's voice.

Jensen strolled into the room, dressed casually—for him—in brown trousers and a cream-colored polo shirt. There was curiosity in his eyes when his brother's gaze slid between him and Shannon. "I didn't realize the two of you were acquainted."

"Shannon showed me around this lovely home," Oliver announced.

"That's, ah, correct." Shannon, who'd appeared relaxed only moments before, now appeared ready to bolt.

The fact puzzled Oliver. He'd been under the impression that while Shannon and Jensen weren't well acquainted, they were on good terms.

"Will you have a cup?" Oliver asked his brother. "I have Fortnum & Mason."

Jensen's smile gave Oliver his answer, while Shannon's brows pulled together.

"Fortnum & Mason is a popular British tea manufacturer. They have a Smoky Earl Grey blend that Oliver—

and almost everyone in the family—prefers," Jensen explained before Oliver could open his mouth.

"I'm sure it's delicious, but I'll have to pass." Shannon appeared to make a great show of looking at her watch. "We can talk another time, Oliver. I have plans and I'm sure you and your brother have a lot to discuss."

Oliver's heart gave an odd lurch. He surprised himself by crossing the room, taking her arm and leading her back to her seat at the table. "Nonsense. You're staying for tea."

"Down," Ollie called out. "Want down."

"I can get—" Shannon began.

Oliver held up a hand, then fixed his gaze on his son. "What do you say?"

Ollie stared at him with innocent blue eyes before his mouth widened into a grin. "Pease."

"Good man." Oliver lifted his son down from the high chair.

Jensen exchanged a look with Shannon. "Amazing."

Shannon cocked her head, but before Jensen could explain, Oliver looked up from wiping Ollie's hands.

"Nothing amazing about it. Child rearing is no different from running a successful business enterprise. Rules and order are essential." Oliver shifted his gaze to Shannon. "My brother expected me to be a bumbling feckwit incapable of rearing my son."

Oliver pulled out a bin containing an assortment of toys, placing several before Ollie on the rug within eyeshot of the kitchen table. The whistling teakettle brought him back to the stove, where he produced three cups of the steaming brew in short order.

"Surely he's seen you in action before?" Shannon

cradled the "I Love Texas" mug in her hands with an unexpected reverence.

"Oliver only recently gained custody of Ollie," Jensen explained. "After Diane…"

Jensen stopped and slanted Oliver an apologetic glance. In their family, private matters weren't usually discussed in the presence of a guest.

"Diane was my ex-wife," Oliver explained. "The divorce was already in process when Ollie was born. Because I believed a child—a baby especially—needed his mother, I didn't fight her for custody. She recently died in a car accident."

"She shouldn't have been out that night." Jensen's voice rose and anger flashed in his eyes. "She should—"

"Enough."

The quietly spoken word was enough to stop Jensen's potential tirade in its tracks.

"She was Ollie's mother." Looking back, the person Oliver blamed most was himself. He should have paid more attention. He should have known that Diane was spending more time with her new boyfriend than with Ollie. "The accident occurred fairly recently."

He felt Shannon's hand on his arm, looked up to find her soft eyes filled with compassion. "I'm sorry for your loss."

"We'd been divorced over a year."

"You were also once married to her. That means you once loved her." She gave his forearm a squeeze, then removed her hand.

Oliver nodded briskly.

Diane hadn't wasted any time finding another man once the baby was born. She'd been with yet another man when she died. That's why the sadness he'd experienced upon hearing of her passing had blindsided him. He finally accepted it was understandable, given this was a woman he'd once known and loved.

Jensen steepled his fingers and his gaze settled on Shannon. "I understand you work for your father."

"I do." She sipped her tea and her smile told Oliver she found it pleasing. "The Triple S is a large spread. I do mostly administrative work, but in a pinch I'm able to do just about anything—feed cattle, vaccinate, castrate..."

"Good Lord." The words popped from Oliver's lips before he could stop them.

"You're in the Wild West now, brother." Jensen grinned. "Oh, and before I forget, I brought you some more names of possible nannies for Ollie. These are from Amelia since you didn't appear happy with any of the ones Amber and I suggested."

"I'm very particular when it comes to my son," Oliver said without apology.

Jensen took a sip of tea, then lifted the mug higher to read the inscription—"This Ain't My First Rodeo." His lips twitched and he shook his head before taking another drink. Seconds later he reached into his pocket and pulled out a sheet of paper. "The latest list."

"Perfect," Oliver pronounced. "We'll take care of this right now."

Jensen tilted his head back. "How do you propose to do that?"

"Miss Singleton knows everyone in the area." Oliver smiled at Shannon. "She and I will go through the names over dinner and decide which ones to interview."

"I'm afraid that won't be possible." Shannon set down

her mug, the flash of irritation in her eyes at odds with her easy tone. "I have plans."

"Break them," Oliver ordered. "This is more important. A child's welfare is at stake."

The men in Shannon's family often told their friends that she was a contradiction: a purring kitten and a ready-to-strike rattler. The consensus seemed to be it was best not to push her too far.

The good humor drained from Shannon's body. Did the rich and powerful Oliver Fortune Hayes really think he could, with a cavalier wave of his hand, dismiss her plans for the evening?

There was no reason for him to know that those plans were fluid. Several friends planned to eat and drink their way through platters of nachos and bottles of Corona beer at the Hollows Cantina during happy hour. They'd told her to join them if she was free.

But as Shannon opened her mouth to reiterate she had plans, his words gave her pause. As much as she didn't want Oliver to think he could bring her to heel with a single wave of those elegant fingers, she wanted him to find a suitable nanny for Ollie.

You'd think after growing up with four younger siblings—and years spent babysitting—she should be tired of children. But she loved them. Not just the small ones. She even got a kick out of the often obnoxious teenagers from Lubbock who came out to ride horses as part of a Country Connection program.

Ollie was such a cute little guy and he'd recently lost his mother…

"Shannon." Oliver reached across the table and took

her hand. "Please. I need your help." His tone was softer this time.

Heat rose up her arm. For a second she forgot how to speak. She licked her lips. When his eyes darkened, her resistance melted into a liquid pool.

"I'd love to stay and chat, but Amber is expecting me." Jensen attempted to hide his grin by raising the cup to his lips for one last swallow. "It appears you two have a lot to, uh, discuss."

Shannon flushed. "Be sure to tell Amber hello from me."

"I will give her your regards." Jensen gave a slight bow of his head, all serious now. One hundred percent British. He turned and handed Oliver the promised list. "The names."

"Thank you." Oliver took the list in his left hand, extended his right. The two men shook.

Shannon blinked at the civilized gesture. She tried to imagine her brothers shaking hands and…couldn't. Punching each other, heck yes. That occurred on a daily basis.

Because the men were standing, she also rose to her feet. Jensen shook her hand before he left.

With a resigned sigh, Shannon turned to Oliver. She had to admit she was curious whom Amelia had recommended. She gazed pointedly at the list dangling from his fingers. "May I see it?"

With paper in hand, Shannon wandered back to the table and sat. Taking a gulp of tea, she narrowed her gaze and scanned the names.

After putting down a few more toys for Ollie, Oliver took a seat across from her.

"What do you think?" he asked when several seconds had passed. "Any good possibilities?"

Shannon laid the paper on the table and sat back. "Do you want tactful? Or honest?"

Oliver's gaze lingered on her face, and a curious energy filled the air. An invisible web of attraction wrapped around them. When he leaned forward, Shannon was sure he was going to kiss her.

Unable to move, she held her breath and stared into those brilliant blue eyes.

His lips were a heartbeat away when little Ollie let out a high-pitched squeal. Shannon turned her head just in time to see him gleefully knock down the stack of blocks.

Though he'd recently lost his mother, the child appeared happy and content, with the dog sitting upright beside him. Right now all was well in his life, and that warmed her heart. But the little boy's world could quickly take a nosedive if Oliver hired any of the women Amelia had suggested.

She shifted her gaze back to Oliver. The moment had vanished. It was almost as if it had never existed. This made Shannon wonder if it had been simply wishful thinking on her part.

"Quinn isn't much for gossip and your sister is relatively new to Horseback Hollow." Shannon strove to keep her tone matter-of-fact. "I grew up here. I keep my ear to the ground."

The expression seemed to puzzle Oliver. His dark brows pulled together.

"I know everything that goes on in this town," she clarified. "Things your sister and even her husband might not know."

Understanding filled his eyes. "Tell me."

"Will you keep it confidential?" Though Shannon liked to have the scoop, she wasn't a gossip. Okay, not much of one. The only reason she was considering sharing what she knew with Oliver was to protect Ollie.

"Most certainly."

Based on what Shannon had observed, Oliver appeared to be an honorable man who loved his son and wanted the best for him.

Hoping she wasn't making a mistake dissing women his sister had recommended, Shannon went through the names on the list one by one. By the time they'd gone through three, Ollie had tired of his toys and was rubbing his eyes and whining. Barnaby sprawled on a nearby rug, snoring lightly.

"Let's break for a few minutes." Oliver rose to his feet. "I need to change Ollie's nappy and put him down for a kip."

He inclined his head, and she knew what he was asking without him saying a word.

"I'll wait."

"Your dinner plans?"

"No worries." Though it was almost five and the start of happy hour was seconds away, Shannon was no longer in a hurry to leave. "While you're taking care of Ollie, I'll make us another cup of that delicious tea."

"Thank you."

When he and his son disappeared down the hall, Shannon sent a quick text to her friends, canceling her appearance, then put the kettle on. By the time he returned from the bedroom, the tea was ready.

"How is he?" She placed the two cups on the table.

"Dry and sleeping." He gestured toward the steaming tea. "Thank you for that…and for staying."

"I let my friends know I'd be late." She raised a hand when he started to protest. "I want to finish this with you. We only have two names left."

He studied her for a long moment before dropping his gaze down to the list and pointing. "What about this one?"

"Sally Steinacher drinks." When Oliver opened his mouth, she continued. "Not just socially. She has a problem. The family did an intervention last year and she went through treatment, but she's fallen off the wagon. Last week when I was in Vicker's Corners, I spotted her coming out of a liquor store with a sack."

"Perhaps she was buying for a friend or a family member," Oliver suggested.

Shannon gave him a pitying glance. "What kind of friend or relative would send an alcoholic to buy them liquor? Even if someone were that stupid, Rachel and I ran into her later on the street and we both smelled alcohol on her breath."

Oliver lined through her name with a single precise stroke of his Montblanc pen, the same way he'd done with the previous three names. "We've now reached the last person on the list. Is Cissy Jirovec a possibility?"

The hopeful look in his eye vanished when Shannon shook her head.

"She used to live in Horseback Hollow. Cissy calls Vicker's Corners home now. She's a nice person and I know she did a lot of babysitting while she was growing up."

"Then what's the issue?"

There was something about having those vivid blue

eyes focused on her that Shannon found unsettling. "The problem isn't with Cissy. It's with her boyfriend."

"I wouldn't be hiring him."

"Wayne used to live in Horseback Hollow. He has a bad temper."

"What does her relationship with this man have to do with her suitability for the position?"

"Wayne has a child from a relationship with another woman in Lubbock. Several years ago he lost his temper and broke his daughter's arm. The doctors in the ER found other healed injuries when they examined the little girl. He was charged with felony child abuse. I read all about it in the Lubbock paper."

"He did this to his own child?"

"He did." Shannon nodded solemnly. "I would hope Cissy wouldn't invite Wayne over while she was watching Ollie. But if Ollie were my son, I wouldn't take the risk."

Just as he had with the previous four names, Oliver drew a line through Cissy's name. With one hand he crumpled the sheet of paper.

"I might have hired one of these women." There was a look of restrained horror on his face.

"On the surface they look good. But, don't despair. The placement agency you're working with is top-notch. They'll do a good job of screening the candidates for you." She offered him a reassuring smile. "You'll find that right someone soon."

Oliver shook his head. "I think I've just found her. I want you to watch Oliver."

"Pardon me?"

"Name your price."

"Mr. Fortune Hayes—"

"Oliver," he interrupted, offering her a smile that turned her bones to liquid. "If we're going to be living under the same roof, it makes sense to be on a first-name basis."

Her breath caught in her throat. "What are you saying?"

"We should be on a first-name basis. Don't you agree?"

"I—I suppose."

"Splendid." The smile that split his face made him look almost boyish. "Shall we shake on it… Shannon?"

Chapter 4

"Shake on what? I haven't agreed to any deal." Shannon stuck her hands behind her back. Thank goodness the words came out casual and offhand.

"Smart woman. It's always best to discuss terms on the front end." He leaned forward in a companionable gesture, resting his forearms on the table.

The gesture somehow made him seem more approachable and appealing. Although if he got much more appealing, Shannon might jump him and rip off that pristine white shirt and perfectly knotted tie.

When Shannon didn't speak, he simply smiled. "You obviously know your negotiating techniques. Okay, I'll toss out an amount."

"We're not negotiating," Shannon protested. "Look, Mr. Fortune Hay—"

"Oliver," he said, once more not playing fair by flashing that enticing smile. "We decided on first names."

"Okay, Oliver." Shannon raked back her hair with her fingers, her heart pounding. Why did she feel as if she was in a race she was destined to lose? A race that, in some ways, she wanted to lose? "I—"

Before she could say more, he tossed out a number that had her forgetting what she'd been about to say.

"I believe that's a fair offer."

"Per…?" She really didn't want to say per month if he meant every two weeks, but it was an amazing sum of money either way.

"Week."

Shannon tried to control her expression by counting to ten in her head. The amount was five times what she'd been making in Lubbock. She swallowed past her suddenly dry throat and shifted in her seat. "If you're offering to pay that much, I'm surprised you don't have women—and men—beating down the door to work for you."

"That's not the salary the agency suggested. They told me the going rate in the area and I agreed to it." His gaze searched her eyes. "I'm a businessman, Shannon. I'm willing to pay for quality. It's as simple as that."

Shannon never considered she could be bought, but then again she'd never been offered so much money for a position she knew she'd enjoy. Working for her father was fine, but he really didn't need her. Little Ollie did.

Oliver turned his head slightly to the side. "What do you say?"

Shannon wiped suddenly sweaty palms on her jeans. "Before we discuss salary any further, I'd like to know your expectations."

He nodded approvingly and studied her for another long moment.

"Timewise, London is six hours ahead of Horseback Hollow." He gestured with an open palm to the clock on the wall in the shape of a rooster. "This means that much of my business will be conducted very early in the morning. That's why living in is nonnegotiable."

"I could come first thing in the morning, say at six a.m." She'd almost said five, but that was her father's favorite time to roll out of bed, not hers.

"That won't work." Oliver tapped a finger on the table. "If I'm speaking with a client at two a.m. and Ollie starts crying and needs attention, I need someone here who can tend to him."

"He could spend the night with me at my parents' home." The words came out in a rush, before she even considered what her folks might think about having a toddler underfoot. All she knew was the idea of being under the same roof with Oliver Fortune Hayes night after night was…disturbing. "That way, you could conduct business without any interruptions at all."

When she finished speaking, Oliver shook his head. The set of his jaw said there would be no changing his mind. "I want Ollie's schedule to be disrupted as little as possible. If I hadn't already canceled other trips to see my family, I'd have canceled this one and remained in London. Ollie has experienced more changes in the past few months than any little boy should have to face."

"You care about him."

Oliver looked perplexed. "Did you think I didn't?"

Well, she wanted to say, *sometimes you treat him like just one more thing in your life you need to handle.* But she knew that wasn't being fair. Her interaction with Oliver and his son had been minimal.

"No, of course not." Shannon blew out a breath. "You're probably right about not injecting more change into his life."

He relaxed in his chair. "Any other concerns you'd like to discuss?"

Shannon cleared her throat. "What about meal preparation, laundry and housecleaning duties? Would those be something you'd expect from me?"

"Negotiable."

"I would need time off."

"I'm not a slave driver, Shannon." His lips lifted in a boyish smile before he became all business again. "At a minimum I would require you to be here between the hours of midnight to noon, Monday through Friday. However, I'd prefer that during the working week you remain on duty until six p.m. That would allow me to have some sleep knowing Ollie is safe under your care."

Though he was proposing some pretty long hours, she *would* have every evening free. Other than Rachel, most of her friends worked eight-to-five jobs, and this really would be no different. "What about weekends?"

"Those days are yours."

She tapped her index finger against her bottom lip. "It's tempting."

"I'd like you to start immediately."

"You're getting ahead of yourself, Bucko." The word, commonly used by Shannon and her sibs, slipped out before her lips could trap it and swallow it whole.

"Bucko?" Oliver raised one dark brow. "I don't believe I'm familiar with the term."

His lips twitched ever so slightly.

Sheesh, the guy was appealing. And that was part of her concern.

Shannon jerked her gaze from those lips and squared her shoulders. There was no getting around it. The elephant in the room had to be addressed. "There's one thing we haven't yet discussed. How you respond may be the difference between my accepting your offer or respectfully declining it."

Oliver's eyes turned flat. He folded his hands before him on the table, his gaze never wavering from her face. "You have my undivided attention."

The fact that Oliver was being so businesslike should have made it easier to spit out the words stuck in her throat. But somehow, having those blue eyes focused so intently on her made her feel like a schoolgirl about to admit to a crush. Dear God, what if she'd only imagined the chemistry between them?

Shannon shifted in her seat and hesitated, despite knowing there was nothing to do at this point but take a deep breath and plunge ahead.

She focused her gaze on a spot over his left shoulder. "Ever since we've met, I've noticed this crazy kind of electricity between us. That's why I think it's important we agree up front to keep things strictly platonic between us. Giving in to the attraction would only complicate the situation."

She was out of breath by the time she finished. Had he been able to understand what she was trying to say? She'd spoken so fast—too fast—the words tripping over each other in her haste to get them out.

"Electricity?"

Of course if he was going to pick one word to focus on, it would naturally be that one. But it was the twinkle in those blue eyes that had her jerking to her feet, a hot flush shooting up her neck.

"Forget it. Forget I said anything. This isn't going to work." To her horror, her voice shook slightly.

It wasn't the hint of amusement in his eyes that had gotten to her. It was the frustration of not being able to make herself heard. Of her concerns and feelings being summarily dismissed.

That's how it had been with Jerry the Jerk. No matter how many different ways she'd told him to back off— that she wasn't interested—he never heard her.

Because he didn't want to hear what I had to say. Because I didn't matter.

As emotions flooded her, Shannon whirled toward the door.

She'd taken only a step or two when Oliver grabbed her arm, his expression contrite.

"I didn't mean to wind you up." He loosened his grip but didn't let go. "You have my word as a gentleman that I will never take advantage of you while you're under my roof and in my employ."

Shannon blew out a shaky breath and swayed slightly, conscious of his hand on her arm. He stood an arm's breadth away, near enough for the intoxicating scent of his cologne to tease her nostrils and make her want to lean close.

Step back, she told herself. She needed to put some distance between her and Oliver. That way she could think. That way she could breathe.

But her feet were as heavy and unmoving as if rooted in concrete. At that moment Shannon didn't have the energy—or the desire—to move.

Instead she tilted her head back and once again found herself drowning in the shockingly blue depths of Oliver's eyes.

Oliver stepped toward her, hand outstretched.

The heat in his gaze ignited a fire in her belly.

A zillion butterflies fluttered in her chest. Shannon moistened her lips and, as she caught another whiff of his cologne, reconsidered her hardline stance of only a moment ago.

One kiss.

What would really be wrong with one little kiss?

After all, people shook hands all the time to seal a deal. How would this be any different? Even as the rational piece of her brain still capable of cognizant thought told her it was indeed *very different*, she extended her hand.

Shannon waited for him to take her fingers and tug her to him. Waited for that magic moment when he would enfold her in a warm embrace before covering her mouth with his…

Her lips were already tingling with anticipation when his hand closed over hers and he gave it a decisive shake. "To new beginnings."

Even as a tsunami-sized wave of disappointment washed over her, Shannon forced herself to breathe and made her lips curve in an easy smile.

Regroup, she told herself.

Her father always said actions spoke louder than words. By his actions, Oliver had shown he was a man of his word. A man she could trust. There was something even more important Shannon had learned today.

She had more to fear from herself than from him.

* * *

Happy Hour at the Hollows Cantina had been going for close to two hours by the time Shannon strolled through the front door. She wasn't surprised to find standing-room-only in the bar area.

Her friends tried to squeeze her in at their table, but even if she could have located a spare chair, there was no room for one more.

"That's okay." Shannon waved a hand in the direction of the bar. "I'll just mingle."

"I'm coming with you." Rachel's heels had barely hit the shiny hardwood before her chair was snatched away.

Good old Rachel, Shannon thought with a warm rush of affection. She could always count on her.

The two women wove their way through the crowd, stopping every few feet to chat with friends and acquaintances while keeping an eye out for a couple of empty spots at the bar. They finally snagged two stools when a young couple got up abruptly and hurried off, hands all over each other.

"Get a room," someone yelled, and laughter rippled through the crowd.

A bartender approached to wipe the counter and take their order.

"The nachos are my treat," Shannon announced.

Rachel narrowed her gaze. "What's got you feeling so generous?"

"Tonight is a special occasion." Shannon smiled her thanks as the bartender placed a bottle of Corona beer sporting a wedge of lime in front of her. Before he rushed off he assured her the nachos would be out shortly. "We're celebrating."

The half-finished bottle Rachel had brought with her

from the table paused midway to her lips and a smile blossomed on her mouth. "You know I adore happy news. Clue me in. What are we celebrating?"

Shannon raised the beer in a mock toast. Initially she'd been hesitant about accepting Oliver's offer. But now she felt confident of her ability to withstand temptation. "My new job."

Rachel's smile froze. Then she clinked her bottle against the one Shannon held and sputtered out her congratulations.

"Thanks. I'm superjazzed." The position was all about Ollie, she reassured herself. She had no doubt she and the boy would get along splendidly. Shannon would not think about the way her heart hammered whenever Oliver was near.

"When did they call you?"

The quietly spoken question came out of nowhere. Shannon blinked and focused on her friend. "Who?"

"The person who contacted you about the Fortune Foundation job." Rachel cleared her throat. "When did you get the good news?"

The bartender, a thirtysomething-year-old with a shaved head, set a plate of loaded nachos in front of them.

"I never thought they'd choose someone this soon," Rachel continued before Shannon had a chance to respond. "But, hey, if it couldn't be me, I'm happy it was you."

"This isn't the foundation job. They won't let us know until the end of the month, remember?" Shannon picked up a chip dripping with cheese and nibbled. "I'm going to be a nanny to Oliver Fortune Hayes's son. It's short-term but the position pays extremely well."

"Oh." The tightness on Rachel's face eased. "When do you start?"

"I move in Sunday night." Shannon popped the nacho into her mouth. "I asked him for a few days to get my stuff together and my bags packed."

"You're moving in with him?" Rachel's voice rose.

Shannon quickly explained about the time difference and the need to be there to watch Ollie while Oliver was conducting business.

"How did your folks take the news?"

A twinkle of amusement danced in Rachel's eyes. Like most Horseback Hollow natives, her friend knew Shannon's parents were a bit on the conservative side.

Shannon grimaced, not looking forward to that conversation. "They don't know. Not yet. I was at Oliver's place until I came here. All I can do is assure them it's strictly business between us."

"Easy peasy." Rachel waved a dismissive hand. "Five minutes in his presence and they'll see it couldn't be anything but business."

Shannon frowned. "What makes you say that?"

"Think about how he stands, so straight and tall. It's like he's got a poker up his a—" Rachel stopped abruptly when she saw Pastor Dunbrook two stools away. She lowered her voice. "I'm just saying that while Oliver may look smokin' hot—and sound just as good as he looks—he has that British thing going."

"British thing?"

"Stiff upper lip and all that. Jolly good and tally-ho." Rachel tapped two fingers against her lips. "Kissing him would probably be like kissing a corpse."

As if Rachel's attempt at a proper British accent

wasn't hilarious enough, her describing Oliver as a cold fish made Shannon laugh.

"What's so funny?" Rachel tilted her head, and a speculative gleam shone in her eyes. "Have you already kissed him?"

"Ra-chel." The name was said with just the right touch of injured emotion and appeared to allay her friend's suspicions. "I barely know the man."

"That wouldn't stop me if I was interested in a guy."

"Well, I'm not interested in Oliver, not in that way. This is strictly a business arrangement."

"Then why did you laugh?"

"Because I don't see Oliver as being a cold fish."

"Yeah, right."

"No. Seriously. He's simply… British."

Rachel rolled her eyes and swiped a nacho off the plate.

"Okay, so maybe he's a bit uptight," Shannon admitted. "But it wouldn't take much to loosen him up."

"You go for it, sister." Rachel's red lips focused on something in the distance then curved upward in a sly smile. "In fact, there's no better time to start than right now."

"Other than I'm occupied, enjoying this scrumptious plate of nachos and—" Shannon lifted the Corona "—this ice-cold beer with you. Oliver, on the other hand, is—"

"Right behind you."

"What?"

"Turn," Rachel ordered.

Shannon swiveled on the bar stool. She inhaled sharply and her heart began pumping in time to the sexy salsa beat.

The man she'd been chatting with less than an hour earlier stood in the lobby. Ollie stood fidgeting at his side while Oliver chatted amiably with Wendy Fortune Mendoza and Marcos Mendoza, owners of the cantina. Wendy, looking as stylish as ever in a wrap dress of bright red with matching five-inch heels, clasped the hand of her three-year-old daughter, MaryAnne.

Even as Shannon's eyes were drawn to MaryAnne's adorable pink-and-white-striped dress, she couldn't help noticing the way Marcos's hand rested lovingly on his wife's shoulder or how hot Oliver looked.

He'd changed his clothes, wearing yet another dark suit but this time coupled with a gray shirt and charcoal tie. Odd he hadn't mentioned he had plans for the evening. He certainly hadn't acted as if he was in a rush for her to leave. Quite the contrary.

"Time to start warming up the iceberg," Rachel said in a low tone.

"Saying hello would be the polite thing to do," Shannon agreed, ignoring Rachel's snort of laughter.

Placing her Corona bottle down, Shannon hopped off the stool and pulled a small round mirror from her bag. Before taking a step, she touched up her lipstick, then flashed Rachel a smile. "Back in five."

Rachel lifted a nacho heavy with beef and cheese and gestured to the platter. "Just warning you, these may be all gone when you get back."

"I will return to find both the nachos *and* my seat waiting." Shannon pointed at her friend and spoke in an ominous voice suitable for any horror flick. "Or you will pay the price."

"No guarantee, Chickadee." Rachel peered over the Corona bottle at Shannon and those baby blues twinkled.

"If some sexy cowboy wants that stool, those chips or me, I'm sayin' yes."

Shannon ignored the warning and turned, anticipation fueling her steps as she headed across the hardwood floor toward Oliver.

Chapter 5

Though Oliver hadn't had the pleasure of meeting Wendy Fortune Mendoza before tonight, he was well aware she was one of his Texas cousins. The minute he walked into the Hollows Cantina, she greeted him warmly. Since she and her husband owned the cantina, Oliver assumed Wendy and Marcos were cohosting the last-minute party his mother, Josephine, had organized.

But Wendy informed him that she and Marcos wouldn't be able to stay. Even though they couldn't attend, they'd made the restaurant's private room available for the impromptu dinner.

"I'm happy to have the opportunity to meet you." Marcos, a tall man in a perfectly tailored suit with piercing dark eyes, gave Oliver's hand a firm shake.

From what Oliver had heard, Marcos was a savvy businessman, yet it was clear, seeing him with his wife and daughter, that family was also important to him. A man would have to be blind not to notice the loving way Marcos's gaze lingered on Wendy.

"I don't know if you heard but I've secured lodging at a ranch house on the Singleton property. I'll be there for the duration of my stay in Horseback Hollow." Oliver dropped his gaze and shot Ollie a warning glance when the child began tugging on his hand. "Stop by sometime. Bring your daughter. Ollie seems to enjoy being around other children."

"Wonderful. I'll call you this week and we'll set something up." Wendy started to say more but shifted her attention and smiled brilliantly. "Shannon. It's been ages."

Oliver turned to see Wendy give his new nanny a quick hug. She slipped an arm through Shannon's and lifted her gaze to Oliver. "I'm not sure if you've had a chance to meet Shep's daughter—"

"Introductions are unnecessary." Oliver offered Shannon a warm smile. "Miss Singleton and I are well acquainted."

Wendy exchanged a glance with her husband.

"Just this afternoon Shannon agreed to be Ollie's live-in nanny," Oliver announced.

Astonishment rippled across his cousin's pretty face. "Why, that's wonderful."

"Live-in?" Marcos's dark eyes narrowed. "Your father approves of this plan?"

"I'm twenty-five, Marcos," Shannon said drily. "I hardly need my father's okay."

"He's your father," Marcos said pointedly.

"Living in is necessary because of the time difference between here and London." Shannon quickly explained the circumstances, ignoring Marcos's disapproving glance and focusing on Wendy instead.

"Because of that six-hour difference, most of Oliver's business will be conducted during the overnight hours," Shannon continued before Oliver could add anything. "As a toddler, Ollie can't be counted on to sleep through the night."

"We know all about sleepless nights." Wendy shot a teasing glance at her husband. "Remember when MaryAnne was that age?"

Marcos nodded but his gaze remained troubled.

For the first time, Oliver considered what Shep Singleton would think of his daughter living under the roof of a man he didn't know. Would he understand that it was a simple business arrangement? Or would he worry Oliver might take advantage of Shannon?

Shep had been pleasant and accommodating when Oliver had called to inquire about the house. A personal visit to the Singleton home appeared necessary. Oliver would introduce himself, explain the situation and allay the man's fears before Shannon moved in on Monday.

He was planning his strategy when his mum, Josephine Fortune Chesterfield, breezed through the door, a vision in pale blue silk. Her gray hair, arranged in a chignon, flattered her handsome face. "I'm here. The party can begin."

She extended both hands and moved quickly to him. "Oliver."

"You look lovely as always." He took her hands in his then bent to brush a kiss against her cheek.

"Good evening, Wendy. Marcos." His mother's curious gaze settled on Shannon. "You're Shannon Singleton, Shep and Lilian's daughter. Am I correct?"

"You have an excellent memory, Mrs. Chesterfield." Shannon smiled at his mother. "How are you this evening?"

"Josephine, please. I'm wonderful, now that my son and grandson have joined me in Horseback Hollow."

Ollie made a sound of displeasure when Oliver tightened his hold on the child's hand.

"There's my little darling." Without warning, Josephine scooped Ollie up into her arms.

Startled, the boy stiffened. His eyes widened and his bottom lip began to tremble. Oliver certainly didn't relish snatching Ollie from his mother's arms. But neither did he want his son to start crying and cause a scene in public.

He was rapidly sorting through options when Shannon stepped forward and stroked the child's arm, diverting his attention.

"Hey, Ollie," she said in a gentle, melodious tone. "Remember me from this afternoon?"

Apparently the child did remember. His trembling lips morphed into a wide smile and he extended chubby arms to Shannon.

Instead of taking him from his grandmother as Oliver expected, Shannon clasped his small hands in hers and jiggled them up and down. "Can you tell your grandma your puppy's name?"

Ollie smiled, showing a mouthful of drool and tiny white teeth. "Barn-bee."

"Is Barnaby a nice puppy?" Josephine shot Shannon a grateful smile before refocusing on her grandson, now content in her arms.

As the two continued their corgi conversation, Oliver touched Shannon's arm, drawing her attention to him. "Thanks."

She shot him a wink. "No prob."

Their gazes locked and that electricity she'd mentioned returned to give him a hard jolt.

Blast it all to hell and back. He was not so crass as to be attracted to the nanny. Okay, so perhaps he was... intrigued. Shannon was different from the London socialites he frequently took to the opera and sometimes to bed.

But *intrigued* didn't translate into action. Correction, *wouldn't* lead to action. Even if Shannon wasn't his employee, Ollie and managing his business affairs were his top priority.

Shannon's eyes widened as Fortunes flooded the lobby, including Oliver's brother Jensen and his fiancée, Amber. "Why is everyone here? What's the occasion?"

"Mum decided to host a last-minute dinner party. She invited all the family in the area." Oliver smiled ruefully. "She didn't want to put my aunt out so she decided to have it here. She's a bit impulsive, but that's part of her charm."

"How fun. I admire spontaneity." A hint of wistfulness crept into Shannon's voice. "I'm not spontaneous. You miss out on a lot when you're always thinking things through."

"So true, my dear," Josephine interjected.

Shannon's cheeks grew pink. Clearly, she hadn't realized that his mother had eyes—and ears—in the back of her head.

"I was surprised to see you here this evening. I didn't know—" Oliver stopped, remembering. "That's right. You told me you had plans."

"I met some friends for happy hour." Shannon glanced over to the bar.

Oliver followed her gaze. A cowboy sat in the seat she'd vacated moments before, munching on nachos. Was the man someone she knew?

Oliver opened his mouth but shut it without speaking. Not his concern.

Strictly business, he reminded himself.

"It was a pleasure seeing you again, Josephine." Shannon's use of his mum's first name earned an approving smile. "Enjoy your dinner party and your grandson."

Shannon shifted her gaze to Oliver, and when those brown eyes settled on him, he experienced another punch of awareness.

"Trust me." She lowered her voice to a conspiratorial whisper. "Go with the enchiladas. They're the best."

Unable to resist touching her, Oliver reached over and lightly squeezed her shoulder. "Thank you…for everything."

Shannon smiled and strolled off.

"I thought someone said we were meeting in the party room," a feminine voice said. "But the lobby works for me."

Oliver turned to find a petite dark-haired woman with an angelic face and a wide smile approaching him.

"You probably don't remember me from the other night." The young woman extended her hand. "I'm Gabi Mendoza. We—"

"He remembers you, darlin'." Jude Fortune Jones, another one of Oliver's Horseback Hollow cousins, stepped forward and pressed a kiss on the top of Gabi's head. "No man forgets you."

Gabi flashed her tall blond fiancé an indulgent smile.

"Aw, thanks, honey. But Oliver saw a lot of new faces the day he arrived."

Though Oliver was exceedingly good with names and faces, Gabi was correct. With so many relatives to meet, including their spouses and significant others, he appreciated her courtesy. "We didn't have much of a chance to chat the other day."

"Tonight we'll get better acquainted over cowboy caviar," Gabi told him.

Oliver pulled his brows together, completely flummoxed. "Cowboy caviar?"

"It's not really caviar." Jude slanted a glance at his fiancée, who simply smiled cheekily.

"It's actually a type of dip," Gabi explained. "It contains black beans, tomato, avocado, onion, cilantro and corn."

"Interesting," Oliver murmured.

Jude grinned. "Let's just say it's a whole lot more tasty than those nasty fish eggs."

"Oliver has a discerning palate," Jude's brother Christopher Fortune Jones tossed out as he strolled past. "And you, bro, are just a hick from the sticks."

Jude's eyes flashed, but then Gabi wrapped her arms around his neck and pressed her nicely curved body against him. "I like you just the way you are, sweetie pie."

Oliver couldn't decide if he'd just witnessed normal sibling interaction or if there was more behind the tension between the brothers.

"Oh my goodness." Gabi pulled from Jude's arms. "I almost forgot."

The pretty Latina turned to Josephine, who still held her grandson.

"I hope you don't mind. I asked my father to join us tonight. Jude and I had planned to have dinner with him. Then you called and—"

"Orlando is here?" Josephine sounded oddly breathless.

"He's on his way. I hope it's no trouble."

"No trouble at all." Josephine's free hand rose to smooth her hair. "Orlando is always welcome."

Jude and Gabi wandered off to speak with Quinn and Amelia.

"I need to freshen, uh, check on a few things." Josephine's long elegant fingers fluttered in the air, sending diamonds flashing in the light.

"Would you like me to get everyone settled before we leave?" Wendy asked Josephine as relatives continued to arrive.

"That would be very much appreciated." Josephine patted her niece's shoulder, even as her gaze remained fixed on the door.

"Everyone." Wendy spoke loudly above the conversational din. "The waiters have appetizers and beverages for you in the party room. The buffet is in the process of being set up. Please make your way down the hall."

"Thank you, dear," Josephine said. "I'm sorry you can't stay."

"Next time," Wendy began.

"Honey, we're late." Marcos took his wife's arm.

After offering Josephine a quick hug, Wendy hurried off with her husband and daughter, stopping for a second where Shannon stood speaking with a couple Oliver didn't recognize. Locals, he decided, noticing the denim and boots.

His mother surprised him by calling Shannon's name

and motioning to her when she began to head out the door with Wendy and Marcos. When Shannon sauntered over, Josephine took one of her hands. "I fear I didn't make it clear—I'd love for you to join us."

"C'mon, Shannon, join us. Please." Gabi had returned. She slanted a glance at Oliver. "Shannon made me feel so welcome when I came to stay in Horseback Hollow last year after my father's accident."

Clearly, the two women were friends. Still, Shannon hesitated. "I don't want to intrude."

"You're not intruding." Oliver's gaze locked on hers. "You're very much wanted."

You're very much wanted.

What was there about the sentiment, said in that delightful British accent, that made her want to giggle like a nervous schoolgirl? The words echoed in her head, even as Shannon gestured to Rachel that she'd call her later. Her friend smiled and nodded, then refocused her attention back on the cowboy who was eating the last nacho.

While Ollie remained tightly clutched in his grandmother's arms, Shannon strolled with Oliver down a wide hallway to a large room that resembled the inside of a Mexican hacienda. It had arched doorways, stucco walls of bold red and spicy mustard and a tile floor that complemented the warmth of the walls.

Oliver slanted a sideways glance. "It was fortuitous, running into you here."

"Fortuitous for me." Shannon shot him an impish smile. "I'm getting dinner out of the deal."

"And I will have the pleasure of your company," Oliver said gallantly.

"You're going to be sick of me very soon," she teased with an ease that surprised her. "Underfoot practically 24/7."

"I'll be working a lot of hours," he said seriously. "Our contact will likely be minimal."

Shannon pulled back a scowl. He didn't have to sound so doggone pleased at the prospect. "Hopefully you'll carve out some time to play with Ollie."

Surprise flashed in his eyes. "Entertaining him, keeping him safe and tending to his needs will now be your job."

Before she could formulate a response, she was handed a margarita and Oliver was swept away.

Though Shannon hadn't done much socializing with the British branch of the Fortunes who'd recently arrived in Horseback Hollow, she'd grown up with Jeanne Marie's children. There were seven of them and they were all here tonight, as was Josephine's sister, Jeanne Marie.

Shannon mingled, accepting an empanada appetizer from a passing waiter before taking a seat at a table with Gabi and Kinsley Aaron. Kinsley was the outreach coordinator for the Fortune Foundation and engaged to Christopher Fortune Jones.

Since both women were set to be wed on Valentine's Day, bridal talk dominated the conversation and continued after they went through the buffet line and sat down with their plates of food.

Oliver stood across the room, caught up in conversation with his brother-in-law, Quinn Drummond. Back in middle school, Shannon had the hugest crush on Quinn. When she was thirteen she'd gathered the courage to ask him to a turnabout dance.

When both Quinn and Oliver turned to look at her,

Shannon smiled and wiggled her fingers in a semblance of a wave, praying Quinn wasn't relaying to Oliver the awful story of how she'd awkwardly asked him out.

Abruptly she turned to Gabi and bared her teeth as her gaze flickered. "All clear?"

Gabi swallowed a bite of salad. "Perfect. Why?"

"Just checking." Shannon glanced at Gabi's chicken taco salad; heavy on romaine, light on cheese, no tortilla bowl. "How's the salad?"

"Delicious." Gabi smiled. "What about the enchiladas?"

"Truly out of this world." Shannon took another bite, savoring the taste. "You should try one."

The suggestion was out before she remembered Gabi was committed to eating nutritionally. Looking at her, it was hard to believe Gabi had needed a heart transplant when she was nineteen.

"This will fill me up, thanks." Gabi flashed an easy smile and gestured to where Oliver now stood speaking with his sister, Amelia. "Give me your take on Oliver."

Though she and Gabi were currently alone—Kinsley had joined her fiancé at another table—Shannon didn't immediately answer. "What do you mean?"

"You must like him well enough to go to work for him, to live with him."

"I think our *business* arrangement will work out well for both of us." Shannon chose her words carefully, knowing whatever she said stood a good chance of getting back to Oliver.

Jude was his cousin, after all. And Gabi didn't seem the type to have secrets from her fiancé.

"I'm asking what you think of him as a man." Gabi waggled a fork at Shannon. Her dark eyes sparkled.

"Admit it. Doesn't that sexy accent make you want to swoon?"

"Who are you swooning over, Gabrielle?" Jude appeared out of nowhere to plop down in the chair Kinsley had recently vacated. "Before you answer, let me warn you that it better be me."

He lifted her hand to his mouth and kissed her knuckles.

"Sorry, Charlie." Gabi wrinkled her nose, her tone teasing. "Your cousin Oliver's accent has us both swooning. Isn't that right, Shannon?"

"That's a kick in the shorts." Though he tried to look stern, Jude failed miserably. Once he got the smile that kept trying to form on his lips under control, he turned and called out, "Oliver, get your ass over here."

Oliver merely glanced over at the sound of his name.

Jude made an impatient "come here" motion with his hand.

After a few final words to his sister, Oliver strode over.

"He was speaking with Amelia." Shannon had a sinking feeling she knew why Jude had summoned Oliver.

"Now he'll be speaking with us," Jude said, suddenly all affable-cowboy charm. He reached over and pulled up a chair when Oliver approached the table. "Join us."

Oliver's brows pulled together.

Beneath Oliver's polished smile, Shannon saw signs of fatigue. Had everyone forgotten that he'd made a transatlantic flight with a toddler only days earlier?

"What can I do for you, Jude?" Oliver asked.

Shannon thought his eyes may have lingered on her for an extra heartbeat, but she couldn't be certain.

"You can stop making the ladies swoon."

Obviously perplexed, Oliver glanced over at Shannon for clarification.

She simply smiled and shifted her gaze to Jude. This was his bronc in the rodeo, not hers.

"These ladies—" Jude gestured to Shannon and Gabi "—are swooning over your accent."

Oliver ignored Gabi to focus on Shannon. Though she'd never been the wilting-violet, blushing type, heat rose up her neck.

"Actually, it was me." Gabi raised her hand like a schoolgirl eager to talk. "I adore your accent. Though I'm not sure the effect would be the same, can you teach me to speak like you?"

Poor Oliver.

Two lines formed between his brows. It was obvious he didn't quite know what to make of his cousin's soon-to-be bride or the plate of cowboy caviar someone shoved into his hand.

"Gabi's teasing you." Shannon spoke in a matter-of-fact tone and took a sip of the margarita.

"Oh."

"I'm in the mood for some dancing," Jude announced. "Mind keeping the ladies company while I get that started?"

"Dancing?" Shannon smiled. "On what dance floor?"

"That will be remedied momentarily," Jude said over his shoulder.

"Don't even bother trying to figure him out." Gabi's tone was filled with warm affection. The smile was still on her lips when she shifted her attention to Oliver. "I was surprised to see Amelia and Quinn here."

"Why?"

"Their baby is so tiny."

"I'm certain whoever is watching her has been cleared by Scotland Yard."

Oliver sat the plate of "caviar" down just as the sweet melody of a romantic ballad filled the air, followed by Jude's booming voice.

"I don't know about the other grooms-to-be, but with the wedding less than two weeks away, I need to practice my dance steps," Jude said.

"Give it up, Jude," one of his brothers called out. "Practice isn't going to change the fact that you have two left feet."

"He does not," Gabi muttered indignantly.

"Shut up, Chris," Jude shot back good-naturedly. "We're going to use this part of the room for dancin', so everyone put down your drinks and grab a partner."

"That's my man," Gabi said with pride. "A real take-charge guy."

Her take-charge guy returned to the table to pull her to her feet and lead her to the area he had cleared for dancing. They weren't the only couple. All around Shannon and Oliver, men and women were pairing up.

When Shannon saw a woman walk by with a toddler, it struck Shannon that she hadn't seen Ollie for a while. "Where's Ollie?"

"Mum is changing his nappy." Oliver grasped on to the topic like a drowning man would grab a life jacket. "I couldn't pry him away from her even if I wanted to."

Do you want to, Oliver?

He looked at her so strangely that for a split second Shannon thought she must have spoken aloud. Until she realized his growing unease was because everyone who'd been seated at their table was now dancing.

Oliver pushed back his chair and abruptly stood.

When he opened his mouth, Shannon found herself anticipating what it would feel like to be held in his strong arms.

"If you'll excuse me." His head inclined in a slight bow. "I must check on my son."

Oliver turned on his heel and strode off, leaving Shannon alone and, just as when she was thirteen, without a date for the dance.

Chapter 6

By ten the next morning, Oliver had fed his son, changed his nappy for the third time and was ready to get down to business. He placed Ollie in his car seat and set off for the Triple S ranch.

He called Shannon's father to make sure he'd be home, indicating he had something of a personal nature to discuss with him. When Shep had bluntly asked what it was, Oliver told him it was a matter best discussed in person. So here he was, on a bright and sunny Saturday morning in early February, headed over to clarify with a Texas rancher that he didn't have designs on his daughter.

Certainly Shannon intrigued him. How could she not, with eyes the color of rich, dark cocoa and a smile that pierced his reserve as easily as an arrow through marshmallow. Was it any wonder that last night he'd been seriously tempted to ask her to dance?

Oliver wheeled the Mercedes onto the highway, remembering how very close he'd come to asking her. But that, he thought rather righteously, was the difference between a strong man and a weak one. No matter how tempted he was to see what it would feel like to hold her in his arms, Oliver hadn't given in to temptation.

In fact, he'd walked away. Not because he couldn't handle the temptation but because he'd seen the way her foot tapped in time to the music and the longing way she glanced at the couples dancing. By leaving the table, he'd made it easier for other men to ask her.

Yet, when he'd watched his cousin Galen stroll over and Shannon had risen to take his arm, Oliver had felt a twinge of unease. He hoped his cousin was an honorable man.

Oliver couldn't help noticing Galen held her a little too closely when they danced. And why was he whispering in her ear? What could they be saying that was so secretive? It had to be a ploy to get even closer to her. And from what Oliver had observed, it worked.

Actually it was something Oliver might have done if she'd been in his arms. But Shannon was his employee. Not that a man couldn't dance with his employee. But he could never hold her close.

The last thing Oliver wanted was to mess up a good working relationship before it even began. Some women could handle a casual, meaningless affair. He had the distinct impression that Shannon wasn't like those women. In fact, she'd made it clear she wanted a business relationship only. He'd agreed. He'd given her his word. And a gentleman always kept his word.

Though right now Oliver didn't feel much like a gentleman.

Thoughts of Shannon occupied him during the rest of the drive to the Singleton ranch. By the time Oliver turned onto the long lane leading to the house, Ollie was fast asleep. Oliver stifled a groan at the sight of the boy's lolling head in the rearview mirror. He'd discovered if Ollie napped throughout the day, he often didn't sleep well at night.

But Oliver couldn't concern himself with that now. He would get through another night of little to no sleep with the thought that tomorrow night Shannon would be there to take care of Ollie. And Oliver would finally be able to get back to business.

For now, he had a different kind of business to attend to, and he wasn't looking forward to it.

Before confirming a time, he'd asked Shep if Shannon was home. According to Shep, she'd left early that morning to attend a "farmers' market" in Vicker's Corners and wasn't expected back until noon. By that time, Oliver's business should be concluded.

The Singleton home was a two-story with white siding, black shutters and a wraparound porch. The bushes on each side of the walk leading to the front steps looked like a sturdy variety with burnished red leaves and tiny thorns.

Oliver noticed the ceiling of the porch was painted blue, like the sky. Seeing the swing made him wonder if Shannon ever sat there and shared kisses with some lucky man while a full moon shone overhead.

Oliver chuckled at the fanciful thought and shifted Ollie's weight in his arms. Though his son was by no means fat, he was sturdy, weighing in at approximately a stone and a half. Not that easy to carry when he squirmed as he was doing now.

Having Ollie with him wasn't ideal but Oliver had brought some of the boy's favorite toys, so hopefully that would keep him occupied during the brief discussion with Shannon's father.

When Oliver reached the front door, he had Ollie stand beside him while he rang the bell.

The door opened several seconds later.

"You must be Oliver." Shep Singleton was a tall man in his late fifties with a thick thatch of gray hair and a lean, weathered face.

Dressing down for the occasion had been a smart move, Oliver decided. Though he considered this a business call, he hadn't worn his suit. Instead he'd taken a page from Jensen's playbook and chosen a pair of khakis and a polo.

Even with the concession, he felt overdressed compared with Shep's jeans and flannel shirt.

Because Shep didn't extend his hand, Oliver kept his own at his side.

"Come in." Shep motioned to him. "Lilian has coffee brewin' and she's cutting some slices of her blue-ribbon banana bread."

Oliver didn't think he'd ever had blue-ribbon banana bread. In fact he was fairly certain he'd never had regular banana bread. He considered asking how blue ribbon differed from regular, just for his own edification, but decided it wasn't important. Not when they had more important things to discuss.

He followed Shep into a foyer that was pleasant but unremarkable, with a staircase straight ahead and a parlor to the right. Because the older man's strides were long, Oliver was forced to pick up Ollie to keep pace.

The kitchen was as old-fashioned as the rest of the

house, with appliances the color of avocado and a chrome kitchen table with a swirly gray-green top. There was an ornamental print on the wall with teapots and kettles of all shapes and colors.

A slender woman who reminded Oliver of her daughter, with warm brown eyes and hair the color of strong tea, turned to greet him.

"It's so good to finally meet you," Lilian said with a warm, welcoming smile. "When Shep told me you were stopping by, I hoped you'd be bringing this little guy with you."

Her gaze lingered on Ollie, and a soft look filled her eyes. She reached inside a clown jar and pulled out what looked like an oat biscuit. The questioning look in her eyes had Oliver nodding.

Lilian moved slowly to the child, who stood looking around the colorful kitchen with a wide, unblinking look of wonder.

"Hi, Ollie." She crouched down with the ease of a woman used to constant movement.

The toddler stared at her.

"Do you like cookies?" Lilian held it up in front of him, and when she was certain she had his attention, she broke off a piece and held it out to him.

A shy smile hovered on Ollie's lips. Still, after a moment, he reached out and took the piece from her hand, shoving it into his mouth.

"Ollie, what do you say to Mrs. Singleton?" Oliver prompted.

"Tank ooh," Ollie spoke around a mouthful of cookie.

Lilian ruffled his hair in a casual gesture and stood. "He's darling. Shannon has four younger brothers, so we're used to boys around this house."

"Four boys." Oliver almost cringed. He had a difficult time managing one. "That must have kept you busy."

"I'll say. For years I didn't know if I was coming or going. I longed for just a couple hours to myself. Even fifteen minutes." She laughed and a wistful look crossed her face. "Now I'd give anything to have that time back."

Her gaze dropped to Ollie. "Cherish every minute with your son. Time goes by so quickly."

Shep cleared his throat. "I told Oliver you had some banana bread for us. And coffee."

Lilian flashed a smile. "What's conversation without coffee and banana bread?"

Without realizing how it happened, Oliver was at the table with a steaming mug of strong coffee before him and a small plate containing delicious-smelling bread still warm from the oven.

He waited for Lilian to dispense the sterling, but when none was forthcoming and he saw Shep pick up the slice and take a bite, Oliver followed suit. When in Rome...

"This blue-ribbon banana bread is excellent," he told Lilian, making her blush.

"Last year it won a purple at the state fair."

Oliver simply nodded and smiled. He made a mental note to ask his sister about a "purple."

"Well, I'll leave you boys to your business." Lilian refilled their coffee cups before her gaze shifted to Oliver. "Being as it's such a nice day, I thought I'd air out some blankets on the line. Would you mind if I took Ollie with me? I promise I'll keep an eye on him."

Oliver hesitated. "He's wanted to stay close lately. Last night he didn't even want my mum to hold him."

Of course, his mother had unthinkingly swooped in, startling him. Still, Ollie had recently become cautious around people he didn't know. Other than Shannon. He'd taken to her right off.

"Do you mind if I give it a try?"

"Not at all." It would be easier to speak with Shep if he didn't have to keep Ollie occupied.

"Ollie." Lilian crouched down beside the boy, who still held the scruffy yellow tiger he'd had when Oliver had picked him up from Diane's parents.

According to Diane's mum, they'd given the stuffed animal to Ollie when he was born, and it was a favorite of his. She'd had tears in her eyes when she'd relayed the story, Oliver recalled.

At the time, Oliver hadn't paid much mind to her. He'd been so angry with them for withholding information of Diane's death. For keeping his son from him.

"Would you like to go outside with me? You can take Mr. Tiger with you, if you like," her voice continued, low, calm and soothing.

There was something about the way Lilian spoke that reminded Oliver of Shannon. An intonation. Or a certain cadence in her speech. Not an accent, though the woman certainly sounded American. He finally concluded it was the warmth that wove through each word like a wool scarf on a foggy morning.

Whatever the reason, Ollie responded the same way to Lilian as he had to Shannon. Instantly and with no hesitation.

Lilian took his hand in hers. The two made it all the way to the door leading outside before they turned back. "Say, 'Bye-bye, Daddy. See you soon.'"

She demonstrated a wave for the child.

"Bye-bye," Ollie said in his high-pitched, sweet baby voice. "See you soon."

Oliver smiled, even though he noticed Ollie didn't call him "Daddy." He never did. Of course his vocabulary was rather limited, consisting of only twenty-five words. Still, if Ollie could say the dog's name, shouldn't he be able to say "Daddy"?

Once the back door banged shut, Oliver decided to get right to the point. "I suppose you're wondering why I'm here."

Shep lifted his piece of bread. "I figure you're fixin' to tell me."

The older man bit into the bread, then washed the piece down with a swig of coffee. He leaned back in his chair and studied Oliver intently.

For a second Oliver felt like one of those young lads in films, meeting his girl's parents for the first time. Oliver had no personal experience in this arena. He'd been sent to a preparatory school when he was thirteen. Functions with suitable girls' schools had been prearranged. No parents involved.

"Your daughter has agreed to be Ollie's nanny while I'm in Horseback Hollow."

"She mentioned something about that the other night," Shep admitted.

Oliver felt a surprising surge of relief. "Then you don't have a problem with her moving in."

The mug of coffee Shep had lifted to his mouth froze in midair. He lowered it slowly until it came to rest on the table.

Unlike his daughter's, Shep's eyes were a piercing pale blue. Oliver felt the full force of his gaze punch into him.

"Move in. With you?"

"Not with me," Oliver clarified, keeping his tone conversational. "Into the house."

"Your house."

"Technically your house," Oliver pointed out.

"Don't give me any double-talk, boy." Shep's eyes narrowed and Oliver felt as if he were in the crosshairs of his father's foul temper once again.

Though Rhys Henry Hayes hadn't remained married to Josephine for long, it had been long enough for them to have two sons together, and for his father to make Oliver's life a living hell.

"Shannon will always be treated with respect when she's under my roof." Oliver met Shep's gaze with a calm one of his own.

As a young boy, Oliver had vowed he'd never be intimidated by any man ever again. "That's why I'm here. To let you know she will be my son's nanny. My employee. Nothing more. She's safe with me."

Shep's expression gave nothing away. He took a big gulp of coffee before he responded. "Shannon is twenty-five. As much as I'd like to, I can't make her decisions. But I will speak bluntly."

"Please do," Oliver said quietly.

"After what happened in Lubbock, after that incident, I don't feel comfortable with her being there with only a baby in diapers as a chaperone."

Oliver cocked his head. "What incident in Lubbock?"

"Oliver."

Shannon paused in the doorway, taking in the cozy scene with her father and Oliver at the table. She let her gaze sweep over the half-eaten pieces of banana bread and coffee mugs in need of refills.

"Your father was about to tell me about some incident in Lubbock," Oliver told her.

* * *

Despite telling herself not to react, Shannon felt her spine grow rigid, vertebra by vertebra. She shot her father a fulminating glance that, as usual, he ignored.

"Correct me if I'm wrong, but I believe that's my story to tell. Or not." Forcing a smile, Shannon shifted her attention back to Oliver. "It's not all that interesting. I had a boss who got a little handsy. It's over and done. I've moved on."

The back door clattered and seconds later, her mother strode into the room, Ollie chattering happily at her side. "Shannon, honey. When did you get home?"

"Just walked through the door," Shannon answered absently, her mind back in Lubbock. She didn't like thinking of that time. It was in the past and she meant what she'd said to Oliver—she'd moved on. "Do you have any more banana bread?"

"It'll spoil your appetite for lunch," her father warned.

Some things never change, Shannon thought ruefully. But instead of being irritated, she found the knowledge strangely reassuring.

"You're eating it," she pointed out. "Won't it spoil *your* lunch?"

"Nope." Shep grinned and popped the last bite into his mouth.

Shannon rolled her eyes. "Oh, honestly."

Oliver's gaze traveled between her and her father, as if he found their simple exchange fascinating.

Out of the corner of her eye, Shannon saw Ollie run across the room to Oliver. He swung the child onto his lap with a welcoming smile.

Shannon's heart swelled. How could she have ever thought this man didn't care about his son?

"I hope the bread didn't spoil your appetite, Oliver. I'd love to have you join us for lunch." Lilian wrapped the rest of the loaf in plastic wrap. "We're having quiche."

Shep grimaced. "Aw, Lil, why not burgers?"

"Too much red meat isn't good for you." Lilian's argument was an old one, repeated daily. She shifted to Oliver. "We're also having a nice salad of dark greens with a balsamic vinaigrette I make myself."

"What happened to the good ole days of iceberg and Thousand Island?" Shep groused.

Lilian ignored the comment to focus on their guest. "If you don't think Ollie would like quiche, I can rustle him up some mac and cheese."

Shannon expected Oliver to make some excuse to leave. Once again he surprised her.

"Thank you, Mrs. Singleton." He gestured to the now-empty plate before him. "If your quiche is as good as your blue-ribbon banana bread, I'm in for a treat."

"Splendid. And please, call me Lilian." Her mother smiled. "If you and Shep have concluded your conversation, why don't you take Shannon and Ollie out to the porch and check out the swing? It's a beautiful day and it'll give me a chance to clear the table and get ready for lunch. Shouldn't be more than a half hour or so."

Oliver rose and smiled at Shannon. "I don't know that I've ever sat with a pretty woman on a porch swing before."

Shep shoved back his chair. "I'll join you."

"Honey." Lilian covered the sharp tone with a laugh. "You're not going anywhere. You're staying right here and helping me."

"I can help you, Mother."

"No, no. Your father will help." Lilian turned to her

husband and looped her arm through his. "Shep, sweetie, I think I may have a bottle of Thousand Island in the pantry after all. Why don't you look for it while Shannon and Oliver head outside?"

Shannon thought about telling her mother she knew exactly where to find the salad dressing, but kept her mouth shut. Her mother had it in her head that she and Oliver were going to have some time alone on the swing, and there was no getting around that.

Besides, Shannon was curious about what Oliver and her father had been discussing when she arrived. For that matter, she wanted to know exactly what had brought Oliver to the Singleton ranch this morning in the first place.

At this moment, she hadn't a clue. Oliver was a difficult man to figure out. Like last night at the dinner party. They'd been having a perfectly lovely conversation when he'd ditched her. Once he'd left the table, she hadn't seen him again all evening.

She'd enjoyed a couple of dances with his cousin, then headed out. Now she arrived home to find him shooting the breeze with her dad.

"Oliver." She looped her arm through his and shot him the same sugary-sweet smile her mother had offered her father only seconds earlier. "Let's swing and you can tell me what brought you all the way out here this morning."

Chapter 7

Though it was only February, the outside temperature felt more like June. Thankfully there was a light breeze from the north and the covered porch shielded Oliver and Shannon from the worst of the midday sun. Shannon took a seat at one end of the swing and Oliver sat down with Ollie at the other.

Almost immediately, the child left his father's lap to scoot over to Shannon. He rested his head on her lap and she automatically began to stroke his soft brown hair. In seconds, his eyelids closed and he fell quickly asleep.

"He shouldn't be that tired." Oliver glanced down at his son with a worried frown. "He slept in the car on the way here."

"Little boys expend a lot of energy." Shannon smiled, then sobered as she remembered there was something they needed to discuss. She met his gaze. "Tell me why you came all the way out here today."

"To speak with your father."

Shannon curbed her impatience and merely lifted a brow. "About?"

"The comments Marcos made last night got me to thinking." Oliver shifted on the white lacquered slats. "I decided to reassure your father you would be safe and respected under my roof."

Shannon pressed her lips together and counted to five. "I am in charge of my own life, Oliver. Whatever goes on, or doesn't, under your roof is our business. Not my father's. Not my mother's. Understand?"

He stared at her for a long moment. "I see your point."

"I appreciate that your intentions came from a good place," she acknowledged. "But this is between us."

She wasn't sure exactly what all "this" encompassed, but for now it was simply the job and taking care of Ollie.

"You went behind my back." Shannon did her best to keep the hurt from her voice. After growing up in a family of men, she'd learned there was no quicker turn-off than to lead from emotion. "You never even mentioned you were considering speaking with my father."

"That's because it was something I decided last night."

"There were opportunities during the evening when you could have discussed your concerns with me," she said pointedly.

He reluctantly nodded, then surprised them both by reaching over and taking her hand. "Apologies. I overstepped."

She searched his gaze and saw only sincerity.

"Accepted." Shannon made no move to pull her hand away as the swing moved slowly.

"What happened in Lubbock?"

She blinked and jerked her fingers free. "I already told you."

"You said your previous employer got 'handsy.' That's not much of an explanation."

Should she tell him? If so, how much should she say? Even though it wasn't all that long ago, in Shannon's mind it was ancient history. She'd moved on. Still, it wasn't as if she had anything to hide, and if she didn't spill, she wouldn't put it past Oliver to do some investigating on his own.

"My last job was with a marketing firm in Lubbock. My direct supervisor, Jerry, was the CEO's nephew." Though Shannon did her best to keep her voice matter-of-fact, it shook slightly. She continued to stroke Ollie's hair and found the motion relaxed her. "He wasn't much older than me, but he was married with two kids."

Oliver made an encouraging sound.

Shannon felt the urge to get up and pace, but couldn't because of Ollie. The twist in her belly told her she wasn't completely over what had happened. Not fully, anyway.

"Jerry seemed nice at first, though there was something about him that put me on alert. Too many compliments of a personal nature, and whenever he was at my desk, he stood too close. I told myself I was just overreacting. At my previous job I'd worked with all women, so overreacting seemed plausible."

Oliver didn't speak, simply inclined his head in a gesture that seemed to indicate she should keep talking.

"Then he started touching me."

Oliver's head jerked up and a muscle in his jaw jumped. "Touching you?"

"It started out innocent enough—a hand on my shoulder while he leaned over to look at my computer screen, brushing back a strand of hair from my face." Shannon gazed down at Ollie's head resting in her lap. She swallowed past the dryness in her throat. "I told him the touching made me uncomfortable. But no matter what I said, he turned it around and made me wonder if I was being too sensitive. You know, making something out of nothing."

"He made you doubt your instincts."

"Yes. He didn't listen to my concerns, didn't acknowledge they were valid. I let the issue drop. That was my first mistake."

"What happened?" Oliver asked in a low, tight voice.

"One night, shortly before Thanksgiving, we were working late. I made a point to never be alone with him. It started out as four of us working on a campaign. The other two ended up leaving. I was almost finished so I stayed behind. That was my second mistake."

Without her quite realizing how it had happened, her hand was once again in Oliver's. The warmth of his strong fingers wrapping around hers gave Shannon the strength to continue.

"He—he pulled me to him, kissed me, told me his wife and kids were out of town and we'd have his house to ourselves. No one would ever know." Shame bubbled up inside Shannon. "He wouldn't let go of me. Finally I was able to jerk away. My shirt tore. I started crying."

"Bastard," she thought she heard Oliver mutter.

"I reminded him he was a married man. He laughed and called me a tease. But when I said I was going to his boss, he turned the tables again and accused me of coming on to him. Said he was shocked and appalled by my behavior. Then he asked who did I think his uncle would believe? Him, an upstanding family man and deacon of his church? Or me? A single woman who'd never complained about his behavior until now?" Shannon lifted her gaze to meet Oliver's. "I turned in my resignation without even giving notice. I returned to Horseback Hollow and put it all behind me."

Oliver's fingers tightened around hers.

She waited for him to say that she should have stood up for herself, should have at least told his uncle the story, but to her relief he didn't.

"I loved my job," she added. "It was hard to walk away. But I didn't see that I had any choice."

"You made the best decision for you."

"I did." Shannon felt herself relax and was sorry when Oliver released her hand. "Though it still makes me angry you went behind my back, it's probably a good thing you spoke with my father. He doesn't have a very high opinion of male employers right now."

"I meant what I said," Oliver told her. "You're perfectly safe with me."

Shannon could only wonder why she found his words more disappointing than reassuring.

When Oliver arrived home later, it was after two. By then Ollie was cranky and out of sorts. After changing his nappy, Oliver sat the boy down on the rug in the living room with his bricks, hoping a little quiet play would relax him.

But Ollie refused to be distracted or comforted. He knocked down the stack that Oliver had arranged, then picked up one and flung it across the room. When Oliver tried to put him down for a nap, he stood at the edge of the playpen and cried, rocking back and forth like a monkey in a cage as tears slipped down his chubby cheeks.

Though Oliver had some catching up to do on market indices, he lifted his son up and settled into the rocker with him. Every time Ollie pulled back, Oliver would bring him back against him. Finally the boy quit struggling, his hands resting on his shoulders as Oliver rocked him. Back and forth. Back and forth.

Oliver wondered if Diane had ever rocked Ollie. Or, for that matter, had Mrs. Crowder, his London nanny? This was a first for him, but he'd been desperate. As he felt his son relax against him, Oliver realized rocking was really quite nice. A connection. Between him and Ollie.

A connection that only served to remind him how much of Ollie's life he'd missed.

Not insisting on regular visitation had been a mistake. Just as Shannon not pressing charges against her boss had been a mistake. In his estimation the man shouldn't be able to harass an employee—hell, *assault* an employee—and get away with it.

Not only get away with it, but make her feel as if the whole thing was somehow her fault. That's why he hadn't added to her guilt by suggesting she could have handled the situation differently. She'd made the best decision based on where she was at the time.

Oliver closed his eyes, realizing he was more tired than he thought. Adjusting to a different time zone while having total care of a small boy had proved more difficult than he'd initially envisioned.

His respect for mothers and nannies had gone up a thousandfold…

Oliver awoke to a small hand pressed against his face. When his lids eased open, he found himself staring directly into Ollie's bright eyes.

"Up," Ollie ordered. "Get up."

The child could say "get up" but couldn't manage "Daddy"?

By the foul smell permeating the air, Oliver knew Ollie wouldn't simply need a nappy change. He'd probably need a bath, as well. His prediction proved correct.

It wasn't until Ollie was changed, bathed and fed that it struck Oliver that the child's schedule was going to be disrupted once again. Tonight was Amelia and Quinn's baby shower. He wasn't certain what to expect, but he assumed a gift was de rigueur. Thankfully, Oliver hadn't had a chance to give them the limited-edition Highgrove baby hamper he'd picked up at Harrods department store before he left London.

Though he wasn't sure if Amelia was still into organic supplies or not, the hamper contained not only a fully jointed antique mohair Highgrove bear, but an assortment of organic baby products created with a blend of oils to be calm and soothing to a baby's skin. The salesclerk had assured him the baby hamper was a popular gift for new mothers.

Diane had been a new mother once. Had she been as thrilled by Ollie as Amelia was by Clementine? Perhaps.

Oliver raked a hand through his hair. Their marriage had already been in trouble when Ollie was born. He'd dealt with the increased tension and Diane's unhappiness in the only way he knew how, by working even harder and giving her expensive trinkets. It hadn't been enough. Oliver expelled a heavy push of air, feeling the full weight of his failure.

He placed Ollie in the Pack 'n Play and watched his son pick up a toy truck with a squeal of delight.

He'd made so many mistakes...

Banishing the unproductive thoughts and emotions, Oliver motioned Barnaby off the sofa and headed for the shower. He'd never been to a couple's baby party. Gabi and Jude were hosting the event, held at his aunt Jeanne Marie's spacious ranch home.

By the time Oliver arrived, cars and trucks lined both sides of the graveled drive. He parked at the end of the long line. A truck immediately pulled in behind him.

He paid little attention, his focus on releasing Ollie from his car seat. They were late and Oliver prided himself on being punctual. However, when he'd let Barnaby outside, right before they were to leave home, the dog had run off. Oliver had wasted precious minutes looking for the animal, who'd received a stern lecture once he returned.

"We're going to have to quit meeting like this."

He turned and there was Shannon, wearing a shirt and skirt the color of mint, her hair pulled back in a casual twist.

"You look amazing," he said.

"You don't look so bad yourself." Her gaze settled momentarily on his gray trousers and open-necked white shirt. "Let me hold your gift while you fumble with the car seat."

"Fumble is right." Oliver gave a laugh. "He's strapped in tighter than most astronauts."

Shannon stood close while he unbuckled Ollie. The light vanilla scent of her perfume was pleasing. "I should have realized you'd be here, what with Amelia being your sister."

"A sister who is a bugger about punctuality."

"We're not that—" Shannon glanced at her watch. "Eek. You're right. We are late. We need to hoof it."

She started down the lane toward the house at a surprisingly fast clip, the gifts hugged to her chest.

Oliver scooped up Ollie and headed after her.

They reached the house at the same time and climbed the steps to the porch in unison. Oliver rang the bell.

It was only seconds before the door opened and Jude waved them inside.

The gifts were lifted from Shannon's hands and Gabi directed Oliver to a temporary playroom set up at the back of the house. Several children were already there, along with two teenage child-care workers.

To Oliver's surprise, Ollie screeched in excitement and hurried over to pick up a plastic bat. Oliver only shook his head. His son's mercurial moods were a constant mystery. He told the teenage babysitter to come and get him if Ollie got scared.

As he didn't want to simply disappear—though the thought was tempting—Oliver walked over to Ollie and told him he was leaving and would be back soon. Ollie blinked, opening and closing his hand in the gesture Lilian had taught him. "Bye-bye."

Before leaving the room, Oliver reiterated to the young woman monitoring the door not to hesitate to retrieve him if Ollie turned fussy. He saw by the look on her face she'd written him off as just another overprotective parent. Especially considering Ollie was now happily banging the plastic bat like a drum on the floor.

His duty completed, Oliver hurried from the room and found Shannon waiting with two flutes of champagne.

She shoved one into his hand. "For you."

"Thank you." He took a sip and found the vintage very much to his taste. As they strolled down the hall, Oliver began to relax. "This evening may not be so bad after all."

"I'll ask how you feel after the games."

"Games?"

"Oh, yeah," Shannon said as they headed into the large double parlor where the guests were congregated. "You can't have a baby shower without games."

Oliver couldn't begin to imagine what kind of games she meant.

"There's the last couple," Gabi called out when he and Shannon entered the parlor. "We can get started now."

For a second, Oliver looked around to see whom she meant until he realized she was talking about him and Shannon. He started to protest until he saw Shannon's friend Rachel had been paired with Quinn's elderly aunt.

Not that he minded being paired with Shannon for whatever games they would play; he simply didn't want to put her in an awkward position of everyone thinking they were a couple.

"What's the game, Gabi?" Shannon smiled easily, looking relaxed among this group of friends.

Even though Amelia was his sister and he was family, Oliver was clearly the outsider today. Though he was proficient at social conversation, he was rather relieved Gabi appeared ready to launch into the scheduled activities.

The first game was a baby word scramble. Each "team" was given twenty words where the letters had been scrambled. Oliver was, by nature, a competitive person. He quickly discovered Shannon shared his must-win attitude.

Sitting beside each other on an overstuffed sofa, they breezed through the first nineteen words. Then they reached number twenty.

"BELOTT." Shannon gazed down at the word. Her brows pulled together.

Oliver knew he should be studying the letters. But the simple task of focusing had become increasingly difficult with each word. He couldn't take his eyes off the side of Shannon's face, off the graceful arch of her neck, off the woman who took his breath away.

Her choice of attire for the evening only made it more difficult for him to concentrate. The shirt she wore was a thin fabric. If Oliver looked hard enough, he could practically see right through it to the smooth expanse of creamy skin and the lacy…

His mouth went dry.

"We've got eighteen," he heard Quinn's aunt announce to the room. "Two more and we win."

"One left," Amber said to Jensen.

Shannon leaned closer, as if she thought practically having her nose on the paper would unscramble the word.

All the closeness actually did was further scramble his brain until he couldn't think of anything but how good she smelled and wonder how good she'd taste.

"Twenty," Christopher called in triumph and high-fived Kinsley, then kissed her thoroughly to cheers and applause.

"The last one was the easiest," Kinsley said when she came up for air.

Oliver exchanged a glance with Shannon. She lifted her shoulders in a wordless gesture.

"What was it?" Oliver whispered.

"I have no idea," she said, her tone low and for his ears only. "But I'll find out."

"I'll pick up everyone's papers." Shannon jumped to her feet, collecting the paper and pencils.

She returned to Oliver's side seconds later. "You'll never guess."

He leaned close. "Tell me."

"Bottle."

He groaned. "How did we miss that one?"

"The question is how could we decipher *diaper genie* and fall apart on *bottle*." She laughed good-naturedly. "I guess you can't win 'em all."

As the evening progressed, Shannon discovered Oliver always played to win, whether it was "pin the diaper on the baby" or making a "baby" out of Play-Doh.

But all the Fortunes were competitive. It wasn't until they announced who'd guessed closest to the number of candies in the three-foot-high baby bottle that Oliver claimed his first victory.

"We did it, Shannon." His wide grin made him look years younger.

Actually, he'd done it. She'd wanted to go lower, but he'd convinced her to put the higher number on the guess.

By the time they got to cake and gifts, Shannon had almost forgotten this was a baby shower, an event she normally avoided like the plague. Mainly because it always reminded her she was still alone with no one special in her life.

Oliver stood across the room visiting with his sister when the babysitter appeared in the doorway holding Ollie's hand. The boy's face was tear-streaked. Drops of moisture glistened on his dark lashes.

"He wants his mom and dad," the girl announced to no one in particular.

"I'll take him." Shannon held out her arms and Ollie lunged toward her. She hefted him up and settled him on her hip. "Hey, bud, what's got you so upset?"

Ollie's only answer was to press his face into her neck.

"Looks like he's already halfway in love with you."

Shannon's heart gave a leap but her expression was nonchalant as she turned toward Rachel. "To whom are you referring?"

"Little Ollie. The kid has you in a death grip." Rachel leaned around Shannon and smiled at the boy. "Hi, Ollie. Remember me?"

Ollie burrowed deeper against Shannon.

"I guess I can't impress all the men." Rachel straightened and gave a little laugh. "By the way, it's totally not fair I ended up with Quinn's auntie and you got Oliver."

Shannon smiled benignly. "You've always told me life isn't fair."

Rachel thought for a second then grinned. "You're right. I'm going to snag one of the leftover baby bottles. Want one?"

Shannon shook her head. The game where the goal was to finish a baby bottle filled with beer had been incredibly frustrating. Who knew bottles emptied so slowly? "No thanks. I've got my hands full right now."

"Later, gator." Rachel gave Ollie a cheeky grin then strolled off.

"Gator." Ollie lifted his head. "Gator."

"That's good, Ollie." Shannon thought for a second. "Can you say… Shannon?"

He stared at her. For a second his oh-so-serious expression reminded her of Oliver. Then he smiled and her heart melted. "Mama."

Shannon chuckled. "Sha-non."

"Mama," he repeated, flinging his arms around her neck.

Though it made absolutely no sense, tears stung the backs of her eyes and she hugged Ollie extra tight. He was so young to be without a mother.

"Amelia is ready to cut the cake." Oliver paused, appearing to notice Ollie for the first time. "What happened?"

"He wanted his daddy." Shannon continued to rub the child's back. "You were busy so we've been bonding. And he's fine now. Aren't you, bud?"

She tickled his ribs and the toddler giggled.

Oliver smiled. "He's pretty heavy. I can take him."

"He's fine." Shannon cuddled Ollie. "Amelia and Quinn sure received a lot of nice gifts for Clementine."

"They did," Oliver agreed, rocking back on the heels of his Ferragamo shoes.

She'd enjoyed watching Oliver mingle with his family in such a relaxed atmosphere. This was why he was in Horseback Hollow. To get reacquainted. To spend time with his sister and his new niece.

"I can tend to Ollie while you socialize." If she could take some of the pressure off him by watching Ollie tonight, she was happy to do it.

"I'm content where I am at the moment," he told her.

"Except, I fancy a cake. And some ice cream. Shall I get some for both of us?"

"A man who knows the way to my heart," she teased.

His slow smile had said heart doing flip-flops.

"I'll take that as a yes." Oliver shot her a wink and everything inside her went gooey. "Be right back."

Shannon watched him cross the room to the refreshment table and realized in only a few short days, Oliver Fortune Hayes's happiness had become important to her.

The question was…why?

The reason, she decided, when he reappeared with a slice of strawberry cake in one hand and chocolate in the other, was one best pondered on a full stomach.

Chapter 8

Spending his Sunday evening grocery shopping at the Superette was not the way Oliver envisioned ending his weekend. Especially after a baby shower had disrupted his normal activities last night.

Oh, whom was he kidding? Nothing had been normal since the day he arrived in Horseback Hollow. But he'd been hopeful that had been about to change. He'd planned on spending the evening preparing for his first full day of work since arriving in Texas. Then Shannon had brought up the serious lack of food in the house.

"What do you think about an asparagus and goat cheese frittata for dinner?" Shannon stopped in front of the dairy case. "I have a great recipe."

"If you're certain it's no trouble."

"No trouble at all." Shannon flashed him a smile. "I love to cook."

She placed a carton of eggs in the shopping trolley, an odd-looking contraption that resembled a red race car. Though Ollie was strapped in, the boy didn't seem to mind. He happily turned the steering wheel in front of him.

As they went up and down the aisles picking out fruits and vegetables, bread and crackers, Oliver realized he and Diane had never gone to the grocery shop together. He wasn't certain she'd ever gone herself. She may have simply had one of the help handle the mundane task. Perhaps she'd called in the order.

Though Oliver wouldn't exactly call the excursion fun, it wasn't altogether tedious. In almost every aisle they'd run across one of his relatives or a friend of Shannon's. They'd talk for several minutes before continuing down the aisle. Then they'd run into someone else and another conversation would ensue.

The "quick" trip to the store was turning into quite an affair. Still, by the number of groceries in the basket, Shannon had been correct in her assessment. They had been seriously short on rations.

The truth was, he'd spent so much time making sure her room was ready that he'd given little thought to the food situation.

"Does Ollie like these organic food purees?"

Oliver stared at the two pouches she held up, one marked Sweet Potato and the other Blueberry. Had Ollie ever had these? Did he like them? Shannon might as well have asked him to name the ingredients in "blue-ribbon banana bread." "No clue."

Shannon tossed them into the buggy. "I have a friend in Lubbock with a little girl about Ollie's age. Her daughter loves them, so we'll take a chance. They're really good for a growing child."

He bowed to her wisdom. As the oldest of five and with friends who had children, she had the experience and knowledge he needed. Yet, it seemed he should know what food his son preferred.

By the time they reached the checkout lane, the trolley was full. He waited for the cashier to call for someone to assist her. But when Shannon began to drop items into the sacks once they were scanned, Oliver stepped up.

"You picked out the food," he told her. "I'll place them into the sacks."

Ignoring her dubious look, he attacked the task with gusto. His logical mind concluded heavier items should go at the bottom and he shouldn't place cleaning supplies next to food items. Shannon offered additional tips as she sorted the groceries into groups.

"I was a sacker in high school," she said when he gaped at her quick hands.

"You held a position while you were in school?" He paused, nonplussed, a bag of organic apples in his hand.

"Of course." She distracted a whining Ollie by having his stuffed tiger zoom toward him like an airplane. "When there are five kids in your family, if you want something extra you have to work for it."

Oliver simply nodded, though he couldn't relate at all to that logic. In his family there were six children. He and his brother Brodie were from his mother's first marriage. There were four children, his half siblings, from her second marriage to Sir Simon Chesterfield. Oliver felt confident all had received the same admonition growing up: excelling in the classroom was the only priority.

Once the groceries were stowed, he pointed the rental car toward home. As had become his pattern, Ollie fell asleep in his car seat. And when Oliver pulled into the driveway of the ranch house, Ollie woke up, all smiles and full of energy.

Oliver rounded the car to open Shannon's door, but she was already out of the vehicle and releasing Ollie from his car seat. She helped the boy climb down, then turned to help Oliver with the groceries.

He held up a hand when she reached for a sack. "I will bring these inside. You can put them wherever you like in the cabinets."

"Okay." Despite her agreement, she snatched a small bag of produce. "I'll take this one in with me. That way you'll have one less bag to carry. Oh, and don't worry about Barnaby. Ollie and I will let him out."

With a sassy toss of her head, she strode to the door with Ollie on her hip and a sack of produce in her arms. She had a terrific figure. The way the denim hugged her backside brought a stab of heat and a plethora of lascivious thoughts.

Belatedly reminding himself that the woman he was lusting after was his employee, Oliver forced his gaze from her derriere and back to the groceries in the boot. By the time he'd brought all of the sacks inside and Shannon had put the food away, they were all hungry.

While Shannon whipped up the frittata, he put Ollie in the high chair and fed him leftover chicken from lunch, apples and a pureed pouch of sweet potatoes.

The boy ate with a single-minded determination Oliver couldn't help but admire. Though the cook had tended to Ollie's culinary needs back in London, Oliver found he enjoyed watching his son dive into the food and learning what he liked…and didn't like.

When Ollie finished eating, the sun had set and the serviceable kitchen took on a warm, pleasant glow. The unexpected sound of rain pattering on the roof only added to the ambiance.

"Looks like we arrived home just in time." Oliver pushed back the curtains. Rain fell in sheets and when the thunder boomed, Barnaby left Ollie's side to dive under the table.

Shannon moved to where Oliver stood and gazed out. The arousing scent of vanilla teased Oliver's nostrils. He wanted nothing more than to see if she tasted as good as she smelled. But if his nearness had a similar effect on her, it didn't show.

She stepped back and turned toward the stove. "I love the sound of rain on a roof."

I love being with you.

Considering that he'd already acknowledged enjoying her company, the sentiment shouldn't have surprised him, but it did.

The frittata, accompanied by a green salad, was soon on the table. Oliver brought out a bottle of Chablis, and once he'd poured them each a glass, he held his up in a toast. "To an enjoyable working relationship."

Her glass clinked against his. She smiled. When she took a sip, he felt a hard punch of awareness. Heat simmered in the air, and once their eyes locked he couldn't look away.

Shannon's eyes darkened until they looked almost black in the light. A splash of pink colored both her cheeks. When she moistened her lips with the tip of her tongue, Oliver nearly groaned in agony.

He wanted her. In his bed. On the floor. Heck, the kitchen table would do quite nicely in a pinch.

He wanted to strip off her clothes, touch her...

"Oliver."

Through his haze of desire, he became aware that she was speaking to him.

"Uh, yes?" His gaze remained focused on her lips, as full and lush as a ripe strawberry. He had no doubt she would taste just as sweet.

"I brought some snickerdoodle cookies with me. My mom and I made them earlier today. Would you like one for dessert?"

His foggy brain fought to process the words. Snicker-doodle? Had she really just asked if he wanted a cookie?

He opened his mouth to say he wanted *her*, not some damned biscuit, but instead found himself nodding.

"You won't be sorry." A pleased smile lifted those delectable lips. "They're delicious."

Oliver was already sorry. Sorry he had to settle for a biscuit instead of what he really wanted for dessert tonight.

After dinner, Oliver surprised Shannon by offering to clean up the kitchen so she could get settled. She immediately accepted the offer. Happy to have the time to get settled, Shannon fled to her room before Oliver changed his mind and decided he needed her to watch Ollie.

As she stood in the bedroom with the pale yellow walls and lace curtains, Shannon felt a twinge of unease. She hadn't realized how personal bringing her stuff into a man's home would feel. Though she and Oliver wouldn't be sleeping in the same room, she was supremely aware that his bed was just on the other side of the wall.

Shopping at the Superette had also felt intimate. Almost as if they were a couple, instead of just employer and employee. Part of it, she knew, was because instead of simply going in and grabbing a few things, they'd strolled up and down the aisle chatting with various friends and family.

She'd seen the look of surprise on the faces of the people they'd run across. Oliver must have seen it, too, because he made a point of explaining she was Ollie's nanny. Still, some had continued to look skeptical.

After all, Oliver was hardly treating her like an employee, laughing and joking and giving her almost carte blanche on choosing what they needed.

Then he'd surprised her by insisting on bagging the groceries. When they reached home, he carried the items inside. Had she even thanked him? She paused, a pair of lace panties in her hand, and tried to recall.

Though her door was partially open, a knock sounded.

"Come in," she said absently and turned.

Oliver stood in the doorway, an odd expression on his face.

It took her a second to realize he wasn't looking at her. His gaze was riveted to the black thong dangling from her fingers.

Lightning fast, Shannon whirled and dropped the scrap of lingerie into the drawer. She cleared her throat. "I was just unpacking."

"I saw."

She flushed.

"Ollie is in his cot." Oliver's gaze slid to the open

dresser drawer. "I thought I'd take a quick shower but wanted to make sure you didn't need the facilities first."

Shannon shoved aside the thought of him wet and naked and her wet and naked with him. She shut the drawer. "I'm fine. I'll just be unpacking."

He gave a curt nod and turned to leave, but stopped when she said his name.

"Uh, hey, I just wanted to say thanks for everything." She waved a vague hand in the air, but his confused look told Shannon she needed to be more specific. "For putting fresh sheets on my bed. For having the house so clean and organized. For your assistance at the Superette. I didn't expect you to pack up the groceries or carry them inside."

His brows pulled together in puzzlement. "I've learned that taking care of Oliver and the home is a daunting task. Be assured I shall attempt to lessen the burden on you as much as possible."

Shannon stared at him for a long moment. Who was this man? She thought she'd had a good handle on Oliver Fortune Hayes, but she was beginning to think she didn't know him at all.

Almost of their own accord, her feet crossed the room to where he stood. Without giving herself a chance to think, she placed her hands on his forearms and brushed a kiss across his mouth. "Thank you."

He visibly stiffened. "What's going on, Shannon?"

She took a casual step back. "I'm not sure what you mean."

"The kiss." A muscle in Oliver's jaw jumped. "You made a point of insisting we keep things between us strictly business. I agreed. I gave you my word."

Embarrassment heated her cheeks. She wasn't an impulsive person and had no idea what had gotten into her. "Technically that wasn't a kiss."

Obviously confused, Oliver cocked his head.

"Take your shower." She patted his cheek. "And trust me. If I ever do kiss you, *really* kiss you, you'll know it."

Over the next few days, Oliver and Shannon settled into a routine. There was no touching or kissing, but neither was ever far from his mind. He made a concerted effort not to dwell on such matters because he didn't want to screw up what was turning out to be an extremely satisfying business arrangement.

In the span of a few short days, Shannon had turned a small, slightly battered house into a home. The smell of baking bread often greeted him when he awoke. Ollie was always fed, bathed and entertained. Oliver didn't take any of this for granted.

The initial plan was for her to be off duty at five, but Shannon insisted he sleep until he woke. When he got up, supper would be waiting. She insisted she loved to cook and had discovered it was fun to make dinner for someone besides herself.

But this evening they wouldn't be eating at home. They'd been invited to her parents' house for dinner. When Lilian had called, Oliver had attempted to decline the invitation, but had felt sorry for her when she told him Shep had sprained his ankle and was making her life miserable. She needed company, a distraction for Shep.

Oliver suggested Shannon go alone but Lilian said quite seriously that her husband would behave better with another man in the house. Though he doubted Shep would be happy to see him, Oliver had reluctantly accepted the invitation.

Now he was faced with what to wear. He glanced into his closet. If he wore a suit he'd be overdressed. He pulled out a pair of dark trousers and a charcoal shirt. But when he saw his reflection in the mirror, Oliver realized he needed to go even more casual.

With one last longing look at his suits, he changed into a pair of jeans and a thin-striped cotton shirt. He pulled out a pair of leather dress boots. Ignoring his unease, Oliver reminded himself this was suitable attire for dinner at a Horseback Hollow ranch.

When he came out of his bedroom shortly before they had to leave, Oliver was surprised to see Shannon wearing a maroon dress with heeled boots.

"You look lovely…and I'm underdressed."

She grabbed his arm when he spun to head back to his room to change.

"You're perfect," she said with obvious sincerity. "You'll put my dad at ease. You know he'll be wearing jeans and one of his flannel shirts."

Oliver narrowed his gaze. "If dinner is casual, why are you wearing a dress?"

Her cheeks pinked. "Mom got on me the other day about my appearance. She said every time she saw me lately, I looked more like a ranch hand than a young woman."

Oliver's gaze slowly slid down her figure, the curves nicely emphasized by the clingy fabric of the dress.

"You could never look like a boy," he said honestly.

She looked totally feminine and all too appealing. She wore a new scent, a sultry fragrance that reminded him of tangled limbs and sweat-soaked sheets.

"I like your new perfume," he said as he helped her on with her jacket.

The pink on her cheeks deepened. "Rachel helped me pick it out. There's going to be some new guys at the progressive dinner on Saturday. She says I'm never going to attract anyone smelling like vanilla."

"Progressive dinner?"

"It's where you have cocktails at one house, appetizers at another, salads at yet another, et cetera," she explained. "Jensen and Amber are organizing it all. I believe they're doing the entrée at their place."

Oliver lifted Ollie from the floor, ignoring his howl of protest. "Who are these new men?"

"Friends of Quinn," Shannon said absently, scooping up Ollie's tiger and handing it to his son. "That's all I know."

"I look forward to meeting them," Oliver said smoothly.

Shannon blinked. "I didn't realize you were going."

Oliver smiled. "Wouldn't miss it for the world."

Chapter 9

"You actually took Oliver home for dinner?" Rachel gave a hoot of laughter, the sound so light and carefree that Shannon couldn't help but smile.

From his perch in the high chair next to their table at the Vicker's Corners ice cream shop, Ollie looked up from rearranging his Cheerios cereal. He garbled out a smattering of words.

Since the boy had eaten all but ten of the "Os," Shannon grabbed the Tupperware container from her purse and put a few more on the table.

"It wasn't so bad," Shannon said, recalling the evening that had started off a bit awkwardly but ended quite well. "Oliver loves my mom's cooking, and he and my dad talked horses. Apparently Oliver not only has a stable of Arabians at his country estate, he also owns a couple of racehorses."

"From what I've heard he's got big bucks. I'm sure he owns a lot more than a few horses." Rachel leaned forward, resting her forearms on the table. "Has he kissed you yet?"

"No," Shannon answered quite honestly. "He's been a perfect gentleman."

She saw no need to add that *she'd* kissed *him*. Despite the havoc it had wreaked on her sleep, that brief one-time brush against his lips barely counted.

"Is he gay?"

"No, he's not gay, he's British." Shannon saw Rachel's lips twitch. She met her friend's gaze. "Sometimes when we're together, I can almost feel the heat between us scorch my skin, but he always shuts it down."

Rachel took a long, thoughtful sip of her soda. "Why do you think that is?"

"My fault. I insisted we keep things strictly business." For a second Shannon dropped her gaze to her hands, before focusing back on Rachel. "I still believe it's for the best."

"Seriously?" Rachel's disbelieving expression was almost comical.

"Yes, seriously. Think how awkward it would be if we hopped into bed together," Shannon pointed out.

"Honey, I'm betting the guy is fairly experienced in the bedroom. I don't think there would be much awkwardness."

"You thought he was gay."

Rachel dismissed this with a flick of her wrist. "I was just trying to get a reaction."

"Like you're doing now."

"Guilty as charged." Rachel sounded not at all sorry as she slurped up the last of her Italian soda.

"If we *did* have a physical relationship, then decide it's a mistake, I'd have to face him every day."

"You're a big girl. You could handle it."

"I don't know, Rachel. He's different from other guys I've dated. There's something about him that—"

"Mama." Ollie reached over and tugged on Shannon's sleeve, then repeated more loudly. "Mama."

Rachel gave an incredulous laugh. "Did the munchkin just call you 'Mama'?"

"It's his word for any woman." She turned to Ollie. "What is it you want, sweet pea?"

"Dink." He pointed to her malt. "Dink."

"You want a drink, sweet boy? What do you say?"

"Pease." Ollie batted his lashes. He had his father's charm in spades, Shannon decided, and let him sip from her straw.

"That kid has you wrapped around his little finger," Rachel said with a sly smile.

"I'm falling hard for both of them, Rachel," Shannon admitted with a heavy sigh. "And I can't seem to do a thing to stop it."

The one thing she'd done right, Shannon decided that Saturday evening, was not attend the progressive dinner with Oliver. When he asked if she wanted to go with him, she'd told him she planned to ride with Rachel.

She and Rachel had decided that in the ice cream shop several days earlier. Her friend insisted it would be good for Oliver to not take her for granted. From Shannon's perspective, it was all about making the two of them seem less like a couple. Not only in the mind of the community, but in hers, as well.

Oliver would soon be returning to England. Once

he left, she'd likely never see him or Ollie again. She couldn't afford to get too attached.

"These Crazy Coyote Margaritas are de-lish," Rachel said, sipping hers.

"They're good...and strong." Shannon couldn't recall the last time she'd had a drink where the alcohol was so prominent. "We'd better pace ourselves."

"Let's pace ourselves right over to those two hunky cowboys Quinn invited."

"Doesn't that seem a bit bold to you?"

"The early bird gets the worm."

"Yeah, and the early worm gets eaten."

Rachel merely shot her a saucy smile. When she started across the room, Shannon hurried to catch up. Rachel looked adorable in her black skinny jeans and a color-block sweater. Shannon had chosen a wrap dress of emerald green but wondered if she should have worn pants tonight instead.

The two men speaking with Quinn were strangers. Shannon had heard through the singles grapevine that both were unattached and each owned large ranches in central Texas.

She and Rachel had almost reached the men, when she felt a hand on her arm. She paused but Rachel continued on without her, obviously wanting dibs on the cowboy of her choice.

"Fancy meeting you here."

Shannon turned and immediately found herself drowning in the liquid depths of Oliver's blue eyes.

"Hello, Oliver."

He looked terrific in dark trousers and a gray shirt. He smelled terrific. Not a scent she recognized but it was nice, very nice. And the spot where his hand now rested on her arm sent waves of heat throughout her body.

"You look lovely." His gaze traveled all the way down from her face to the tips of her heeled boots. "You should wear that color more often."

"I'll keep that in mind." Get off the personal, she told herself. "How did Ollie do when you dropped him off at your mother's?"

Josephine had been thrilled when Oliver had asked her to watch Ollie overnight. It would be the first time the toddler had spent the night since arriving in Horseback Hollow. Though Oliver hadn't appeared concerned, Shannon was worried.

A troubled look appeared in his eyes. "He cried. I felt like a heel walking out the door and leaving him there."

"I wonder how he's doing."

"Better. I called before I came in. Mum said they were playing with his trucks." Oliver expelled a breath. "Bedtime may be difficult."

Shannon had gotten into the habit of rocking Ollie to sleep at night. She knew she should probably just put him in his crib—or cot as Oliver liked to call it—and let him cry. But he'd been through so much in his young life, and the closeness seemed to comfort him. "Did you tell your mother he likes to be rocked to sleep?"

"I did." His lips tightened. "I got the feeling she thought it unnecessary."

When someone took her empty glass and handed her another Crazy Coyote, Shannon accepted it automatically. "I hope she at least gives it a try."

"I hope so, as well."

"What are you two talking about?" Jude stopped beside them, one arm looped around Gabi's shoulders. "You look way too serious."

"Nothing important," Oliver said smoothly.

"Those Crazy Coyotes pack a punch," Gabi said to Shannon. "Watch yourself."

Shannon glanced down, surprised to find the second drink in her hand. "I will. But I'm safe anyway. Rachel is the designated driver."

"Rachel?" Gabi glanced curiously at Oliver. "You two didn't come together?"

"Nope," Shannon said, taking a gulp of her drink.

Gabi frowned. "How odd."

"Not so odd, sweetheart." Jude smiled. "Shannon works for Oliver. They're not dating."

Though she couldn't have said it better herself, for some reason the words stung.

The fact that Oliver merely sipped his glass of wine, his eyes dark and unreadable, only made it worse.

Time to seek out Rachel and those two gorgeous cowboys. Men who'd grown up in Texas and would *stay* in Texas. One of them was bound to be just the kind of man she was looking for.

But as Shannon crossed the room, she found her mind drifting to the two men she couldn't have, one a handsome charmer with dark hair and wicked blue eyes, the other a miniversion of the first, a little boy with a toothy grin who called her "Mama."

Oliver watched Shannon flirt and laugh with a tall blond-haired cowboy at every house on the progressive dinner circuit. The evening was coming to a close, and by the way the guy was looking at Shannon, baked

Alaska wasn't the only thing he wanted for dessert this evening.

He'd started the evening with a glass of wine but had since switched to water. Not Shannon.

In addition to dessert, Christopher and his fiancée, Kinsley, had made a variety of after-dinner drinks available to their guests.

Not only had Shannon drank a couple of Crazy Coyote Margaritas earlier, she'd enjoyed wine with dinner and had another glass in her hand now. The cowboy, Oliver noted, had switched to coffee.

Though Oliver told himself Shannon wasn't his concern, there was something about the man he didn't like. When they'd been introduced, he'd noticed an arrogant immaturity, a meanness that he hid quite well behind a charming smile.

"Your nanny and the cowboy look like they're having a good time," Jensen observed, coming to stand beside him and noting the direction of his gaze.

"Her name is Shannon." Even as he spoke with his brother, his gaze remained focused on her. He saw her glance around as if searching for someone. "She's looking for Rachel."

"Rachel left. I heard her tell Kinsley she wasn't feeling well."

"She was Shannon's ride home."

"Rachel probably assumed you'd take her home." Jensen took a sip of wine, gazed up at his brother. "Or the cowboy."

Oliver's lips tightened. "I don't like the way he's looking at her."

"You mean like she's a piece of meat and he hasn't eaten in a week?"

"Excellent summation."

"What are you going to do about it?"

Oliver exhaled a ragged breath and turned away. "Nothing. Shannon's personal life is her business. Not mine."

That feeling lasted until it was time to leave and he headed toward his car. Most of the others had already left, but he'd stayed behind to speak with Chris about the work of the Fortune Foundation.

There was a shiny red pickup truck parked not far from his car. As Oliver drew closer to his car, voices resounded in the still night air.

He realized one of those voices was Shannon's. Oliver stopped and listened, his fingers on his key fob.

"I told you no."

There was frustration in her voice. Anger, too. And fear?

"C'mon, you've been teasin' me all night. No need to play the shy virgin."

"I don't want you to touch me. No. Wesley, stop."

Oliver saw red. Not even conscious of covering the last few feet to the truck, he jerked the door open and yanked the cowboy off Shannon.

Taken by surprise, the man fell to the ground with a hard thud.

"Are you okay?" he asked Shannon, her eyes too bright and her face pale.

She nodded, her lips trembling.

The cowboy was now on his feet, hands clenched into fists at his sides. "What the hel—"

Oliver took a step toward the man. He wasn't a street fighter but he had displayed a talent for boxing in his younger years. He resisted—but barely—the urge to tear the man apart. "When a lady says no, she means no."

The man's mouth turned sulky. "We were just havin' us a little fun."

"When a lady says no, she means no," Oliver repeated, his words like ice.

By now Shannon had scrambled from the car and moved so that she stood behind him.

"I don't have a beef with you." Wesley raked a hand through his shaggy blond hair. His gaze slid to Shannon. "Didn't mean no disrespect."

Oliver watched as Wesley turned, jumped back in his truck and roared off.

"There goes my ride."

Oliver whirled and gave an incredulous laugh. "You're upset he's not driving you home?"

"It was a joke." Shannon offered a shaky smile. "A poor one."

He extended his hand to her. "Let me take you home."

"He wouldn't listen to me." Her lips began to tremble in earnest now. Tears welled in her eyes. "I think if you hadn't come along, he might have..." She faltered, her breath coming in gasps. "He might have—"

Suddenly Oliver's arms wrapped around her and he pulled her to him, holding her tight while her tears drenched his shoulder. "He didn't. Shh. You're okay."

The words were soft and gentle, as soothing as the ones he said to Ollie when the boy cried. Thankfully, the man hadn't injured her. Or had he?

"Did he hurt you?" Oliver asked abruptly, holding her at arm's length, his gaze desperately searching her still-moist eyes.

"My wrist." She held up her right hand and he could see the red marks from pressure. "But no, I'm okay."

She trembled all over now; even her teeth chattered. "Could you hold me again? J-just for a s-second. I'm s-s-so c-cold."

"Certainly."

With great gentleness, Oliver wrapped his arms around her and held her close. Her body fit perfectly against his.

They stood there in the quiet, with the full moon shining overhead and the crickets chirping, until the trembling and the tears subsided.

She was the one who broke the connection, sniffling and swiping at her eyes as she took a step back. "I— I'm sorry."

"He's the one who should be sorry," Oliver said, a grim note in his voice. "And he will be. I doubt Quinn will want to do business with him once he hears about this incident."

"Oh, Oliver, please don't tell Quinn." She lifted her pleading gaze to his. "I shouldn't have kissed him. It— it gave him ideas and—"

"You listen to me, Shannon Singleton, and listen carefully. There is no excuse for a man to force himself on a woman. You said no. You said stop. I heard you and he heard you, too. He chose not to listen."

"He wouldn't listen," she said morosely. "No one ever listens."

"Not people like him." Oliver pressed his lips together and fought for control over his anger. "I know his type. All charm and full of compliments, underneath cold calculation. He saw you, he wanted you, and by God he was going to have you…regardless of your feelings on the matter."

Shannon pressed a hand to her belly. "I feel sick."

Without warning, she sprinted to the bushes and was violently ill.

When she returned, looking pale as death, he handed her a precisely folded handkerchief.

A ghost of a smile lifted her lips. "Where'd this come from?"

"My pocket," he told her. "A gentleman never leaves home without a handkerchief."

His words had the desired effect of bringing a smile to her lips.

"I believe—" Oliver held out his arm to her "—it's time to head home."

She met his gaze. "There's nowhere else I'd rather be."

Chapter 10

Shannon kept her eyes closed during the trip home. She couldn't believe what a mess she'd made of the evening. For a second, before Oliver had pulled Wes off her, she feared she wouldn't be able to stop him.

There had been something in the cowboy's gaze only seconds before Oliver had arrived that had chilled her to the bone. For a second white-hot terror resurfaced and threatened to overwhelm. Nothing happened, she reminded herself. Still, she shivered.

"You're shaking." Beneath the calm, well-modulated tone, Shannon heard the concern. "Shall I turn on the heater?"

"The temperature is fine." Even as she said the words, her teeth began to chatter.

Oliver shook his head. He pulled the car to the side

of the country road. Reaching over into the backseat, he grabbed a jacket. "Put this on."

She didn't argue. Shannon shrugged into the cashmere coat and let the comforting warmth surround her. The exquisite softness coupled with the faint scent of Oliver's cologne that clung to the jacket soothed her jangled nerves. By the time they'd gone a couple of miles, the trembling stilled.

Oliver had been amazing; a white knight riding— well, more like running—to her rescue. He'd stood strong against Wesley, stared the cowboy straight in the eye and told him what he did—what he'd been about to do—was wrong.

Now, being with Oliver in the luxurious confines of the car with the strains of classical music playing on the radio, Shannon felt as if nothing could ever harm her. Not as long as Oliver was with her.

When they pulled into the driveway, relief washed over her. She was home.

Shannon wasn't sure exactly when she'd started thinking of the old ranch house as home, but it didn't matter. This was another place she felt safe.

"Thank you, Oliver." She unbuckled her belt and shifted to face him. "For everything."

He surprised her by leaning close and cupping her face in his broad palm. "I'll never let anything—or anyone—hurt you."

The fierceness of his tone was at odds with his gentle touch.

Her heart thudded against her chest so loudly it was a wonder he couldn't hear.

Or perhaps he did. Oliver's hand dropped away and he sat back. "Let's go inside. You've had a long day."

When he opened her car door, Shannon stepped out, slipping her hands into the pockets of the jacket.

His palm rested lightly against the small of her back as they traversed the short distance to the house. Barnaby met them at the door, wagging his tail and offering several welcoming woofs before racing outside.

While the corgi's welcome had been loud and exuberant, without Ollie, the house seemed too quiet.

Seconds later, Oliver let Barnaby back inside. The corgi did his best to herd Shannon deeper into the house, but her feet remained firmly rooted in the foyer. She knew she was stalling, but couldn't bear the thought of going to her bedroom and being alone with her thoughts.

"How are Ollie and your mother getting along?" she asked, conscious of Oliver's concerned gaze riveted on her.

"Step into the kitchen and have a seat. I'll tell you everything I know." Oliver gestured to the table. "It's a fascinating tale."

The kind understanding in his eyes told her he knew exactly why she was hesitating. Her heart swelled in gratitude.

"I want to hear it all. He's been on my mind all evening." Right now, it felt good to focus on someone other than herself.

Oliver crossed the room, flipped on the lights in the kitchen and then turned back to Shannon. "May I get you a cup of tea? I have chamomile infusion. It has no caffeine. According to Amelia, drinking it before bedtime practically guarantees happy dreams."

Though Shannon's stomach was still unsettled, he

looked so eager to comfort her, she couldn't refuse. "I'd love some."

As Oliver proceeded to fill the kettle, Shannon finally got her feet to move. She glanced longingly at the sofa, but her mouth held a foul taste.

"I'm going to freshen up a bit," she told Oliver.

"Take your time. The tea will need to steep."

She felt his gaze follow her as she headed to the bathroom. After brushing her teeth, she splashed her face with cold water and got rid of the raccoon smudges below her eyes. Obviously waterproof mascara wasn't the same as tear-proof.

Shannon pinched her cheeks to add color to the pallor, then sat on the edge of the tub and took off her boots and tights. Her legs were bare when she padded back into the living room. She hung up his cashmere storm jacket then took a seat at the table.

Oliver kept the conversation light until he handed her a steaming mug emblazoned with Don't Mess With Texas.

Wrapping her hands around the ceramic, she gave him a grateful smile while he sat across from her.

"You look as if you're feeling better."

"I am." Even as she said the words, Shannon realized they were true. She rested her elbows on the table and fixed her gaze on Oliver. "Now, tell me all about Ollie's evening."

"According to Mum, it was a bit of a rocky road at first. He kept crying out for 'Mama.'" Oliver's brows pulled together. "It's difficult for me to believe he meant Diane. From everything I heard, she hadn't spent much time with him those last few months. And she's been gone for some time now."

"He calls me 'Mama' sometimes," Shannon admitted. "I think it's a term he uses for women in general."

"I wasn't aware…" Oliver rubbed his chin. "That explains a lot."

"Did he finally settle down? Have fun?"

"Ah, yes, indeed he did." Oliver seemed to shake off whatever thoughts had pulled him away and refocused on her.

"Tell me," she prompted. "I want deets."

"Deets?" He lifted a brow.

She laughed. "Details."

"Ollie ate well," Oliver told her, sipping his tea. "Mum said he appeared to enjoy all the attention. He asked for Barnaby numerous times."

Hearing the sound of his name, the corgi rose from his dog bed, stretched and then moved to Shannon.

"Good boy." She patted his head and gave him a brief scratch behind his ears.

Oliver watched the interaction with interest, smiling when the dog finally left Shannon to mosey over to him.

"I checked with my mother right before I left the party. She said Ollie went to sleep—after being rocked, I might add—and was sleeping like an angel." Oliver's gaze took on a faraway look. "She told me many times how much she enjoyed having him over."

"Sounds like you may have a babysitter for life."

He lifted the mug of tea, appearing to consider the statement. "While I'm in Horseback Hollow, anyway."

Shannon's heart plummeted. It was so easy to forget that Oliver didn't belong here, to think this was his home. To imagine him being here forever. With her.

But he wouldn't be staying and putting down roots. In fact, by the first of April he'd be back in London. She'd likely never see him again.

It was something she had to keep in mind, or an April Fool's Day joke would be on her.

First thing the next morning Oliver called Quinn. He'd promised the sleeping beauty in the other room that he wouldn't tell Quinn what had gone on last night. And he kept his promise. But that didn't mean he couldn't let Quinn know that his potential business partner was a scoundrel of the first order.

While Oliver scrambled eggs and fried bacon, he issued his warning in words that had been carefully chosen prior to placing the call.

As expected, Quinn pressed for solid details. Oliver only reiterated if he was going into business with someone, Wesley should never be considered, no matter how perfect a partner he appeared to be on paper.

Oliver heard Amelia in the background telling Quinn that her brother rarely issued such warnings and they should heed it. He appreciated his sister's confidence and support. By the time he ended the call, Oliver felt certain he'd squashed any business deal between Quinn and Wesley.

"Good morning."

Oliver slid the phone into his pocket and glanced up. Shannon stood in the hallway, looking a bit heavy-eyed—but just as beautiful as always—in jeans, a long-sleeved T-shirt and cowboy boots. Her hair, normally loose around her shoulders, had been woven into some sort of complicated braid.

He rose from the table. "Would you like some breakfast?"

"I believe that's supposed to be my line." A smile lifted the corners of her lips. "But I have a different question for you this morning."

Intrigued, Oliver inclined his head. "What is it?"

"You like horses, right?"

"I do. Very much."

"I just spoke with my mother." Shannon shifted uncertainly from one foot to the other. "My dad's ankle isn't any better. It seems to be a pretty bad sprain."

"I'm sorry to hear it." Oliver was not only sorry for Shep but for Lilian, as well. It couldn't be easy keeping an active man like Shep Singleton down.

"The thing is, my parents ride every day. It's something they've done for years." Shannon crossed the room and picked a piece of crisp bacon from the frying pan. "Knowing Ollie would be at your mother's this morning, she asked if I would come over and exercise the horses. If we went together, both horses would get a workout. It wouldn't take long."

There had been a period, years ago, when Oliver had ridden every day. Once he moved to London, riding had been confined to visits to his country estate. He'd missed it, he realized.

"My mother said she'd like to keep Ollie all morning," Oliver mused.

"We'd easily be there to pick him up by noon."

Oliver thought, considered. There were things he needed to do to prepare for his workday. But he sensed

Shannon needed a ride in the great outdoors more than she needed almost anything else.

He glanced down at his dark trousers and dress shirt. "Give me five minutes to change and I'll be ready."

Shannon reined the horse to a halt at the top of a hill that overlooked a large swath of her parents' property. Though the sun shone brightly, the temperature was in the upper sixties, perfect riding weather.

Beside her, Oliver sat easily on her father's horse, a spirited roan named Bucky. Right before he mounted Bucky, she'd plopped a black cowboy hat on his head.

He'd muttered a protest, but she knew it was only for form when he'd left on the Stetson headgear. Though comfortable outside, the sun could be intense to an un-shielded head.

They'd ambled through fields, then galloped to-gether down a well-worn path by the stream. When they'd reached the hill—okay, so it was more of a small mound—she enticed him to the top by telling him the view would be worth it.

"What do you think?" She relaxed in the saddle, gaz-ing out over the valley where cattle grazed.

"Beautiful."

"That's what I think—" But when Shannon turned, thrilled he saw the peaceful serenity and beauty that many overlooked, she realized his gaze wasn't on the land, but on her.

Her face had to be dusty, her hat tipped back, and some of the hair that she'd woven into a side braid now hung loose against her cheek. Not to mention her eyes had to be puffy from last night. But the way he looked at her, well, she couldn't remember any man looking at her in quite the same way.

Her heart swelled until she thought it would burst from her chest. "Thank you."

A startled look crossed his face. "For what?"

"For being so nice to me."

"I don't understand."

"You were my knight in shining armor last night." Shannon refused to let embarrassment quash the words she desperately needed to say. "You saved me from an evil sorcerer. You comforted me. Not once did you make me feel stupid, though I had been very stupid."

"No," he said forcefully. "What happened was all on him."

"I just want you to know that I appreciated you coming to my rescue and being so…nice. If there's anything I can ever do for you, all you need to do is say the word and I'm there."

"Thanks is hardly necessary," he began. "I—"

"It's very necessary," she insisted. "I also realize what you gave up to come here today. Being on horseback under the bright blue skies has made me feel better. You knew it would."

"How could anyone not feel better with all this beauty as far as the eye can see?" He gestured with one hand, though his gaze remained on her.

"You're a special guy, Oliver. I hope one day you find a woman back in London who can appreciate all you have to offer."

"This is the one," Rachel said with the authority of a seasoned shopper. "It's you."

Shannon studied the simple, yet sexy, black dress.

All evening they'd searched for just the right dress for Shannon to wear to the Grand Fortune wedding ceremony Friday night.

When one Fortune got married it was a big deal. But when four Fortune siblings decided to tie the knot on the same day, the event took on epic status. The evening would be the talk of the year, no, the decade. Not just any dress would do for such a wedding.

The stores in Lubbock had an abundance of dresses in every style and color. A few had caught Shannon's eye enough to try them on. But none had jumped out and proclaimed, "I am the one."

They'd headed back to Horseback Hollow, empty-handed and discouraged. At the last minute they decided to check out a couple of boutiques in Vicker's Corners.

At boutique number two, they hit the jackpot. Amazed, Shannon gazed at her reflection in the triple mirror. "It makes me look positively skinny."

"Forget skinny. It makes your boobs look ginormous," Rachel said, and the sales clerk laughed.

"The dress is very flattering," the clerk concurred. "Is this for a special Valentine's date?"

"Actually," Shannon said, "I'm attending a wedding on Valentine's Day."

"Ah, *the* wedding. Wear that dress and your date won't be able to take his eyes off you," the clerk assured her before hurrying off to help another customer.

"She's right." Rachel relaxed in the dressing room chair while Shannon slipped off the dress. "It's perfect for the weddings."

Rachel's overemphasis of the plural made Shannon smile.

"Seriously," Rachel continued, "how often do you get one dress that will cover four weddings?"

Shannon slanted a glance at the price tag and tried not to wince. While the cost was definitely more than she wanted to spend, the dress *was* gorgeous. She thought about the clerk's words.

Would Oliver think she was lovely? Would he look at her—

"Especially four Fortune weddings."

Shannon reined in her thoughts. While she'd been daydreaming, Rachel had been chattering about the upcoming nuptials.

"I don't know about you," Rachel continued, "but I wouldn't want to share my special day with three other couples."

"It wouldn't be for me," Shannon acknowledged. "But I think the Fortune siblings must view this grand event as even more special because they're sharing it with the ones they love."

"I bet Jeanne Marie and Deke are celebrating."

Shannon raised a brow.

"Think about it, four weddings for the price of one," Rachel explained. "What a deal."

"For them maybe," Shannon said with a laugh. "I'm just grateful you agreed to go in with me on four gifts."

On Friday, at Jeanne Marie and Deke's sprawling ranch, four of their children would say their vows: Jude and Gabi and Chris and Kinsley, as well as Stacey Fortune Jones marrying Colton Foster and Liam Fortune Jones marrying Julia Tierney.

They'd had the large red barn on their property converted into a reception area. Outside, a huge stage had been constructed for the ceremony itself. Shannon had no doubt the quadruple wedding ceremony and reception would be a night to remember in Horseback Hollow.

"Did I tell you my parents are watching Ollie?" Shannon stepped out of the dress and handed it to Rachel.

"Your parents are such good friends of Deke and Jeanne Marie." Rachel placed the dress on the padded hanger, a look of surprise in her eyes. "I thought for sure they'd be invited."

"They are close friends and they planned to go." Shannon pulled on her jeans and tucked in her shirt. "But my dad's ankle is still bothering him. Because it's so difficult for him to get around, they decided to stay home."

Shannon reached down to pick up her bag. When she straightened, she found Rachel staring at her with a curious expression.

"What's wrong?" she asked her friend.

"I know we've planned to go together for ages." Rachel spoke slowly, as if choosing her words carefully. "But if you'd rather go with Oliver…"

"No. No way. I'll have more fun with you." The moment the words left her lips, Shannon wished she could pull them back. It sounded as if she was dissing Oliver, when nothing could be further from the truth.

She'd only meant to reassure Rachel their plans were solid and she wasn't doing a last-minute about-face.

"You're right. He may be hot but he's a little uptight." Rachel spoke cheerily, her good humor back. "Did you hear that all four of Gabi's brothers will be there? Orlando showed me pictures the other day. All I can say is, wow. Not a dog in the bunch. Tall. Dark. Hunky. They look like fun guys. We should consider hanging with them at the reception."

"Perhaps." Shannon did her best to summon some enthusiasm even though the only hunky man she wanted to hang with was Oliver.

Of course, Oliver would soon be an ocean away. She supposed it wouldn't hurt to consider other possibilities.

But even as the thought crossed her mind, Shannon knew she wasn't interested. There was only one man she wanted. Only one man she loved. And that man was the one who could never be hers.

Chapter 11

After making sure his tie was precisely knotted, Oliver strode down the hall. When he reached the living room, he came to an abrupt stop. For a second, all he could do was gaze at the vision of loveliness in black lace before him.

Shannon had bent over to give Ollie a toy. The angle gave Oliver an excellent view of her breasts—er, her dress. In his thirty-seven years, Oliver had seen his share of short black dresses. Cocktail parties, gallery openings and charity galas were filled with women wearing what many considered the classic party dress. Never had he seen one that took his breath away.

Though it didn't show an obscene amount of skin, something in the cut of the dress made Shannon's legs look longer, her waist impossibly tiny and her breasts…

His mouth went dry. When he cleared his throat, hoping to get some fluid to the area, she straightened and shot him a brilliant smile.

Then her beautiful eyes widened.

"Oh, my." She pretended to fan herself. "You're really rockin' that black suit, mister."

For the weddings of his four cousins, Oliver had chosen a slim-fit Armani, coupling it with a crisp white shirt and dark skinny tie. His favorite pair of Paul Smith black oxfords completed the outfit.

Though the phrase "rockin' that suit" wasn't familiar, the admiration in her eyes said she approved of his choice of attire.

"Your dress," he said, unable to keep his gaze from dropping to the lacy vee that showed the ivory swell of her breasts, "is…unbelievable."

"In a good way, I hope?" Though her tone was light, he saw concern in the brown depths of her eyes.

"You will be the prettiest woman there."

She gave a pleased laugh and lifted Ollie into her arms. "That's nice to hear, but with four gorgeous brides, I sincerely doubt that."

"The prettiest woman there," he repeated, happy her plans to attend with her friend had fallen through and she was his for the night.

A flush rose up her neck, but he saw his words had pleased her. She dropped her gaze to Ollie, who was attempting to pull the tiny silver necklace from her neck.

"Did you hear that, Ollie?" she asked the toddler. "Your daddy thinks I'm pretty."

With chubby fingers still wrapped around the necklace, Ollie lifted his gaze and stared at her for several seconds. He grinned.

"Pretty Mama," he said clearly, then repeated the words. "Pretty Mama."

Oliver stared, startled. "I think you have another admirer," was the best he could manage.

"Yeah," she said with a self-deprecating smile. "I'm a big hit with the toddler set."

"He called you 'Mama.'"

"That's his go-to word for females," she reminded him.

Oliver didn't argue but he was fairly certain Ollie knew exactly who he was calling "Mama." He glanced at his watch. "We should leave."

"You're right. It's not going to be quick and easy getting away from my parents." Shannon offered a wry smile. "Be prepared. They'll want you to go through Ollie's bedtime routine in excruciating detail."

She never overstepped, Oliver thought. Shannon always made it clear Ollie was ultimately his son, his responsibility, not hers. The trouble was, Shannon was such a natural with him it was easy for him to forget.

Mrs. Crowder, his London nanny, was efficient and kind to his son. But Ollie had never called her "Mama." He wondered if the older woman rocked Ollie to sleep every night or sang silly songs with him. These were things Shannon did as part of the daily routine. Oliver made a mental note to pay more attention to those details once he was back in London.

On the drive to her parents' ranch, Ollie and Shannon sang a song about monkeys jumping on the bed. Actually Shannon did most of the singing, with Ollie occasionally yelling out "no more" or "monkey" several beats too late.

The foolishness of the tune coupled with the sound of his son's giggles made Oliver smile.

As Shannon had predicted, Shep and Lilian wouldn't let them leave until they'd been apprised of every nuance of Ollie's schedule. When they returned to the car, Oliver had no doubt his son would be well cared for during the evening.

"That was kind of your parents to offer to keep Ollie overnight." Oliver exited the long drive and turned the car in the direction of Jeanne Marie and Deke's ranch.

"My parents adore children." A tiny smile lifted her lips. "They can't wait to have grandchildren. Watching Ollie gives them a taste of what that will someday be like."

"Happy to be of service."

Shannon's expression turned thoughtful. "I'm glad you brought Ollie to Horseback Hollow. It's good he had this chance to get acquainted with your family and them with him."

Oliver realized with a sense of chagrin that he'd never thought of the trip in those terms. In his mind, coming to Texas had been about seeing Amelia and meeting his new niece.

"Thanks to modern technology, even after you return to London you'll be able to video chat with your mother and other family members," Shannon continued. "That way they can stay close to Ollie."

"Good suggestion." But Oliver found he didn't want to talk about leaving Horseback Hollow. Not tonight. "Do you like weddings?"

Shannon blinked at the abrupt change of subject but went with the flow.

"What woman doesn't? I enjoy seeing the dresses and

the hair. I like seeing what kind of flowers the bride and groom chose and how they structured the ceremony." She paused for a second. "With four brides and grooms, I wonder how they decided everything. Majority vote?"

Oliver lifted a shoulder in a slight shrug.

"I can see the advantages of all of them getting married at the same time but…" This time, it was her turn to shrug.

"Not for you?"

"Never say never," she said with a little laugh, "but I don't believe it would be for me. Anyway, marriage is so far down the road for me it doesn't even bear thinking about."

Oliver slanted a sideways glance. "You'll find the right man."

Having Oliver mention her with another man in the same breath gave Shannon a bad taste in her mouth. "When you married Diane, you must have thought she was the right one for you."

Oliver's only reaction was a tightening grip on the steering wheel. "At the time, I was convinced we made an excellent match. We socialized with the same people, had similar interests and backgrounds. I thought she'd be happy if I gave her what she wanted. I was mistaken."

His lips clamped shut.

"What did she want?" Shannon asked quietly into the stillness.

"What most women want—a lovely home, designer clothes, jewels."

"I'd settle for a man who loves me," Shannon murmured.

Oliver continued as if she hadn't spoken. Perhaps he hadn't heard her. His gaze had taken on a faraway look.

"She wanted a child, so we had Ollie. He was an infant when she began a relationship with another man."

"She cheated on you?" Shannon's voice rose, despite her efforts to control it.

"She left me for him." Oliver spoke in a tone one might use to report an expected change in stock prices. "They were together approximately six months when she replaced him with the man she was with at the time she died."

"It sounds as if she wasn't sure what she wanted."

"Perhaps." His expression gave nothing away. "All I know for certain was she no longer wanted me. I couldn't make her happy."

"I'm sorry." Impulsively Shannon reached over and squeezed his hand.

"It was the failure of our marriage that bothered me more than losing her," he said almost to himself. "Up until our divorce, I believed if I worked hard enough at something, I would be successful."

Shannon heard the disappointment in his voice. She knew what it was like to not live up to your own expectations. If only she could pull him close and comfort him as he'd comforted her not all that long ago.

"I never heard what happened to your plans to attend the weddings with Rachel." By the change in subject, Oliver made it clear the discussion of his failed marriage had come to a close.

Shannon understood that, too. She often did the same thing when the subject of Jerry and how she'd handled that whole situation came up.

"Rach is supergood with hair. A couple of the brides asked if she'd come early to help with final touch-ups." Shannon waved a dismissive hand. "She was concerned about leaving me in the lurch, but I assured her it was no problem. I told her I'd probably catch a ride with you. If not, there was always Wesley."

His gaze shot to her. "Surely you would not consider—"

"Not in a bazillion years." She made a face. "I just wanted to see if you were listening."

"I always listen to you."

He'd listened to her that night when that scumbag had attacked her. And Oliver had held her while she cried...

"I've decided if Wesley is there tonight—" Shannon swallowed her trepidation and forced a bright smile "—I'll simply ignore him. There'll be so many people that it shouldn't be difficult."

"He won't be there."

The words were said with such confidence Shannon had no doubt they were true.

"How do you—" Shannon frowned. "You promised you wouldn't say anything about what happened to anyone."

"You should know by now I'm a man of my word," Oliver said stiffly, appearing affronted. "I didn't mention your name or any specific incident. I merely told Quinn that Wesley was not the type of man he should have as a business partner or a friend."

Incredulous, Shannon could only stare. "He didn't ask why you felt that way?"

"Of course he did." A slight smile lifted Oliver's lips. "But he quit pressing for details when Amelia told him to trust me."

"Oh."

"I would never betray your confidence. Or my promise to you." Oliver slanted a speculative glance in her direction. "Enough talk about that. Did I mention my brother Brodie will be attending the wedding?"

"I don't believe I've met him."

"He's flying in for the ceremony." A look of fondness crept into Oliver's gaze. "Knowing Brodie, he'll return to London as soon as possible."

As if sensing her curiosity, Oliver smiled. "Brodie enjoys the finer things in life. This town would not be his cup of tea. Too small and too rustic."

Shannon pulled her brows together, trying to remember the family history. "Is he older or younger than you?"

"Four years younger."

"That means he's between you and Jensen?"

"Yes. Brodie and I are from our mother's first marriage. Jensen is from her second."

Shannon tapped a finger against her lips. "I knew Jensen's father had died and Josephine was a widow. Is your dad still alive?"

"No."

There was a wealth of emotion contained in the single clipped word.

As irritating as her father could be at times, Shannon knew she'd be devastated if anything happened to him. She reached over and placed a hand on Oliver's arm. "I'm so sorry."

"Don't be. He was a mean SOB who was not liked by most people, including his sons."

"Then I'm doubly sorry," Shannon said softly. "Growing up with such a father had to be—"

"I consider my mother's second husband, Sir Simon Chesterfield, my father. He was a good man. The best, actually." Oliver met her gaze. "You don't have to be related by blood to be a parent."

"I agree." For some reason Shannon thought of Ollie. She could easily love him as if he were her own. Heck, she was already halfway in love with the little guy.

As the car slowed, Shannon glanced out the window. "Oh my goodness, look at all the people."

A man Shannon recognized as working for the Horseback Hollow Sheriff's Department motioned for Oliver to turn into a large field that was now a parking lot.

White golf carts, festively decorated with ribbons and fresh flowers, zipped up and down the rows of cars, transporting attendees to where the ceremony would be held. The drivers—many of them locals—looked quite impressive in black pants, crisp white shirts and red vests.

Shannon wasn't sure how many carts were running but had a feeling anyone golfing today would be walking eighteen holes.

She waited for Oliver to help her out of the cart, anticipating the moment he'd take her hand and she'd get to touch him—however briefly—once again.

To her surprise—and pleasure—the contact wasn't short-lived. Instead of immediately releasing her fingers, he entwined his with hers and retained the hold while they waited for the cart. Unfortunately, once they stepped inside the open vehicle, he released her hand. But she felt encouraged when he rested his arm on the top of the seat.

"I hear Jeanne Marie and Deke had the interior of the barn completely renovated for the reception and dance," Shannon said as the large red structure came into view.

"Mum told me the work has been going on for weeks." As they drew close, Oliver's gaze lingered on the large number of people waiting to be seated. "Apparently the carpenters just finished the outdoor stage where the wedding ceremony will take place earlier this week."

"It's fortunate rain stayed out of the forecast."

"I have no doubt there was a contingency plan in case of bad weather."

"I can't wait to see what everyone in the wedding parties is wearing." Shannon could feel her excitement build the closer the cart got to the drop-off point. "I heard each bride has two attendants, a maid or matron of honor and a bridesmaid."

"More than adequate."

Typical man, Shannon thought. She bet he'd had a whole slew of attendants at his wedding. From the little he'd told her, his ex-wife had liked the finer things in life. Shannon briefly considered asking for details, then tamped the impulse down almost as quickly as it had surfaced.

Right now she couldn't handle thinking of Oliver marrying another woman.

As if sensing her turbulent mood, Oliver took her hand. With a single touch her world, which for the moment had tilted on its axis, righted itself.

Sounds of a Bach concerto filled the air as the cart drew to a smooth stop. When Oliver took out his wallet to tip, the driver shook his head. "We're being well compensated for our services. Enjoy the ceremony."

Oliver took her arm to steady her as she stepped from the vehicle in her heels.

"Oh, my" was all Shannon could manage to say when her gaze fell upon the elaborate stage.

Shannon expected a simple raised wooden platform large enough to hold four sets of brides and grooms and a minister. She hadn't expected something that looked as if it had been carved from stone and borrowed from the Parthenon. Four fluted Ionic columns formed a semi-circle, topped with an ornate frieze containing four vertically channeled tablets depicting hearts.

Two steps led to the stone platform. Four tall urns filled to overflowing with gypsophila and delphinium were strategically positioned on the stage. The heavy mass of the white flowers was accentuated by deep red roses.

In the center aisle leading to the "temple," a white tapestry had been placed, flanked by red rose petals. White wooden chairs lined both sides of the center aisle. The ends of each row held bouquets of roses and greenery.

"This is more elaborate than I imagined." Though there was no need to speak softly, Shannon spoke in a hushed whisper.

"It's a Fortune wedding." Oliver responded with a chuckle. "Prepare to be impressed."

Chapter 12

As the lovely strains of another piece of classical music from the string quartet filled the air, Shannon's eyes turned dreamy. "I take back what I said about not wanting to share my day with three other brides. If I could have this, I'd happily share the day with a dozen others."

Though Oliver could see how Shannon might be awed by the sumptuous arrangements, he thought how it paled compared with his wedding at Saint Paul's Cathedral.

Diane had wanted a formal, elegant affair, complete with trumpets and royalty in attendance. But the marriage that was supposed to last a lifetime had barely made it to the three-year mark. Diane bore her share of the burden for the failure, but he now realized that he did, too.

"Oliver."

His name, said in that cultured British accent, had

him banishing any thoughts of the past and smiling even before he turned. "Brodie."

Though normally too much of a buttoned-up Londoner for public displays of affection, Brodie Fortune Hayes surprised Oliver by giving him a manly half hug with a thump on the back.

"Good to see you." His brother glanced around. "Where's the little guy?"

"Ollie is with a baby minder for the evening. A couple I trust."

"Undoubtedly." Brodie's gaze slid away to settle on Shannon.

"Brodie Fortune Hayes, I'd like to introduce Miss Shannon Singleton. Shannon is a friend. She's also graciously consented to help me out by serving as Ollie's nanny while I'm in Horseback Hollow."

"Miss Singleton." Brodie extended his hand.

"Shannon, please." She smiled and shook his hand. "I knew you were brothers the moment I saw you."

At six feet tall, both men were the same height, with brown hair and vivid blue eyes. Like Oliver, his brother was dressed in a hand-tailored dark suit. Though, in Shannon's estimation, Oliver was the more handsome of the two.

If Rachel thought Oliver was a true Brit, Shannon couldn't wait until her friend got a load of Brodie. The man gave new meaning to the term "stiff upper lip."

"If you're not sitting with anyone, perhaps you'd like to sit with us," she offered.

Brodie's brow shot up and his gaze shifted to Oliver.

Shannon felt herself color. She hadn't meant to imply she and Oliver were a couple. The question now was how to backtrack without making everything worse.

Oliver didn't seem to notice the faux pas. "Yes, Brodie, you must sit with us."

"You two are…together?" Brodie spoke cautiously, as if feeling his way through a minefield.

"Has the transatlantic flight addled your brain?" Oliver spoke with more than a hint of exasperation. "Shannon is standing right here. I just introduced her to you. Of course we're together."

Brodie let the subject drop, though Shannon was aware of his speculative gaze as an usher took her arm to escort her to their seats.

She was amazed how close to the front they were seated until she realized that, of course, they'd be near the front. Oliver and Brodie's cousins were being married today.

Shannon had to admit she'd grown so used to chatting with Oliver that it was difficult to stay silent. But, as they waited for the ceremony to begin, she bit her tongue each time she was tempted to share an observation or impression.

It had been a while since Oliver had seen his brother. She wanted to give him a chance to speak with Brodie without having her in the middle of the conversation.

As guests continued to be seated, Shannon struck up a conversation with Cisco Mendoza, one of Gabi's brothers, who was seated to her right. He was a handsome man with dark hair and eyes, and a charming smile.

She was laughing at something Cisco said when Oliver touched her hand.

"The processional is ready to begin," he said in a low tone for her ears only.

Feeling as if she'd been caught doing something

wrong—though she wasn't sure what it was—Shannon shifted her attention.

The bridesmaids moved slowly down the aisle, in dresses ranging from deep wine to seashell pink. Shannon wondered if Oliver noticed the color of the grooms-men's boutonnieres matched the respective bridesmaids' dress color.

Soon it was time for the maids of honor and best men to make their trek down the aisle. When they reached the stage, little MaryAnne Mendoza appeared holding a white wicker basket filled with rose petals of every hue. The three-year-old waved to people she knew and flung the petals with great gusto on her way to the plat-form, making more than a few in the audience chuckle.

Finally, the audience rose and one by one the four brides began their walk down the aisle on their fathers' arms. Shannon thought Gabi's father, Orlando, looked incredibly handsome in his dark suit. Oliver's mother, Josephine, must have thought so too, because Shannon caught her giving the handsome Latino a second glance.

"They're all so lovely," Shannon whispered to Oliver as the last bride joined her groom at the front.

Oliver simply smiled and squeezed her arm as they took their seats.

Considering there were four brides and four grooms to keep track of, everything proceeded seamlessly. Shannon found herself especially moved by the minister's sermon. He urged the couples to continue to nurture the love they now shared and to move from a "me first" attitude to "us first."

The ceremony continued with the lighting of the unity candle. The recitation of vows made Shannon sigh. Each set was so very personal and unique to the couple saying them. Love wove through the vows like a pretty ribbon, bringing a lump to Shannon's throat and a tear to her eyes.

Soon the radiant brides and grooms were making their way down the aisle. Shannon had no doubt each couple would enjoy the blessing of a happy marriage.

As thrilled as she was for all of them, Shannon couldn't stop a stab of envy as she wondered if she'd ever find such happiness.

If she did, one thing was certain, it wouldn't be with Oliver. In a matter of weeks, he'd be back in London. The thought was a dark cloud on the sunny day.

It didn't help that Shannon felt like a third wheel strolling with Brodie and Oliver to the barn for the dinner buffet and dance. It was obvious—to her at least—that Brodie was puzzled by her presence, probably wondering why she was intruding on his time with his brother.

Catching sight of Rachel, Shannon seized the out. She tapped Oliver's arm. "I need to speak with Rach. I'll catch you later."

She ignored his puzzled expression and shifted her gaze to Brodie. "It was a pleasure meeting you. I hope you enjoy your stay in Horseback Hollow."

Then she was gone, disappearing into the crowd.

Oliver couldn't stanch a surge of irritation. It wasn't as if he expected Shannon to spend every moment of the reception with him. Though he *had* given her a ride and stepped up to be her escort when she'd been left high and dry by her friend Rachel. The same friend she was now scurrying off to meet.

"Your nanny is very attractive," Brodie said in a slightly bored tone.

"She's not my nanny—she's Ollie's nanny," Oliver snapped.

"No need to get testy." Brodie narrowed his gaze. "Are you falling for the cowgirl?"

"She's an employee," Oliver said pointedly.

"So, you wouldn't mind if I got something going?" Brodie raised a brow. "A quick shag might make my brief stay in this backwoods town more palatable."

Oliver rounded on his brother, barely resisted the urge to grab him by the lapels of his Hugo Boss suit coat. "Stay away from her, Brodie. Shannon is off-limits. Understand?"

Brodie merely laughed. "I knew you had a thing for her."

"What are you talking about? I've already told you she's my—"

"Employee. I heard that part. But I have eyes. I see how you look at her. When she was talking with that man on the other side of her, you looked as if you wanted to punch him."

"I'm merely concerned about my employee's welfare." Oliver's penetrating gaze dared his brother to disagree.

"Whatever you say." As they entered the barn, Brodie's cynical look eased. "Whoever was in charge put a lot of time and money into planning this reception. It might be tolerable."

This time it was Oliver's turn to laugh. "It's good to have you here, Brodie. Let's get a glass of champagne."

The reception was in full swing, the dance floor was crowded and Shannon still hadn't crossed paths with

Oliver. But she'd connected with almost everyone else in the entire county.

She'd even done her part by helping Gabi's four brothers, Matteo, Cisco, Alejandro and Joaquin, feel welcome by introducing them to all the single women she knew.

They were a good-looking bunch who had all the women swooning. Moments earlier she'd been leaving the dance floor with Cisco when they'd run into Delaney Fortune. She'd introduced the two, then hurriedly excused herself. She'd promised Galen Fortune the next dance.

She'd known Galen since childhood. He was her buddy. Because there was only friendship between them, spending time with him was always easy and comfortable.

"You're a good dancer," she told Galen. "How is it that I didn't know that about you?"

He maneuvered her around the crowded dance floor with quick, sure steps. "Another one of my many hidden talents."

Shannon smiled and caught sight of Oliver speaking with his mother at the edge of the dance floor. She waved but he disappeared from view when Galen spun her around.

"It's kind of weird, isn't it?" Shannon said, relaxing in his arms.

"What is?"

Her lips twisted in a wry smile. "Being single when everyone around you is getting married."

Galen's brows pulled together. "Some just aren't lucky enough to find the right person. Me, I'd rather stay single than settle."

"Me, too," Shannon said, relieved to hear she wasn't

the only one who felt that way. "I can't imagine anything worse than—"

"May I cut in?"

A thrill ran down Shannon's spine. Oliver wanted to dance with her.

Galen stepped back. "Thanks for the dance, Shannon."

She smiled warmly at him. "Any time."

Before she could catch her breath, she was in Oliver's arms. She loved the way he smelled, a woodsy mixture of cologne and soap and maleness that had heat percolating low in her belly. She let the intoxicating scent wrap around her.

"You two looked quite friendly."

"Galen? We're buddies from way back."

"Did you ever date?"

"No." Shannon laughed. "He's like another brother."

Was it only her imagination, or did Oliver's shoulders relax slightly?

"Have you enjoyed the festivities?" he asked.

"It's been fun. I've danced a lot."

"I noticed. You seemed to have developed a particular affinity for Gabi's brothers."

"They're nice guys." She lowered her voice. "The women all think they're incredibly hot."

He stared at her for a long moment. "What about you?"

She wasn't sure what made her be so bold, but she let her fingers caress his neck. "Let's just say I prefer a different type of man."

His eyes darkened to stormy pools of blue and he surprised them both when his hand flattened against her lower back, drawing her up against the length of his body.

He held her so close she could feel the evidence of his desire against her belly. The hardness ignited the flame that had been simmering inside her for days.

Slow it down, she told herself. It might simply be the romance in the air that was causing him to react to her this way.

But she had to admit, whatever the reason, she liked having him stare at her with such blatant hunger in his gaze.

"My brother thinks you're hot," he murmured, twining strands of her hair loosely around his fingers.

It took Shannon a second to find her voice. "He—he's not my type, either."

"Who is your type, Shannon?" he asked in a husky voice.

There was a beat of silence. "I believe you know the answer to that question, Oliver."

Even as his mouth relaxed into a slight smile, he tightened his hold.

Shannon sighed with pure pleasure. Dancing with Oliver, being held so firmly in his strong, capable arms, was all she wanted, all she needed. Forget Galen and Brodie. Forget the Mendoza brothers.

Forget our agreement.

Shannon opened her mouth to tell him she'd been wrong to insist things stay strictly business. But as they dipped and swayed to the romantic melody, she found it impossible to think, much less speak. The world around her disappeared and all she knew was they fit together perfectly and she was right where she wanted to be…

Reluctant to give up the intimacy, she lost herself

in the music, drifting on a cloud of pure pleasure until the jarring ring of his cell phone shattered the moment.

Shannon lifted her head as he slipped the phone from his pocket and glanced at the readout.

"Working on a Saturday night?" she teased.

"It's your parents' number."

Her breath caught, then began again. They wouldn't call unless it was important. A jolt of uneasiness went through her.

Oliver pressed the phone against his ear and talked with her mother as he maneuvered them to the far edge of the dance floor, where it wasn't so noisy.

"How high?" His mouth tightened into a grim line. "I'll be right there."

"What's wrong?"

Shadows played in his eyes, making them unreadable.

"Ollie has a fever. One hundred and three." His brows knit together as he calculated. "Thirty-nine point four Celsius."

"Fevers that high aren't uncommon in a child his age."

"I can't stay." His gaze darted to the exit. "I can have one of my family members take you home."

"No need." Shannon snatched her bag up from the table where she'd left it earlier. "I'm going with you."

Chapter 13

Oliver unbuckled Ollie from the car seat and carried him into the house, his strides so long and quick that Shannon had to run to keep pace. Once inside, he flipped on the lights with one hand and sat the boy down on the sofa. Barnaby immediately jumped up to sit beside him.

"Let the dog be," she told Oliver when his arm moved to swipe the animal off the sofa.

Confusion turned to understanding when the boy wrapped his arms around the corgi, resting his head against the dog's soft fur.

"I'll get the thermometer so we can recheck his temperature," Shannon told Oliver. Thankfully, after a recent trip to the store, she'd stocked the medicine chest in the bathroom with all the necessities. "Mom gave him some acetaminophen before we got there so it should start coming down."

"Stop," Oliver ordered, pushing up from the sofa. "You sit here with Ollie. He needs someone to comfort him."

Shannon moved to the sofa. She didn't argue, though she could make a good case that it should be his daddy comforting him rather than a relatively new nanny. But Ollie had taken to her from the start and now, even as she took Oliver's spot on the sofa, the child cuddled against her.

In less than a minute, Oliver returned with the temporal scanner. Shannon talked him through how to use it. A lethargic Ollie only whimpered.

Some of the grimness around Oliver's mouth eased at the readout. "One hundred and one."

Shannon exhaled the breath she didn't realize she'd been holding. "Better."

She brushed Ollie's hair back from his face and Barnaby licked her hand. The boy's eyes were closed now and his respirations were easy and regular.

"He's asleep," Shannon spoke softly, her voice barely above a whisper. She glanced up at Oliver. "Think we should try to put him in the crib?"

"Let's give it a few more minutes." Oliver sat on the other side of Ollie and the dog. His gaze lingered on her dress, a bunch of lace clutched between Ollie's fingers. "You can take my car if you'd like to return to the reception."

"Are you crazy? I'm not leaving Ollie."

Or you, she thought. His son's unexpected fever had clearly shaken Oliver.

Shannon brushed back a lock of Ollie's soft brown hair. Tears stung the backs of her eyes. Oliver wasn't the only one who'd been shaken. With his eyes closed and his skin so pale, Ollie looked so little, so defenseless.

"Children are such a responsibility," Oliver said quietly as he gazed at his sleeping child.

"And such a joy." Her heart rose to her throat. Shannon realized she wasn't halfway in love with Ollie. She was totally in love with the little guy.

"You like children." Oliver's gaze never left hers. "The first time I saw you interact with him, I knew."

She nodded, feeling oddly embarrassed by the blatant admiration in his eyes.

"I've always loved children," she admitted. "Do you know when I was a little girl, I told my parents I wanted half a dozen kids when I grew up? Truth is, I'd still like a whole houseful."

As she'd hoped, the statement distracted Oliver from his worry. His eyes widened. "Seriously?"

"Yep." Shannon gave a little laugh, then lowered her voice to a confidential whisper. "Let's keep that our secret. Something like that gets out and any potential suitors will run screaming away into the night, never to be seen again."

He gave her a dubious glance. "You're kidding."

"I wish I were. Let me give you an example." Shannon shifted slightly and repositioned Ollie in her lap. "I dated this guy when I lived in Lubbock. We had fun together. Things were going well, until the subject of children came up. One night I said to him what I just said to you. You'd have thought I'd exploded a grenade under him."

Oliver cocked his head, his eyes bright with interest.

"His reaction made more sense when he told me he wasn't sure he even wanted kids…ever." Shannon expelled a breath and shook her head. "He called me once after that, but it was over. Now, if a guy asks, I just say I like children and hope to have a couple someday."

Oliver rubbed his chin. "Why not be honest?"

"I am being honest. I do like children. I do hope to have a couple. But having more would need to be something my husband wanted, too." Shannon gave a little laugh. "I have my doubts that I'll find any man who wants six."

"My mother had six," Oliver reminded her.

"Mine had five," Shannon said. "But I think things were different back then. Big families were more the norm."

"I don't know how they did it." Oliver glanced at his son. "Being a parent is exhausting."

"You even have household help," she pointed out.

"It's not only the physical care," Oliver said, almost to himself. "I'm organized and disciplined. Though I certainly don't know how I'd do it without a nanny and a housekeeper. But..."

He paused for a long moment then continued.

"Being a parent makes me feel vulnerable in ways I don't particularly like." His gaze lingered on his son. She saw the love in his eyes...and the fear. "I never thought I was capable of loving so deeply. It would kill me to lose him."

How had she ever thought Oliver was a cold fish or that Ollie was simply an obligation?

"That's the downside of caring for someone," Shannon said solemnly. "It makes you vulnerable. My grandmother used to say love isn't for the faint of heart."

She wasn't sure how the phrase translated into Brit-speak, but from the look that crossed his face he got the gist.

"It can be frightening to have such intense feelings." Oliver raked a hand through his hair. "Especially when you aren't certain if the other person feels the same way."

Shannon was fully prepared to tell him Ollie wouldn't go to him so easily or let himself be comforted if there wasn't love and trust between them.

Then Shannon realized his gaze wasn't on his son, but on *her*. It wasn't Ollie's feelings he was wondering about, but hers. The knowledge gave her a subtle, plea-surable jolt.

She dropped her gaze to the boy, feeling warmth rise up her neck. "I think we can put him to bed now."

"Let me." Oliver rose, then bent over and carefully lifted his son from the sofa.

A second later, Barnaby hopped off the sofa, hitting the floor with a thud.

"While you get Ollie settled," Shannon said in a low tone, "I'll take Barnaby outside."

Oliver's brows drew together. "Stay close to the house and in the light. I heard howling out there."

"Coyotes." Her tone was matter-of-fact. The animals were a fact of life in the area. "They normally don't venture close to the house, especially when the flood-lights are on.

"C'mon, Barnaby." She started toward the door, the dog padding behind her.

"Shannon."

She turned, raised a brow.

"Wait a minute. Once I get Ollie settled, we can take Barnaby out together."

"Sure. That'll work." Shannon didn't mind waiting.

Not because she was some wussy who couldn't stand being in the dark by herself, or because she was fearful of a few coyotes. But because it'd be nice to have the company. Especially on such a beautiful night when the moon was full and a plethora of stars filled the clear night sky.

Instead of remaining in the living room, Shannon followed Oliver into Ollie's room. She turned on the Mickey Mouse night-light and removed the stuffed animals from the crib.

Oliver laid the boy down, removing his jeans, shoes and socks with now well-practiced movements, leaving the child clad only in a T-shirt and diaper.

After checking the diaper, Oliver looked up. "Dry."

"Good. I know my mom said she'd changed him right before we got there, but still—"

"A soggy nappy would have awakened him for sure."

"Right. And what he needs right now is uninterrupted rest." After checking his temperature one last time, Oliver motioned Shannon out of the room.

"It's down another degree," Oliver confided, relief etched on his face.

"Good." Shannon squeezed his hand.

After they were a safe distance down the hall, Shannon turned to the dog. "It's time, Barnaby. Let's go outside."

The dog emitted a low woof and sped to the back door, his short legs moving surprisingly fast.

But speed disappeared once Barnaby was outside. The corgi took his time sniffing every bush and tree in the area. Though the night air had a bit of a bite, Shannon wasn't cold. Oliver stood beside her on the bricked patio and heat rolled off him in waves.

"I want to kiss you," he surprised her by saying as the silence lengthened.

Her stomach felt as if it had dropped three feet straight down.

"Then why don't you?" Even though her heart raced wildly, she spoke in the same matter-of-fact tone he'd used.

Oliver studied her for several seconds before he spoke, his steady gaze shooting tingles down her spine. "We have an agreement."

"I release you from that agreement," she said in a solemn tone. If she'd had a magic wand, she'd have tapped his shoulder for good measure.

Oliver shook his head. "You're still my employee."

Her heartbeat hitched. "I'm not."

"Unfortunately you are." He expelled a heavy breath but didn't take a step away. Instead Oliver moved closer.

Shannon recognized the signs. He was waiting, hoping, for her to convince him. Lifting her chin, she shook her head slowly from side to side, a tiny smile lifting the corners of her mouth. "You may be the one who signs my paycheck, but actually I work for Ollie."

For a second those blue eyes were simply astonished. "Ollie is a child. You can't work for him."

"I beg to differ." Her voice had taken on a playful edge. "He's my focus. So, technically I work for him."

"Let's say I accept that premise, which by the way is quite a stretch of logic. It doesn't negate the fact that if we begin an affair…"

Shannon held herself very still, firmly ignoring the unsettling flutter his words caused in her midsection.

"I thought we were talking about a kiss," she said with a studied nonchalance that deserved an acting award.

The look he shot her fried every brain cell she possessed, and then some. "We both know where one kiss will lead."

Yes, and Shannon wanted him so desperately it was a wonder she hadn't ripped his clothes off before now.

Not sure of the steadiness of her voice, Shannon settled for a jerky nod.

"This—" He paused, as if searching for the words. "Whatever happens would be a temporary thing."

Her heart performed another series of flutters. When she opened her mouth to say she didn't care, to say—

"I'm not looking for a relationship." She saw a flicker of challenge in his eyes. "And I won't be in Horseback Hollow that much longer."

Even with shadows playing in his eyes, making them difficult to read, she swore she saw regret lurking there. Nonetheless, his words were clear. He'd spelled it out, leaving no room for fanciful thoughts of happily-ever-after.

Though Shannon had grown up in a traditional home and had been taught intimacy was only coupled with love, and then only after marriage, this was her life and her decision.

She cared deeply for Oliver, she respected him and she was physically attracted to him in a major way. What would be the harm in stealing some moments of pleasure? Especially if they both went into an affair with eyes wide open.

Apparently misunderstanding her hesitation, Oliver reached over and squeezed her hand. His voice was soft, reaching inside her to a raw, tender place. "Refraining is the wisest course of action."

Yet, at his simple touch, sensation licked up her

arm, down her breasts and on down to pool between her thighs. Heat simmered in the night air.

When he started to pull his hand back, she brought it to her mouth and placed a kiss in the palm. "Depends I guess on your definition of *wise*."

His blue eyes darkened. "What are you saying?"

The intoxicating scent of his cologne wrapped around her senses. Her gaze met his.

"I'm saying I want you." Her eyes searched his. "I'm okay with it not being forever. I'm not sure I'm ready for forever, anyway."

"I don't want to hurt you."

She gave a little laugh, her pulse a swift, tripping beat. "Uh, correct me if I'm wrong. I believe it's pleasure—not pain—on tap tonight."

Still, he made no move toward her. "Are you sure?"

Shannon took a step closer, wound her arms around him and planted a kiss at the base of his neck, his skin salty beneath her lips. Then she lifted her face, and met his dark gaze with what she hoped was a sexy smile. "Very sure."

"Well, then…" He folded her more fully into his arms, anchoring her against his chest as his mouth covered hers in a deep, compelling kiss.

He continued to kiss her with a slow thoroughness that left her weak, trembling and longing for more. When his tongue swept across her lips seeking access, she eagerly opened her mouth to him, her tongue fencing with his.

The warmth in her lower belly turned fiery hot and became a pulsating need.

Barnaby's deep woof barely registered.

Another bark and the dog sprang. The unexpected

impact of the solid body against the back of her knee knocked Shannon off balance. Only Oliver's strong arms saved her from a tumble.

"Barnaby." She dropped her gaze to the dog, who now sat at her feet. "What is your problem?"

"He's ready to go inside." Oliver's mouth skimmed the edge of her jaw. "It's a good plan."

Keeping a firm grip on her arm, Oliver opened the sliding glass door. The dog bounded inside, nails clattering against the hardwood, and made a beeline for Ollie's room.

With her fingers linked with Oliver's, Shannon followed the dog down the hallway. When Barnaby plopped down on the rug next to the crib, Shannon stepped around him to lean over the rail.

Oliver joined her.

"His cheeks aren't flushed anymore," he said, his voice filled with relief.

Shannon placed the back of her hand on Ollie's forehead. "His skin is cool."

She and Oliver exchanged a smile, then eased silently from the room. They stood in the hall and Shannon fought against a sudden wave of awkwardness and uncertainty. "I don't know about you, but I'm ready for bed."

"You took the words out of my mouth."

She tilted her head back, met his gaze. She'd never seen such beautiful eyes. Or such compelling eyes. Or eyes that had a weakening effect on her knees.

Oliver reached out and touched her cheek, one finger trailing slowly along her skin until it reached the line of her jaw. "I can't wait to have you in my bed."

Then, before she even had a second to breathe, his

lips were on hers, exquisitely gentle and achingly tender. He took the fingers of her hand and kissed them, featherlight. "Unless you've changed your mind?"

"Race you there," she said and, with a breathless laugh, started to run.

Chapter 14

Oliver caught up with Shannon just as she reached the doorway. She giggled like a giddy teenager when he spun her around.

"Caught you," he said.

"I let you catch me." How was it that standing here, both of them grinning like two fools, felt so right?

She'd had two other love affairs, one in college and one when she lived in Lubbock. While in both cases she'd had high hopes for a future with the guy, being with them had never felt quite right.

Now, here she stood beside a man who'd made it clear whatever they shared would be very short-term, and she had no hesitation or doubts.

Like now, having him scatter kisses down her neck felt natural and oh-so right.

"Hmm." Shannon tilted her head back, giving him

full access to the creamy expanse of skin. "I love the feel of your arms around me."

"I love the taste of you." His lips continued their downward journey. Only when he reached the vee of her dress did he lift his head. "This dress drives me absolutely bonkers."

She gave a pleased laugh. For that one compliment alone, the dress had been worth every penny she'd spent. "Oh, so it's the dress you fancy, is it?"

Oliver chuckled, then kicked the bedroom door shut with his foot, reaching around her to lock it. "I fancy every part of you."

The sentiment, coupled with the wicked look in his dancing blue eyes, sent warmth sliding through her veins like warm honey.

"Locking the door seems a bit excessive," she said, her tone light and teasing. "Concerned about Barnaby doing some spying?"

"I don't want anything to disturb us," he said, then his smile turned rueful. "Except—"

Shannon didn't know what to think when he abruptly released her and strode to the bedside stand. When she saw him flip on the baby monitor, her admiration for him inched up another notch.

"Just in case Ollie needs us." In several long strides he was back beside her, pulling her to him.

"I must admit I find your concern for Ollie—" she leaned close to whisper in his ear "—incredibly arousing."

"I'll remember that." His eyes twinkled. "All I ask is you do your best to restrain any carnal urges while I'm checking his temperature or changing his nappy."

Shannon realized she was seeing a playful side of

Oliver that up until now she'd caught only glimpses of. "This relaxed, fun side of you is also sexy."

"I'm beginning to think," he said, brushing back a strand of hair that had fallen across her cheek, "that everything about me turns you on."

Shannon pretended to think for a second, then grinned. "Pretty much."

"We're going to take our time tonight. No rushing allowed." His expression turned serious. "That will be difficult, considering I've wanted to kiss you for a very long time."

"Well, what are you waiting for?" She lifted her face to him and placed her hand on his chest, toying with a button. She slipped it open. "What do you say? Let's get this party started."

Shannon felt her knees grow weak at the fire in his eyes. An answering heat flared through her, a sensation she didn't bother to fight.

"Oliver." She spoke his name, then paused, not sure what she wanted to say. Her eyes, which seemed to suddenly develop a mind of their own, zeroed in on the area directly below his belt buckle.

He chuckled, a low pleasant rumbling sound.

"Slow," he murmured, twining strands of her hair loosely around his fingers the same way he had when they'd danced earlier, "means keeping our clothes on a little while longer."

Shannon stuck out her lip and pretended to pout. The effect was spoiled by the smile that kept forming on her mouth. "I don't like this game."

"Oh, but you will." His voice was like a promise.

Shannon lifted her gaze and their eye contact turned into something more, a tangible connection between the two of them. Could he hear her heart pounding? How could he not?

"You're pretty full of yourself, mister," she managed to sputter.

Oliver winked. "That's a Fortune for you."

Shannon's laughter disappeared when his hands spanned her waist. He ran his palms up along the sides of her dress, skimming the curve of her breast, and she forgot how to breathe.

Her nipples stiffened, straining against the fabric toward his touch.

"You are so lovely," he whispered into her ear right before he took the lobe between his teeth and nibbled.

Shivers rippled across her skin.

Without warning, he shifted and pressed his mouth against hers. When his tongue swept across her lips seeking access, Shannon eagerly opened her mouth to him, her tongue fencing with his.

He tasted like the most delicious decadent candy she'd ever eaten. And she couldn't help wanting more.

Still, as he promised, Oliver didn't rush. He simply continued to kiss her. Testosterone wafted from him like an invisible tether, tugging at Shannon, keeping her feet anchored to the floor and her mouth melded to his.

The feeling of his mouth on hers was like nothing Shannon had experienced before.

She ached for him, desired him, with her entire being. The need quickly became a stark carnal hunger she hadn't known she was even capable of feeling.

"I want—" she whispered against his mouth, when they came up for air "—you."

"I'm not going anywhere," he said, his voice a husky caress.

"I want you naked." In a display of unexpected boldness, she pushed her hips against him, rubbing his erection.

"I planned to take this slow," he reminded her, his breath hitching. "Savor every moment."

"Plans have changed," she said. "Next time we'll go slow. For now, get naked."

"Heaven protect me from a bossy woman." But his eyes glittered and his clothes quickly landed in a heap next to hers on the floor.

She'd been hot only seconds before, but now, when his gaze shifted to her naked body and lingered, Shannon felt exposed and vulnerable. She almost embarrassed herself by trying to cover her most private parts with her hands…until she saw the stark desire in his eyes. Desire…for her.

To realize he wanted her as much as she did him was a heady feeling and a confidence booster. Her hands remained at her sides.

"You are…magnificent." He breathed the words and took her hands loosely in his.

"You're not so bad yourself." An understatement, but the best Shannon could manage at the moment. Broad shoulders, hard chest, lean hips, Oliver Fortune Hayes was every woman's fantasy.

Though a businessman, Oliver had a workingman's body, corded with muscle, lean and tan. Dark hair converged on the flat planes of his stomach into a line that…

She inhaled sharply and her knees suddenly felt weak.

Without warning, he scooped her up and carried her to the bed.

"Hey," she laughingly protested, "what do you think you're doing?"

"Something tells me you're going to be at your best horizontal."

The bed was soft and luxurious, and the tiny part of her brain still capable of rational thought registered the fact that he must have had a new mattress delivered.

Rational thought disappeared as Oliver settled beside her and once again began to kiss her. Not slow and easy as he had before but with a voraciousness that showed a mounting hunger.

The same hunger that was rapidly consuming her.

She could have cheered when his thumbs brushed across the tight points of her nipples. His stroking fingers sent shock waves of pleasure through her body.

"Oh, Oli—"

Whatever she'd been about to say died away on a soft little whimper as he found one sensitive part of her body after another. His hands continued to move, to search; touching, stroking, caressing until her heart pounded and she didn't even know her own name. All Shannon knew was she needed him to continue touching her.

"Your breasts are perfect," he whispered. "I need to taste you. Open your eyes."

Shannon opened her eyes. As she watched, he touched the tip of his tongue to the tip of her right breast. The combination of seeing and feeling brought her up off the bed and had her crying out in delight.

He smiled, then circled her nipple with his tongue before drawing it fully into his mouth. The gentle sucking had her arching against him. At the same time, his hand slipped between her legs.

She parted for him, catching her breath as he rubbed against her slick center. Then his head was moving down to where his fingers still caressed, scattering kisses down her belly.

The tension filling her body continued to increase exponentially with each warm, moist kiss against her bare skin until she stiffened, realizing just where those wickedly clever lips were headed. Part of her suspected what Oliver was going to do while the rest of her couldn't believe it was really happening. She'd heard…she'd read… but she never had…

His openmouthed kiss between her legs had her writhing in pleasure. He found her sweet spot and licked it over and over again until all she could do was dig her heels into the mattress and clutch the sheets with her hands.

How could it be she'd lived this long and had never known such pleasure existed?

"I want you inside me," she said even as her muscles tensed and collected and her breath came in ragged pants.

She didn't have to ask twice.

Oliver pulled away briefly and she heard the sound of foil tearing. Then he was over her.

She reached between them and guided him inside.

He was large and stretched her in the best way possible. Her legs swept around his hips as he began to move slowly inside her in a rhythm as old as time.

Shannon felt filled, yet the need—that all-encompassing need for him—propelled her to want more. She clung to him, urging him deeper.

The rhythmic thrusting grew faster. As she surged against the pleasure swelling like the tide inside her, Shannon heard herself groan, a sound of want and need that astonished her with its intensity.

Her blood had become a fire in her veins, her pulse throbbing hard and thick.

Seconds later, the orgasm ripped through her, hitting with breathtaking speed. Her entire body convulsed then released.

As she cried out, Oliver caught her mouth in a hard kiss.

He continued to thrust until every last drop of pleasure had been wrung from her. Only then did he take his release, shuddering in her arms and calling out her name.

For a moment he simply lay there on top of her, a sweet heavy weight. When he rolled off, she murmured a protest.

In answer, his arm slipped around her, not confining, but comfortable. With a contented sigh, Shannon snuggled against his chest and discovered her head fit perfectly just under his chin.

He was warm and solid. A man she could hold on to, a man she could count on. At least for another few weeks...

Shannon fought to keep her eyes open.

"You kept your promise," she murmured before she fell into a sated slumber. "It was so very good."

Oliver waited until Shannon's breathing had turned easy and deep before he slipped from her embrace to check on Ollie. Even after he confirmed his son's fever had remained down and the child was resting comfortably, he didn't return to bed.

Instead he headed to the kitchen and poured himself a glass of whiskey. Sipping from a tumbler shaped like a boot, he stared into the darkness.

He'd had sex with a number of women, but tonight

had been different. Shannon had touched a part of him that Oliver had always kept well hidden. From the time Oliver had been a small boy, his father had taught him to guard his emotions. Although the man had never struck him, Rhys Henry Hayes's tongue had been a potent weapon; sharp as a knife and capable of drawing blood.

His father had been fond of saying he didn't tolerate fools. To Rhys's warped way of thinking, a fool was anyone who cared too much and let it show. That included little boys.

Taking another sip of whiskey, Oliver thought of the words Diane had flung in his face the day she moved out. She'd accused him of being as cold as his father and told him it was no wonder she had looked for love elsewhere.

At the time, he'd shrugged aside the arrow that had been aimed to wound, concluding it was her way of excusing her own poor behavior. Now he wondered if there might have been some truth to the statement. Still, something had kept him from fully trusting his wife, and in the end Diane's duplicity had shown his instincts had been spot-on.

Shannon, on the other hand, was a different story. It would be easy to let her get too close, and that would be disastrous for all concerned. She was a small-town girl who loved living close to family and friends. Her home was in Horseback Hollow. His home—his life— was in London.

Her mind, her heart, the person she was fascinated him. Her body tempted him. She was the total package, and that's what made her so hard to resist, both in bed and out. That's what would keep him coming back for more. He knew there was so much more of this fascinating woman left to plumb.

The thought made him smile, remembering all he'd plumbed tonight—

Arms slid around his bare chest. "I hope that smile means you're thinking about me."

When Oliver turned, he found Shannon wearing one of his shirts, hanging open save for a single button. Her hair was a tangled mass of curls and her gaze was sloe-eyed and sensual.

He flipped the button open, then eased back the shirt and let it slide to the floor. His mouth skimmed the edge of her jaw, testing the sweetness of her skin. "You must be a mind reader."

She laughed softly and wound her arms around his neck, lifting her face for a kiss.

Though it hadn't been all that long since he'd left her side, it felt amazingly good to hold her again. To taste her. To smell her. He spread his hands over her buttocks and pressed her against his erection.

"Well, hel-lo there," she said, her eyes teasing.

He bent his head and kissed her softly on the mouth. "I haven't had nearly enough of you."

"You stole the words right out of my mouth."

"I love your mouth." Once again his lips closed over hers.

She kissed him back, and the kisses quickly became more urgent and fevered. Then abruptly she stepped back, swaying slightly.

He reached out and took her arm, concern deepening his voice. "Problem?"

"Just a couple shaky knees that aren't going to hold me up much longer." She grasped his hand, tugging and gesturing with her head toward the bedroom. "Remember, I'm at my best horizontal."

Oliver chuckled. Locking his hand around her elbow in a secure grip, he propelled her into the bedroom. Once the door was shut and locked, they tumbled onto the bed.

Though his body responded with breathtaking speed, this time, he took it slow. He wanted it to be perfect for her.

When the last shudder had left her body and she lay spent beneath him, Oliver held her close and savored the moment.

Still, his last thought before he joined her in sleep was that he had to keep up his guard. It would be far too easy to pretend he never had to let her go and start to believe this was exactly where he belonged.

Chapter 15

Oliver pulled the rental car into the long driveway and mentally calculated the hours until he'd be able to leave. He couldn't use the excuse that their baby minder wanted them home early. Ollie was spending the night with Oliver's aunt Jeanne Marie.

Though he'd hoped to spend some quality time with his mother this weekend, Oliver never imagined it would involve attending something called a "card party" on a Saturday night. Especially a party held at the home of Shannon's parents.

The monthly event had been rescheduled from last weekend. Apparently too many of the "regulars" had wanted to attend the Fortune weddings, so they'd voted to move the card party back a week.

Oliver hadn't seen Shep or Lilian since the night of

the wedding. Which meant he hadn't had to look in Shep Singleton's face since he'd begun shagging his daughter.

Though initially Oliver had told himself that what had happened after the wedding had been a one-time— okay, a two-time—thing, it had seemed so natural to go to her the next day. By Wednesday, a romp between the sheets had become a daily affair.

Of course, because of his crazy work hours, any love-making had to occur before midnight or after lunch. So far that hadn't been an issue. When he wanted something, he was pretty adept at making it happen.

And Oliver wanted Shannon Singleton. He wanted her with an intensity that continued to amaze him. It wasn't just physical. Shannon made him laugh and feel things he hadn't let himself feel in years.

Like with Ollie. Oliver hadn't realized it until she'd casually mentioned that she'd noticed he never told his son that he loved him.

"It goes without saying," he said, recalling his exact words. "I take care of him. I work hard to put food on the table and give him what he needs."

"He needs to hear the words," she'd insisted.

When he hesitated, she'd taken his hand and marched him into the living room, where Ollie had sat playing with his bricks.

"Tell him," she urged in a low voice.

Feeling incredibly silly, Oliver had crouched down beside his son. He opened his mouth, then closed it and cleared his throat. Why did something that should have been so easy come so hard to him?

"Ollie."

The boy looked up, his smile wide. He held up an *A* brick for Oliver to admire. "See."

"It's very nice." If Oliver had been alone, he'd have simply patted the boy on the head and stood up.

But Shannon stood there, looking at him with such encouragement—and confidence—he couldn't back down. Not even with his father's words rolling around in his head.

It really wasn't a big thing, he told himself, just three little words. People said them all the time, even if they didn't mean them. But Oliver would mean them. He loved Ollie, more than he'd ever thought possible.

Just. Say. The. Words.

"Ollie." He gently touched the little boy's face and gazed into his eyes. "I love you."

The boy's smile was like a flash of sunshine warming everything it touched, thawing out a part of his heart that had been frozen for too long. Though Oliver was fairly certain the toddler hadn't understood what he said, Shannon had been right. He'd needed to say the words.

Oliver scrubbed the boy's head with his hand and then stood.

"Go ahead and play with your bricks." His voice had been thick with emotion and had shaken slightly. He'd felt foolish and more than a little angry that he couldn't seem to control the intense feelings welling up inside him.

Then Shannon had wrapped her arms around him and given him a big kiss. When she'd stepped back, the pride in her eyes washed away everything but joy.

"Earth to Oliver." Shannon's voice broke through his thoughts. "I think we should go inside."

Oliver pulled his thoughts back to the present. "I'm not looking forward to this evening."

"The fact that you pulled up and have yet to turn off

the engine tells me you're still considering making a break for it."

She knew him so well. Why did he find the thought so disturbing?

"Forgive me if I don't want to spend a Saturday playing cards with my mother." His tone was curter than he'd intended.

Her cheery smile faded and she stiffened. "If you didn't want to come, you shouldn't have accepted the invitation."

"It's not just that," he reluctantly admitted.

"What then?"

"It's your father."

"My dad?" Her eyes widened then narrowed. "What has he done now?"

"I told him I wouldn't touch you when—"

"You've been doing nothing but touching me for the past week and in every possible place."

Just the words said in that throaty whisper had him going hard. He shifted uncomfortably in his seat.

"I'd promised him he had nothing to worry about." Oliver set his jaw in a hard tilt. "I assured him you would be totally safe living under my roof."

"I am safe living under your roof." Shannon reached over and wrapped her fingers around his hand.

The simple touch eased a little of the tension that held him in a stranglehold.

"You would never let anything bad happen to me. If someone broke in, you'd protect me. If I hurt myself, you'd tend to me." Her voice was low and soothing. "I *am* safe. The sex, well, that's something private between you and me."

Oliver frowned, realizing he didn't like hearing her refer to what they shared as *sex*. *Shagging* also didn't fit.

But that left *lovemaking*, and that didn't work either. There was warmth, there was caring, but love wasn't part of the equation.

"My father will never suspect," she assured him.

But halfway through the evening, when they were between games and Oliver had unconsciously slid his arm around Shannon's waist and she'd leaned into him, the look in Shep's eyes could have cut steel.

Oliver should have known better than to get too close to Shannon. Though he'd never been a demonstrative kind of man, she was very much the opposite. She was always finding excuses to touch him, and he'd discovered he liked it.

He'd also seen how it pleasured her when he unexpectedly reached over and took her hand or gave her a hug when she came in the door. It had seemed such a little thing to do to make her happy.

He'd also been more demonstrative with Ollie, and the boy had become more openly loving with him. Yesterday his son had even called him "Daddy" for the first time. Just recalling the moment brought a lump to his throat.

"When will you be leaving our little town, Oliver?" Shep asked pointedly during a brief conversational lull.

"Oh, Shep, must you bring up such a disturbing topic?" Josephine's brows knit together in a frown. "It feels as if Oliver and Ollie just got here, and now you're bringing up their departure."

"Can't ignore the facts." Shep took a swig of beer straight from the bottle. "Thought I heard you'll be returning to London in just a couple of weeks."

Beneath his arm, Oliver felt Shannon stiffen. They'd

agreed not to talk about when he would leave, and Oliver inwardly cursed Shep for bringing up the topic. But the man's comment required an answer.

"Not that soon." Oliver kept his tone easy. "Closer to the end of March."

"Several weeks then, but not that long off." Shep shot a pointed look in his daughter's direction, as if making sure she was listening, before his gaze returned to Oliver. "You have a girl back home?"

"Pardon?"

"A girl. A woman you're seeing."

"No," Oliver said coolly.

"My son has been much too busy the past year to do much socializing," Josephine interjected. "His brokerage firm keeps him extremely busy, and now that he has Ollie to care for, I doubt there'll be much time for dating."

"Oh, I'm sure he'll find a few free moments now and then." Shep took another swig of beer. "Your son seems like the type to take advantage of every opportunity."

Oliver heard Shannon's quick intake of breath. If they'd been alone, Oliver would have had no hesitation in calling Shep on his comment. But the rest of those in attendance seemed oblivious to the conversation's undertones.

To make a scene would serve no purpose, he told himself even as his spine stiffened.

Oliver met Shep's gaze. They would talk, his eyes told her father, soon.

"Did I tell you Ollie has now started calling Oliver 'Daddy'?" This time it was Shannon who filled the silence. "It's so cute. He clearly says 'Daddy,' not 'Dada.'"

"Shannon called Shep 'Da' until she was three."

Shannon gave a little laugh. "Oh, Mother."

Lilian lifted her hand as if swearing an oath. "True story."

"Tell them what the boy calls you," Shep said to Shannon.

The slight pink across her cheeks deepened, but she acted as if she hadn't heard.

Josephine took a sip of tea, considered. "I believe 'Shannon' would be difficult for a child to say."

Shep opened his mouth.

"He calls me 'Mama,'" Shannon said, then quickly added, "I think it's what he calls all females."

"He calls your mother 'Lil,'" her dad said.

A lightning bolt flashed in Shannon's eyes. Oliver couldn't believe her own father hadn't noticed his daughter's mounting irritation. Perhaps Shep didn't care. Perhaps he wanted to get a rise out of her.

Or perhaps this was his way of making a point. Steer clear of Oliver Fortune Hayes. He'll eat you up and spit you out and never look back.

Shannon pushed to her feet and flashed a smile that didn't quite reach her eyes.

"I'm really tired. Ollie was up a lot last night." She slanted a glance at Oliver. "I hope you don't mind leaving early."

"Not at all. It's embarrassing when your own mum trounces you." Oliver bent over and brushed a kiss against his mother's cheek. "May we give you a ride home?"

Josephine smiled and glanced over at Orlando Mendoza, who'd been her partner most of the evening. "Thank you, but I believe I have that covered."

Oliver and Shannon made their exit in record time.

Once they were in the car, Shannon rested her head against the back of the seat and huffed a frustrated breath.

"My father was in rare form tonight." Her lips tightened. "No doubt about it. He's figured out we're sleeping together."

There was no reason to disagree. That fact had been very obvious. "You're his little girl. He's concerned I'm going to hurt you."

"I'm a woman, not a child," she snapped. "We both went into this with our eyes wide open."

Oliver didn't want to ask, but knew the question would fester if he didn't. "Any regrets?"

The anger fled her eyes, replaced with another kind of heat. She leaned over and brushed a kiss against his cheek. "Only that we're not at home right now so I can have my way with you."

The next week passed swiftly. Shannon kept her days so full she didn't have time to think. It was at night, when Ollie was in bed and Oliver was working, that her mind raced and she did nothing but think.

She thought about the fact that the Fortune Foundation would soon be choosing its new marketing executive. What would she do if the foundation offered the position to Rachel and not her? She couldn't continue to stay in Horseback Hollow and simply help out around the ranch. But the thought of returning to Lubbock filled her with dread.

But what weighed most heavily on her mind was the knowledge that each passing day brought her closer to the time when Oliver and Ollie would leave her and return to England.

Barely aware of the fragrant aroma of vegetables and meat cooking in the pot before her, Shannon automatically stirred the soup and blinked back tears.

This time spent with Oliver and Ollie had been the best of her life. Living under the same roof with Oliver had given her extra insight into the man behind the British stiff upper lip. He wasn't cold and off-putting as Rachel thought. He was a warm, caring man with a huge capacity for love.

At her encouragement, Oliver had become more demonstrative with Ollie. The increased openness was already bearing fruit. Ollie now ran to his father as often as he ran to her. And just yesterday, when Ollie had fallen on the rocky driveway and skinned his knee, his father had been the one he wanted to comfort him.

Oh, how she was going to miss them both. Shannon sighed and picked up the spoon.

She started to stir the soup again and felt a tug at her pant leg.

"Mama, up." Ollie stood beside her, arms held high.

Setting the spoon down, she lowered the heat even more, then stepped back and lifted the boy into her arms.

He smelled like soap and shampoo. Shannon wished she could hold him tight and never let him go. Instead she smiled. "Are you hungry?"

The little boy nodded vigorously. "Want ice cream."

"That's my boy."

Shannon whirled to find Oliver standing in the doorway, his hair mussed from sleep, Barnaby at his feet.

She glanced at the clock on the wall. "You didn't sleep very long today."

It wasn't even six and he hadn't gotten to bed—or

rather to sleep—until noon. Ollie had been taking an extra-long nap and they'd been…occupied.

Oliver's normal pattern was to sleep until seven, then they'd have a late supper. She usually fed Ollie earlier, as the child preferred to eat smaller, more frequent meals.

"Couldn't you sleep?" she asked, when he didn't respond.

"Too much on my mind" was all he said, but she could see his expression was troubled.

Shannon set a now-squirming Ollie to the floor. He immediately ran to his father.

Oliver scooped him up and a smile lifted his lips. "You getting some loving from Shannon? Smart man."

The child turned his head and smiled at Shannon. "Mama give ice cream."

Oliver raised a brow, but there was laughter in his eyes. "Now I see what goes on while I'm sleeping."

"Give ice cream, Mama," Ollie repeated, pointing in the direction of the refrigerator.

Neither she nor Oliver paid any attention to the boy calling her "Mama." After the night they'd played cards, Shannon had tried again to get Ollie to call her by her given name—even a shortened version—but she'd had to concede defeat.

"Ollie may want ice cream," Shannon said easily, casting a playful glance at the child, "but he'll be getting yogurt."

Oliver grimaced.

"Hey," she told him, "it's healthy and it tastes good."

"I'll take your word on that." He sniffed the air. "Whatever is in that pot smells good."

"Homemade vegetable beef soup," she told him. "My

mom gave me her old bread machine, so I made tomato basil bread to go with the soup."

"Sounds delicious."

"I thought we'd start off with a glass of wine and antipasto. Then a green salad, soup and bread." Shannon, who'd practically kicked and screamed while her mother taught her to cook, had discovered she actually enjoyed cooking…when she had someone to cook for besides herself.

Oliver swung Ollie through the air, and the boy erupted into giggles. When he set him down, Ollie began to protest until Oliver flicked on the television to a *Daniel Tiger's Neighborhood* rerun.

Mesmerized, the boy crawled up onto the sofa and Barnaby jumped up with him. Shannon got him a tube of yogurt and the child took it, his eyes firmly focused on the television.

"What do you say?" Oliver said automatically.

"Tank you," came the response from the child.

Oliver moved to the table and pulled out a chair. "I got another email from Diane's mother."

Ah, so that's what has him so troubled.

Shannon went to the counter where she'd placed two wineglasses and poured each of them a glass. She set the plate of antipasto on the table and took a seat opposite Oliver.

As she munched on an olive and sipped her wine, she thought back to when he'd received the first email. It had been right after the card party. Though he'd mentioned it in passing, she could see he was troubled by the contact.

She hadn't pressed, knowing he would tell her the specifics in his own time, or he wouldn't. As then, she had to resist the urge to push.

"She wants to video chat with Ollie. Says he's their only grandchild and they want to be a part of his life." Anger, at odds with the calm delivery, simmered in the air.

Unsure how to respond, Shannon took a bite of ham.

Oliver set down his wineglass and leveled a gaze at her. "They expect me to go out of my way when they couldn't be bothered to tell me about Diane's death. I had to hear about her death at a bloody cocktail party."

"I assume you asked why they hadn't told you when you picked Ollie up." Shannon kept her tone nonchalant, as if totally unaware of the hostility vibrating in the air.

"Celeste—that's Diane's mother—said she hadn't been thinking clearly. That her daughter's death had devastated her."

"Sounds…logical."

As if he'd finally found an outlet for his rage, Oliver pinned his gaze on her. "You're on their side. You think I should forgive them."

"I think—" Shannon carefully picked up another olive, though her stomach was so jittery she didn't dare put it in her mouth "—that losing a child *would* be horrific. It seems logical she wasn't thinking clearly."

"They had Ollie for two months." He shoved back his chair and jerked to his feet. "Two months without notifying me."

Let it go, Shannon told herself, *you're the nanny. This isn't your business.*

But even as the thought crossed her mind, she realized that she couldn't let it go. She cared for Oliver and for his son.

Ollie deserved to know his grandparents. And no

good would be served for Oliver to harbor such anger. Still, how to proceed was the question.

Shannon took a long drink of wine. "What was your impression of Diane's parents? Prior to her death, I mean?"

He turned back from the kitchen window where he'd been gazing—or rather *glaring*—out into the twilight.

"Nice enough," he said grudgingly, as if it pained him to say the words. "Father is a barrister. Mother is involved in a lot of civic activities."

"Any other children?" she asked casually.

"Just Diane."

"Did you see her parents often after you were married?"

"At holidays. Occasionally they'd come to London and we'd go to the symphony or the theater."

"No backyard barbecues or card parties?" Shannon teased, relieved when he smiled.

"Not their cup of tea." His smile faded. "I can see where you're headed with this, what you're trying to do."

"Really?" She lifted the glass to her lips, but didn't drink. "Tell me. What is it I'm trying to do?"

"You want me to think about what they were like before, to give them the benefit of the doubt." He twirled the stem of the glass between his fingers.

"Someday Ollie will want to know about his mother. He'll have all sorts of questions. Who better to give him that information than her parents?"

His jaw jutted out at a stubborn angle. "They should have told me."

"Life is full of should-haves," Shannon said with a

heavy sigh. "I should have confronted Jerry, but I didn't. Cut them some slack, Oliver. Not only for Ollie's sake, but for your own."

Chapter 16

Shannon rested her head against the seat of Oliver's luxury Mercedes sedan and let the soothing tones of a Mozart piano concerto wash over her. As the car continued smoothly down the highway toward town, she slanted a glance at Oliver. Her heart tripped when he returned her smile then reached over to squeeze her hand.

She liked that they didn't feel the need to talk all the time. They'd both gotten comfortable with occasional silence. And she liked how when she did say something, Oliver listened to her, really and truly listened. Though Shannon still didn't know what he planned to do about the situation with Oliver's grandparents, it had been empowering for her to realize that he seriously considered her opinions.

Tonight she planned to simply sit back and enjoy her date with Oliver.

It *was* a date, she told herself. How could it be considered anything else?

Oliver had asked if she was busy Saturday night.

She'd said she was free.

He asked if she wanted to check out the recently renovated theater that had opened in Horseback Hollow.

She told him she'd love to see a movie.

While Horseback Hollow wasn't big enough to support a first-run theater—they had to go to Vicker's Corners or Lubbock for that—this week the local theater was running the classic *Back to the Future*. Shannon hadn't even been born when the movie had been made, but since this particular science-fiction comedy was one of her father's favorites, she'd seen it many times.

The thought of sitting in a dark theater with Oliver, eating popcorn and candy, perhaps even sharing a soda, made seeing the movie for what had to be the zillionth time very appealing.

Josephine had been desperate for what she had taken to calling her "Ollie time," so the boy was spending the night with "Nana," whom he now adored. Thinking of the vibrant woman brought to mind something Shannon had meant to bring up earlier.

"Have you noticed that lately your mother is always texting?" she asked Oliver after he parked and they started down the sidewalk of Horseback Hollow's main street.

Earlier when they dropped off Ollie, Josephine had been in the process of sending a text. Though Shannon's parents both texted occasionally, lately it seemed every time she saw Oliver's mother, the phone was glued to her hand.

"Mum likes technology," he said a bit absently. His eyes suddenly widened and a grin split his face. "Brodie."

Shannon hadn't seen much of Oliver's brother, although she knew he and Oliver had gotten together several times since Brodie had arrived in Horseback Hollow. From the few things Oliver had said, Shannon had the distinct impression his brother didn't think much of her hometown.

Brodie strode over. As always, he was impeccably dressed in a dark suit, his shoes shined to a high gloss. He cast a disapproving gaze at the jeans and cotton shirt Oliver wore.

"At least you're not wearing cowboy boots," Brodie said with a sniff.

"No," Shannon said with an impish smile, extending one foot so he could see her Tony Lama footwear. "I am."

A pained look crossed Brodie's face.

"We're going to view a movie at the cinema," Oliver told him. "Would you care to join us?"

"They're showing *Back to the Future*," Shannon added. "It's considered a classic."

A hint of a smile lifted Brodie's lips and then it was gone. It was as if he wasn't sure if she was putting him on or not. "I appreciate the invitation, but I have other plans."

"Would those plans involve Alden Moore?" Oliver lifted a brow. "I saw you coming out of the Hollows Cantina yesterday with him."

Shannon glanced at Oliver in surprise. He hadn't mentioned anything to her about his brother and Mr. Moore. Not that Oliver was required to tell her everyone he saw or spoke with during the course of the day. But Alden Moore was big news in Horseback Hollow.

The president of Moore Entertainment, Alden was the man charged with opening Cowboy Country USA, a theme park currently under construction at the edge of Horseback Hollow. The last Shannon heard, the park was scheduled to open Memorial Day weekend.

"The Hollows is one of the few places in town I can tolerate." Brodie gave a dismissive wave. "Thank heavens I leave for London in a few days, where I can get some real food."

"What were you and Alden discussing?" Oliver pressed.

"Business. That's the only topic that interests me." Brodie shifted his gaze to Shannon, not missing the way his brother's hand circled her waist. "It appears you two are enjoying an evening out, leaving my nephew to fend for himself."

Oliver laughed. "Mum has him. Trust me, he'll be spoiled rotten by the time we pick him up tomorrow morning."

Surprise had Brodie's eyes widening. "You're leaving the tyke in her care overnight?"

"She insisted." Oliver's lips twitched. "You know how determined she can be."

"He'll be asleep by the time the movie is over," Shannon added. "We'd just have to wake him to take him home."

"Well—" Brodie inclined his head "—enjoy the cinema."

"Stop by before you leave," Oliver called after him.

Brodie nodded and continued to walk.

"Odd," Oliver said, almost to himself.

"What?"

"Brodie isn't usually so reticent." Oliver lifted a shoulder in a slight shrug. "It's of no importance."

He took Shannon's hand, a gesture that had come to

seem so natural to him. Oliver assumed it was because there was a lot of touching going on at home.

Shannon's capacity for pleasure astounded him, as did his need for her. As their trust in each other had grown, they'd become even more adventurous in bed. Oliver had discovered that lovemaking could be passionate and intense but also casual and fun. Last night he'd even laughed aloud while tussling with her on the bed.

As they strolled down the sidewalk, under the glow of the streetlamps, they spoke of Ollie and Barnaby, of his mother and other family members. She didn't mention Diane's parents and he didn't bring them up either. Though he was becoming more reconciled to the idea of letting them be a part of Ollie's life, he wasn't quite there yet.

Once they reached the box office, he paid for the tickets. Shannon tried to pay for hers but that was never an option. He had invited her and he would pay.

Though the show was ready to begin, Shannon insisted she couldn't watch the movie without candy and popcorn. He hurriedly bought the refreshments and they found a couple of seats toward the back of the darkened theater. The place was only a third full, so there were plenty of choices.

"I love Junior Mints," Shannon whispered halfway through the show, popping another of the dark candies into her mouth.

The merest hint of chocolate remained on her lips. Leaning close, he ran a finger across her lips, heard her quick intake of air.

"Chocolate," he said, in response to her questioning look. "Your lips are sweet enough. They don't need any enhancement."

Instead of looking at the screen, where a truck of manure was being dumped on Biff's car, Shannon's gaze remained focused on Oliver. His groin tightened when she slowly ran her tongue across her lips.

Oliver had never condoned public displays of affection. But lately he found himself reaching for Shannon's hand or placing his palm against her back…simply for the contact and because the connection to her felt so good.

Taking her arm to steady her when getting out of the car made perfect sense. Reaching out to grab her if she stumbled was totally appropriate.

Kissing a woman in a public theater? Unthinkable. But now, as Oliver's gaze lingered on Shannon's full, soft lips, he found he couldn't think of anything else.

Wait until you get home.

He'd never last that long.

Wait until you get in the car.

He'd never last that long.

Kiss her now. It seemed the best option. The *only* option.

Societal rules be damned.

"Shannon," he spoke softly while his gaze traveled over her face and searched her eyes.

Was that harsh, uneven breath coming from her? Or him?

With great tenderness, Oliver brushed his fingers against her cheek then slowly lowered his head and closed his mouth over hers.

The kiss was warm and sweet and touched a place inside him that had been cold for so long. He heard sounds of laughter coming from the big screen but paid it no mind. All that mattered was him. And her. The closeness. The love.

The thought had him jerking back.

Even in the dim light, he could see the startled confusion in her eyes. Her lipstick was smudged from his kisses, the hair she'd intricately braided pulling loose.

Though his heart galloped in his chest, he casually gestured with his head toward the screen. "They're getting to the good part."

Since he'd paid little attention to the film, he had no idea what had happened or was about to happen. Neither did he particularly care.

Shannon gave a jerky nod and turned her attention back to the screen, but he sensed her puzzlement. When she straightened in her seat and leaned ever so slightly away from him, her withdrawal was like an ice pick to the heart.

Oliver slid his arm around her and pulled her close. When she relaxed and rested her head against his shoulder, his world that had tipped so precariously only seconds before righted itself.

He knew they were back to normal when she lifted the box of Junior Mints from her lap and offered him one.

Though Oliver wasn't a fan of the candies, he took one and realized when it hit his tongue that it tasted like her kisses. And he simply had to have another taste. The rest of the movie passed by unwatched.

Shannon blinked as they stepped from the darkened theater into the light. She looked, he thought fancifully, like a sleeping beauty waking up. *His* sleeping beauty.

Her lips were swollen from his kisses, her hair mussed. He hadn't been able to keep from slipping his fingers into the silky strands as their mouths melded together. And though they'd just stopped kissing when the credits had begun to roll, Oliver was seized with an overpowering urge to kiss her again.

Actually, he wanted to do a whole lot more than kiss her.

"Instead of going for ice cream in Vicker's Corners as we discussed, how about we go home and have...dessert there?" Though Shannon spoke casually, he recognized the look in her eye.

"Great minds think alike." He took her arm as they stepped out of the theater and onto the sidewalk.

Oliver resisted—barely—the urge to hurry her along. There was no need to rush. With his mum watching Ollie, they had all night.

"Oliver, what a pleasant surprise."

He pulled up short. "Amelia."

Looking young and carefree in a dress more suited to a college girl than a new mum, his sister quickly closed the distance between them. Quinn was with her, their baby bound to his chest in some kind of flowery fabric.

Oliver shot him a sympathetic glance.

Quinn simply grinned.

"What are you two doing out?" Oliver asked. The baby seemed far too small to be exposed to the cool night air.

"We could ask you the same question." Amelia's de-cidedly curious gaze slid from him to Shannon.

"We wanted to check out the new theater," Shannon said, then seemed to reconsider her words. "I mean, I wanted to check it out so I asked Oliver if he'd be in-terested in joining me. He said he was, so here we are."

She was chattering, Oliver realized, the way she tended to do when she was nervous. Why, he wondered, was she so nervous? And why was she making it sound as if he'd simply tagged along for the evening?

"It was very nice, wasn't it, Oliver?" she added, when no one spoke.

"It was very enjoyable." The only part Oliver remembered of the movie was the rolling credits, but the kisses had been exceedingly pleasurable. "What about you?"

"Wendy and Marcos wanted to see Clementine, so we stopped in for dessert."

Oliver resisted—barely—slanting a glance at Shannon. They had a different kind of dessert planned once they reached home. And he had no doubt he'd enjoy his more than whatever his sister and her husband ordered tonight.

"Where's Ollie?" Amelia glanced around as if expecting the toddler to jump out from behind a tree.

"He's with Mum this evening."

"Ollie is such a sweet little boy." Amelia's lips curved, her look one of fondness. "I was telling Quinn just the other day how much I wished you and Ollie would stay in Horseback Hollow."

"Am, you know that's—" Oliver began.

"Oliver was such a good big brother to me," Amelia told Shannon. "I couldn't have asked for better. I know our children are just cousins, but if Ollie grew up here, he'd be like Clemmie's big brother."

Amelia shifted her gaze back to Oliver. "Wouldn't that be nice?"

"Most certainly." Oliver knew his sister too well to argue. "But my home is in London."

"It doesn't have to be," Amelia said, her expression earnest. "Technology makes it possible for people to work from anywhere. Quinn and I watched an episode on the telly about that quite recently."

"Did you?" Oliver said, vaguely amused at the thought of his former jet-setting younger sister sitting at home watching the telly and discussing changing work habits with her rancher husband.

"You're conducting your business right now from Horseback Hollow," Amelia reminded him, as if she somehow thought that fact had slipped his mind.

"He is, but it's very difficult for him." Shannon spoke up for the first time since Amelia had started her discourse. "Because of the time difference, Oliver has to do all his work in the middle of the night."

"Granted, it's probably not ideal," Amelia conceded. "But if you wanted, you could make staying here work."

Once again, Oliver avoided arguing and simply agreed with his headstrong baby sister. "You're right, Amelia. If a person wants something badly enough, they can make it happen."

Though it was past midnight and Oliver had a lot of calls to make, he sat back in his desk chair, his mind on everything but stocks and bonds.

The words he'd said to Amelia—primarily to placate her—continued to haunt him. Three days might have passed, but he couldn't stop thinking about them.

He believed what he'd said. If he wanted something badly enough, he could make it happen. In his case, Oliver wanted Shannon.

Though he hadn't yet said the words, he realized somewhere along the way, he'd fallen in love with her. Here was a woman he could trust, a woman who cared for him as much as he did for her.

He'd learned a lot from his failed relationship with Diane. Oliver accepted part of the blame for the demise of his first marriage. Back then he'd showed his love the only way he knew how—by providing the material things she so desperately craved.

They'd had the house in the country, the one in London. He'd given her expensive jewelry and household help to make her life easier. But he realized now those were only things. He'd held back his heart. Or perhaps it was simply that his heart had been waiting for someone else.

Though he'd never say that aloud—it was much too Lord Byron-ish—he believed it. While it was still difficult for him to verbalize emotions, Shannon had taught him that actions had to be coupled with words.

That's what Oliver planned to do tonight. His fingers closed around the small jeweler's box in his pocket. When he'd been in Lubbock yesterday, he'd seen the perfect ring for Shannon in a small jewelry store's window.

A large marquis-cut diamond solitaire, comparable to anything the Harry Winston jewelry company would carry, had caught his eye.

Oliver had never been a foolish man, or an impulsive one. He and Diane had dated for several years and he'd spent a lot of time considering whether he should propose. Only now did he realize that if he had to put so much thought into it—at one point he'd even drafted a list of the pros and cons—she hadn't been the one for him.

He'd settled, plain and simple. He'd been past thirty, he wanted a home and a family, and on paper they appeared well suited. But not once had Diane made his heart beat faster simply by walking into a room. Even worse, their house had never felt like a home.

With Shannon, Oliver could fully relax and be himself. No pretense, no posturing. She loved and accepted him as he was and, because he had her unqualified support, he wanted to be a better man.

She's never said she loves you.

The doubt surfaced and though he tried to brush it away, it kept returning to buzz around in his head, like a troublesome fly.

Oliver recognized this hesitation—knew the fear arose from those early years when his father had slapped down any talk or show of emotion.

It was no wonder his mother had left the man. Soon enough for Brodie not to have been tainted by his father's cold harshness, but not soon enough for Oliver.

But he'd gotten past that, Oliver told himself. Telling Ollie he loved him now came easier. And, once he said the words to Shannon, he vowed never to stop saying them.

In his mind, the only thing standing between them now was her affection for Horseback Hollow. But he felt confident of his ability to convince her she could find happiness in London with him and Ollie.

Tomorrow, he would confess his love. They would marry and meld their lives together.

For now, he had a business to run.

Oliver picked up his mobile phone and got back to work.

Chapter 17

"I'm so happy you stopped by this afternoon." Shannon opened the oven door, releasing the delicious aroma of cinnamon into the kitchen. "Otherwise I'd have to eat this coffee cake all by myself."

"You've got Oliver," Rachel reminded her, sipping her coffee. "What time will he be up?"

Shannon lifted the pan to a cooling rack, then took off the oven mitts and tossed them to the counter. She glanced at the clock, saw it was just past four. "He didn't go to bed until almost two, so I don't expect him up until seven. Perhaps even later."

She saw no reason to mention Ollie had been taking a nap when his father had concluded his business dealings at noon. She and Oliver had taken advantage of the opportunity. Though Oliver had been in bed—with her—there had been no sleeping involved.

Rachel studied Shannon over the rim of her cup. "I thought you were supposed to get off at five."

Shannon dropped into the chair opposite Rachel. "Oliver would never get any sleep if I left so early."

Her friend clucked her tongue, reminding Shannon of her mother. "Some things never change."

The coffee cup Shannon had been raising to her lips returned to the table with a clatter. "What's that supposed to mean?"

"It means you let people run all over you."

For a second, Shannon was stunned. She wasn't sure how to respond. Could she have misheard? Transposed some of her mother's words into Rachel's mouth? "What did you say?"

"I meant no disrespect. I care about you." Rachel reached across the table and took Shannon's hands. Before speaking, she slanted a sideways glance where Ollie sat playing with his blocks, Barnaby supervising. "Think about it. Jerry comes on to you. Sure, you tell him you want none of it. But not forcefully enough to make him understand you mean business. He persists. Instead of filing charges or even threatening to, you ran away."

Heat flooded Shannon's face and she pulled her hands back. She rose and moved to the counter. Though the coffee cake was still too warm, she cut it anyway. It gave her something to do with her hands while her thoughts tumbled like clothes in an out-of-control dryer at the local Laundromat.

Though what had occurred at her previous job had happened pretty much the way Rachel described it, she *had* tried to speak with Jerry.

"I was forceful," Shannon protested. "I told him so many different ways to bug off, it wasn't even funny.

But he didn't hear me. He didn't want to hear what I had to say, because I didn't matter."

"Now you're doing the same thing with Oliver." Rachel leaned forward, resting her forearms on the table. "You set up parameters—like you're off at five every day—but then you don't hold him to them. He walks all over you, and worse yet, you don't seem to notice or care."

Ollie let out a shriek when his blocks came crashing down.

"Ollie, shush, your daddy is sleeping," Shannon said automatically, then refocused on Rachel. "What you said about Oliver, it's not like that between us."

"Of course it is. You just don't want to see it."

"You're wrong." A tightness filled Shannon's chest, making it difficult to breathe. "I want to help him out. I like taking care of Ollie."

Rachel's gaze searched her face. "You're in love with the Brit."

Shannon started to deny it, then decided why bother. Rachel knew her too well and would simply see right through her denial. She sighed. "I am."

Rachel inclined her head, her gaze speculative. "Does he love you, too?"

Ah, that was the question.

She thought about what Amelia had said, that if you wanted to make something work, you'd do it. She'd give up her life in Horseback Hollow for Oliver…all he had to do was ask.

But what is he willing to give up for you? To do for you?

Shannon frowned. Maybe she was a pushover. She shoved the troubling thought aside.

"C'mon, Shannon," Rachel pressed. "Be honest, with me and with yourself."

"It feels as if he cares," Shannon said slowly. "When he looks at me, there's this warmth in his eyes. When he touches me, there's heat but something more, something deeper."

"Heat. Warmth. You did it, babe." There was admiration in Rachel's voice. "When we made that bet, I thought for sure I'd win, but sounds like you heated up the iceberg. I owe you a drink."

Oliver paused in the hallway. He'd been jolted awake by the sound of Ollie crying out. But by the time his brain had cleared and he'd reached the living room, his son was happily playing with his bricks.

He'd intended to go back to bed until he heard Rachel's words. She and Shannon had a bet. A bet that involved him.

He clenched his stomach. How had he missed the signs? It wasn't as if this was a first. He'd been targeted before by women who wanted him for his stock portfolio and social position.

But Shannon hadn't been after his money. She'd done it simply for sport. Just to see if she could. And to his shame, she'd succeeded.

His father had been right, after all. A man who trusts was a fool.

Well, he wouldn't make that mistake again.

Though he returned to his bedroom, Oliver didn't sleep. Instead of the quiet candlelit dinner followed by a proposal tonight, once Rachel left, he would send Shannon on her way.

No one made a fool out of Oliver Fortune Hayes.

Not even the woman he'd been foolish enough to love.

* * *

Rachel left shortly after five and Shannon had just fed Ollie when Oliver walked into the kitchen.

"Hey, I thought you wouldn't be up for another two hours." She crossed the room to him, lifting her face for the expected kiss.

Instead, he brushed past her. Opening the kitchen cupboard, he took out the bottle of whiskey and poured himself a shot. He drank the amber liquid as if it was water and he was dying of thirst.

"Is something wrong?" she asked tentatively.

"Has Ollie been fed?"

"Just finished. He ate like a little piggy, so he's probably going to need changing soon." She shut her mouth before she could ramble even more.

Oliver was clearly upset over something, and all she could talk about was his son's diapers?

"What's wrong?" she asked quietly.

Though she longed to wrap her arms around him and hold him close, she stayed where she stood. It was as if he had this invisible force field around him warning of danger should one get too close.

"It's not working." He poured another shot, downed the contents of the glass again in a single gulp.

A cold chill slithered down her spine. "What isn't?"

"This." He gestured wildly, the empty glass in his hands. "You. Me. You taking care of Ollie."

"Wait a minute." Breathe, she told herself. Stay calm and breathe. "Things are good between us. Ollie is happy and I thought—" her voice trailed off slightly before she reined it back in "—things were good between you and me, too."

He turned and met her gaze, his eyes looking more gray than blue, and cold as steel. "I know about the bet."

"Bet?" She pulled her brows together. "What bet?"

"The one you made with Rachel." His fingers tightened around the glass until his knuckles turned white. "How you were going to thaw the iceberg, as you ladies put it. Well, congratulations. You may have won the bet but you lost the job. You're fired."

Shannon stared at him, trying to process what he was saying. "That thing between Rachel and me was just a joke. When you first came into town, Rachel said—"

"I'm not interested in your excuses." His voice sliced like a knife through the air.

"I want you out of here in—" he glanced at his watch "—ten minutes."

For a second, Shannon thought she might faint. Or burst into tears. Instead she simply stood there, her body frozen in place.

This was all a simple misunderstanding, she wanted to say. But what would be the point? She'd tried to explain but he wouldn't listen.

Oliver didn't want to hear what she had to say. Because she didn't matter.

That was the one thing she hadn't been able to make Rachel understand.

That when you don't matter to someone, you might as well talk to the wind.

Fully aware that her unexpected appearance at the Triple S ranch would bring a ton of questions she preferred not to answer, instead of going home Shannon drove to Vicker's Corners. She rented a room at a quaint old Victorian B and B that had caught her eye when she and Rachel were shopping.

Last week, she'd hoped that before Oliver left town, they could carve out some time and spend the night here.

Well, she was here. But she was alone.

Shannon put her suitcase on the floor and flopped back on the bed, still dry-eyed. The tears were there, all balled up inside her. For now she was keeping them under tight control, afraid if she started crying, she might never stop.

Coming to a parting of ways was for the best, she told herself. Oliver would soon be returning to London anyway. By then she'd likely have her new job with the Fortune Foundation.

She tried to tell herself she'd been prepared for the fact that Oliver and Ollie would eventually leave, but she knew that was a lie. The truth was, she'd been secretly hoping Oliver would stay or ask her to go with him and Ollie to London.

Boy, had she been off the mark. He hadn't even cared enough to listen to her. No way was that love. Not the kind of love she wanted, anyway.

It was for the best, she told herself for the zillionth time.

When a stray tear slipped down her cheek, she hurriedly brushed it aside. She always felt like crying when she was tired. Perhaps, if she closed her eyes for just a second…

Shannon woke to sunlight streaming through the lace curtains. Groggy, she turned and saw that it was morning. The vintage alarm clock on the nightstand read 8:00 a.m.

The proprietress, a perky woman named Bea, had gone

into great detail when Shannon had checked in about the lovely breakfast served daily between six and ten.

The last thing Shannon wanted to do was make small talk with strangers. She felt hollow and empty inside. But she refused to sit in the room all day and mope. She would visit her favorite Vicker's Corners café, the one that served the best granola pancakes in the entire state.

Even if the mere thought of eating made her stomach churn, she could sit outside in the sunshine and enjoy the fresh air. She would order a cup of their special coffee—a dark roast and chicory blend with steamed milk.

Feeling better now that she had a plan, Shannon headed for the shower. Minutes later, feeling decidedly more human, she pulled her hair back from her face with a couple of clips, grabbed a pair of jeans and a cotton shirt in heartbreak red—totally appropriate for today—and left the B and B via the back door.

The air held a crisp edge and walking briskly calmed her. It took her less than five minutes to reach the café. Though the café's outdoor seating was surprisingly full for a weekday, Shannon snagged a small wrought-iron table for two. She ordered pancakes—just in case her appetite came back—and coffee. She was scrolling through Facebook pages when her phone rang.

For a second her heart leaped. But it wasn't Oliver's name on the readout—not that she wanted to speak with him anyway—it was Rachel's. Better, she decided, and although they weren't on a FaceTime video call, she smiled. She'd read somewhere that even if you didn't mean it, a smile could be heard in your voice. "Good morning, Rach."

"Are you busy?"

"Not at all." Shannon smiled her thanks to the waiter

who placed a steaming cup of coffee in front of her. "What's up?"

A long moment of silence filled the air.

"You haven't heard."

Shannon's heart seized. She set down the coffee cup with carefully controlled movements. "Heard what?"

Another few heartbeats. "I thought for sure they'd have called you."

Was it her parents? Oliver? Or, oh dear God no… Ollie? Her heart stopped, then began to gallop. The toddler was so quick, she didn't even know if Oliver realized how fast. If you didn't watch him every second, he could easily be hurt.

"Who?" Shannon's voice rose despite her best efforts to control it. "Tell me."

"Christopher Fortune."

Shannon's breath came out in a whoosh and she slumped back in her seat, relief leaving her weak. "Thank God."

"What did you say?"

"I said, that's great." But the moment the words left her lips, Shannon wondered why Christopher Fortune would be calling Rachel. She didn't have to wait long for the answer.

"I got the job." Rachel spoke quickly, as if she wanted to get it all out before she was interrupted. "In fact I'm at the Foundation office now. They have a bunch of employment forms for me to fill out."

"That's…wonderful. Fabulous news." Shannon did her best to force some enthusiasm into her voice, even as the realization hit. They'd hired Rachel, a woman with no marketing experience, instead of her. "I'm— I'm happy for you. Congratulations."

"You're probably wondering why they hired me and not you." Rachel's voice held a nervous edge.

Shannon paused. "Uh, maybe just a little."

The waiter delivered her pancakes and Shannon offered him a brief smile of thanks as her mind raced.

This didn't make sense. Sure, Rachel was pretty and smart, but so was she. And Shannon had three years of experience in the field. Christopher had been impressed by that fact, Shannon recalled.

"Well, I found out something that I think you need to know."

"I don't know, Rachel." Shannon expelled a heavy sigh. Did she really want to know that Christopher thought she'd blown the interview? Because what other reason could there be for her not getting the position? "What's done is done."

Rachel gave a disgusted snort. "How are you ever going to stand up for yourself when you insist on keeping your head in a hole?"

Shannon dumped some syrup on the pancakes. "Okay, tell me."

"The temp who's been working here is real chatty. She told me I almost didn't get the job because I didn't have the experience."

The piece of pancake that had been halfway to Shannon's mouth froze in midair. Her heart began to thud.

"She told me the other person they were considering got a bad reference from her previous employer," Rachel continued. "Apparently that swayed the decision in my direction."

"May I join you?"

Shannon looked up, startled, when a man's hand closed over the empty seat at her table.

* * *

Brodie Fortune Hayes may have asked Shannon the question, but he'd decided to join her regardless of the answer.

This morning, when Brodie had called his brother and asked Oliver if he wanted to check out how the Cowboy Country theme park was coming along, Oliver had nearly bitten his head off.

Something was clearly troubling his older sibling. When Brodie saw Nanny Shannon sitting alone, so far from home and without her little charge, he decided to do some investigating. While Brodie hadn't been able to get anything out of his closemouthed brother, he believed he'd have better luck with the woman.

Shannon covered the phone with her hand. "Sorry. Not in the mood for company this morning."

Ignoring her, he sat and motioned to the waiter for some coffee.

She shot him a venomous glance. He responded with a bland smile, pulling out his phone to check the stock reports. Oliver wasn't the only Fortune Hayes with a healthy portfolio.

"Jerry torpedoed me," Shannon muttered into the phone.

Brodie kept his gaze focused on his mobile unit, sensing she'd watch her words more carefully if she knew he was listening.

"It had to be that, Rachel. He's the reason I didn't get the job." Shannon breathed in and out, and Brodie watched in fascination as she fought for control. "If he thinks I'm going to let him get away with doing this to me, he's got a surprise coming. I—"

Shannon turned her back to Brodie and listened for several seconds.

"I don't think he'd physically harm me. I'll be fine, Rach. You told me to stop being a doormat…okay, maybe you didn't use those exact words, but that's what you meant. I'm just telling you. He's not getting away with this. Okay, bye."

Shannon set the phone down on the table and fixed her gaze on Brodie.

"Are you worried someone might do you physical harm?" Brodie demanded. "Is Oliver aware you might be in danger?"

"I'm not in danger." Her tone was as flat as her eyes. "Even if I were, I can take care of myself."

"Does Oliver know?"

"There's nothing to know. Besides, your brother and I aren't exactly on speaking terms at the moment."

"Oh?" Brodie lifted a brow and feigned surprise. "What happened?"

She hesitated for so long he wondered if he needed to ask again. But just as he opened his mouth to press a little more, she began to speak.

"You want to know? Well, I'll tell you. Oliver used some ridiculous teasing bet I made with Rachel as an excuse to get rid of me. He couldn't even listen to my explanation. You know why?" Obviously the question was rhetorical because she plowed ahead, not waiting for his response. "Because I don't matter to him. He knows me. He knows my heart. But he doesn't care and he just wanted me gone."

Shannon jerked to her feet. "Thanks for breakfast, Brodie." She gestured to the waiter, who'd arrived to take the man's order. "He'll take my check, too."

Without a backward glance, she strode off.

Strange, Brodie thought, *yet very interesting.* He pulled out his phone to call his brother.

Chapter 18

He had behaved abysmally.

For a man who prided himself on his integrity, it was hard for Oliver to admit that what his father had done—what he'd given the man the power to do—had caused him to overreact and treat the woman he loved in such a despicable manner. Shannon had seen through him. Her accusations had been spot-on.

He'd used the "bet" as an excuse to push her away, even though he knew in his heart she wasn't capable of such duplicity. It had been the move of a coward.

What he and Shannon shared didn't have anything to do with a wager. Even if their physical relationship had started that way—which he didn't believe it had—what was between the two of them, the closeness they shared, was one hundred percent genuine.

Oliver now faced the task of righting a very large wrong.

But he firmly believed the words he'd said to his sister; that if a man wanted something badly enough, he could make it happen. He would win Shannon back. He would show her he could be the man she deserved.

He was on his way to the Triple S when Brodie called and relayed the puzzling conversation he'd overheard. Oliver pulled over to the side of the road. His mind raced as he put the pieces together.

"Daddy, cookie," Ollie called from his car seat.

"In a second, son," Oliver said, despite knowing he hadn't packed any biscuits. Even as he ordered Amelia's number to be dialed, he decided the tiger Diane's parents had given Ollie would have to do in place of a biscuit. He leaned over the seat and tossed the well-loved soft toy to him.

The boy squealed with delight and hugged the tiger to his chest.

Oliver stared thoughtfully at his son, at the toy given in love, then shifted his focus as the ringing stopped and Amelia answered. As he'd hoped, she had Rachel's mobile number. Another call confirmed his greatest fear. According to her friend, Shannon was already on her way to Lubbock to confront her former boss. And she'd gone alone.

Oliver dropped off Ollie at his sister's house, then attempted to ring Shannon again. She didn't pick up. He hadn't really expected her to and was once again on the highway headed to Lubbock.

His hands clenched the steering wheel in a death grip. If that sod touched one hair on Shannon's head, Oliver Fortune Hayes would make him sorry he was ever born.

The rental vehicle's GPS led him directly to a large office building of steel and glass in the downtown business district. The lack of parking in the area was of no concern to a Fortune. Oliver simply pulled the Mercedes sedan into a loading zone in front of the building and hopped out.

He barreled through the front door…and straight into Shannon.

He wrapped his arms around her, holding her so tight, she squeaked.

"Oliver, let go, you're crushing me."

Loosening his hold, he stepped back, studying her from head to toe. "Are you okay? Did he hurt you?"

"Who?"

"Your former boss. The one you came to see."

"I told him what I was going to do and I did it." For a moment, a smile of smug satisfaction lifted her lips. "I went to human resources and filed a sexual harassment complaint against him. Apparently the company takes such charges very seriously."

For a moment, it was as if yesterday had never happened. The connection, the warmth was still there. Had yesterday been a bad dream? Perhaps they would simply move forward, relegating his bad behavior to the past.

"You're a strong and brave woman." Oliver gave a little laugh. "Although, you may have taken several years off my life during the drive here."

For a second she returned his smile, then seemed to remember how things were between them. She took several very deliberate steps back.

It appeared forgiveness wasn't going to come so easily.

When Shannon turned abruptly on her heel and started walking, he followed.

She whirled and narrowed her gaze. "What is it you want, Oliver? Why are you even here?"

The coolness in her gaze sent a chill down his spine.

"I should think it'd be fairly obvious." He moved to adjust his cuffs, then realized he'd left the house in such a hurry he'd grabbed the nearest item of clothing. He looked down and saw he'd pulled on an old gray sweatshirt that Shannon had borrowed from her father the other night.

Though he tried to ignore the fact he was dressed like a country bumpkin, his confidence was shaken. "My brother called. I spoke with Rachel. I feared for your well-being."

She offered a tight smile, one that didn't come close to reaching her eyes. "As you can see for yourself, I'm quite fine."

"Well, I'm not quite fine. I haven't been since you left."

"You mean since you ordered me from your home? Since you fired me without even listening to me? When you didn't even give me a chance to say a proper goodbye to Ollie?"

That *had* been a mistake. His son had been distraught. All Oliver could think of to placate the boy was to tell him Shannon's mum needed her for a few days.

Oliver raked his hand through his hair. "We need to talk."

She opened her mouth, then shut it and considered. "There's a park just around the corner. I guess there are a few things I need to say to you."

Her tone wasn't promising, but he consoled himself that at least she was willing to hear him out. But when they reached the small green oasis and took a seat on an ornate metal bench beside an evergreen that had been cut to resemble a dragon, she lifted a hand when he started to speak.

"You had your say yesterday. It's my turn." Shannon lifted her chin, her brown eyes flat and cool. "You were completely out of line. You overheard only part of a conversation, yet you ran with it. I've spent a considerable amount of time thinking why a logical man such as yourself would do something so illogical."

She jerked to her feet and began to pace. "I concluded you were scared of what had been building between us. You were looking for a way to run. That bit of conversation you overheard gave you the out you were seeking."

Oliver opened his mouth to respond but shut it when she glared and continued. "That may have made you feel all justified and righteous, but it was devastating to me. To have the man I loved think so little of me. Worse, I just took the abuse and slunk away. Well, no more. Shannon Singleton is no one's doormat. Not anymore. Not ever again."

Though her voice was steady, she was visibly trembling.

He stood and would have stepped closer, but once again she held up a hand. The coolness in her eyes was like a knife to the heart. And the worst of it was, he had only himself to blame for the distance between them.

Oliver cleared his throat. "First I want to say, I'm proud of you, Shannon."

"Well, doesn't that make me feel all warm and fuzzy inside."

The sarcasm had him raising his brows. "I mean it. I know what it took for you to come down here. You're right about my behavior. I was out of line last night.

Please come home with me. And Ollie. It's where you belong."

"News bulletin. I don't belong anyplace where some-one can order me out of the house when they get angry or scared or whatever." Shannon leaned over and picked up her bag, which she'd set by the bench, then straightened. "That's not a home, that's a job."

"Shannon," he called out when she headed to the ornate entrance gate.

After a slight hesitation, she stopped and turned.

"I'm sorry," he said.

She paused for the briefest of seconds, as if waiting for him to say more. After a long moment she gave a little laugh that somehow managed to sound incredibly sad. "Yeah, well, I'm sorry, too."

Before Oliver climbed the porch steps of the Single-ton house, he cleaned off the bottom of his shoes. Who knew a walk through a corral could be so...unsavory?

Though it wasn't even ten in the morning, he'd already managed to cross two items off his agenda, as evidenced by the conciliatory email winging its way across the Atlantic to Diane's parents and his visit to the corral to speak with Shep.

His future father-in-law had been shocked when Oliver had shown up to ask for Shannon's hand in marriage. Actually, he thought, the man seemed vastly amused that Oliver wanted to marry a woman who wasn't even speaking to him at the present time.

Still, Shep had laughed and clapped him on the shoulder, telling him to "go for it." Oliver took that to mean he had the man's blessing.

Now came the hard part. After taking several deep breaths, he rang the bell.

Through the screen door, he watched Lilian approach. This time there was no broad welcoming smile, only a slightly wary one. Oliver didn't blame her. Shannon was her daughter and he was, well, the cad who'd hurt her.

"Hello, Oliver." Lilian glanced nervously over her shoulder. "I didn't expect to see you here."

"Mrs. Singleton," he said, reverting back to the more formal address. "I was wondering if you could fetch Shannon for me. I'd like to speak with her."

"Who is it, Mom?"

A second after he heard her voice, Shannon stood beside her mother and close enough to touch.

Oliver's heart slammed against his chest. She was breathtakingly beautiful in blue jeans, a simple white shirt and bare feet.

Her eyes widened. "What are you doing here?"

Oliver met her confused gaze with a slightly unsteady one of his own. "I'm here to listen."

Shannon blinked. Her initial instinct had been to order him off the property. Until he said he'd come to *listen*. After she'd left the park, she'd thought of several other things she wanted to say to him.

In fact, she'd planned to call him today. She considered. For what she had to say, face-to-face would definitely be better.

"Okay, we'll talk." Shannon glanced at her mother. "Give us a few minutes."

Her mother's eyes softened. "Take as long as you need, dear."

Shannon stepped out onto the porch and, after a momentary hesitation, moved to the swing.

Oliver followed, taking a seat on the far end then swiveling to face her.

She had to admit he looked quite dashing in his dark suit, crisp white shirt and red Hermes tie. Once, when she told him wearing her favorite cowboy boots made her feel more confident, he'd sheepishly confessed he felt that same way about a suit and tie.

Her heart softened slightly. "You said you came here to listen."

He nodded.

"Well, then, I'd like to see Ollie." Shannon folded her hands in her lap, hoping he didn't notice the slight tremor. "I think it's important he understands I didn't leave because of anything he'd done."

"You can see him anytime you want," Oliver said. "Ollie has missed you. We both miss you."

The last was said so quietly, but with such emotion, that for a second Shannon found it difficult to speak. She took a moment to clear her throat. "I—I left a few things behind, too. Let me know when would be a good time to stop by."

"You're welcome anytime."

Tears stung the backs of her lids, but Shannon blinked rapidly and kept them at bay. "Okay, fine. Thanks."

He reached out as if he intended to take her hand but let it fall when she sat back.

"Is there anything else you want to say to me?" he asked.

Shannon thought for a moment, a task that was becoming increasingly difficult. His nearness appeared to have turned her brain to mush. Of course, five minutes after he left she'd likely recall a dozen things she wanted to say. "No. No. That was all."

"In that case, would you mind listening to me for a second?" When she opened her mouth, he lifted a hand. "If at any time you want me to leave or to stop talking, just say the word."

"Are you saying if I ask you to leave and never come back, you'll do it?" Though her insides shook like jelly, her voice came out steady.

"I can't promise I'll never come back." Oliver shifted in his seat. "You're too important to me to make such a promise."

"What do you want to say, Oliver?"

"You were absolutely right."

"About?"

"Deep down, I was fearful of allowing you to see how much you mattered to me. My father told me numerous times anyone who loves or shows emotion is a fool."

"You were married, Oliver. You'd taken that leap once before." Shannon's chuckle held no humor. "I'd have thought love would come easier to you the second time around."

"I was never able to give my heart totally to Diane." A red flush rose up his neck. "Since coming to Texas, I've come to believe my heart was waiting for you."

Shannon gaped. Never had she thought she'd hear such flowery prose come from Oliver's mouth. Yet he seemed sincere…if slightly embarrassed.

"I'm not proud of my behavior." His eyes closed for a second and she watched as he clenched and unclenched one hand. "When you walked out the door and drove off, I realized I'd been a berk."

"A what?"

"A—a fool." He gave her a lopsided smile. "You have my heart, you know. You will always have it." He reached over and took her hands in his. "Believe me. I love you. I trust you. Completely. Totally. Without reservation."

Tears welled in her eyes and slipped down her cheeks.

Oliver wiped them away with the pads of his fingers. "I'm sorry I hurt you."

"I love you, too." The emotion squeezing her heart made her voice husky.

"You realize Ollie and I are a package deal."

"I love Ollie." This time it was *her* fingers swiping at the tears that seemed determined to fall. "Your little guy stole my heart within seconds of meeting him."

"If we were to be together permanently, what is it you'd want, Shannon? Tell me what it is and it's yours."

Puzzled, she pulled her brows together. "What do you mean?"

"If we were married, where would you like to live?"

Married? Her breath caught. If they were *married*?

Shannon thought of how she'd insisted to Rachel she wouldn't wed any man unless he agreed to settle in Horseback Hollow. "What if I said I wanted to live in Horseback Hollow?"

"Then that's where we'll live," he said without hesitation. "I want you to be happy. If being here makes you happy, this is where we'll live."

"But your business," she protested. "The hours—"

Capturing her hand, he brought her fingers to his lips and kissed them one by one. "Don't worry. It won't be a problem."

He might be able to make it work, but she knew it'd

be difficult not only for him, but for them as a family. Still, it appeared he was willing to make the sacrifice.

Because he loves me. Because he wants me to be happy.

Shannon loved her friends, her family and her little town. But there was a whole, wonderful—slightly scary—world out there she'd yet to explore. Was it fear that had made her so adamant about remaining in Horseback Hollow?

"Would we build a home in town? Or would you prefer living on a ranch? If you could pick," Oliver prompted, "tell me what your dream home would look like."

His blue eyes were focused on her. She had his full attention.

"In my perfect world—" she slid closer to him "— you'd have your arm around my shoulders during this discussion."

Before she'd finished speaking, Oliver closed the remaining distance between them and slipped an arm around her shoulders, pressing a kiss against her hair. "Better?"

"Much." The heat from his body mingled with hers and the coldness inside her began to thaw. "Actually, I'd like two homes."

He smiled. "That could be arranged. One in town, the other in the countryside, I presume?"

"Actually, I was thinking of one home here, the other in London. We could spend part of the year in England and the other part in Horseback Hollow. When Ollie is school-age, we might need to reconsider, but for now, that's what I'd like."

His brows pulled together. "Are you certain?"

"Yes." She kissed him on the lips. "Absolutely certain."

"Then that's what we'll do."

"Just like that?"

"Just like that." He smiled. "What about children?"

"What about them?"

"How many would you like?"

She hesitated.

"Be honest."

"Six," she said. "I've always wanted six."

His smile widened. "What a coincidence. That's how many I'd like, too."

"Seriously?"

"Seriously."

Tears flooded her eyes. "This is overwhelming."

"Oh, sweetheart, there's more."

"I don't know if I can handle more," she said with a shaky laugh.

It appeared, in this, he would give her no choice. Oliver rose, then dropped to his knee before her.

Shannon's breath hitched when he pulled out a velvet jeweler's box and flipped it open. The large diamond glittered in the sunlight. Smaller diamonds, but no less brilliant, surrounded the large marquis-cut stone.

"Shannon." He spoke her name softly, and in the quiet she heard the love, saw it reflected in his eyes.

"It's…it's the most beautiful ring I've ever seen."

His smile flashed and she knew her response had pleased him. He took her hand and focused those blue eyes directly on her as he began to speak.

"When I first saw you at the Superette, I was impressed by your kindness, your willingness to help a stranger find his way. Being around you, getting to know you, I realized just how special you are, and I began to fall in love." He squeezed her fingers. "If you count the days since we first met, we haven't known each other that long, but it feels as if I've known you forever. I've been waiting my whole life for you. Without a single doubt I know what we share is right and true and strong enough to last a lifetime."

It was quite a speech from a man not prone to verbosity. And she knew without a doubt the words came straight from his heart.

"Oh, Oliver." Joy sluiced through her veins. If this was a dream, Shannon prayed she'd never wake up.

"I promise no one will work harder to make you happy or cherish you more than me." His gaze searched hers. "And I will listen. Always. My life will never be complete without you beside me to share it. Will you marry me, Shannon? Will you be my wife and Ollie's mother?"

For several heartbeats, Shannon struggled to find her voice, to put into words all she was feeling.

"When I look into my heart, I see only you," she said finally. "I can't imagine growing old with anyone else. I love you so much. So yes, Oliver, I will marry you. And I'll be proud to be Ollie's mother."

Then the ring was on her finger. When he stood and pulled her into his arms, Shannon knew with absolute certainty there was no other place she wanted to be.

Not only for now, but for eternity.

Epilogue

The opulent hotel room on Buckingham Palace Road surrounded Shannon in a sweet cocoon of luxury. But the true treasure was the man sleeping beside her. She glanced at her husband, then at the large diamond solitaire on her left hand, now made complete by a wedding band.

Last week she and Oliver had tied the knot in Horseback Hollow, surrounded by family and friends. Two days ago, they'd flown to London, accompanied by her parents and brothers.

Oliver had insisted on paying for her family's trip to England and had gotten them all seats in first class. While in the UK, her parents and brothers were staying at his home in Knightsbridge. Shannon and Oliver would join them there at the end of the week.

She'd never thought she'd get her father on an airplane, much less out of the United States, but Shep had taken to England like a duck to water. Once he'd figured out how to use the Tube, her dad had been unstoppable. For her mother, this was the honeymoon she'd never had, but Oliver had waved aside her thanks, telling her that they were family now.

His family had embraced her just as easily. Last night, Brodie had hosted a reception for them, inviting not only family but Oliver's UK friends and business associates to celebrate their marriage at the swanky Savile Club in Mayfair.

The best part of the evening for Shannon was having the opportunity to get to know Brodie better. He wasn't as uptight as she first thought. She'd come away from their lengthy chat knowing she and Oliver's brother were destined to be good friends.

She was trying to decide whether to get up or go back to sleep when she felt Oliver stir.

"Can't you sleep?" he asked, pushing himself to a sitting position.

"Just admiring the view." She glanced around the sumptuous bridal suite in one of London's premier hotels. "This sure beats the B and B in Vicker's Corners."

"It's lovely here," he admitted. "I'm enjoying the view myself."

She turned to see what part of the room had captured his gaze. Was it the paintings? The mural on the ceiling? Or the opulent fixtures?

Instead she found his gaze focused directly on her.

Her skin heated beneath his gaze.

"The B and B was nice, too," he said, offering her

a lazy smile. "I'll never forget that first night with my beautiful wife."

The images from their wedding day—and night— were forever etched in a special place in Shannon's heart. There were the vows they'd written and the scent from the orchids Oliver had had flown in because she'd mentioned once they were her favorite. Most of all, she'd never forget the look of love in his eyes when he'd seen her walking down the aisle on her father's arm.

"I like hearing you say 'my wife,'" she admitted. "Almost as much as I like saying 'my husband.'"

She snuggled beside him, her fingers toying with the hair on his chest. "Brodie mentioned last night he's taking full credit for us being together."

Oliver rolled his eyes and chuckled. "I don't know how he arrived at that conclusion, but it sounds like something my brother would say."

"Brodie is really very sweet." Shannon paused thoughtfully. "He's not nearly as stuffy as he first appears. I believe with a little help from the right woman…"

"You really think he just needs the right woman to warm him up?" Amusement ran through Oliver's voice like a pretty ribbon.

"I do."

"You know, I'm feeling a bit stuffy right now."

Shannon couldn't keep from smiling. "Is that code for you need some *warming up* yourself?"

"It is, indeed."

Oliver clasped her face gently in his hands, lowered his mouth to hers…then jerked back as the door to the bedroom was unceremoniously flung open.

Shannon gave a little yelp. "I thought we locked the door."

Oliver sat up straight, just in time to see his son race across the room, the nanny hot on his heels.

"Mama, Daddy," Ollie called out happily as he ran to his parents. "I come see you."

When he reached the bed, Ollie pulled himself up, then crawled over the covers, as quick and agile as a little monkey.

The drama continued when Barnaby appeared, zipping past the nanny, emitting deep woofs with each step. He reached the bedside and began to bark. Because of his short legs, the corgi required Shannon's help to make it to the top of the silk duvet.

"I'm so sorry, sir, ma'am. The little tyke got away from me." The distraught nanny's face was flushed and a strand of gray hair had come loose from her serviceable bun.

Though many relatives had offered to watch Ollie during their honeymoon, Shannon and Oliver had wanted the boy close, so they'd secured a suite and enlisted the help of Mrs. Crowder.

Ollie flung his arms around both parents, burrowing against them. He giggled as Barnaby reached him and began licking his face.

Nanny Crowder wrung her hands, obviously unsure if she should snatch her young charge and his pet out of his parents' honeymoon bed or simply beat a hasty retreat. "Oh, my. Oh, my. This will never do."

Oliver caught Shannon's eyes and they exchanged grins. It may have been a chaotic scene, at least to anyone unused to small boys and dogs, but this was his new reality.

He'd been blessed with a beautiful wife whom he adored, a son who brought joy to his life every day and a corgi that could always be counted on to liven things up.

"No worries, Mrs. Crowder," Oliver told the nanny, his heart overflowing with love and thankfulness. "This is all quite perfect."

* * * * *

Amanda Renee was raised in the northeast and now wriggles her toes in the warm coastal Carolina sands. Her career began when she was discovered through Harlequin's So You Think You Can Write contest. When not creating stories about love and laughter, she enjoys the company of her schnoodle, Duffy, as well as camping, playing guitar and piano, photography and anything involving animals. You can visit her at amandarenee.com.

Books by Amanda Renee

Harlequin Western Romance

Saddle Ridge, Montana

The Lawman's Rebel Bride
A Snowbound Cowboy Christmas

Harlequin American Romance

Welcome to Ramblewood

Betting on Texas
Home to the Cowboy
Blame It on the Rodeo
A Texan for Hire
Back to Texas
Mistletoe Rodeo
The Trouble with Cowgirls
A Bull Rider's Pride
Twins for Christmas

Visit the Author Profile page
at Harlequin.com for more titles.

WRANGLING CUPID'S COWBOY

Amanda Renee

For my superagent, Pamela Harty
of The Knight Agency.

Thank you for your unwavering faith, support
and guidance.

Chapter 1

"I know women love shoes, but isn't this taking it a little too far?"

Delta lowered a freshly shod horse's hoof to the ground and straightened to acknowledge the lame wise-crack. She half expected to find a cocksure ranch hand looking to score. Instead, a rugged cowboy with deep maple-brown eyes and hair to match rested casually against the work truck she'd parked in the Silver Bells Ranch's wide stable entrance.

"Garrett Slade." He took a step toward her and extended his hand. "I'm the ranch's new partner. My brother Dylan has told me you're the best farrier in the state. It's a pleasure to meet you."

"Delta Grace." His muscular fingers encircled her palm, sending a tingle down to the tips of her toes. "Dylan's much too kind, but I appreciate it just the same.

And the pleasure is all mine," she drawled. Delta inwardly cringed at the unfamiliar licentious tone she had never heard come out of her mouth. He was the most attractive man she'd laid eyes on since heaven knew when, and she found it most unsettling.

She stepped around Garrett and gave the draft horse's bristly muzzle a rub. The animal inquisitively nudged the pocket of her pink-and-black plaid flannel shirt until she unbuttoned it and rewarded him with the baby carrots she had tucked away earlier. She returned to her truck and packed up her tools before removing her heavy-weight apron chaps under the heat of Garrett's gaze. "I'm finished here for the day, but I'll need to return tomorrow for Lightning Bug, the quarter horse with navicular disease. I need to be here when Dr. Presley radiographs the hoof so we can discuss further shoeing modifications. He's improved significantly since the early fall when Jax first noticed it."

A flicker of sadness crossed his features at the mention of Garrett's uncle, who had died six weeks earlier. They were almost halfway through January and the ranch's future precariously balanced on the newly formed partnership between the two Slade brothers. They had managed to avoid foreclosure on the 730-acre guest ranch, but they still had major renovations to undertake for them to profitably compete with the more modern ranches cropping up around them.

"I am truly sorry for your loss. Jax was a great man."

Garrett nodded wordlessly and led the Belgian horse to his stall. Delta secured the side compartment of her truck while trying to ignore the way his fawn-colored barn coat framed his broad shoulders. If the Silver Bells Ranch wasn't her largest account, she would have asked him to join her for a drink in Jax's memory. But she wasn't willing to cross that line under any circumstances.

Delta firmly believed her professional and personal life should remain independent of each other. She'd successfully maintained that balance back in Missoula, but it proved more difficult since she had moved to Saddle Ridge in northwestern Montana. A town forty times smaller meant running into customers no matter where she went. Lucky for her, Missoula was a two-hour straight shot south and she visited her family and friends whenever she wanted.

She had a few single girlfriends in town, but Liv was pregnant with triplets and Maddie was so in love with the baby thing she spent all her free time helping Liv prepare for their arrival. Weeknights had become lonely and it didn't help that Saddle Ridge had already gone head over boots for Valentine's Day. She never understood the fervent commercialization of the blasted holiday. Back home she could escape it. Not in Saddle Ridge. Everywhere she turned, there was another cupid aiming an arrow at her heart. She'd like to shove that arrow somewh—

"I wanted to discuss a few things if you have the time to spare." Garrett's voice shattered her mental assault on the chubby cherub.

"Sure. Silver Bells was my last stop today." Delta folded her arms tight across her chest as a bitter wind blew into the stables. "Just let me move my truck out of your entrance." Minutes later, she was back inside as Garrett slid the tall wooden doors shut behind her. The cold lingered on her body, causing her to regret leaving her jacket on the front seat.

"Let's talk in my office where it's warmer."

His office? Delta found it interesting that Dylan had handed over the responsibility of the horses to Garrett. They had been his greatest pride, but she understood the necessity to move into his uncle's position of managing the ranch along with the lodge and staff.

Snorts and nickers coupled with the lone scrape of a shovel against a stall floor masked the awkward silence that grew between them as she followed him down the center corridor. The friendliness that had transpired between them only moments ago seemed to fade with each stride.

The office door creaked as Garrett opened it for her to enter. Fluorescent lights swathed the large room with the flick of a switch. She had been there before, but it had resembled more of a cozy den. Not anymore. A row of chest-high filing cabinets with shelves above them replaced the oversize leather couch along the rough wood wall opposite the desk. And the kitchenette now consisted of a coffeepot and nothing more. Dylan had faithfully stocked boxes of cookies, chips and other nibbles for his employees to snack on during the day. It appeared those were a thing of the past, too.

"Have a seat." Garrett removed his hat and hung it on the freestanding rack behind his desk before shrugging off his coat and hanging it on the other side. He waited for her to sit in the chair across from him before doing the same. "I'm not sure how much you know about the changes the ranch is undergoing, but I'd like to discuss a few cost-saving ideas with you."

"Okay." Cost-saving automatically registered as less compensation in her brain.

"I've only been here a week, so I haven't had the

chance to review all the stables expenses, but I have seen a handful of your invoices." Garrett fanned out five of her itemized bills across the worn black walnut surface. "Our farrier costs seem high."

"You have almost a hundred horses. Thirty of which are Belgians. And you have to factor in all the therapeutic shoeing, too." Delta hadn't known what to expect from their conversation, but this wasn't a good start. "I realize it's none of my concern, but since we're on the subject, I don't understand why you're maintaining this many horses when you don't have the business to support them any longer."

"Because Dylan doesn't want to thin the stables. I've agreed to give the ranch six months before revisiting the idea." Garrett removed a pad from the top drawer and scanned his neatly written notes. "In the meantime, I need to reduce the ranch's overhead at once so we can balance their expense. Please don't think you're my only target. But since you're here today, I'd like to tackle this expense first. Had Dylan or Jax discussed cold-shoeing with you? The cost is significantly lower."

Target? Tackle? They weren't playing a sport. She was a fourth-generation farrier and she took her job seriously.

"The quality is lower, as well." Delta only cold-shod a horse when the animal had an intolerance to the hiss of firing up a forge or the smoke produced when a hot shoe met the hoof. "It's much easier to hammer and shape a hot shoe than file a cold one and it provides a more exacting fit. In my opinion, cold-shoeing is done by less experienced farriers. Some do exceptional work, but they're not equipped to handle the corrective or specialized work I do for your horses. As you've already said, your brother considers me the top in the state."

She'd had to justify her prices in the past, but Delta hadn't anticipated having to defend her value, as well.

"I think we're getting off on the wrong foot, no pun intended." Garrett gathered her invoices and stacked them in front of him. "I'm not looking to replace you as Silver Bells' farrier. I'm asking if we can cold-shoe from this point forward and hot-shoe only when necessary."

Delta weighed her options carefully. Just as Garrett had said, cold-shoeing was significantly cheaper. It also forced her to do twice, if not three times, as many jobs to offset the difference.

"I prefer not to, but you're the customer. If you want cold-shoeing, then that's what I will do."

"You are capable of cold-shoeing, right?"

"I beg your pardon." Delta abruptly stood, inadvertently shoving her chair backward into a filing cabinet. "I assure you I'm more than capable of any shoeing requirements you might have. But I will also assure you, I'm the only farrier around that will work on your Belgians."

"Why is that?" Garrett asked, without a single muscle in his body reacting to her outburst.

"Because they're obstinate and they weren't trained from the beginning to lift their feet. The ones that do tend to lean on me. Since Silver Bells doesn't have a proper shoeing stall where I can secure their foot to work on it, my back takes a beating."

"Good to know." He jotted down a note.

"If that's all, I have another appointment to get to."

"I thought you said this was your last stop of the day," Garrett challenged.

"I was mistaken. I have one more to make." Delta had

an imminent date with a bar stool after this conversation. She marched to the door and willed herself to open it nicely. "See you tomorrow."

"I'm looking forward to it," Garrett called after her as she stormed toward the exit.

"I'm not," Delta mumbled to herself. She hated when a perfectly good man went from sexy to infuriating in a matter of minutes. It was a waste of nice-fitting Wranglers.

The sound of Delta's boots reverberated against the floor as she barreled out of the stables. Garrett had hoped she would have been more sympathetic to the ranch's difficult financial position. And maybe she already was. He didn't know enough about her to say one way or the other. But a small part of him wanted to know a lot more about the mahogany-haired beauty that couldn't get away from him fast enough.

According to Dylan, Delta had extended their payment terms out to ninety days from her usual fifteen. That alone had been generous, but it still wasn't enough to help their bottom line. Now here he was, a total stranger, asking her to take more of a financial hit for him.

He respected Delta's need to earn a living. Hell, he could even understand her getting upset at the prospect of less money. Her attitude was a bit much, though. Answering his questions was part of the job, and she shouldn't have been insulted by them or his request.

Back in Wyoming, his farrier had cold-shod their horses to his satisfaction. So then why did he have a strong desire to call Delta and apologize? He had done nothing wrong. He just wished he hadn't made her mad.

Although making people mad seemed to be his new norm.

His in-laws were mad at him for moving their grandkids thirteen hours away from Wheatland, Wyoming, back to his hometown of Saddle Ridge, Montana, with only two days' notice. Garrett had been living with his in-laws and managing their three-thousand-acre cattle ranch for the last three years, after his wife had passed away from pancreatic cancer. He'd known for a while it was time for him and the kids to stand on their own, but he didn't know how or where.

When Dylan offered him a chance to partner with him on the Silver Bells Guest Ranch, he hadn't had to think twice. They weren't quite on their own, but he needed to be near his own family again. Plus, Garrett's brother-in-law had been more than ready to take over the cattle ranch and he was confident he'd left it in capable hands. Moving back to town was the best choice for him and his kids. If only his seven-year-old daughter felt the same way.

Kacey was mad at him. He had torn her from her friends and grandparents during Christmas vacation and then told her they were moving a few days later. She had cried all night after her first day of school almost two weeks ago. The crying had stopped, but she no longer spoke to him. The silent treatment was alive and well in the Slade household. Except for his four-year-old son, Bryce. The kid found happiness everywhere and loved his new preschool.

Garrett fired up the snowmobile and headed for the ranch's main entrance. Even the biting wind against his cheeks didn't help erase the flash of Delta's bright smile when they first met...or her resentment toward him when she left. She was the last person he needed to be thinking about. His kids were his first priority, the ranch second. There was no room for hurt feelings.

He arrived at the front gate and waited. The school bus would drop Kacey off in a few minutes and he hoped a ride to the house would cheer her up. The scowl on his daughter's face when the bus doors opened told him that wouldn't be the case. He needed to stick to horses. At least they liked him.

"Get on, baby," Garrett said as she marched past him. "It's too cold to walk."

"You're embarrassing me in front of the other kids," Kacey ground out. She gripped the straps of her backpack tighter and trudged down the ranch road. "Now they're going to pick on me tomorrow."

"No they won't." Garrett wondered if all girls were this dramatic at her age. "Get on. The bus left and I'm not taking no for an answer." He scooted back for her to sit in front of him.

"What about my bag?"

"Give it to me." Garrett lengthened the straps on the yellow *Beauty and the Beast* backpack and slung it over his shoulder. Appropriate considering he felt like the Beast this afternoon. "Now get on."

Kacey climbed over his legs, doing her best not to hold on to him for support. Garrett grinned and revved the engine, causing the snowmobile to lurch forward a few inches. She immediately leaned against him and gripped his arms. "And away we go."

Dylan hopped out of his lifted black pickup before helping Bryce down as Garrett drove up to the small two-bedroom log cabin. It had been Dylan's until he'd moved into their uncle's house. Garrett had given each of the kids a bedroom and he'd taken the loft. It served his needs, plus it wasn't like he was bringing anyone home to share his bed. He doubted he'd ever be ready for that again. Rebecca had been his entire world for nine years until Kacey came along. And then Bryce. His family had been perfect.

The second the snowmobile stopped, Kacey slid out from under his arms and stomped up the front porch steps. He was getting tired of seeing the back of his daughter's head all the time.

"Daddy!" Bryce ran to him. "I can write my name."

Garrett lifted him into his arms. "You can? You'll have to show me when we get inside."

"Hey, man, I like the new look." Dylan nodded to the backpack. "Kind of clashes with your jacket, but I think you wear it well."

"I thought it complemented my eyes." Garrett laughed as he climbed the stairs. "Thanks for picking up Bryce from preschool. I appreciate it."

"No problem." Dylan followed him into the house, just in time to hear Kacey slam her bedroom door. "It gives me a chance to prepare myself for when Holly's this age."

"I think you have a while considering she's only a few weeks old."

"You and Harlan keep telling me they grow up fast." Dylan glanced down the hall toward Kacey's room. "I take it there hasn't been any improvement."

Garrett set Bryce down and helped him out of his snow boots and jacket. "I made it worse. I embarrassed her in front of the kids on the bus because I picked her up on a snowmobile." He eased Kacey's backpack from his shoulders and tossed it on the armchair. "My kid hates me."

"Has she really said that?"

"No, but she thinks it." Garrett kicked off his own boots.

"I can remember us hating Mom and Dad a time or two when we were kids. It's growing pains and the stress of starting over in a new place while trying to make friends. We were lucky. We went to school with the same kids year after year. You and I don't have a clue how hard it is for her to adjust."

"I know you're right. It's just difficult to take sometimes. I hate knowing she's hurting. She barely eats and stays locked in her room." Garrett grabbed a box of crayons and a stack of paper from the kitchen counter and set them on the coffee table. "Show me what you learned in school today, champ."

Bryce chose a blue crayon and began drawing a large letter *B*. His tiny tongue stuck out between his teeth as he concentrated on his letters.

"How did things go with Delta this afternoon?" Dylan sat cross-legged on the floor across from Bryce. "That's the most perfect *B* I've ever seen."

"She's mad at me, too." And that bothered him more than it should. He peered over Bryce's shoulder as he drew a *C*. "Very good, you're almost there."

Dylan's brows rose. "You better not run off my farrier. She's one of the nicest people I've met. She stays mostly to herself, but she's a real sweetheart."

"Look, Daddy." Bryce handed Garrett the paper.

"Wow!" He ran his fingers over the printed letters. "I'm so proud of you." He gave Bryce a hug and held it up proudly for Dylan to see. "My son did that."

"Way to go, little man." Dylan high-fived the boy.

"Can I go show Kacey?" Bryce asked.

"We'll show her when she's feeling better. Go hang it on the refrigerator for me while I talk to your uncle Dylan for a minute." His son's sock-covered feet thumped across the hardwood floor as he ran from the room. "The farrier bills are astronomical. With you wanting to keep the horses, I had to cut costs. So, I asked her to cold-shoe them from now on."

"No wonder she was mad." Dylan eased off the floor and onto a chair. "That's not her style. She hasn't been able to take on new customers in months. She's in high demand because of her superior craftsmanship. I like her work. Her knowledge has prevented a lot of problems. When our last farrier retired, she effortlessly slid into the position. Let her do her job the way she sees fit."

Garrett sagged against the back of the couch. "If you wanted a silent partner, then you should have said so ahead of time."

"I didn't say that."

"You asked me to go in fifty-fifty and that's what I did. My fifty percent needs to cut costs in those stables, but you're making it impossible. I can't sell any horses. I can't ask the farrier to save us money. You told me last week you're happy with our feed distributor. What's left? The veterinarian?"

"Don't you dare." Dylan braced his hands on his knees. "Lydia Presley knows each of my horses by name."

"Our horses," Garrett corrected. "A partnership shouldn't be difficult to grasp considering you had one with Jax."

"I accept our partnership, but I need you to focus on

moving forward and making us money. I cut back all I could last year. When I asked you to run the stables, I didn't mean for you to change anything. We have guests booked into the ranch the first of the month and we need to stick to our renovation schedule. Let's try to avoid any further hiccups, please. I've had enough of those around here."

"Fine." Now Garrett needed to apologize to Delta tomorrow. He'd spent twenty minutes around the woman and already made an ass of himself. Not that he should care. The ranch employed her services and that was the extent of their relationship. "I need to feed my kids. At least the one that will eat." He started for the kitchen and tripped over Bryce's boots, causing him to stub his toe on the fireplace hearth. Totally his fault. He'd left them there. "Dammit, that hurts."

"I have an idea." Dylan slapped him on the back. "I'll take the kids to my house, feed them and help Kacey with her homework. You need to let off some steam tonight and Kacey would probably enjoy spending time with Holly. Go into town, get a drink and a bite to eat and then pick them up when you're ready."

It was the best idea he'd heard all week. He needed to clear his head of the ranch, and that included Delta. The woman had already stuck in his mind like a fly to honey, and he didn't need any more complications in his life.

Chapter 2

Complication must be Garrett's middle name. No sooner had he walked through the doors of the Iron Horse Bar & Grill, when he spotted Delta at the far end of the dimly lit bar. Alone. Apparently, her next stop hadn't been a customer.

Garrett weighed his options. Walk out before she saw him, grab a booth in the back and pretend he never noticed her, or eat crow and get it over with. Delta's gaze met his as she lifted a drink to her lips and froze. He could have sworn her shoulders sagged at the recognition, but between the neon beer sign behind her and the waitress temporarily blocking his view as she swept under the stools, he wasn't a hundred percent certain. Delta lowered her glass and shook her head, destroying any illusion of subtlety, and then waved him over. Garrett had hoped for a burger and a beer, but it looked like he was eating crow for an appetizer. So much for unwinding.

Johnny Cash's "Ring of Fire" played on the jukebox as he crossed the room and he couldn't help but notice his boots hit the floor in time with the beat. Before Kacey was born, he and Rebecca had spent every Friday and Saturday night dancing around this very floor. He hadn't expected the memory to be so vivid eight years later.

"I hope our conversation earlier didn't drive you here." Garrett pulled out the corner bar stool next to hers and sat down. "It's not even five o'clock."

"I could say the same to you." Delta sipped at her drink. "I was hungry, frustrated and this is the only place in town that's not decked out for Valentine's Day." Her face soured at the mention of the holiday.

"Bad breakup?" he asked.

"Something like that," she mumbled, staring down at the amber liquid as she swirled it in the glass.

"I hear you." Garrett motioned for the bartender. "It's not my favorite either." His wife had died four days before the holiday, reminding him every year of what he'd lost.

"Bad breakup for you, too?"

"Something like that." If only it had been a breakup, maybe his heart would have survived.

Delta nudged a platter of nachos toward him. "Help yourself. I can't eat all this on top of the sandwich I ordered."

"Thanks." Garrett took her cordiality as a positive sign and reached for a few of the neatly stacked napkins along the back edge of the bar.

"What can I get you?" the bartender asked.

"I'll have whatever she's drinking."

One of Delta's brows rose. "Brave man."

"Why's that?" Garrett couldn't help noticing how naturally beautiful she was without a lick of makeup. Truth was, he'd noticed it the moment he first saw her, but he forced it to the back of his mind. He had no business admiring anyone the ranch conducted business with. It was unprofessional and he wasn't interested in anything more.

"I'm drinking chipotle whiskey." Her mischievous smile presented more of a dare than a warning. "I don't know if you can handle it."

"I'm sure I can handle it. I'm a man. We're rugged." Garrett hooked his boots on the stool's footrest and followed Delta's eyes to the television she remained transfixed upon…sports scores from last night's games.

"If you say so," she said, her attention still unwavering from the screen.

"Seriously?" If Dylan thought Delta was one of the nicest people he had ever met, his brother needed to get out more. "I guess I gave you some first impression, huh?"

"Listen, don't get me wrong. I get it." Delta leveled her gaze to his. "You're trying to save money wherever you can. But are you aware I had started charging your uncle twenty percent less than all my other customers over a year ago to help ease some of the ranch's financial burden? Then I extended your payment terms six months later. I've taken two significant hits from my largest customer and now I'm taking another one. I won't lie to you. It hurts. But, I shouldn't have acted or reacted the way I did."

Well, if that hadn't made him feel like more of a jerk he didn't know what would. "I knew about the payment terms, which I hope to amend sooner rather than later, but I had no idea about the discount. I should be the one apologizing. I was a bit overenthusiastic earlier."

"Just a bit." Delta's smile tightened.

The bartender set Garrett's drink on the bar top. "Did you want to place a food order?"

Garrett looked over the glossy double-sided menu. "Bacon cheeseburger, medium rare with fries."

"Sure thing." The man turned to Delta. "Your order's almost up. Do you want them to hold it and serve it with his or bring it out when it's ready?"

"Please don't wait on my account." Garrett had ruined enough of her day. He didn't want to add dinner to it.

"I still haven't made a dent in these nachos." Delta sighed down at the plate. "Go ahead and hold mine."

"You didn't have to do that."

"Yeah, well, I can't sit here and eat with you watching me."

"I could leave."

"You could, but that would be rude of me to ask. Besides, I ordered a turkey club. It's not like it's going to get cold." Delta nudged the nachos closer to him. "Please help me eat these."

Garrett lifted a heavily topped tortilla chip. "Think we can start over?" he asked before popping the gooey piece of heaven into his mouth. "Man, these are awesome. You never used to be able to get nachos here. A basket of chips and salsa was about all you could order outside of a burger or a bar pie."

"Been away for a while?"

"Almost five years. I visited my brothers when I could, but it's been even longer since I came in here."

Garrett lifted his drink. "You still haven't answered me about starting over."

"Hard to forget being asked to do my job differently."

"We'll forget about that, too. Fresh start. This is our first meeting, and you can go back to doing what you do best."

"I'm not even going to question why you changed your mind, but I'll take the do-over." Delta raised her glass to his. "It's a pleasure to meet you, Garrett Slade."

"Same here." Garrett's eyes had already begun to water from the scent of the whiskey, but he took a man-sized swallow anyway. "Good Lord, woman!" He exhaled slowly, surprised that flames didn't shoot out of his mouth. "How do you drink this stuff?"

Delta's impish laugh rose above the music. "I can take the heat."

Garrett froze. He hadn't heard those five words in years. He squeezed his eyes shut against the memory, wishing he'd chosen someplace other than the Iron Horse tonight.

"Are you all right?" Delta's warm hand upon his arm snapped him back to the present. "You need to take it easy with that stuff. It's meant to be sipped, not chugged."

Garrett shook his head. "It's not that." The concern reflecting in Delta's caramel-brown eyes touched his soul in a way he hadn't thought possible again. "This is the first time I've been here without my wife. We practically lived in this place before we moved to Wyoming."

"Where is she now?"

"She died." He took another sip of his drink, needing the heat to numb the pain of the memory. "Pancreatic cancer."

Delta's grasp tightened. He could have sworn he heard her swallow hard at the revelation, but when he lifted his gaze to hers, only sympathy greeted him in return.

She eased her grip. "Her loss must have been devastating for you."

"Thank you." Garrett patted her hand and shifted on his stool, effectively breaking all physical contact between them. He stared down at the gold band he hadn't found the will to remove. In his heart, Rebecca would always be his wife. There could never be anyone else. "You reminded me of her when you said you could take the heat. Rebecca used to say those exact same words."

"Really? Wow." Delta rubbed her hands up and down her jean-clad thighs.

"Chemotherapy killed her taste buds and she constantly bet that she could out heat me."

Delta stilled. "I've heard that."

"Some things just stick in your mind, you know?" He folded his napkin into a tiny triangle. "It's been almost three years and sometimes it feels like yesterday. Coming here is just hitting me harder than I expected."

"I can imagine." She picked up a chip and broke it in half before setting it back down on the platter. "So, this was your spot, huh?" Sadness reflected in her eyes as she spoke.

"Up until the day we moved away." Garrett straightened his shoulders. "But enough about that. Tell me about yourself. I don't remember you when I was growing up here, although you're definitely younger than me."

"I'm from Missoula, born and raised." She cracked a knuckle against her glass. "And I'm thirty, so if I'm younger, it isn't by much."

"I have three years on you." Garrett watched the

kitchen door, hoping their orders would come out soon. He already felt he had said too much. "So...what brought you to Saddle Ridge?"

"Henry, Silver Bells' former farrier. I don't know how well you knew him."

"We spoke a few times in passing. Dylan and Jax always talked about him, though. Seems like a good guy from what I've heard."

"He and my dad apprenticed together way back in the day." Delta swiveled slightly to face him, causing her knee to brush against his. "Oh, I'm sorry. I didn't mean to bump you." Her hand rested lightly on his leg for a brief second, but it was long enough to send his blood coursing quicker through his veins. "When Henry decided to retire, he called and asked if I was interested in taking over his customers. Before that, I was working for my dad. Coming here gave me a chance to have my own business. And Missoula is still close enough for me to visit my family on weekends and holidays."

Garrett tried focusing on her face as a whole, but he kept wandering down to her mouth as she spoke. Her lips were full and naturally darkened, as if she'd just been kissed. Not that he needed to be thinking about kissing Delta or anyone else. His heart was permanently shuttered. *Stick to the topic, Garrett.* "How long have you been here?"

"A little over a year." She sipped her whiskey with ease. "Where were you in Wyoming?"

"Wheatland." Garrett rolled the glass slowly in the palms of his hands. Oddly enough, he found the liquor less intoxicating than Delta. "My wife and I moved there almost five years ago to be closer to her parents. I managed their cattle ranch up until a few weeks ago."

A waitress set both of their meals in front of them. She was one more person he didn't recognize. It used to be he knew everyone and their brother. When did he become a stranger in his own hometown? At least he'd made one new friend tonight.

"Silver Bells must be a big change from a cattle ranch."

"It is." Garrett took a bite of his burger and nodded. "It was time, though. I love my wife's family, but we were living with them. I appreciated their help with the kids, but the place had a shroud of grief hanging over it. They talked about Rebecca all the time and her mother still set a place for her at the table." Garrett didn't even have to close his eyes to envision that empty seat across from him. It made every meal almost unbearable. "My kids are mad because I refuse to do that here, but I don't want them growing up in a constant state of depression. That's not to say I love Rebecca any less." His voice began to rise. "She'll always be my wife. No one will ever replace her."

Delta reared back at the declaration as if he had physically shoved her. The force of his words had startled even him.

"I can't imagine anyone would try." She inched away from him and turned her attention to her sandwich.

"I'm sorry. You're the first woman I've really sat down and spoken with outside of family. Apparently I left my manners back in Wyoming."

"Let me make this easy for you." Delta side-glanced him. "I'm just one of the guys where you're concerned. I can assure you it will never be anything more. I'm assuming you're okay with that."

"Suits me just fine." Then why did her matter-of-fact

attitude on the subject sit on his chest like a bobcat on a briar bush? He certainly wasn't interested in her.

"Good. Now that that's out of the way…how old are your children?"

"Bryce is four and Kacey will be eight next month. Rebecca died just before her fifth birthday and she hasn't wanted to celebrate since. I'm hoping this year will be different. And I need to stop running on about myself and my problems." Garrett ordered a beer before returning his attention to Delta. "I've monopolized the entire conversation."

Delta dabbed her mouth with a napkin. "We all need a friendly ear sometimes."

"At least I've wandered into the friend zone and out of enemy range."

"Friends, huh?"

Her bemused expression gave him pause. "It's a start, at least."

"I'll give you that much."

Over the rest of their meal Garrett continued to tell her about his kids. She'd listened intently as he spoke and had carried on their conversation as if he hadn't made a repeated ass out of himself earlier. By the time their plates were empty, he realized he hadn't asked much about her. Guilt over Rebecca forced him to tamp down the desire to make plans to have dinner with Delta again. Tonight was a one-time deal stemming from a chance encounter. That was it.

"Buy you another round?" The question was out of his mouth before he could stop it.

Delta rose from her stool, tugged a few bills from the pocket of her jeans and tossed them on the bar. "Thank you, but I need to get going. Jake's waiting for me."

Jake? "Oh, okay. At least allow me to pay for your dinner to make up for this afternoon."

"Nah, I got it. Besides, I thought we just met tonight." Delta winked. "I'll see you tomorrow when we meet with Dr. Presley." She began to walk away and then turned toward him. "Welcome home, Garrett. I hope you find the peace you're looking for."

By the time he arrived at Dylan's to pick up Kacey and Bryce, he felt more certain moving back to Saddle Ridge had been the right decision for him and his family. He could hear his kids from the great room as he climbed the steps of the log cabin's front porch. Peering in the window, he saw Kacey dancing around the room with his brother while Bryce and Emma—Dylan's fiancée—clapped along with the music. It had been a long time since he'd heard his daughter laugh so freely. And it was better than any song playing on a honky-tonk jukebox.

Dylan caught his reflection in the window and waved him inside.

"Daddy we had pasketti!" Bryce ran over to him.

"Spaghetti," Kacey corrected. "You're old enough to say it right."

Wise beyond her years, his daughter still hadn't relinquished playing mother to her brother. She'd taken on the role herself the moment he and Rebecca told Kacey she was sick. In hindsight, they never should have told her. She'd barely had a chance to be a child.

"I see that." Garrett knelt on the floor next to his son. He tried to give his daughter a hug, but she slipped under his arm and sat next to Emma on the couch. He didn't want to pressure Kacey, but damned if it didn't kill him to see her happy up until the moment he walked

in the room. "Looks like you wore most of your pasketti, little man."

Kacey huffed at him. "You're not helping, Dad."

"He refused to wear a bib." Emma frowned. "Or a
towel or a napkin. I wanted to get him changed and wash
his shirt before you got back, but I didn't have anything
that would fit him."

"It's no big deal. He's always been a messy eater. I
keep hoping he'll grow out of it soon."

"How was dinner?" Dylan asked.

"Good. I ran into Delta at the Iron Horse. And don't
worry. I apologized and told her she can continue to do
her job as she sees fit."

"Thank God for that."

"We wound up having dinner together although I'm
afraid I did most of the talking. She seems pretty nice."

"Dinner together, huh? You sly dog." Dylan nudged
his arm. "You went on a date with Delta."

Garrett put a finger to his lips and glanced over at
his daughter, who continued to ignore him. "Please," he
whispered. "Kacey's mad at me enough. And I have absolutely zero interest in pursuing anything with Delta.
It was just two people sharing a meal."

"Okay, okay." Dylan held up his hands in surrender.
"One question, though. When she left, she said Jake
was waiting for her. Who's Jake?"

"He wasn't with her today?"

"No." Garrett hadn't spent much time with Delta in
the stables, but as far as he knew, she was there alone.
"Does he work for her?"

"Work for her? No." His brother laughed. "They, um,
live together. I'm sure you'll meet him soon. When you

see one, you usually see the other. Why the curiosity about Jake if there's nothing between you and Delta?"

"Just wondering." He hadn't expected her to have a boyfriend after her comment about Valentine's Day. Garrett lowered Bryce to the floor. "Run and get your stuff together. I need to get you home and into a bath, then it's off to bed." He tried to shake the flip-floppy sensation growing inside him. He was fine two seconds ago. It had to be from the chipotle whiskey. "Kacey, honey, time to go." Garrett gave Emma a hug as she stood up from the couch. "Thank you for entertaining them tonight. I really appreciate it. I know you have your hands full with Holly."

"Holly's been a dream baby so far." Emma held Garrett's face between her palms and smiled up at him. "I know this move hasn't been easy on you or the kids. They're welcome here anytime. Don't you ever think twice about it."

Garrett took her hands in his and gave them a gentle squeeze. "My brother struck gold with you. He's a lucky man."

"Holly and I are the lucky ones. We inherited an amazing family."

"Enough already," Dylan called out from the kitchen table. "I swear you two are the ones who are related. I've never seen two more sentimental people in my entire life. Emma still has the baby hormone thing going on, but you, dear brother…" Dylan's head tilted questioningly. "That must have been some dinner."

Garrett ignored his brother's comment and walked out to bundle the kids into the car. He'd been feeling nostalgic ever since Christmas when he first came home. He had so many memories in this town. Most good. One life-shattering.

He still hadn't been able to drive past their old family ranch. The place where their father had died at the hands of their brother, Ryder. Shortly after the funeral, their mother sold the ranch and moved to California where she remarried and rebuilt her life. He and Rebecca had left from Saddle Ridge to escape the pain of the past, and years later he'd come back to escape even more pain. His grief emotionally drained him every day. He had to work—to continually stay active to keep his mind occupied and remain strong for his children. He refused to let them down.

Tonight, despite the bittersweet memories of Rebecca, some of the weight had lifted from his shoulders. He'd enjoyed taking time away from the ranch, and being in Delta's company, even though the tension that still hovered between them. He'd been able to relax for a few short moments, and somehow that new beginning he needed finally seemed possible.

"There's my boy!" Jake ran across the yard and jumped into Delta's arms. At fifty-five pounds, he was no lightweight, but she didn't care. He licked the side of her face as his body wriggled against hers. "I missed you, too. Did you have fun today?"

Delta's Australian shepherd loved ranch life and her clients enjoyed having him around, but twice a week she treated him to BowWowWowzer's Doggie Daycare where he could be among his own kind. It was her way of giving back to the animal who gave her so much unconditional love and support through the darkest days of her life.

That darkness had come flooding back when Garrett told her about Rebecca. Not that it was ever completely gone, but on most days, she managed to keep those memories neatly tucked away.

"Thanks for taking such good care of him, Anna." Delta pulled a folded check out of her back pocket and handed it to the daycare's owner. "I think I was paid up until today. This should cover the rest of January and all of February. If not, let me know next week."

"No problem. My Sugar and Banjo can't get enough of him. I swear the three of them together rule the play yard." A chilly twilight breeze blew between them, causing Anna to pull her jacket tighter across her chest. "The temperature is expected to drop tonight. Why aren't you wearing a coat?"

Delta glanced down at her flannel-covered arms. "I guess I forgot to put it on. It's in the truck. I have Jake to keep me warm."

"Far be it from me to pry, but are you all right? You look kind of pale."

Delta lifted her gaze to see two sets of blue eyes studying her closely. Jake's and Anna's.

"What? No." Delta hugged Jake closer to her. "I mean yes, I'm fine. I have a lot of work stuff on my mind tonight."

"If you're sure that's all it is. I know Jake's a good listener but I can lend an ear if you ever need one."

"I appreciate that. You better get inside before you freeze. I'll see you soon."

Delta carried Jake to the truck. He was perfectly fine to walk, but she wasn't willing to release her hold on him. She needed the comfort only he could provide. Once tucked away in the warmth of the cab, she eased her grip on him, but he refused to budge from her lap. He sensed her hurt and grief and protectively shielded her from the world just as he'd done from day one.

Anna stood watching her from the daycare's front door. If she didn't leave now, Delta was certain the woman would knock on her window next. She backed out of the drive and started down the road with Jake plastered to her side. Turning on the radio, she tried to forget her conversation with Garrett. It was impossible when guilt wrapped its icy fingers around her heart. Delta was all too familiar with cancer. She had survived stage IIIb Hodgkin's lymphoma after it had almost killed her three years ago. That was when Jake had come into her life.

Her father had heard about a litter of puppies from one of his customers. Cute as Jake was, the last thing she'd wanted was an animal to care for. She'd been back living with her parents and couldn't even take care of herself. But once she looked into the dog's big blue eyes, her heart had melted. From that point forward, they rarely spent time away from one another. He'd gone with her to the hospital, giving comfort and support not just to her, but to other patients. Once she had kicked cancer's ass, she worked with Jake to have him become a certified therapy dog. They visited hospitals and nursing homes in Missoula, and still did, whenever she went home. But they'd also continued their routine here in Saddle Ridge.

Jake wasn't just her dog. He was her best friend and had never let her down.

She pulled down the ranch drive to her small home and parked. She rented the former caretaker's home on an older couple's ranch. They were on one side of the property and Delta on the other. In exchange for the use of their barn to house her farrier equipment and work truck, she shod their horses free of charge.

She opened the truck door, allowing Jake to jump over her lap and onto the ground. Every night he ran to her landlord's door for a cookie, then back to her house for dinner.

Delta slid into her jacket and sat in one of the rockers on the back porch. The brisk January air felt good against her warm skin. Between the nachos and her dinner, she felt a food coma coming on. She leaned her head back, closing her eyes. Garrett's face immediately came to mind. The sadness in his eyes as he spoke of Rebecca had just about broken her. If she hadn't left when she had, she never would have made it out of there tear free. Why had she survived when so many others had died? People with families. People like Rebecca. They'd both battled cancer at the same time, yet she—the one with no family—had survived.

A soggy tennis ball landed in her lap, jarring her out of her thoughts. "Ew, Jake!" Delta held up the filthy ball. "Is this the one you lost last summer?" Jake ran down the steps and barked, waiting for her to throw it. "I'll take that as a yes. One more time then we're going in." She stood and threw the ball of crud toward the empty pasture before unlocking the back door. Within seconds, Jake had returned with his treasure. "You're not bringing that in the house. Drop it." If she didn't know better, she would have sworn he rolled his eyes at her. "Yeah, I know. Mean mommy. Now come inside for dinner. I have a date with the TV remote."

She wondered what Garrett was doing tonight. She imagined him curled up on a couch, reading to his kids. Did they look like him? Not that it mattered. She couldn't

go there. She made a point to avoid any personal involvement with a client. This was still a new business
and she wouldn't screw it up. There wasn't room or time
for dating.

She sagged against the kitchen counter. She'd never
missed the touch of a man more than she did right now.
And only one man would do. Garrett Slade. The most
off-limits man she knew.

Chapter 3

The following morning, Jake beat Delta into the Silver Bells Ranch stables. Normally she wouldn't have minded, but not knowing how Garrett would react, she quickly caught up to her over-curious dog. She didn't want anything to rekindle yesterday's tension.

Delta turned the corner and saw Garrett crouched down in front of Jake scratching his ears and talking to him. "Where did you come from?"

"I'm sorry. He's with me."

Garrett smiled up at her and then ruffled her pup's long blue merle fur. "Let me guess." Her dog panted happily at the attention. "This is Jake."

"The one and only." Delta patted her thigh, signaling for him to come to her side. "I hope it's okay that he's here. He goes to work with me on most days."

"It's fine. Dylan told me. I wish my daughter was

here to see him. She would be in love. I keep thinking about getting a dog to help her adjust to the move." Garrett took off his hat and raked his hand through his thick brown hair before setting it back on his head. "And I'm rambling again."

"Good morning, Delta," Dr. Lydia Presley said as she and her assistant exited Lightning Bug's stall. "I'm glad you could be here today."

"Hey, Lydia." Delta was thankful for the intrusion. "No problem. I'm anxious to see how he's progressing."

"I just finished taking the x-rays. I got here a little early." She held out a slender, deeply tanned hand to Garrett. "We haven't met yet. I'm Lydia Presley, your veterinarian, and this is my assistant, Selena. I hope you don't mind that we went ahead and got started."

"Not at all. I'm Garrett, new co-owner of the ranch. It's a pleasure to meet you. My brother speaks highly of you."

"Same here. I've heard a lot about you, as well."

Apparently, Lydia had heard more about Garrett than she had. She had known the brothers had partnered but that had been the extent of it. It would have been nice to know something about him before they met, not that anyone owed her that. But the man piqued her curiosity in the worst possible way.

"Garrett, how familiar are you with navicular disease?" Lydia asked.

He shook his head. "I've heard of it, but I've never had to deal with it before."

"Let's begin with the basics, then. It's a degenerative disease of the navicular bone. Don't think of it as a disease the horse contracted. It's more of a syndrome of abnormalities and it's commonly misdiagnosed, which is why x-rays give a more definitive picture." Lydia tugged her iPad out of her bag and flipped open the cover. Tapping on the screen, she opened a series of digital x-rays and pointed to a small bone located on the backside of the front hoof. "It also affects the tendon behind it, and this little sac between the bone and the tendon. It's not something that happens overnight. While many times it's attributed to incorrect shoeing, that wasn't the case here."

"Then what caused it?"

"We don't know for sure. Quarter horses like Lightning Bug are more prone to it. They have large bodies on small feet. It was probably a trauma of some sort that resulted in an interruption of the blood supply. There's no cure, but we can manage it with drug therapy, exercise and the use of a nerve block. We've already discontinued drug therapy due to his improvement. Today we're looking to see what adjustments need to be made to his shoe."

"Which is where I come in," Delta said. "In this case, I used a light plastic and aluminum glue-on shoe with a foam insert, similar to our own running shoes. It's critical the hoof angles and balance are correct so Lightning Bug has the correct foot support. That's why we're checking to see if any adjustments need to be made since the hoof is continually growing."

"And you're sure you can handle all of this?"

Delta ground her back teeth together. She knew he didn't mean anything derogatory with his question, but somehow she doubted he would have asked it if he had been dealing with her father instead.

"I've been handling it," she answered. "I have quite

a bit of experience with corrective shoeing and navicular disease."

"And we've successfully managed it together on several horses." There was a slight edge to Lydia's voice. "It's not that uncommon. We treated one of your sister-in-law's rescues before Christmas. I want Lightning Bug to continue with daily light exercise to keep him moving. This is not something you want to baby, because stall rest will do more harm than good. I'll be back to check on him midweek. Since Delta's modifying the shoe, we like to make sure everything is doing what it should."

Delta wasn't upset but she appreciated Lydia's support. If Garrett picked up on the women's tension, he didn't show it. The man had a lot on his shoulders now that he was the ranch's co-owner. It had to be difficult being a single parent and starting over.

Delta checked her watch. It wasn't even nine o'clock and she had already emptied her thermos of coffee. She left Lydia and Garrett to discuss the other horses in the stables and headed toward the new lounge area he'd told her about last night over dinner, praying there was a freshly brewed pot.

Delta yawned, cursing herself for staying awake half the night. It hadn't exactly been her choice. She couldn't get her conversation with Garrett out of her head. Every time she had closed her eyes, there he was. The man was good-looking, she'd give him that. But that didn't mean she wanted him invading her every waking thought.

Jake trotted along next to her as she entered the lounge. She had expected one table and a handful of chairs, not several tables and a mini cafeteria setup. The mismatched furniture gave it a cozy feel. There were even Crock-Pots plugged in along the back wall, most likely courtesy of some of the ranch hands' wives that worked up at the lodge.

"Great." Delta looked down at Jake. "Now he's given me a reason to like him. I don't want to like him." The dog nudged her hand with his wet nose. "Don't you get too attached to him either."

She'd met many widows and widowers over the last three years. She'd visited with children too young to understand what was happening to their bodies. Those were the hardest. But out of everyone she'd met, Garrett was different. The people she sat with were going through cancer or had gone through it repeatedly. Garrett had suffered through the ordeal long-term, and three years later the loss of his wife still haunted him. Maybe that was why she couldn't get him out of her head.

"Delta, do you have a minute?" A shiver ran up and down her spine at the sound of his voice.

"Sure." Delta reached for a tall paper cup and filled it to the top. "Coffee?"

"Yes, please."

She watched him shift uncomfortably from the corner of her eye. "Tell me when. I always take mine black so I never know how much creamer people use."

Garrett waved his hand. "That's good." Delta handed him the cup. "About before… I don't want you to think I'm questioning your abilities."

"Aren't you?" Delta faced him. "I'll admit, I was a little miffed, but I realize you're concerned about Lightning Bug. I don't know how much Dylan told you about my experience, so I'll fill you in because you should know who's working for you."

"Delta, you don't have to do that." Garrett set his cup on the table behind him.

"Yes, I do. It's the only way you'll begin to trust me."

"If Dylan trusts you then I trust you." He sighed and jammed both hands in his pockets. "But if it makes you feel better, tell me."

"I'm a Certified Journeyman Farrier by the American Farrier's Association. I have both my forging and therapeutic endorsements. I also make a point to continue my education on a regular basis and I consistently work closely with equine veterinarians and hospitals throughout the state. I'm a fourth-generation farrier and this is more than just a job to me. It's my life. It's been ingrained in me since I could walk. And if there's anything I'm uncertain about, I have an extensive network to confer with."

"Wow, no wonder my brother was afraid I'd run you off." There was a nervous lilt to Garrett's voice. For a man who had greeted her so cocksure yesterday, she rather enjoyed the softer side of him. Maybe too much so. He stiffened as if reading her thoughts. "I appreciate your understanding. And I wanted to thank you for last night. It was nice having a friend to talk to."

There was that word again. She didn't want to be in the friend zone. Friends did things together. Friends relied on one another. The only thing she wanted to rely on Garrett for was a paycheck.

"If you need to talk, I'm available to listen, but—"

"That's what I had started to say before Dr. Presley joined us. I enjoy talking to you. I felt human for the first time in a long time last night. So, yeah, I'd like to take you to dinner sometime soon."

"Garrett." One of the ranch hands poked his head in the door. "We have a grain delivery coming in."

"Okay, be right there."

"Thanks for understanding about earlier." Garrett slapped a plastic top on his coffee. "I'll call you and we'll make plans."

And then he was gone.

"What the heck just happened?" She slumped in one of the chairs and began scratching Jake's scruff. "Did he just ask me out on a date?" Jake lifted his paw and rested it on her thigh. Delta groaned and closed her eyes. This was not how she planned to start the morning.

By the time Kacey stepped off the school bus, Garrett was ready to call it a day. He still had a few hours of work to do, but it would have to wait until tomorrow morning. He wanted to spend a few hours with Kacey before they went to his brother Harlan's house for dinner. Over Christmas, he had promised Kacey and his seven-year-old niece Ivy that once they moved to town they could have regular weekend sleepovers. This was supposed to be his turn to host, but the girls were staying at Harlan's since Garrett wasn't finished unpacking. That was next on his agenda.

Emma had offered to babysit Bryce on Saturday while Dylan helped him finish setting up the house. By the time Kacey got home on Sunday night, he wanted their place looking like a real home. They hadn't had a home of their own since Rebecca died. He loved living close to family again. They could support him when he needed it. He'd missed that in Wyoming. Rebecca's family was wonderful, but it wasn't the same as having his own nearby.

Instead of embarrassing Kacey again on the snowmobile, he opted to pick her up in the SUV. Surely that had to be okay. In spring, he'd allow her to walk from the ranch's front gate to the house, but it was just too cold in mid-January.

Kacey slammed the passenger door and glanced in the backseat at Bryce. "Are we going to Uncle Harlan's now?"

"Not until later." Garrett stared at his daughter. "You could try saying hello first." Once again he was met with radio silence. "Kacey, look at me." When she refused, he cut the truck's ignition.

"What are you doing?" she screeched and looked toward the school bus pulling away from the ranch. "Just drive."

"Listen, young lady. I realize you're having a difficult time accepting this move. But this is home now. I suggest you find a few things you like about it and focus on those because we're not moving back to Wyoming. And from now on, when you get in this car you say hello to me and your brother. And you need to stop yelling and slamming things. Do I make myself clear?"

"Yes," she murmured, still facing the window.

"Can you look at me, please?"

Kacey turned her body slightly toward him, and stared at the floor.

"Looking at me involves me seeing your eyes."

Slowly she lifted her gaze to his. Tearstains streaked her cheeks and her eyes were pink-tinged and puffy.

"Have you been crying?"

She blinked once as her bottom lip began to quiver. "I'm just tired, Daddy."

Garrett wasn't buying that excuse. "If you're too tired, then maybe we shouldn't go to Uncle Harlan's tonight."

Kacey's eyes grew wild. "You said every weekend

Ivy and I could have sleepovers. You can't break your promise."

"Well, honey, if you're so tired that you were crying on the way home from school—"

"I just need a nap."

His daughter had never once asked for a nap. When she was little, she always fought her mother when she tried to get her to take one. Something was wrong and he wanted to know who or what had upset his daughter.

"I wish you would talk to me and tell me what's bothering you."

"Can we go home now?"

Garrett wanted communication with his kid that went beyond one-line answers. A few weeks ago, this hadn't been a problem. Now it had become their normal routine and he hated it.

"Yeah, we can go." Garrett started the truck. "Do you have homework this weekend?"

"A little."

"How about you start on it before we go to your uncle's house." At least that would keep her in the kitchen where he could help her.

"Ivy and I were going to do it together."

"Together better mean you do your homework and she does hers. Not you do one subject and she does another, then you copy off each other like you did last week." That was a problem with having cousins in the same grade.

"We won't copy." Kacey already had her fingers wrapped around the door handle as they pulled up in front of the house. No sooner did he park than she was out of the truck and up the stairs and jiggling the knob. She would just have to wait a minute because the door was locked and he still needed to get Bryce out of his car seat. "Daddy, I have to go to the bathroom. Can I have the keys?"

Garrett sighed, not knowing whether to believe her or not. She did have an hour-long bus ride home. Deciding he'd had enough battles with his daughter for one day, he tossed her the keys. "Leave them on the kitchen table, please."

By the time he got inside with Bryce, she had firmly shut herself behind her bedroom door. Just as he figured. He wanted to knock. Hell, he wanted to drag her out of her room and hug her until she opened up to him, but he knew she'd have no part of it. He missed his sweet little girl.

She used to be the perpetually happy kid. He always knew where she was by her laughter. That all changed when Rebecca died. The anniversary was eleven days before Kacey's birthday, and his in-laws always made such a production of the date, it clouded Kacey's special day. This year he had decided his daughter deserved to have a happy birthday. Maybe then he'd hear her laugh again.

Three hours later, Garrett helped his brother clear the table while his sister-in-law tried to teach Bryce how to eat and not wear his dinner.

"Good luck with that, Belle." He laughed. "I used to think it was a hand-eye coordination issue, because he appears to miss his mouth, but he's been tested for everything under the sun. One doctor told me he thinks Bryce likes the feel of the food, that's why he wears it. It's also the reason we never eat at a restaurant."

Belle held a forkful of food out to Bryce. "If you can

eat this nicely, then you'll get another." Bryce frowned and reached for the plate, but Belle pulled it away. "One mouthful at a time, sweetheart. Finish this first."

"Daddy, can we go play in my room?" Ivy asked. Kacey hadn't said two words to him since their talk earlier, but she'd chatted nonstop with her cousin since they walked in the door.

"Go ahead, but be back in a half hour for dessert."

"No copying each other's homework," Garrett reminded them.

"You seriously don't think they went upstairs to do homework, do you?" Harlan asked.

Garrett waited until he no longer heard the girls' footsteps on the stairs before answering. "Has Ivy mentioned anything about Kacey being upset in school or on the bus?"

"Not to me." Belle wiped Bryce's face with a napkin and handed him a spoonful of baked beans. "Did something happen?"

"When she came home today, she had obviously been crying. I tried to talk to her about it, but I couldn't get anywhere. I just thought maybe she had said something to Ivy."

"No, but I'll see what I can find out," Harlan said.

"Just don't let on that I put you up to it." The last thing Garrett wanted was his daughter thinking he was spying on her. He was, and owned that, but she didn't need to know about it.

"Please." His younger brother nodded to the sheriff's hat hanging by the back door. "I have my ways of getting people to talk without them knowing it."

"Yeah, that's why you were so successful getting Ivy to confess to taking the neighbor's bunny last year."

Belle shook her head. "Kids are complicated. I was one of the worst."

"You sure were," the men said in unison.

"Now, that's not right." Belle wadded up her napkin and threw it at them. "Let me tell you, growing up around you two was no picnic. Now hand me a dish towel. I think I'm getting somewhere with this one."

Garrett admired Harlan and Belle. They had grown up together, gone their separate ways and then found their way back to each other last year. Now they were expecting a baby in May. Despite their playful digs at one another, they were the happiest couple he knew, outside of Dylan and Emma. Garrett had been the first of the five Slade brothers to get married, and he'd never been more sure of something in his entire life. And he'd thought it would last at least fifty years, if not seventy-five, considering they married straight out of high school. He missed that companionship. He missed those knowing glances across the table. Having someone to hold all night long. He missed his old life, and if Kacey felt a fraction of the way he did, he understood where she was coming from.

"In all seriousness," Harlan began, pulling him out of his thoughts. "I'll see what I can find out and let you know. How's it going at Silver Bells this week?"

"Better. I think I'm finally getting to know everyone's names and what they do. I need to get creative on where we can save on the renovations. I think the biggest savings will be in sweat equity and bartering. Maybe a week or weekend at the ranch in exchange for services rendered."

"That's a great idea. I did quite a bit of that when I built the rescue center." Belle's Forever Ranch opened last year on the other side of their property. The non-profit rescued animals and provided desperately needed medical care. Once they were rehabilitated, they helped give comfort to abused and neglected children who had suffered similar fates. "I can give you some of my construction contacts. Maybe they can help you, too."

"I'd appreciate that, thank you." Garrett poured a cup of coffee and sat across from Belle at the table. She had the patience of a saint and didn't coddle Bryce the way his mother-in-law had. Dawn had blamed his messy eating on Rebecca's death, and she'd taken to spoon-feeding him at every meal over the past three years. Garrett had repeatedly asked her not to, but she insisted on feeding him the way Rebecca had. His son had been sixteen months when Rebecca passed. It didn't matter that he'd grown old enough to eat by himself.

"Dylan told me you and Delta had dinner together last night." Harlan grabbed another dish towel from the drawer and set it on the table for Belle. "I really like her. I'm glad you're getting out."

"You're seeing Delta?" Belle's face lit up brighter than the sun on the horizon. "Just in time for Valentine's Day. She is so nice. I can't even begin to tell you how much she's done for my rescues."

"Whoa!" Garrett pushed away from the table, almost taking his coffee with him. "I am not seeing Delta. I made that clear to Dylan last night. Let's not perpetuate that rumor."

"Calm down, bro." Harlan wiped up the coffee that sloshed onto the table. "No need to get all defensive. I'm just telling you what Dylan told me. But if you enjoy being around one another, why not see where it goes."

"Because I'm married." Garrett hated that people

automatically assumed that because his wife died the marriage was over. Maybe it was in the eyes of the law, but it wasn't for him. He'd always hated the phrase "'til death do us part." He didn't believe in it and had asked the minister to remove it from their wedding vows fifteen years ago. They vowed to love each other for all eternity instead, and he would never break that promise, even though she had told him she hoped he would find someone new one day. There wasn't room in his heart to love another woman. "We're just friends."

"Okay, fine." Harlan shrugged at Belle. "Just make sure she knows that."

"Of course she does." Garrett shook his head. "I didn't even know she would be at the Iron Horse when I went there. I saw her at the bar, and we ate a meal together. It's not like I asked her out." Garrett froze, remembering his earlier conversation with Delta. "Oh, no."

"What's wrong?" Belle asked.

"I think I accidentally asked Delta out to dinner."

Harlan slapped his brother on the back and laughed. "The heart wants what the heart wants."

Garrett closed his eyes. This couldn't be happening. How could he have been so cavalier with his dinner invite? Maybe she hadn't taken it that way. He replayed the conversation in his mind. What exactly had he said? Something along the lines of wanting to take her to dinner. *Shit!* He had asked her out and hadn't even realized it. He scrubbed his hands down his face. He needed to straighten that out and fast.

Chapter 4

"Why do I get the feeling you're avoiding me?" Garrett startled her as she exited Lightning Bug's stall.

"Good Lord." Delta flattened herself against the wall before realizing who it was. "You would have been in for the surprise of your life if I'd been carrying a hot shoe."

"I knew you weren't since your truck is outside and the back was shut." He crossed his arms in front of his chest. "No forger, no hot shoes. I also saw Jake waiting patiently behind the wheel for you."

Okay, so he was observant. "I've been here almost every day to check on Lightning Bug, except for Sunday when I visited my family. I was only stopping in for a minute."

"I know you've been here." He widened his stance and tilted his hat back. "I got your notes, Delta. It's just I haven't seen you in a week."

Five days, but who was counting. But he was right. She had been avoiding him. Luckily for her Garrett was a creature of habit and it didn't take long to figure out his routine. She'd been able to get in and out without running into him, except for today, when he beat her at her own game.

"Listen I think we should—"

"I have to tell you—" they both said at the same time.

"Ladies first." Garrett removed his hat and bowed slightly before her. The gesture, however goofy, was actually charming in a Garrett Slade sort of way.

"Look, I—I like you," she began, trying to find the words to let him down easy.

"Okay." Garrett quickly donned his hat. "Let me stop you there. I gave you the wrong impression the other day. I think you're very nice but I don't want to date you."

Delta started to laugh. "Oh, thank God for small favors."

"Excuse me?" Garrett stepped back and frowned slightly. She hadn't meant to wound his ego, but those were the best words she'd heard all week.

"I don't want to date you either." Delta patted her chest in relief. "I've been wracking my brains trying to find a way to tell you. I mean you're good-looking and all that, but I refuse to date anyone I work with or for."

Garrett began to smile, seemingly satisfied with her explanation. "I still would like to take you to dinner, though. But it would be strictly platonic. Just friends. Nothing more."

"Yeah, about that." Delta gnawed on her bottom lip. "Don't get offended, but I kind of make a point not to hang with anyone I work with either. If the friendship goes south, it affects my business. If you don't mind,

I'd like to keep that part of my life separate. Unless you need someone impartial to talk to about your wife or something like that."

"Okay, now I'm confused." Garrett stared at her as if she had three heads. "It's okay for me to talk to you about something painfully personal but we're not allowed to be friends? I think your logic is a little backwards."

"No, it's not." Delta sighed. She hadn't meant to hurt his feelings. "Listening to someone talk is different. It's what I do, well, we do. Jake's a certified therapy dog and I volunteer at the convalescent home in town. I understand the need to talk. Your loss was devastating and I'm always available if you just need someone to hear you out. That's a given. But it can't be more than that."

"How do you make friends, then?" Garrett's face contorted.

"I have friends." Delta didn't like having to defend her reasons for not mixing work and pleasure. "Here and back home."

"Back home, huh?" He rested an arm on a stack of hay bales. "You sound like my daughter."

"I don't understand." And she didn't care to. This was exactly why she kept her personal life private.

"You live in Saddle Ridge. You've been here for—what did you say—a year?"

Delta nodded and played along. "What does that have to do with anything?"

"You've established a business and a reputation here. Quite a good one from what I understand. Whether you want to admit it or not, this is your home. Missoula is where you're from."

Delta opened her mouth to argue and quickly shut it. Okay, so he had a slight point. But, Missoula would always be home, no matter where she lived or for however long. "How about we agree to disagree and leave it at that."

He studied her for a few seconds before answering. "Sure." She began to walk away when he continued, "One of the Belgians threw a shoe. Do you think you might be able to fit that in today?"

Delta inwardly groaned. There were a lot of things she loved about her job but shoeing an uncooperative draft horse wasn't one of them. It would have been nice if he had at least considered her comments about the ranch not having a shoeing stall. She realized he was trying to save money, but a shoeing stall worked to Dr. Presley's advantage, too. It gave them both much more control over the animal while keeping stress to a minimum.

She checked her watch. "Yeah, I can squeeze it in. I'll have to open up the doors and back my truck in."

"Thank you. Let me know if you need anything."

Delta watched him walk away. She was okay with her decision to not be friends. Wasn't she? He was a customer. Her largest. Going out and having a few drinks or dinner would be unprofessional. People in town would talk and assume they were dating. Or that Silver Bells was getting a special rate. Well…they *were* getting special treatment. Garrett did just want to be friends. Nothing more. And he was still in love with Rebecca. Maybe it wouldn't be so bad. Then again, she already found herself drawn to the man, and she didn't need any more temptation. It would only lead to heartbreak. Hers.

An hour later, Garrett cursed himself for allowing Delta to get under his skin. Not because she'd done something wrong, but because he couldn't get her scent out of his nose. It was a combination of cinnamon and nutmeg, and he couldn't figure out if it was her hair, or some sort of body wash she had used. Either way, he'd never smelled that scent on another person before. It was uniquely Delta and it drove him crazy.

Fresh air. Now, that was what the doctor ordered. The day had been unseasonably warm, to the point where excessive runoff from the snow melt had begun to flood one of their stables. Luckily it was the side where they stored some of their equipment, so none of the horses were standing in water. They'd had to rush-order a load of sandbags to prevent any further flooding. It was one more expense they didn't need.

Garrett rechecked the grounds surrounding all three stables and then fired up one of their four-wheelers to tour the ranch's perimeter. Normally his ranch hands made the trek around the 730 acres, but he wanted to distance himself from all things Delta. He saw her truck drive toward the main gate as he crested the first slush-covered hill. The last thing he needed was to start changing his routine to distract himself from a woman. There was no other woman. Only Rebecca. Then why did he feel so damn guilty?

Garrett's sanity began to return by the time he finished riding fence. He checked the time—something he did constantly since they'd moved to Saddle Ridge. When he'd lived with his in-laws, he hadn't paid attention to his children's routines. They were just there when he finished working for the day.

It pained him to realize how unaware he'd been until he was a hundred percent responsible for them. He had always considered himself a great parent, when in reality, he hadn't been. He'd blamed Dawn and Terry for many of the kids' problems but he'd waited to rectify the situation, and that had also affected his kids. If they'd moved sooner, even to a home of their own in Wheatland, it would've been better than doing nothing.

On his way back to the stables, the shrill ring of his cell phone interrupted his thoughts. He tugged the phone from his breast pocket and checked the display. It was Kacey's school.

"Garrett Slade speaking."

"Mr. Slade, this is Darcy Malone from Saddle Ridge Elementary. We just wanted to check on Kacey since she wasn't in class this morning."

"What do you mean, she's not in class? I watched her get on the school bus this morning."

"Kacey's homeroom teacher reported her absent." Garrett heard the muffled sound of somebody covering the phone. "Mr. Slade, I'm going to personally check each of her classes and call you back in a few minutes."

"What? You expect me just to wait when you have no idea where my daughter is? I'm on my way there."

Garrett jammed his phone in his pocket and pinned the throttle as far as it would go. His tires spun before they gripped the ground. He skidded the four-wheeler to a stop beside his truck and hopped off, fishing in his pocket for the keys before realizing they were already in the ignition.

He dialed Harlan first. "The school just called me. They said they haven't seen Kacey today but I saw her get on the bus."

"Where are you now?" Garrett heard Harlan's police siren through the phone.

"Heading to the school."

"I'll call it in and meet you there. Try to stay calm.

She's probably somewhere in the building. I'll have them pull Ivy out of class and see if she knows anything."

Garrett threw his phone on the passenger seat. He knew something was off with his daughter. He had tried to be her friend, hoping she would talk to him. Maybe he should've just demanded she tell him what was going on. Even after her mother's death, Kacey hadn't been this withdrawn. Dylan had been right. There was no way he could've comprehended the difficulties of switching schools and making friends when he'd never had to do it. Had he pushed her too far?

His phone rang again. "Mr. Slade, it's Darcy. Kacey is not in school."

Garrett's heart stopped beating as the world went silent around him. He tried to breathe as the phone slipped from his fingers, but his lungs no longer functioned. He pulled his truck off the road, unable to feel the steering wheel beneath his palms.

"Mr. Slade? Mr. Slade…"

Garrett fought for air.

"Mr. Slade. Are you still there?"

"Where's my daughter?" he whispered. "I can't lose her, too."

"I think I can hear him. I don't know if he got into an accident or what. Mr. Slade, if you're still there, we've notified the sheriff's department."

"Harlan." Garrett shook his head and sucked in a deep breath of air. "My brother's the sheriff's department," he said as he patted the driver's side floorboard for the phone.

"Mr. Slade, I can barely hear you."

His fingertips grazed the hard plastic of the phone. He inched it toward him until he could grip it. He pressed the Bluetooth button and waited for the familiar chime. "I'm here. My brother Harlan is the deputy sheriff. He's already on the way. I'll be there in two minutes."

Garrett pulled onto the road as Harlan's police SUV flew up behind him. He lowered the window and signaled for his brother to pass. *Harlan will find her.* He had to. *This is fixable.* It had to be. *This isn't like when Rebecca died.* It can't be.

An hour after she had left, Delta returned to Silver Bells in search of her phone. The stables seemed eerily quiet as she walked through the door with Jake by her side. Come to think of it, she hadn't seen a single soul when she drove onto the ranch, which was odd for that time of day.

"I wonder where everyone is." Delta's boots against the cement corridor and an occasional neigh were the only sounds to be heard. "Maybe they were having a company meeting up at the guest lodge. You need to help mommy find her phone."

She scanned the center corridor as Jake trotted ahead of her. Stopping at Lightning Bug's stall, she started to unlatch the door when she heard the faint sound of music coming from the next stall down. The stall that had been empty since she started working on the ranch.

"Hello?" Delta called out. She peered through the upper bars of the stall wall, not seeing anyone, but the music was definitely louder. It almost sounded as if it was coming from under her. She tried to look down along the wall, but the stall was partially swathed in a dark shadow. "Hello?" The stall door creaked as she opened it and the music grew louder. "Is someone in here?"

She allowed her eyes to adjust to the dim light before slowly peering around the corner. She made out the faint outline of a child's shoe.

Oh, my God. There's a kid on the floor.

Delta rushed into the stall and reached into the darkness. A scream pierced the air and sent her to her knees. Jake rushed in, barking incessantly in the dark. A tiny figure scampered past her and into the corridor as Delta regained her footing. She gripped the stall's bars, pulling herself to her feet only to be standing in front of a very much alive little girl who was equally as startled as she was. It didn't help that Jake was continually circling her.

"Come here, Jake. She doesn't need to be herded. She's okay." Delta bent forward. "You are okay, aren't you?"

Delta heard the music again, and realized it was coming from the girl's earbuds. She'd had her iPod on so loud she hadn't heard Delta coming. The girl nodded, but her frightened face said otherwise. Her eyes wildly looked up and down the corridor but not at her and Jake. She didn't seem afraid of them. But she was afraid of something.

"My name is Delta, and this is Jake. Jake, say hello." The dog sat in front of the girl and waved his right paw at her. "Jake's a therapy dog, so if you're scared, you can hold on to him and he'll make you feel better. Do you want to touch him?"

Delta wanted to get close enough to the child to make sure there weren't any visible signs of trauma. The girl lifted her hand so Jake could sniff her. He pushed his head under her fingers until they were buried in his long thick coat. The corners of her mouth began to lift as Jake pressed his body against hers.

"What's your name?" Delta asked.

"Kacey," she whispered.

Kacey? Garrett's Kacey? "Don't you have school today?"

She shook her head. "We have off."

Hmm. Delta could have sworn she passed the school bus in town earlier. "How would you like to help me find my phone. I think I dropped it here earlier when I was checking on Lightning Bug."

"Are you a vet?"

"No, sweetie. I'm a farrier. I put shoes on horses."

"How come you had to check on Lightning Bug?"

"Because he has a limp and needed a different type of shoe, so I had to make him one. You could say I'm a shoe designer for horses."

Kacey's smile began to grow. "I know where your phone is."

"You do? Where?"

She disappeared into the stall and returned carrying a yellow *Beauty and the Beast* backpack. So much for her not having school today. She unzipped the front pocket and removed Delta's phone. "I found it when I came in before. I was going to give it to my dad later."

"Thank you for taking care of it for me." Delta punched in her security code and saw a missed call from Garrett. She also noticed the time on the top of the screen. It wasn't even one-thirty and school didn't get out for another hour. "Sweetie, did you walk home from school?"

Kacey shrugged her shoulders and then sat on the floor next to Jake.

"School's a long way from here." It had to be at least three miles. That was a long walk for a child, especially in the cold. Delta pressed the voice mail screen and read the transcribed message. Even without hearing Garrett's voice, the tone was frantic.

She typed a quick text message to him: Found Kacey in your stables. She is okay. I'll stay with her until you arrive.

She pressed Send and slid the phone in the pocket of her jeans.

"How about a snack and a cup of hot chocolate?"

Kacey's eyes brightened at the mention of food. Considering how long it had to have taken her to walk to the ranch, she probably hadn't eaten since breakfast.

"Come on, Jake. Let's get Kacey something to eat."

They both followed her into the new employee lounge. Delta opened the upper cabinets and pulled out a small pack of cookies and a granola bar. She set them on the table, hoping Kacey wouldn't try to run. Although, the way Jake kept body checking her, she didn't think the kid would get very far if she did. That was the one problem with owning an Australian shepherd. They always had to be working, and sometimes that meant herding people.

Delta tore a packet of hot chocolate open and dumped it in a cup before filling it with water. She popped it in the microwave and waited. Kacey unzipped her ski jacket. That was a sign she was staying. Delta stirred the cocoa when the microwave dinged and topped it with a dash of vanilla creamer to cool it down a bit.

"Here you go." Delta set the cup on the table.

Kacey had already slipped out of her coat and was seated. When she reached for the cup, Delta saw tiny bruises on the girl's forearm. They looked like grip marks, about the size of a child's hand. Delta knew them well.

"Kacey, is someone bullying you at school?"

The little girl's eyes flew open. Her panic had returned. Jake instantly sensed her anxiety and began nudging her hand. She reached into his thick fur again and gripped it.

"It's okay to tell me. You should always tell a grown-up when other kids pick on you." Delta sat across from Kacey at the table and watched her expression, seeing parts of Garrett in her tiny features. The same dark hair and eyes. "When I was your age, there was a girl who used to pick on me something terrible. She'd wait until we went into the bathroom and would always push me against the wall and hit me. She did it every day for two years before a teacher caught her. I used to go home and cry. I couldn't understand why she didn't like me."

Kacey's hands stilled. "Really?"

"Really. When the teacher walked in on her doing it, I was so relieved. But you know what I found out? I could have told my teacher or my parents and they would have put a stop to it much sooner."

"Weren't you afraid?" Kacey began to bite her thumbnail.

"Yes, I was. I thought if I told, then other kids would start picking on me. But that didn't happen. The teacher made sure of it. They moved that girl into another class." Delta wondered what the policy was at Kacey's school. Maybe the kid would even be expelled. The bruises on her arm were pretty dark. Whoever did this to her used force. "Have you tried talking to your daddy?"

Kacey shook her head. That would explain why she was hiding out. She didn't want to get in trouble for skipping school.

"Kacey!" Delta heard Garrett's voice boom through the stables.

Kacey wrapped her arms around Jake. "He's going to be so mad at me."

"He's not mad, he's scared." Delta stood. "Stay here with Jake and I'll explain it to him first, okay?" She scanned the room to make sure there wasn't a back door she might have overlooked earlier. Nope, just one door. She stepped into the corridor, almost slamming into Garrett. "Slow down, cowboy. We need to talk first."

Garrett tried to step around her, but she blocked him again. Flattening her hands on his chest, she pushed him out of the doorway. Delta saw fear reflecting in his eyes.

"She's okay, but you need to listen to me for one second before you go in there, please." Delta refused to let him in, afraid he'd yell at her for cutting class. "Someone has been bullying your daughter and from the bruises I just saw on her arm, I think it's been pretty bad. I'm assuming she headed home shortly after the bus dropped her off at school."

"What?" Garrett's body stiffened. "Somebody hurt my baby?"

"What's going on?" Harlan joined them, out of breath. "Where's Kacey?"

"I want to know who hurt my kid." Garrett stared down at Delta, willing her to move.

"I think the bruises are from another child's grip," she said as she moved aside and let him pass.

Garrett crossed the room in three long strides and lifted his daughter into his arms, sobbing into her hair. "You scared me, baby. Don't you ever do that again. I can't lose you."

Delta turned away to give him privacy and faced Harlan. "She didn't say much, but she was very interested when I told her I had been bullied as a kid. I'll leave the rest to you guys."

"Thank you, Delta." Harlan tipped his hat and entered the lounge.

She patted her thigh and Jake trotted out of the room to her. "Come on, boy. You did good today. You deserve an extra cookie tonight."

Her heart broke for Garrett. Their family had suffered enough and now they were struggling once again. They may have moved from Wyoming for a fresh start, but that didn't always come easy. Maybe Garrett needed a friend more than she needed her rules.

Chapter 5

"I know you're scared, sweetheart, but you can tell me anything. No matter what it is." Hours later, Garrett still fought to remain calm. He was finding it increasingly difficult when he still didn't know who'd hurt his daughter. And until he found out, she wasn't going back to school. "If you don't want to talk to me, you can always talk to your uncle Dylan or Emma or your uncle Harlan and aunt Belle."

"What about Delta?" Kacey shifted on the couch and looked up at him.

"When someone hurts you, I want you to tell any adult." He hadn't expected Kacey to include Delta in her circle of trust. Then again, Delta had been the one to get her to finally open up. "Did you like talking to her?"

Kacey nodded. "She told me someone had bullied her, too."

The revelation surprised him along with the anger coursing through his veins at the thought of somebody hurting Delta. He had no right to feel anything for her except gratitude. He wanted to tell his daughter she could talk to Delta whenever she wanted. While he didn't think Delta would be opposed to it, their conversation earlier about not being friends reverberated in his head. His heart told him she'd make an exception for a child.

There was a knock at his front door before Harlan entered. "I wanted to check on you two before I headed home." Harlan joined them on the couch. "How are you doing, buttercup?"

His brother looked over her head and nodded toward the door.

"Kacey, why don't you go get ready for bed. I'll be in to read you a story in a little bit."

Wordlessly, she slipped off the couch and trudged up the stairs to her room.

"Good night, Kacey," his brother called after her.

"Good night, Uncle Harlan."

As soon as her bedroom door clicked shut, Harlan turned to him. "Belle and I were able to get more out of Ivy tonight. It's not just one kid bullying her, it's a group. A little mean girls club. And they've not only attacked her physically, they've been saying things about her online. Ivy couldn't tell me what, because we don't allow her to have any social media accounts. She had only heard about it from her friends. I went on there pretending to be one of her classmates and I saw some pretty hateful things."

"What the hell is wrong with kids today?" Garrett slammed his fist into the couch. "We didn't do this when we were their age."

"We didn't have social media back then, but there was bullying." Harlan got up and walked into the kitchen. "I remember quite a few kids getting beat up on the playground and not saying anything. Delta told me earlier that she had been on the receiving end as a kid."

"Kacey just told me that, too." Garret was beyond thankful Delta had revealed what had to have been a painful past to his daughter. "I think it's the only reason Kacey's talking tonight. She finally realizes she's not alone. How long has Ivy known about this?"

"From what we can gather, from the beginning." Harlan grabbed two beers from the fridge and handed one to Garrett. "They had made a pact not to tell anyone. She didn't want to betray Kacey's trust so she kept it secret and had been trying to defend her. I explained that not saying anything was part of the problem and she promises to tell me or another adult whenever she sees bullying of any kind from now on. I wish I'd had this conversation with her sooner, but at seven years old I didn't think I had to. And I of all people knew better. I hear about this stuff all the time on the job. Children committing suicide because they're being viciously attacked at school. I saw my daughter's name in some of those posts tonight and it sickened me."

Garrett held his head in his hands. *Suicide?* They were talking about little kids. How did he miss the signs? How did he miss the bruises?

"It's hard. She is this little woman so I respect her privacy and let her pick her own outfits and bathe on her own. I never once thought to say show me your arms and legs so I can see if somebody has beaten you up."

"You couldn't have known."

"I should have known." Garrett slammed his beer

on the table. "The signs were there. I'm a single father and I took away her only female role model by moving here. I can't help but wonder if she'd have told her grandmother, or if her grandmother would've noticed it earlier and could've put a stop to this."

Harlan patted his brother on the back. "In my experience on the force, kids are pretty good at hiding things. I've seen all sorts of abuse that teachers and neighbors or other parents and siblings had missed. I know you're upset, but don't drive yourself crazy over this. Kacey has other female role models. She's just not used to them yet. She only met Belle and Emma over Christmas. And there's Delta. Kacey clearly trusts her. Maybe they could spend more time together."

"How is that supposed to happen?" Garrett couldn't even get her to agree to dinner. "It would be different if Delta had a kid, too. Then there would be a reason for Kacey to see her. But Delta is long gone before Kacey gets home from school." School. Garrett groaned. "What am I supposed to do now? I can't send her back there. What do I do about these other kids and the stuff online? Whatever's on there, I want it down."

"I've already taken care of her attackers. I reported them to the school board and there is a formal police report on file. I need a statement from you, which is the other reason I'm here. I'll also need a victim statement from Kacey, but that can wait until tomorrow."

"My daughter will be eight in a few weeks and she's already a victim giving statements to the police. When I moved back here, I thought I was moving my kids into a safe environment."

"You have to be vigilant," Harlan said.

"Oh, believe me. Nothing is getting past me again."

Garrett wanted to wring the necks of his daughter's tormentors' parents. There was no way kids came by this on their own. They learned it somewhere.

"Maybe Kacey needs to spend more time with Belle at the Forever Ranch. Belle swears by animal assisted therapy."

"So does Delta. Jake is a certified therapy dog."

"I've heard that. Delta has made quite an impression on Saddle Ridge in the year she's been here. She volunteers a lot of her time to various organizations."

"And once again, you're trying to sell me on her."

"Would it be such a bad thing? Dating again doesn't mean you have to stop loving Rebecca. Your heart has more room than you think. Valentine's Day is less than a month away and I'd like to see you happy again. I'm not telling you to marry her. I'm saying explore the possibility of a relationship, whether it be friends or more."

"Please tell me Belle hasn't turned you into one of those people. Valentine's Day is nothing but a greeting card holiday. Even Rebecca didn't buy into it. She felt our love deserved to be celebrated year-round. And you're wrong. There's no room left in my heart."

And there never will be.

A little more than a week had passed since Delta had found Kacey hiding in the stables. She had wanted to call Garrett a few times and ask how she was doing, but she'd decided against it. The kid had a huge support system and she was sure they were taking good care of her.

And it just so happened her next stop was part of that support system. Every six weeks she trimmed hooves at Belle's Forever Ranch along with Harlan's personal stable of horses. She was sure Belle would update her on Kacey.

Delta parked and hopped out of the truck. Jake was at doggie daycare chillin' with his buddies for the day. She missed him when he wasn't with her, but sometimes he just needed to be a dog and not a best friend.

Delta fastened her apron chaps around her waist and gathered her tools before heading to the backside of the stables. "Good morning, darling." Delta rubbed The Fuzz's muzzle. Harlan had named his horses after outlaws and Belle had countered with police ones. She had The Fuzz and Colombo, two rescued former race horses, and Joe Friday, a donkey that had doubled his weight since living at the rescue center.

"Hey, Delta," Belle called to her from the chicken play yard. And it was a real play yard, complete with toys and a little obstacle course. She had never seen a chicken play before she met Belle. "I'll be there in a second. I just need to make sure this one heater is still working on the chicken coop."

"The new coop is adorable." Delta loved Belle's attention to detail. She had built the birds an exact replica of the ranch's red barn, right down to the trim and metal roof.

"It came out good, didn't it?" Belle admired her own handiwork. "I didn't think I'd ever get it finished considering I have to pee every two minutes. I'm with Emma—this pregnancy thing is for the birds." She laughed at her own joke. "Oh, crap." She sighed. "I have to pee again. I'll be right back."

Delta forced a smile as her chest began to tighten. She was happy for Belle, just as she was happy for her friend Liv. But that happiness didn't fill the increasing void in her life. She had dreamt of having children for as long as she could remember. Being one of three kids, she thought she'd at least have that many, but chemotherapy had robbed her of that chance.

Delta inhaled sharply as tears filled her eyes. It had been years since the doctor had confirmed her sterility and the pain never eased, especially since she wasn't eligible to adopt until she was cancer free for five years. Even a private adoption, which she couldn't afford, would be doubtful. It was one more way the big C had kicked her in the teeth. She had a little over two years to go before she could apply and she had the actual date programmed into her phone's calendar.

Some days were more agonizing than others. Today was heading in that direction. Delta wiped at her eyes and turned her attention to The Fuzz.

"Are you ready for me, handsome?" Delta snapped a lead rope to his halter and led him out of the stall. As they walked, she listened to the sound of his bare hooves against the ground. This allowed her to hear any abnormalities in his gait. The fifteen-year-old quarter horse had been shod all his life, but no longer tolerated any form of shoe after his hooves had been so severely neglected they had grown in the shape of a corkscrew. Delta had worked closely with the equine hospital in nearby Kalispell, both donating their services to save the poor animal. Since he spent the majority of his time grazing, they opted to keep his hooves natural to prevent further stress. She stopped by every couple of weeks just to see him and check on his progress. Four months later, he had improved greatly, but still had a long road ahead of him.

She tied him to a nearby hitching post and ran her

hand down the front of his leg until she reached his fet-
lock. She lightly pinched the chestnut on the back of his
leg causing him to lift his foot.

"Good boy." She praised him. A race horse would
have been trained to lift their foot on command, and at
one time, The Fuzz probably had. But he wouldn't do it
anymore without a little coaxing on her part. "Let's see
what we have going on here." She reached for her hook
knife and began cleaning his hoof. "You're doing won-
derfully, my dear."

"I'm back." Belle scratched The Fuzz's neck as Delta
continued to work. "Have you spoken with Garrett at
all?"

That didn't take long to bring him up. "Not since the
incident with Kacey. How is she doing?"

"Hard to tell. The kids who bullied her were expelled,
but because of what happened, Garrett enrolled her in
a private school. It's a lot smaller and she gets more
one-on-one instruction, which she desperately needs to
bring her grades back up. It didn't help that one of the
bullies' parents tried to enroll her daughter in the same
place as Kacey."

"They didn't get in, did they?" Kacey deserved a
safe learning environment. A kid couldn't concentrate
when they constantly had to look over their shoulder.
She knew that firsthand.

"No, the school denied the application. They also
offer counseling services, but so far, Kacey refuses to
participate. We all thought a new school would be a nice
do-over for her, but she's starting fresh again." Belle bit
her lip. "At least in public school she had Ivy. She was
her lifeline. Harlan wants to transfer Ivy to the same
school since the kids were cyberbullying her, too. She

seems open to it. He and Ivy's mom are planning to sit down this weekend and discuss it further."

"I can't even imagine that whole aspect of it." Delta had thick skin, but she didn't know if she would have been tough enough to handle cyberbullying as a kid. "It's bad enough in school, but when it follows you everywhere you go… Wow."

"I do know that Garrett is grateful to you."

Delta stilled the knife in her hand. "Me? Why?"

"If you hadn't figured it out, who knows how long this would have gone on. Besides, Kacey has asked about you, and she's smitten with Jake."

That thought made Delta smile. "He has that effect on people."

"Kacey is spending the weekend here." Belle walked around the front of the horse until she was standing in front of Delta. "You're more than welcome to stop by. Our door is always open."

"I'm working most of the weekend, but I might be able to squeeze it in."

"Bryce is also staying with us this weekend, in case you wanted to stop by Silver Bells and see Garrett." Delta noticed a sudden lilt in Belle's voice. "I'm sure he wouldn't mind seeing you."

Delta lowered The Fuzz's foot and slowly straightened her spine. "I never figured you would be one to play Cupid."

"Who's playing Cupid?"

Delta lifted one brow and cleared her throat.

"Okay, so maybe I am. Can you blame me? You two would be good for each other. You're both single."

"Yeah, well you're forgetting two things." Delta lifted the horse's foot again and examined it. No further cracks, but the outside was still slightly asymmetrical. "He's still grieving his wife and I'm happily divorced."

"I never knew you were married." Belle pulled a carrot from her pocket and fed it to the horse. "I guess it didn't end well, huh?"

"You think?" Delta glanced up at her. "Thanks but no thanks. I don't date clients."

"He said that, too."

"Garrett did?" She lowered the hoof. "Wait a minute. Have you also suggested us dating to him?"

"I may have mentioned it the other night…and the week before." Belle looked skyward. "But Harlan started it. Well, actually, Dylan. They both thought you two were seeing each other."

"Why would they—" Then the realization hit her. This was why dating in a small town was next to impossible. Everyone knew your business. "It was just dinner."

Delta returned her attention to The Fuzz and lifted his foot for the third time, determined to finish it.

"He's a really great guy," Belle said under her breath.

Delta chose to ignore the comment. If she didn't engage her, maybe she'd drop the conversation.

"I'm just saying," Belle added. "Wouldn't it be nice to have someone to go to the movies with or take little day trips with?"

"My day trips consist of driving hom—back to Missoula to visit my family, and I'm not big on the movie theatre." So much for not engaging her. "Even if I was, I have friends I could call. I don't need a man to complete me."

"But don't you want one to share your life with?"

"If and when the right man comes along, I will consider it." She lowered the horse's hoof. "But Garrett is not that person. He's not ready. And neither you, or Harlan, or anyone can determine when he will be. He'll know when the time is right. So put your arrows back in their quiver, Miss Cupid."

"Okay." Belle rested her head against the horse's neck, making it almost impossible to tell where her platinum hair ended and his light mane began. "But please think about seeing Kacey."

"That I'll do." She needed to swing by Silver Bells to check on Lightning Bug anyway. "I'll pick up Jake early from BowWowWowzer's and go today. I'm sure he'd love to see her, too."

She was only doing this for Kacey. It had nothing to do with wanting to see how Garrett was handling everything. Her parents had blamed themselves when it had happened to Delta. It wasn't always easy to ask for help as a kid. And at the time, a part of her blamed them, too. How could they not have known she was in so much pain? But she had done everything in her power to hide it from them and her brothers.

As an adult, she understood both sides of the equation. Okay, so maybe she could bend her friend rule and offer some comfort to Garrett. If she could just manage to keep her heart out of it, she'd be fine. Delta sensed another test of her will coming on and she wasn't so sure she'd pass this one. She wasn't Wonder Woman. She didn't have a shield to protect her. And Lord knew she needed one against Garrett Slade.

Chapter 6

Jake barreled down the stable corridor toward Kacey. Garrett hadn't seen her smile that big in—he didn't know how long. His daughter knelt on the floor and wrapped her arms around the dog's neck, burying her face in his long blue merle coat. He glanced toward the entrance, but didn't see Delta. If Jake was there, she had to be somewhere nearby.

"Daddy, where's Delta?"

"I'm sure she'll be in shortly."

When fifteen minutes had passed, Garrett's concern grew. Where was she? Could Jake have gotten away from her and run to the stables? He told himself not to worry, but lately it was all he did.

"Sweetheart, you stay here with Jake. I'll be right back."

Garrett's strides lengthened as he headed for the door.

He swung it wide and saw Delta lying on the ground, next to her truck.

"Delta!" he shouted as he ran to her.

She scurried to her feet, holding a long pipe like a Samurai warrior. "What?" She glanced around her. "What is it? What did Jake do?"

"He's fine. He's with Kacey. I saw you lying on the ground. Are you all right?"

She rubbed her forehead, leaving behind a dirt-streak. He fought the urge to wipe it away. The last thing he needed was to come in contact with her skin, which he imagined was silkier than silk itself.

"I am, but I can't say the same for my tire." Delta stepped to the side. "I knew something didn't feel right when I was parking. My jack keeps slipping so I can't raise it enough to change the damn thing. Getting a new jack has been on my list for months and I never do anything about it."

Garrett crouched next to her truck and saw two nails sticking out of the tire. Probably courtesy of the renovations they had been doing on the ranch's outbuildings. "Let me change it for you. I'll pay for your new tire, too. This is our fault. I told those guys to go over the ground with a magnet to pick up all the nails. Not just for the cars, but for the horses and our guests. I don't need someone or something impaled on a nail."

"I appreciate that, but I've been all over the place today so I could've picked those up anywhere. All I need right now is a heavy-duty jack. You wouldn't happen to have one around here, would you?"

"Yep. I have one in the barn." Garrett hadn't noticed the flecks of gold in her eyes before. They reminded him of a piece of amber he'd found as a child. Alluring yet mysterious.

"Um, if you tell me where in the barn—"

"I'm sorry. My mind was elsewhere for a second." Garrett stepped around her, careful not to accidentally brush against her body. "Let me go get it. And don't argue with me... I'm changing that tire."

Delta held up her hands in surrender. "Okay. My bones are aching from working this week anyway, so be my guest."

Garrett enjoyed the sight of a woman who didn't mind getting her hands dirty. Probably too much so where Delta was concerned. It didn't help that the woman smelled dark and delicious. As if that was even a scent. He still couldn't pin down what she was wearing. A woman who worked around horses all day should smell like horse. And hay. He would even settle for manure. Anything to distract him from the allure that had begun to draw him toward her. He had Belle and Harlan to thank for that. Every time Kacey had mentioned Delta's name over the past week, they had taken every opportunity to remind him she was single.

A half hour later, Garrett let the jack down and removed it from under her truck. "You're all set. Please let me take your tire into town so I can get a new one put on this rim."

She stepped closer to him. "You don't have to do that. I'll just have it patched."

"Nonsense." Garrett swore he could feel the heat emanating off her body in the cold Montana afternoon. "You, uh—you do way too much traveling to ride around on a patched tire, especially with a truck this size." Garrett reached for the tire and began rolling it toward his truck. "I'm not going to discuss it further," he called over his shoulder, grateful for the distance between them. "I'm getting you a new tire and I'll have it back to you on Monday."

"Absolutely not." Delta ran to block him, causing Garrett to slam into her and push them both against the bed of his truck. He grabbed her waist to steady her, allowing the tire to wobble to the ground. Delta's lush, full lips were inches from his as they parted slightly. As she inhaled, her breasts pressed against his chest, sending his mind in numerous directions. "But, I will take you up on your dinner offer, if it still stands."

Garrett tried to open his mouth to speak but feared any movement he made would be toward her, especially toward kissing her.

"Garrett." Her hands wrapped around his, which were now resting on her hips. "Did you hear me?"

"Ye— I— Yeah— Yes!" Garrett released her and took a step back, tripping over the tire instead.

"Watch out!" Delta grabbed hold of his arm and steadied him before he hit the ground. "Don't you go falling head over boots."

Too late.

"I'm good." He lifted the tire and set it in his truck bed. "This is coming with me." He grabbed two bungee cords from his cab and began to tie the tire in place. If he kept his hands busy, they wouldn't wind up back on her. "So, what's this about dinner?"

"I heard what you had said and maybe I have been a little too rigid with my rules. Dinner with a friend never hurt anyone."

Garrett looked up just as she tucked her hair behind one ear, exposing the delicate side of her neck. It was one of his favorite places to kiss on a woman's body. Well, Rebecca's body. He'd never been with anyone else. That fact alone was enough to temper his libido. Despite his attraction to Delta, if it came down to it, he wouldn't be able to follow through. He couldn't betray Rebecca that way.

"Harlan and Belle are taking the kids this weekend. We have a little arrangement going on. Why don't we go over there?" *Safety in numbers*, Garret thought to himself.

"I was thinking someplace a little more private. Where we could talk...alone."

Garrett's pulse quickened. "Isn't that living a little too dangerously? You're just tossing all your rules out the window."

"This has nothing to do with rules." Delta inched closer as he jumped from the truck bed. "It has everything to do with you and what happened with Kacey. I can relate to how she's feeling. But I also understand how you're feeling because I watched my parents go through the same thing."

Garrett couldn't deny wanting to talk to her about Kacey. He had picked up the phone repeatedly during the week and set it back down, uncertain how to ask her to relive a painful time in her life just to give him some peace of mind.

"I'd like to get your input on the situation, if you're sure it won't bring up too many bad memories."

"Undoubtedly it will, but the more I thought about it, the more I realized you need a friend who's been there. I want to help you, if I can. Heck, maybe if we spend some time together, Belle and Harlan will lay off the matchmaking. With Valentine's Day coming up, maybe we can duck and dodge Saddle Ridge's cupids together."

Her idea wasn't half bad. It would keep his brothers at bay. He wasn't so sure about Belle, but it might work. "Sounds like a plan."

"Great. Oh, and as for my tire, I'm going to deduct the price of a new one off your next invoice." She lifted her chin defiantly.

Garrett laughed. He should have known it wouldn't be that simple. "You'll do no such thing."

"Oh, please, you'll never even know. I'll just leave something off an invoice and you won't be the wiser."

"Are you challenging me?" Garrett watched her draw her bottom lip inward, renewing every urge to kiss her.

"Daddy, what time are we going to Uncle Harlan's?"

Garrett stepped back from Delta and clenched his fists. That was close. Too close. He was a fool for thinking of kissing her, even for a second. "Not for a few more—"

"Delta!" Kacey ran down the walkway with Jake in tow and threw herself into Delta's arms. "I missed you."

"You missed me?" She looked at Garrett questioningly as she hugged his daughter.

He shrugged, surprised at Kacey's attachment to someone she'd only met once.

"I wondered when I would see you again. Daddy, can Delta come with us tonight?"

"Oh, honey. You don't put someone on the spot like that." He wanted to spare Delta having to say no to his daughter.

"Your father just asked me the same thing. I would love to." Delta smiled up at him and shrugged. "How could I possibly turn down an invite from you?"

"Yay!" Kacey jumped up and down. "Can Jake come, too?"

"I don't know about that." Delta laughed nervously. "I think one extra guest for dinner is enough. Jake's been at doggy daycare all morning so I'm sure he won't mind staying home and catching up on his beauty sleep tonight." She held Kacey by the shoulders and lowered her face to hers. "I'll tell you what, though, you are welcome to play with Jake whenever you want. If it's okay with your father, I'll give you my number so you can call me and we'll set up a playdate."

"Did you hear that, Daddy?" Kacey tugged at his arm. "It's okay, isn't it?"

It was more than all right. If Delta could make his daughter this happy by allowing her to spend time with Jake, she could move in for all he cared. "Sounds good to me."

"We're going to have playdates, Jake." The dog jumped up and down on his hind legs in front of Kacey and if he didn't know better, he'd swear the animal understood what they were saying.

Kacey stopped jumping and ran over to Delta's rear passenger-side window. She climbed on the running boards and pressed her face against the glass. "Is that a guitar?" She expectantly looked at Delta for a response. "Do you play?"

"Yes."

"Are you in a band? Can you teach me to play?"

Delta threw her head back and laughed. "I'm not in a band. But I do bring it with me to the convalescent home here in town. Sometimes when I visit the people there, they ask me to sing songs for them."

"What is a con-con-val—"

"Convalescent. It's a nursing home." Kacey didn't realize it, but she had been to one before. Rebecca had spent two months in one before they brought her home to die. Garrett swallowed hard. "People stay there when they need 24-hour care. Delta goes there to cheer them up. If you want to learn how to play guitar, I'm sure Dylan will teach you."

"I want Delta to teach me." She turned away from him. "Can I go with you to the con-va-scent home?"

Garrett didn't want his daughter visiting a nursing home. Not this close to the anniversary of her mother's death.

"Not tonight, honey." Delta seemed to sense his anxiety. "Jake and I wanted to stop in and see you and Lightning Bug and then I need to shower and get cleaned up. I'll stop by the home and then I will meet you both for dinner. When is dinner? I don't want to be late."

"Not until seven, seven-thirty. By the time Harlan gets home from work and I get out of here and clean up myself, and then wrangle my two, it takes us a while to sit down and eat."

"Sounds perfect." Delta wrapped an arm around Kacey's shoulders and began walking toward the stables as Jake fell into step beside them. "How would you like to help me examine Lightning Bug's foot."

"I'd like that." Kacey wound her arm around Delta's waist in return. "You still didn't say if you would teach me guitar or not."

"If your father says yes, then I will." She turned to him. "I wouldn't mind at all."

"Daddy, can I?" Kacey's doe-eyed expression made it impossible to refuse.

"If Delta is willing to teach you, sure." Garrett had

been trying to think of the perfect birthday gift for his daughter. He had already considered a puppy, but now he was thinking about a puppy and a guitar. Were his ears ready for that kind of assault? If it made her happy again, he didn't care. He'd like to see his daughter stick with something. She bored easily and he didn't know if that had been because of the somber environment they had been living in or if she genuinely hadn't found something she really cared about. Maybe animals and music would be her thing.

"Thank you, Daddy." Kacey ran over and gave him a quick hug before running back to Delta and grabbing her hand. "I can't wait to tell Ivy."

"I heard you're in a new school." Delta unlatched Lightning Bug's door and stepped inside while Kacey climbed up on a hay bale and watched her through the stall bars. "How do you like it?"

"It's okay." Kacey shrugged. "I still haven't learned everyone's names yet."

"Yeah, that's always hard," Delta said as Garrett sank farther into the shadows of the tack room doorway. A part of him felt like he was spying on his daughter. The other part felt if he had done more spying, she never would have been bullied to the extent she had been. "I went through that when I went to a new school, too."

"You did?" Kacey lifted her head.

"Things were a little different back then. They didn't kick my bullies out of school like they did yours. All they did was move us to different classes, which didn't help on the playground, so my parents put me in a private school, too."

"Did you like it?" Kacey asked.

"Not at first. I was scared. And like you, I didn't

know anyone. But the teachers were nice and the kids were even nicer. Some of my best friends to this day were from that school."

"Really?"

"Yep. It's just like when I moved here from Missoula and started a new job. I knew one person in town. I had to start all over again. And you know what? It was so much harder as an adult than it was as a kid. At least when I was your age, I had classmates to talk to and get to know. Here I had to go out to strange places and make a point of meeting people. I was nervous."

"You were?"

"Oh, yeah. But I did it, and I have some great friends here, too."

"Like Daddy?"

Delta paused. "Your daddy and I are getting to know one another a little better."

"Are you still nervous around him?"

Now there was a question he wanted answered himself. He leaned farther into the corridor to hear Delta's response, but of course she wouldn't make it easy on him. The two had taken to whispering like two schoolgirls. Curiosity be damned, he was just happy Delta got his daughter talking freely about school. She hadn't been as forthright with him. The woman may pose a serious risk to his heart, but she was good for Kacey. And her needs came before his. As long as he kept all of *his* wants and needs where Delta was concerned in check, he'd survive.

The following night, Delta stood in front of her open closet door and stared into the emptiness. She had nothing left to wear. *It's just dinner.* Then why was she nervous? *It's just dinner.* For the second night in a row.

She turned to the mound of clothes on the bed and sighed. She had tried everything on. Twice. And she still couldn't decide what to wear tonight. Yesterday had been easy. They had gone to Harlan and Belle's with the kids. That was a jeans-and-sweater-type event. One she had enjoyed more than she'd anticipated.

Oh, and that Bryce. She just wanted to eat him up. He had such a cherub face, with pink rosy cheeks, beautiful blue eyes and white-blond hair. That was how she pictured Rebecca. She had no idea what the woman looked like, but that image had come to mind before she'd even met Bryce. She and Garrett had created two beautiful children.

And Delta needed to remember that.

Garrett was in love with Rebecca. There would never be anything more than friendship between him and Delta. She grabbed the empty hangers from the closet and began plucking items off the bed one by one. Black jeans, a pale blue denim shirt and her leather motorcycle jacket. There. Done.

It's just dinner. With a friend. On a Saturday night.

Delta arrived at the Iron Horse Bar & Grill ten minutes before six and parked her red hardtop Jeep Wrangler near the entrance. It was still a bit too early for the evening crowd and she figured she'd be able to get them a table near the bar so they wouldn't risk being stuck in a dark, cozy corner booth. Probably a booth he had shared with Rebecca when they were younger. Knowing Garrett's history with the place, she was surprised when he had suggested it. Then again, maybe that was why he had. It was someplace old and familiar, a place guaranteed to remind him of what he'd had and lost.

She walked in the door and was immediately hit in the chest by Cupid's arrow. *Seriously?* She stared at the foam arrow lying on the floor.

A rather attractive twentysomething cowboy with piercing blue eyes knelt before her. Her breath caught in her throat until he opened his mouth. "I'm so sorry, ma'am. My aim is way off tonight." Then he retrieved the arrow and joined the rest of his pretty twentysomething friends.

Ma'am? You've got to be kidding me. The one place she thought had escaped the Valentine fervor had transformed their game area into Cupid's lair. The pitch penny bench was covered in red leather. Giant diapered cherub butts covered the dartboards that people shot foam and Velcro arrows at and the Cornhole platforms had been painted red and had baskets of red and white beanbags next to them. At least they had left the billiard tables untouched.

She sighed and turned to find a table when she saw Garrett waving to her. So much for her arriving first. He wasn't quite in the dark corner she had feared, but it was the next booth over. Booths were intimate. Especially at the Iron Horse. It was where you brought your date after a movie or before a night of dancing. It wasn't a hey-let's-talk-about-horseshoes type of table.

Garrett stood and removed his hat as she approached. "You look nice tonight," he said as she slid into her side of the booth. "I hope this is okay?"

"Thank you and it's perfect." She couldn't help admiring the snug cut of his jeans and the way they hugged every single curve of his body. And the man had curves.

He didn't have those straight, spindly legs that some men had. He had very defined muscular thighs with...bulges. Garrett Slade had nice bulges. "You look nice, too."

And he did once he sat down and his bulges were out of her direct line of sight. He had on a fawn-colored flannel shirt that made her want to snuggle against it. She could just imagine what it would feel like to be enveloped in his arms with her face pressed against his chest.

Shirt. Her face pressed against his shirt.

Nope. That didn't work either. She didn't need to be pressing any of her parts against any of his. If he hadn't cleaned up so well, these thoughts wouldn't be invading her brain. And it wasn't as if she'd ever seen Garrett get really dirty. The man changed her truck tire and barely got anything on him. He was rugged. He had an air of I'm-ready-to-get-dirty-at-any-moment quality about him, but there was always a flicker of something mischievous behind his dark eyes.

"I ordered us two chipotle whiskeys and a couple of beers. I hope you don't mind."

"Oh no, definitely don't mind." A drink couldn't come fast enough. "What's with the Valentine's Day onslaught when you walk in the door?"

"I was going to ask you the same thing." He leaned closer so she could hear him over the music, bringing with him a heady scent of woodsy aftershave. *Lord help me he smells good.* "It's bad enough I have to deal with this stuff at the ranch."

"The ranch does Valentine's Day? I don't remember that last year."

"It's all Emma's fault. Her wedding planning with Dylan is turning everything into one big Silver Bells lovefest."

Delta tried not to laugh but the way he said *lovefest* looked like he'd swallowed a pinch of chewing tobacco.

"I'm serious." He leaned back as the waitress set their drinks on the table between them. "We have a week-long Valentine's couples-only retreat coming up and it's making everyone in an amorous mood up at the lodge. Thank God my job is in the stables. I don't even go up there for breakfast anymore. Considering half our employees are married to each other, everyone is hand holding or sneaking in a kiss here and there. We're running a business, not a lover's playground."

"Remind me not to step foot in there until that's over with." She raised her whiskey glass. "Here's to avoiding Valentine's Day."

"I'll drink to that." Garrett clinked her glass.

Waylon Jennings' "Good Hearted Woman" played on the jukebox and Delta found herself itching to get on the dance floor. If it had been any other place with any other man, she would have. She looked up at Garrett, fully expecting him to be lost in his memories of what once was. Instead, his eyes met hers and he smiled.

"You want to dance, don't you?"

"No, I'm good." The truth was, she had been wiped out most of the day. Work had been a struggle, but somewhere around four o'clock, she found her second wind. "Kicking back with good company and good food is about all I can handle tonight."

"Long day?"

"Busy. Many small jobs all over the county. What about you? How are renovations going?"

"I wish I had more to do with them." Garrett flipped open his menu. "Dylan's acting general contractor and I'm maintaining status quo in the stables. Thanks to

Belle's help, I've managed to barter some construction services in exchange for riding lessons and a few free stays at the ranch once the cabins are finished."

"That's a great idea."

"It's managing to save us more than I had expected, but that's been the extent of my involvement. My brother runs all the ideas past me and we decide on them together, but I always get the feeling he thinks I'll break if he gives me too much work to do. I want to do more. Our staff is thin, but it's also winter. I can easily appoint someone to manage the stables while I work with Dylan. But he won't give."

"Working with family can be tough." Delta sipped at her whiskey. "When I worked for my dad, I never thought I'd make it out of apprentice mode. Even after I had become a journeyman, I still felt like I was apprenticing under him."

"It dawned on me the other day who your father is. I hadn't put two and two together before. Luther Lloyd Grace is a legend. He's a master blacksmith, too, isn't he?"

"Don't ever let him hear you call him by his real name. Luther Lloyd makes him cringe. You be sure to call him Buck. And yes, he is a master blacksmith. You know the man, you know the legend that is the man, and how could I complain about working under someone with his world-renowned expertise? It's also a hell of a lot to live up to when you're the only kid who followed in his footsteps."

After four generations of Grace farriers, she was also where the legend ended, since she couldn't have kids of her own. One of her brothers worked for the Missoula County Sheriff's Department and the other was a Montana Travler horse breeder. Even if they had kids of their own and they chose to become farriers, it would have skipped a generation.

Her father and grandfather had been so proud to pass the torch, and then her body betrayed her by single-handedly snuffing it out. Her father would never admit to his disappointment, but she knew it was there. A few months ago, she'd overheard him trying to convince Trevor to stop breeding horses and apprentice under him. He hadn't given any reasons. He hadn't had to. But she knew. They all knew.

"Can I offer you a piece of advice?" she asked.

"Sure." Garrett sipped at his whiskey. "This stuff is pretty good once you get used to it."

"I'm glad to see that lesson stuck with you."

He leaned forward on the table and smiled a slow easy grin that caused her heart to skip a beat. "Give me your advice."

Delta rolled her shoulders. She didn't know if it was the man or the heat of the whiskey that made her feel deliciously warm. "Be honest with your brother. If you want more, tell him. He may think he's doing you a favor. Once I told my dad I wanted my own business, he supported me. And when Henry called and told him about Saddle Ridge, he practically pushed me out the door. You might be surprised at his reaction."

"You know what, I will do just that. Tomorrow. Tonight is about friendship."

He raised his pint of Guinness.

"To friendship." She clinked her glass against his.

"And ice skating."

"And what now?" Delta froze before the dark liquid touched her lips. "I am not drinking to that."

"Why not?" Garrett frowned. "The rink is a few blocks down and I thought we could pop over there after dinner."

"The only popping would be my butt bouncing across the ice. I do not skate. I've tried it and I'm not good at it. And no amount of lessons will help me either. I've already gone down that slippery path."

"I didn't think there was anything Delta Grace couldn't do."

"Yeah, well. We all have our limitations."

"Hold on to my hands." Delta hadn't been kidding when she'd said she couldn't skate. The woman could barely stand. "I've got you."

"I cannot believe you talked me into this." Her eyes narrowed at him. "This is not my idea of a good time. What if we fall through?"

"Then you'll be standing in an inch of water." He skated backwards, pulling her with him. "We're skating on a parking lot. It freezes quickly when the temps drop. I promise you won't fall through the ice and drown."

"Oh, you're funny."

"Where's that confidence I know you have?" Garrett enjoyed challenging Delta. She was a little bit of a bad girl mixed with a little bit of sweet. Once he cracked through her hard exterior, he enjoyed getting to know her softer side.

"If I fall—"

"I'll catch you."

"Forget that. I don't want you to catch me. If I fall, you owe me ten more dinners."

"Such a hardship. I don't know if I can handle that."

"Daddy!" a tiny voice called from behind him. "Look, Belle. It's Daddy and Delta."

He dropped Delta's hands when he turned to see Kacey skating toward them.

"What the—erm— Ow."

"Delta!" Kacey skidded to a stop beside Delta sitting on the ice. "Daddy, why did you let go of her?"

"Yeah, Garrett?" Delta snarled. "Why did you let go of me."

"I—I...give me your hand." He reached for her, but she refused to budge. He hadn't meant to drop her. Kacey startled him and he didn't want her to get the wrong idea. He didn't think Delta would fall that fast. Or that hard. "I'm sorry, really I am."

"Go away." She swatted at him.

"Lean on me, Delta. I'll help you," Kacey said.

"No, honey, if I fall again—and I'm sure I will—I don't want to crush you. I am not a skater."

"Sure you are." Belle's arms slid under hers from behind and within seconds, Delta was standing on her feet. "What do you say, Kacey? How about we teach her how the Slade girls skate. Come on, Ivy."

"Yeah!" Kacey grabbed hold of one hand and Belle the other and off they went gliding over the ice at warp speed while Ivy skated in front of the team cheering them on.

"I bet you five this doesn't end well." Harlan held out a gloved hand.

"Nah, I think she'll get it. She just needed the right teacher. She wasn't born on the ice like our kids." Bryce skated around them.

"First dinner last night at my house, and then tonight we find you out here together. Balk all you want, but whatever is going on between you two looks like a relationship to me."

Leave it to the deputy sheriff to dig for information. Hey, at least if he and Belle suspected they were dating, they'd lay off the matchmaking.

"We went out to dinner and then I talked her into coming here."

"Slow down," Delta cried as they flew by. "You're going too fast."

"Open your eyes and move your feet," Kacey ordered. "It's the only way you're going to learn."

The men started to laugh. "You can see how well that worked out for me."

"You're skating, Delta," Ivy shouted.

"Well, I'll be damned," Garrett said. "She is skating." With Belle's and Kacey's help. But she was skating nonetheless.

"Daddy, look at Delta." The women slowed to a stop in front of Harlan, Bryce and Garrett.

"See, we knew you could do it." Belle nudged Delta's arm. "All it took was a Slade to open your eyes."

There was no hiding the double meaning of that statement. But it had also been a Slade who allowed her to fall because he didn't want to risk his daughter seeing them together. Delta's reaction afterward told him there was no hiding that meaning either.

"You're a better teacher than I am, sweetie." Garrett flicked the pompom on his daughter's hat.

"Ain't that the truth." Delta stuck out her tongue at him, making the girls giggle.

"Daddy, do you think you can manage to skate with Delta again, and not let her fall? Or do I have to supervise?"

"Oh, snap!" Delta laughed. "She told you."

"I guess she did." If Kacey didn't have a problem with them skating together, then why should he? He bowed before Delta and extended his hand. "May I have this skate?"

"Do you promise not to let go?"

Kacey joined their hands together. "He promises."

"I promise. I won't let go." And he didn't for the rest of their time on the ice. Belle and Harlan had left long before they did. The hour had gotten away from Garrett, and when they stepped off the ice when the rink shut off the lights for the night, Garrett found himself fighting the urge to kiss Delta good-night as they walked back to where they had parked.

"I guess I owe you ten more dinners."

"I guess you do." Delta opened her truck door. "Thanks again for tonight," she said before climbing in.

"It was my pleasure. Drive safe." He patted the hood of her Jeep as she backed out of the space. He stood on the curb and watched her taillights disappear into the night. Tonight had been more fun than he had anticipated. And much lonelier than he could have ever imagined. There was no one waiting for him at home. No wife, no kids. Just emptiness. And in that moment, he wished he hadn't let Delta drive away.

Chapter 7

Delta awoke Sunday morning to a head on her shoulder and a hot breath against her cheek. She glanced at the clock on the nightstand. It wasn't even six in the morning and she didn't have anywhere to be. Days like these were a rare treat. Normally she had jobs lined up, or if she had gone to visit her parents, she would be driving home. Today her schedule was clear and it was hers to do as she pleased.

The body next to her shifted and yawned, followed by a long lazy stretch and a paw to the face. "Easy with the right hook there, bud." Jake's breathing deepened until it became a steady snore. "And Belle thinks I need a man to share my life with. I don't need a man. I have Jake." Between his gas and snoring, he was as close to a man as she wanted to get.

Delta smiled, remembering last night with Garrett.

It had been completely unexpected and more fun than she thought it would be. At the end of the night, she had thought he was about to kiss her. He didn't, and she still wasn't quite sure how she felt about that.

She sat up in bed and looked around the room, realizing she didn't know how to start her day without an alarm clock ringing in her ear. She should be enjoying her day off and sleeping in, but her body betrayed her. Swinging her legs over the side, Delta groaned as she stood. Between the muscle aches and stiff joints, she felt a hundred years old. Who knew ice skating for hours would hurt so much the next day?

She padded downstairs and filled the coffee carafe with water. Her parents had given her one of those single-serve coffeemakers for Christmas, but it was still sitting in the box on top of her dryer in the laundry room. She was a creature of habit and her habit was making a thermos of coffee every morning and taking it with her. But, she wasn't going anywhere and she certainly didn't need a thermos of caffeine to do nothing.

"What the heck." She walked into the laundry room, picked up the box and sat it on the kitchen table. Today was a good day to change things up.

An hour later, Delta was on caffeine overload. It was her mother's fault. She had included six different kinds of coffee with the gift and Delta had to try them all. After she showered and dressed, it was still only seven thirty in the morning.

"What do people do with all their free time?" She didn't exactly have any hobbies. There was guitar, but sitting around the house didn't appeal to her today. It was too early to call Liv or Maddie. Even the convalescent home frowned on visitors until after nine o'clock.

And it was too cold to go for a hike. "What are we going to do, Jake?"

She stared at her phone, willing a customer to call… willing Garrett to call. And that wasn't right. He didn't need to call her. He had no business calling her. Unless of course, it was for business. Try as she might, she couldn't get him off her mind. It didn't help that he had held her hand while they skated. She hadn't had that kind of intimate contact with anyone since her husband and she missed it, but she certainly didn't miss him.

The man she had spent most of her life loving couldn't handle what the chemotherapy had done to her body. It hadn't just been the hair loss or the constant sickness. It had been the harsh reality that she may not survive. And even if she did, knowing they'd never conceive a child together had driven a huge wedge between them. The turmoil they had experienced was common. Many marriages went through it. There were support groups, but Eddie had refused to attend a single meeting. Regardless of how strong their love had been, it hadn't been strong enough.

If he had told her he wanted to end the marriage she would have still been devastated, but she would've respected his honesty. Instead, he had chosen the coward's way out by distancing himself from her and having an affair with a mutual friend of theirs. Some friend. While Delta fought for her life, Eddie had knocked up his girlfriend. Her world had collapsed around her and she had lost the will to fight. Until Jake.

The dog nudged her knee with his nose, sensing her tension. "What is it, boy? You're bored, too, huh? Come on, let's take a ride into town and see what trouble we can get into."

Delta zipped her ski jacket to the top of the collar. She wished the weather would make up its mind. This morning had to be thirty degrees colder than yesterday afternoon. Jake ran ahead of her and waited patiently by the passenger door of her work truck.

"Not today. We're going in the Jeep." Without hesitation, Jake ran to that vehicle and waited for her by the other passenger door. His intelligence scared her sometimes. "How about we pick you up some dog food?" she asked as he jumped onto the seat.

The only place dog-friendly at that hour of the morning was Saddle Ridge Feed & Tack. She wasn't out of food yet, but she would be by the end of the week. Apparently, half the town had the same idea because the parking lot was almost full. Jake sat still so she could snap a leash on his collar before they stepped out of the Jeep.

A blast of hot air from the heater above the automatic double doors instantly dried her eyes as they entered the store. Jake trotted happily by her side, scanning the floor for bits and pieces of kibble and grain that inadvertently fell out of bags when people brought them up to the register.

"I have a bone to pick with you, Miss Grace," a man said from behind as they were turning down the dog food aisle.

"I beg your pardon." The hair on the back of her neck rose as she spun on him. Garrett. He glared at her with his arms folded across his chest and a scowl the size of Montana plastered across his face. "Oh, hey." Garrett's expression didn't change, nor did he move. "Okay, I'll bite. Why do you have a bone to pick with me?"

"I took your advice, and I spoke to my brother this morning."

"Judging by the look, I'm assuming your conversation fell on deaf ears."

"Oh, no." Garrett tilted back his hat. "Dylan thought it was a great idea."

"So that's good, right?" Garrett shook his head. "It's not good?" Delta wasn't following.

"He put me in charge of the Valentine's week couples-only retreat I told you about last night."

"Ew." Delta wouldn't want that job. "I don't understand. Why isn't Emma planning the retreat? I thought she was running the guest lodge."

"Her daughter's only four weeks old and Emma's not ready to work full-time yet. She's been handling all the marketing from home. She got local TV and radio stations to advertise the retreat in exchange for placing their advertising on our revamped website. Plus, she's planning a wedding. So instead of Dylan putting me in charge of the lodge and having her work on this, they thought it would be great for me to organize all the events, work with the chefs on creating the menus and sprucing the place up so it looks more romantic. All on a tight budget."

"Don't take this the wrong way, Garrett, but you don't exactly scream Mr. Romance." Delta carefully chose her words, not wanting to add insult to injury. "Let's put it this way, a couples-only retreat requires a more feminine touch. I'd think Emma would want to handle that herself."

"I got the impression Dylan's afraid she might make things too sophisticated. It wasn't all that long ago when her plans for the ranch involved turning it into a high-end resort."

"I remember your uncle Jax telling me about that. I never could envision those changes for Silver Bells."

"Neither could Dylan, which is why he fought so hard to keep it. This event is a soft reopening of sorts." Garrett rubbed the back of his neck. "We haven't had any bookings since the first of the year, since Jax had planned to sell the ranch. His death threw everything into a frenzy. Emma sent out a newsletter to everyone on our mailing list to let them know we weren't closing, but we don't reopen until February 1. This Valentine's event sets the tone for the couples-only vacation packages we plan to start offering."

"All the more reason for you not to handle it."

"This retreat has to appeal to men and women. Silver Bells has always been a family guest ranch and that's great in the summer. Newer ranches took a huge chunk of our business. The romantic getaway aspect would be something they don't have, especially when most of our competition is closed during the winter months."

"I still don't see where you come in."

"Emma's goal is to add at least one couples-only week or weekend a month depending on the time of year, but if we don't appeal to the male client, the concept fails. Dylan doesn't want to contradict his soon-to-be wife's ideas, so he put me in charge to eliminate them from the equation. Much to Emma's dismay."

"That's a lot to take on alone. Can't you get somebody there to help you?"

"Oh, somebody's going to be helping me. You."

"Me? Why me?" Delta held up her hands in protest.

She refused to play any part of someone else's romantic vacation. "I hate Valentine's Day."

"Yeah, you and me both. Your advice got me into this mess and you're going to help me clean it up. That's what friends are for."

"Garrett, I don't have a romantic bone in my body." He'd have better luck with Jake helping him.

"Well, you better find one. You better find lots of romantic bones because I don't have a lot of time to get everything planned and ordered before February 10 when the retreat begins. We already have regular guests coming in a few days from now."

Delta quickly did the math in her head. "The tenth is only two weeks from now."

"It sure is, sweetheart. So—" Garrett wrapped his arm around her shoulder. "What are your plans for the rest of the day?"

"Apparently, I'm planning a romantic Valentine's retreat with you." She forced a smile. "I just have to pick up a few things and then I will meet you in your office."

"Make it my house. I'd like at least one day away from my office. The kids won't be home until later tonight and we'll have room to spread out. If we need to go up to the lodge, we can. I'll wait and you can follow me home."

Great. Delta hefted a bag of dog food into her arms. Just what she needed. Being alone, in a house, with a man she was trying to convince herself not to fall for. Her and her big mouth.

Garrett checked the rearview mirror to make sure Delta was still following him and hadn't decided to make a break for it. Not that he could blame her. He didn't know any sane single person who would want to plan for a couples-only Valentine's retreat. And it irked him that Dylan even thought this was a good idea.

He didn't want to think about Valentine's Day. He didn't want to think about love and romance. He didn't want to think. He just wanted to do *real* ranch work. Hard work that left him too tired to think at the end of the day. That had been part of the reasoning behind moving to Saddle Ridge.

Silver Bells had offered him a clean slate. Rebecca had visited Jax's house and the lodge, but she'd never been in this house. He didn't picture her sitting on his couch or lying in his loft bedroom. He didn't see her standing at the kitchen sink or having dinner at the table. His home was Rebecca free and that hurt equally as much as his need for that freedom.

He parked in front of the house and waited for Delta and Jake. He wanted to make a joke about the mission they were about to embark upon, but his mouth became cottony dry as they climbed the front steps. Maybe taking her to his house wasn't such a hot idea. There wasn't anything wrong with two friends working on a project together, because they were just friends.

Just. Friends.

Yep, that was why he'd almost kissed her at the skating rink. And guilt from that had kept him up most of the night. It didn't matter that Rebecca had given him her blessing to move on after she was gone. It felt like a betrayal. And he was a fool for even thinking Delta would want anything romantic to do with him. She was single and beautiful. She could have any man she wanted in town. She was also standoffish. The reality was, he didn't know anything about her beyond her dog and her working for the ranch. He sensed she had a story to tell. There had to be some reason she didn't like mixing friendship with work. It was an extreme response. And Garrett knew all about extreme.

He silently held the front door open for her. She white-knuckle gripped Jake's leash as she cautiously stepped inside, as if uncertain what she might find. He had spent a few hours cleaning up last night, trying to burn off his guilt. The house bordered on spotless, his conscience on the other hand did not.

He closed the door behind them and hung his hat on the hook beside it. "I hadn't thought to ask if you had eaten yet. We could've stopped somewhere on the way and picked up something to bring back. Or I can fix breakfast. If you're okay with bacon, eggs and toast. It's about all I have. Unless you're a vegan like Belle and Ivy, then I can offer you toast and blueberry jam. Or, if you'd like something else, I can run back into town."

Delta and Jake stood frozen in the middle of his living room staring at him with their mouths open. Jake looked up at Delta and then to Garrett and back. She unclipped his leash and nodded. The dog crossed the room and sat in front of him, before lifting his paw and waving. He couldn't help but smile at the gesture. He knelt in front of Jake and scratched the dog behind both ears.

"You did that on purpose, didn't you?" he asked Delta.

"You needed to breathe." She smiled warmly at him. There was no judgment. No fear. Just friendship. And that meant everything right now.

"Thank you. I know this might sound weird but you're the first non-relative female to come into my home."

"Nah, it's not weird. I get it. I've been divorced for almost three years and I still haven't had a man over to my place. Friend or otherwise. What you're feeling is normal. Believe it or not, we're normal."

Now there was something he hadn't known. She'd been married before. And divorced. That must be the bad breakup she'd mentioned their first night together at the Iron Horse.

"Speak for yourself. I haven't felt normal in years." He stood and walked to her. "Here, let me take your jacket, unless you want to get something to eat in town."

"Whatever you're more comfortable with. But by the time we drive there and back we would probably waste over an hour or more. I'm brave enough to try your cooking." She eased out of her jacket and handed it to him. "What can I help you with, because I insist on helping."

"How about you start on the eggs while I defrost the bacon." Garrett led the way to the small but functional galley kitchen. "There's a fresh loaf of bread on the counter if you don't mind slicing it. The knife is in the butcher block next to the sink."

"This wouldn't happen to be Belle's bread, would it?"

"Yes, it is. She's been on a bread-making kick ever since she got pregnant."

"Oh, my God, I love Belle's bread. She gave me a loaf a few weeks ago and I am not ashamed to admit I had intended to share it with my family, but I wound up eating half the loaf on the way to Missoula. It was so good, I didn't feel like sharing the rest with them, so I ate the other half on the way home."

"Should I make the whole pound of bacon, then?"

"Hey, now." She swatted him on the shoulder. "I don't eat that much. I mean I could, but I try not to. Unless it's something really good."

Garrett watched her remove the eggs from the refrigerator and set them on the counter. She opened the glass-front cabinet, grabbed a ceramic mixing bowl and began cracking eggs into it. She looked natural standing in his kitchen. And he found that comforting and scary at the same time.

"Garbage disposal or trash can?"

"I'm sorry, what?" Garrett stepped around her to get the bacon out of the freezer.

"Do you want the shells in the trash can or do you have a garbage disposal?"

"I have a disposal, but Belle composts everything and asks us to keep all scraps." He opened the fridge and removed a large covered coffee can and sat it on the counter next to her. "The shells go in there. I'll drop it off later when I pick up the kids."

"Your family is really close, isn't it?"

"Yes and no." Garrett unwrapped the bacon, set it on a plate and popped it in the microwave. "Harlan, Dylan and I are. After our other brother—Ryder—went to jail for running over and killing our father, the family kind of split in half." He stabbed the buttons on the front panel, causing the entire microwave to slide backwards and bang into the backsplash.

Delta gasped. "That's terrible."

"Supposedly it was an accident, but Ryder was drunk and they were arguing." Garrett sighed. "I still don't know what to believe."

"I can't even fathom what that must be like for you and your family. What about your mom?"

"She moved out to California and remarried. My youngest brother, Wes, stayed on the road bull riding most of the time until he moved to Texas a few weeks ago. And Rebecca and I moved out to Wyoming."

"Were you happy there?"

Garrett ran his hands under the faucet and dried them, willing himself to talk about Rebecca without breaking down.

"We found out Rebecca had pancreatic cancer shortly after my father died."

"Oh, Garrett. I am so sorry." She lifted her hand to reach for him, then hesitated. This was the one time he wished she followed through.

"And then she was gone. I had two major deaths within two years. I didn't really know what to do or where I belonged, so that's when I moved in with my in-laws. And then here." Garret checked the remaining time on the microwave "What about you? Do you have a big family?"

"My mom, dad and my two brothers—Trevor and Cooper—live in Missoula. None of the kids are married and none of us have kids of our own. It's just the five of us."

"Earlier you said you had been married. Mind if I ask what happened?"

Delta stiffened at the question. "My husband cheated on me while I was battling cancer."

Garrett felt as if someone had kicked him in the gut and then sucked all the air out of his body. "You had cancer?"

Delta randomly opened and closed drawers until she found a whisk and then began furiously beating the eggs. "I had stage IIIb Hodgkin's lymphoma."

He reached for her hands and stilled them. She turned toward him and looked up. Tears brimmed her eyes, threatening to spill at any moment. "Why didn't you tell me this earlier when I told you about Rebecca?"

"Because you needed someone to listen. And I didn't want you to think I was being selfish or trying to diminish what had happened to your wife by telling you I fought cancer, too."

"Honey, that's not selfish. Cancer is selfish. Hell, it's the greediest son of a bitch I've ever met. But telling me you had cancer is not selfish. How long ago?"

Delta stepped away from him and washed her hands in the sink. She sighed deeply before answering. "Three years ago."

Garrett felt his heart shudder. "The same time as Rebecca?"

"Please forgive me for not telling you sooner." Her voice cracked as she gripped the edge of the sink. "I just didn't think you would want to hear that I had survived when the person you love more than life itself had died."

"Oh, Delta." He grabbed her hands and held them. "Rebecca died so Bryce could live. We found out she had cancer when she was six weeks pregnant. The doctors gave her options. And she chose life—Bryce's life over her own."

Delta pulled away and covered her mouth with her hands. "She made the ultimate sacrifice."

"She did and there was nothing I could do about it. I begged—I begged her to terminate the pregnancy and start treatment immediately. She refused. Do you know how guilty I feel whenever I look at my son?"

"Oh no, no, no, no. You can't think that way. You're allowed to want your wife to live."

"If she had listened to me, he wouldn't be alive but she would." Garrett sniffled and wiped at his eyes. "It's a sickening feeling. She wouldn't allow me to make any decisions. Rebecca made her choice and I had to accept it and pray. But some prayers don't get answered."

"But mine did." Delta choked back a sob. "Rebecca's should have, too."

"Her prayers were answered. She gave birth to a healthy child that she got to love for sixteen months. By the time she gave birth and started chemo it was too late. The cancer had already spread too much. But that was her choice. Your choice was to fight to survive and that's exactly the way it should be. Please don't think for even one second that I would have wanted you two to trade places. I would never think that, Delta. Never."

"I'm so sorry this happened to you." The tears she had fought so hard to keep in check streamed down her cheeks. "I'm so sorry."

Garrett wrapped her in his arms and held her tight. "I'm sorry, too." He buried his face in her hair, and for the first time in years, he allowed himself to cry.

Chapter 8

Delta ran into the Silver Bells stables a half hour late on Tuesday. She was scheduled to meet with Lydia Presley to review Lightning Bug's new scans. She had purposely scheduled the appointment for late afternoon so she could take care of customers and meet with various vendors about the guest ranch's Valentine's event first. She had only been helping Garrett a few days and she already wanted to strangle Cupid more than she had before Garrett had roped her into helping him.

"I am so sorry. I got tied up." Delta dumped her tote bag on the floor outside Lightning Bug's stall.

"No biggie. I'm just pulling the images up on the screen now." Lydia eyed the fabric swatches and bridal magazines spilling out of the top of Delta's bag. "Are you getting married?"

"Who, me? Oh, hell no. Never again."

Lydia almost dropped her iPad at the comment. "Then what's with the bridal stuff?"

"They're for Garrett."

Lydia tilted her head to get a better view of the top magazine's cover. "I don't think a gown that low cut will look good on him. He doesn't have the cleavage to pull it off."

"Very funny." Delta tried to push the magazines down farther in the bag, but it had already reached its maximum capacity. "We're working together on a Valentine's week event for the ranch. I'm sort of partially responsible for Dylan designating him as the event planner, so he asked me to help him."

"I bet he did." Lydia winked. "Isn't he single?"

"Not you, too."

"What?" Lydia feigned innocence. "You're single. He's single. You're planning a Valentine thing together. Does Cupid have to hit you over the head with his arrow?"

"Me and Cupid had a falling-out a long time ago. Besides, Garrett isn't ready to date, which is why I've taken on so much of the responsibility. He's having a hard time with this. It reminds him of his wife. Plus, I'm not looking. This event is for people who are already together."

"Maybe they should consider a singles weekend. I could see where that would generate some interest."

"Then be my guest to discuss it with Dylan and Emma. I'm up to my eyeballs in trying to find budget-friendly ways to decorate the guest lodge and rooms for the event. I spoke to some of my friends last night and they told me to pick up some bridal magazines for romantic inspiration. I've already spoken with a few places today."

"You can rent everything from tableware to bedding nowadays."

"I already found some place settings I think will work. But I didn't realize you could rent bedding?" Garrett had given her a tour of the lodge and cabins the other day. While the guest ranch was meant to be rustic, the rooms definitely needed some freshening up. There wasn't enough time or money to replace any of the furniture, but bedding would make a huge difference.

"You can rent everything down to the pillowcases and guest towels." Lydia enlarged the first scan of Lightning Bug's hoof. "Everything looks good on this one." She loaded the next image and studied it. "A lot of resorts use rental services to avoid having on-site laundry facilities. Look up linen rental online and I'm sure you'll find a few places nearby. You may even want to call some of the ski resorts and ask who they use."

"You just gave me an idea." Delta tugged her phone out of her back pocket and typed in a quick note before returning her attention to the scans. "What do you think?"

"Your corrective shoeing is doing exactly what it's supposed to. The inflammation is down, his limp is gone. I'm really pleased with his progress."

"Great!" Delta loved her job. It was backbreaking work, but at the end of the day she made a difference in a horse's quality of life. Especially when it came to corrective shoeing. A lame horse could face death if not treated quickly and properly.

"Good afternoon, ladies." Garrett greeted them in the corridor as they exited the stall. "How is he doing?"

"By spring he should be ready to ride the trails again. We'll revisit it more then. Just keep in mind he'll never be able to work every day like he used to. Not at his age. And he shouldn't carry more than eighty pounds, but I think he'll be happy getting back out there with his friends."

"What about if we retire him and let him spend the rest of his days grazing on the ranch."

"You can do that, too. Just keep in mind this is an animal that's used to human contact. If you retire him, make sure he's still handled and touched on a daily basis. Without that interaction, he can begin to experience a form of depression, much the same way humans do when we remove physical contact from our lives."

"I will definitely make sure he is spoiled rotten." Garrett reached into the stall and rubbed the horse's muzzle. "He was one of my uncle's favorites. He would want him to be happy." He turned to Delta. "Speaking of happy, I have something that should make you the happiest woman on this ranch."

"You have something for me?" She heard Lydia giggle behind her. "You didn't have to do that."

"Yeah, I sort of did." Garrett held out his hand. "But, you have to close your eyes and I'll lead the way. I don't want you to see it until we're there."

His strong, firm grip encircled her palm. She fought the urge to entwine her fingers in his, knowing that wasn't the reason he was holding her hand. This was no different than ice skating. There was nothing romantic about it.

"What is it, what is it?" Delta bounced up and down.

"You're worse than my kids. The man told you to close your eyes," Lydia chided.

"Do you know what it is?" Delta asked her.

"No, now close your eyes," she ordered. "Take baby steps so you don't trip and break something."

"How far away is it?"

"Daddy, Daddy." Delta heard Kacey's footsteps run down the corridor. "Are you giving Delta her surprise now?"

"I sure am, sweetheart. Why don't you take her other hand and we'll guide her there together?"

A small hand slid into hers and held on tight.

She squeezed her eyes shut in anticipation as they led her around in what began to feel like circles. "Hey, what are you two up to?"

The sound of Lydia's giggling behind her confirmed what she thought. They *were* going around in circles. The stable corridor wasn't that long and they hadn't gone outside. They stopped and Garrett squeezed her hand.

"You can open your eyes now."

Delta blinked a few times to adjust to the bright overhead light. "Oh, my God!" Her hands flew to her mouth. There at the end of the stables stood a new Amish Belgian shoeing stall. The craftsmanship was exquisite. When she had mentioned the ranch getting a shoeing stall she had envisioned a very basic tubular metal enclosure, never anything this grand. She stepped onto the platform and ran her hand over the smooth white oak. She wouldn't have to hold the Belgians' hooves up any more or deal with them leaning on her while she tried to work. "This is the nicest stock I have ever seen. And the lighting?" Delta looked up at the ceiling. "I don't remember you ever having lights this bright in here."

"Those are new, too." Garrett lifted his chin proudly. "I wanted to make sure you had everything you needed to do your job comfortably."

"Maybe you should look into buying the white dress," Lydia whispered behind her.

Delta swatted her away. "This was very sweet of you, Garrett. You have no idea how much I appreciate it. Thank you." Women could keep their fancy jewelry and expensive shoes. A shoeing stall was the way to this farrier's heart.

A tinge of pink crept into Garrett's cheeks. "There's no need to thank me. I'm embarrassed we didn't have what you needed before now."

"It may not have bothered Henry, so he probably never mentioned it."

"I'm glad you did and I'm glad you're happy. It's the least I can do for all you have done for this ranch over the past year."

She knew Garrett's gift didn't have any romantic undertones, but it was by far the sweetest thing anyone had done for her in years.

His darling daughter had twisted Delta's arm into joining them for dinner. It wasn't that he minded, he just didn't want Kacey's enthusiasm to overwhelm her. Ever since Kacey had opened up to Delta about being bullied he had seen a big change in her personality. The private school had been rough at first, but she was beginning to adjust and had begun coming home from school happier. Her confidence and determination had markedly improved. Homework used to be a battle, but last night, she started working on it without any prodding from him. That had been a definite first.

School had never been easy for Kacey. She always had to work twice as hard to keep up with the other kids. Her teachers had thought it was due to a lack of focus and concentration, but Garrett knew there was more to it than that.

Kacey had just entered preschool when Rebecca got sick. She had designated herself Bryce's primary caretaker shortly after his birth. She'd been changing his diapers and feeding him before she was five years old. It was too much for a child to handle. He hadn't wanted her taking on that responsibility, but she fought him with everything she had.

Kacey had believed if she took care of Bryce, it would free up his time to take care of her mother and she could get better. Her determination broke his heart, because they knew months before Rebecca had died that she wouldn't survive. It wasn't until Belle and Emma came into the picture that she began to relinquish some of her mothering role. But he still found her in Bryce's room most mornings getting him up and dressed for preschool.

"Are you sure you're okay teaching her guitar?" Garrett asked as Delta helped him clear the table while Kacey showed Jake her and Bryce's bedrooms. "I don't want you to feel obligated, especially when my brother plays."

"I'm fine with it. I enjoy spending time with Kacey." Delta set the rest of the dishes in the sink. "But if you're uncomfortable with it, I can make an excuse to leave."

"I love the idea." Garrett turned on the faucet and squirted a few drops of detergent into the sink. "Kacey's never expressed interest in a hobby before you came along. I think you're a good influence on her. It's nice to see her be a kid instead of trying to be so strong for everyone else, including me. I haven't been the best parent. I wore my grief on my sleeve and Kacey paid the price."

Her fingers rested on his bare arm, radiating warmth

straight to his heart. "I think you're doing a remarkable job."

"Thank you." He covered her hand with his own. "I love that you're getting close to Kacey. My daughter has done a complete one-eighty since you walked into her life. I can never repay you for that."

"I don't expect you to."

Her gentle smile drew him into the depths of her charms. "You're wonderful with children, so I have to ask…have you given any thought to having any of your own?"

Delta's shoulders sagged. "Chemo destroyed any chance I had of having children." Delta raised her hand to stop him before he spoke. "Please don't say you're sorry. There's nothing to be sorry about. I made peace with it years ago. There are enough children out there in need of a good home that it makes me okay with not being able to have one biologically. I want kids and I'm prepared to do that without a partner. I just wish I didn't have to wait."

Garrett couldn't fathom being told he'd never be able to have a child of his own. The joy that came from the realization you helped create another living being was like no other. But he could also see himself loving a child that wasn't biologically his, as well.

"Why do you have to wait?"

"Adoption agencies won't consider my application until I'm cancer free for five years. And I get that. In the meantime, spending time with your kids helps fill that void. They really are wonderful children."

"But what if you got involved with someone who already has children?" Garrett froze as soon as he said the words. He hadn't meant to imply himself and he knew that was probably how it had sounded. Not that there was anything wrong with the idea, he just wasn't in the market for a wife. "I just mean there are plenty of single dads out there."

"Oh okay, because for a second there I thought you were—"

"Yeah, sorry, no. I—I don't think I'll ever be ready for that. Not with you."

"What?"

Oh crap! "I meant I'm not saying I'll never be ready for that with you. I'm trying to say I don't think I'll ever be ready, period."

"That makes me feel a little better." She started to laugh. "God, could you imagine?"

"What? Us?" Garrett pulled the drain stopper from the bottom of the sink. "I don't think there would ever be a dull moment."

Delta smiled and nodded. "That's for sure. You don't ever think about it? I don't mean us, I mean like ever with anyone?"

Garrett checked to make sure the kids hadn't wandered into the kitchen. "Rebecca told me to move on, so yeah, I do sometimes. But I don't know how to do that without feeling guilty. And maybe I'll get there someday, but I don't see it."

"You've got this, Garrett." Delta wrapped an arm around his shoulder and squeezed. "Give yourself time."

Garrett slid an arm around her waist, tugging her into a hug. "Thank you. That means a lot to me." He buried his head in her hair and held on. He hated to admit it, but he needed her strength to lean on tonight. The closer it was to the anniversary of Rebecca's death, the more he felt the need to let some of his grief go. After almost three years of keeping it inside, he needed...wanted the release.

"Can we have dessert now?" Kacey asked from the kitchen doorway as Bryce barreled past her and wrapped his arms around him and Delta, making it next to impossible for them to completely break their embrace.

"What about you, little man?" Garrett lifted Bryce into his arms, creating a makeshift barrier between himself and Delta. If Kacey had been bothered by their hug, she didn't show it. That was almost more concerning than if she had said something. He already knew how capable she was at hiding things from him. "Would you like some dessert?"

"Can I have cookies?" his son asked.

"We don't have cookies. Aunt Emma sent you home with brownies. You like brownies, don't you?"

"I thought she wasn't our aunt until she married Uncle Dylan."

Garrett shifted Bryce onto his other hip and smiled at Delta. "They're getting married in June, sweetheart. They have a baby and it's close enough."

He was already dreading the day his daughter asked him where babies came from. And considering her ever-growing attachment to Holly, he had a feeling it would come sooner than later.

He and Rebecca had expected her to ask when Bryce was born, but her mind had been more on her mother's illness than wondering how her baby brother came to be. A part of him hoped the school would beat him to it. But that was the easy way out and his daughter deserved to hear it from him first, regardless of how difficult the conversation would be.

Good Lord. The thought of that alone made him

cringe. He still felt like they were learning how to com-
municate with one another without Terry and Dawn.
He'd never had to explain anything when they'd lived
in Wheatland. It was all done for him. And that was just
as much his fault if not more than it was his in-laws'.
He still loved them dearly, but he had given them way
too much control. While he was grieving, they had kept
his life very neat and tidy. Now it was anything but.
And in a way, he liked that better. He was slowly learning that sometimes you had to shake things up to make
them better.

Garrett lowered Bryce to the floor. "Daddy's going
to finish cleaning up the kitchen and then we'll have
dessert."

"Can Delta start teaching me guitar while we wait?"

"That's a great idea." Garrett smiled at his daughter.
"You keep her busy in there so she won't forget she's
a guest in our home because she doesn't need to clean
up after us."

It would give him some much-needed distance away
from her. Twice now, he'd found himself hugging his
farrier in the kitchen. All right, his friend the farrier.
Either way, it was beginning to feel familiar. He wanted
to fight against it. He didn't want to feel anything other
than friendship toward Delta, but the more time he spent
around her, the more he looked forward to the next time.
Hell, as they were eating dinner tonight he'd caught himself thinking about what he would cook the next time she
came over. He had no right to assume she even wanted to
come back. Although, she did seem to enjoy their time
together as much as they enjoyed having her.

"Okay, okay. Message received," she said to Garrett.

"Let me grab my guitar from the Jeep and take Jake out for a potty break and then we'll start your lesson."

"Can I come with you?" Kacey asked.

"Me, too!" Bryce ran into the living room.

"Stay inside, you two. It's too cold to go out without jackets and I don't have the energy to bundle the two of you up right now. Delta is only going outside for a minute. Unless you plan on making a break for it." He winked and instantly regretted it. He was flirting and he had no right to.

"You're not going to get rid of me that easily." She winked in return. Okay, they were both flirting and maybe he didn't regret it so much after all.

For the next hour, he and Bryce colored at the table while Delta taught his daughter guitar in the living room. Kacey's million and one questions were enough to try anyone's patience, but Delta's laughter dispelled any concerns he might have. He peeked in at them a few times, and was surprised to see Kacey laser focused on the instrument. He had never seen her that interested in anything. Ever. He'd give it a few more lessons before he asked Delta to help him pick out a guitar for her birthday. More and more, he liked the idea of an instrument over a puppy. One adjustment at a time.

They were finally beginning to settle into somewhat of a normal routine in Saddle Ridge. Emma had volunteered to pick Kacey up from school every day, since the private school didn't provide bus service like the public school had. She had already been watching Bryce after preschool, now she had taken on his daughter.

The arrangement was fine for now, but he needed to find a more permanent solution. Emma would eventually be working full-time at the lodge and she would have her hands full between that and her own child. He felt as if he was taking advantage, but she said Kacey was a big help to her with Holly.

The past few days had given him hope. Hope they would survive as a family. There had been times after the move when he'd wondered if his kids would have preferred if he'd walked away and left them with their grandparents. In the back of his mind, he wondered if that had been Dawn and Terry's master plan.

When he had taken over as their ranch manager, he quickly began to lose touch with his children. He didn't bond with Bryce until he was almost a year old. Before that, in all the grief and depression, Bryce was just a baby he was responsible for. But when the fog lifted, it was as if somebody had flicked a switch. That was when he'd decided to take back control of his children. Garrett needed his kids, and his in-laws didn't want to alienate him for fear he would leave with the children. Which ultimately was what happened—not because he was angry or felt threatened. But because it was time.

"Daddy!" Kacey ran into the kitchen with an ear-to-ear smile. "Did you hear me play?"

"Yes, I did. You sounded great, sweetheart."

"My fingers are sore from pushing the strings down on the frets but Delta said I'll grow calloused after a while."

"You'll form calluses," Delta gently corrected. "Let's hope you never grow calloused."

"And Delta said she will loan me one of her guitars to play on since I don't have one."

"That's awfully generous, Delta, but are you sure you want to take that risk?" He feared his daughter would damage the hollow body of an acoustic guitar. "Maybe you should take a few more lessons first."

"I have an older travel guitar at the house that will fit her perfectly. I don't use it that much anymore. I take my parlor guitar back and forth to the convalescent home since it's smaller than the one I normally play." She smiled up at him. "It will give her something to practice on until she decides if this is what she really wants."

"Thank you." Her generosity with his kids continued to amaze him. He'd be lying if he said he didn't sometimes wonder what life would be like having her around more often. "Now, who wants brownies and ice cream?"

"I do, I do!" Bryce climbed on top of his chair.

"Be careful, peanut." Before he could even react, Delta reached over the back of the chair, lifted Bryce up and reseated him. "You don't want to fall and get hurt."

With every minute that passed, every movement she made, Garrett saw her fall in step with their lives. And while the timing was wrong, maybe someday there would be a chance of more.

"I found out not only can we rent linens and place settings, we can rent red, pink and white aprons." Delta poured coffee for her and Dylan while he unwrapped the platter of brownies and sat it on the center of the table. "But we need to get our order in right away because some of the Western designs aren't in stock locally. They'll need a few days to ship them in. I brought the catalog and swatches with me."

Garrett blew out a breath. "Great, thank you." He still hadn't forgiven Dylan for dumping Valentine's Day on him especially when it was so close to the anniversary of Rebecca's death. He'd taken notice of how careful Delta had been to keep their plans simple and tasteful. "When

I wrangled you into this, I hadn't expected you to do so much. You've gone above and beyond."

"You have your hands full with kids and work."

"You have a pretty packed schedule yourself."

"Yeah, but my four-legged child is easier to take care of."

"I want a doggie!" Bryce shouted across the table.

"Yeah, Daddy, when can we get a dog?"

Delta looked at him and started laughing. "Looks like your hands are going to be fuller than I thought." She ruffled Bryce's hair. "How about I loan you Jake from time to time. Would that make you happy?"

"Yay!" The kids cheered from their chairs.

Good save, Garrett mouthed to her.

"I'll add it to your tab." Delta set the cups on the table and grabbed a stack of napkins from the drawer near the fridge. "I also found out there's a hospitality service in Kalispell that will come in daily and handle the laundry service. I'm thinking white. Luxurious white Egyptian cotton sheets, white fluffy towels and bathrobes, and white bedding. I think the higher-end bedding will contrast the rustic wood in the rooms and cabins, giving it a Western flair without being in-your-face obvious."

"I wouldn't have chosen white, but I can picture that." A flash of the two of them sharing one of those rooms played in his mind. He shook his head to clear the thought. "Sounds great."

"I printed out some amazing menus from similar guest ranches in California. Maybe we could elevate the menu just a little bit for this event." Delta crossed the room and picked up the overstuffed tote bag she had left against the wall when she'd come in. She rummaged through it before removing a thick folder. "This should

be a great start for you and the staff." She traded him
the folder for a gallon of milk and two glasses for the
kids. "Maybe pick one thing from each menu and create
your own? The chefs may even want to add their spin
on it. How about asking them to create a special Valentine's Day menu and just use these as ideas. Delegate it
to them. They're the chefs."

He watched her lovingly tuck a napkin into Bryce's
third shirt of the day and set a small piece of brownie in
front of him before opening the ice cream. "Don't worry,
peanut, there's more where that came from." Why was
it the women in his life knew to feed Bryce in small in-
crements yet he and his in-laws had struggled with getting him to eat like a child should?

"Red roses are at a ridiculous premium." She spooned
out a scoop of ice cream in each of the kids' bowls before putting the carton away. "A friend of mine suggested white roses. They're a little more elegant, will go
perfectly with the white theme and will look beautiful
against red table linens. Oh, I know!" She jumped up and
dove into her bag again. "There is a warm red plaid linen
I saw in a catalog. Think flannel shirt. White rose cen-
terpieces would look stunning on them." She thumbed
through the catalog before finding the page, and handed
it to him. "This one. And I had three florists send me
centerpiece ideas along with pricing. Two of them said
they could provide long-stem roses every evening for
turndown service. That would be a nice touch to add to
a bed on top of your standard chocolate."

Once again, he envisioned sharing a room with Delta,
only it wasn't at a hotel. It was at home. Their home. A
home he'd never been to but one where she fluttered
around the kitchen tending to his children as she was

now. A home free of pain and filled with his children's laughter. A home with a master bedroom and a door they could tuck themselves behind at night.

"Daddy." Kacey tugged on his arm. "Delta's talking to you."

"What, oh, we don't have turndown service." Garrett pulled out a chair and flopped down on it. He didn't understand what was happening. He wasn't ready to daydream of a future with Delta. It was still too soon.

"Well, you will for Valentine's week. Figure two staff members can quickly run around and do it while your guests are dining." Delta pulled Bryce's ice-cream-covered fingers out of the bowl and wiped them off. "That's not a finger food." She gently wrapped his hand around a spoon and guided him to the bowl. "Hold it like this and take a small spoonful." She returned her attention to Garrett. "What have you found by way of entertainment?"

Garrett forced his brain to focus on the Valentine's retreat and not the loving and helpful way she attended to his kids. "Um, most of the people I contacted were already booked that week. I think anything structured will detract from Silver Bells' ambience, if we can call it that at this stage. People who come here don't expect to be serenaded while they're eating."

"So you have nothing?" she questioned.

"I just thought we could take it in a different direction. Dylan does sing-alongs in front of our big stone fireplace and I wouldn't mind adding something similar outside around our fire pit in the back. We serve hot chocolate out there at night and the guests make s'mores. A guitarist out there would be nice, too."

"I saw something online the other day about ele-

vated s'mores." Delta's face brightened with each idea.
"Some had bacon, others had strawberries. Maybe the
staff could make some sort of fancier base to replace
the Graham crackers. Maybe a cookie or even a pastry."

"You have good ideas, Delta." Kacey's chair was
inches from hers and Garrett couldn't help but smile at
the way his daughter hung on her every word.

"Thank you, sweetie." Delta gave her a quick hug.
"I wish I could take credit for all of them, but my girlfriends had a lot of ideas from when they planned their
weddings."

"Do you want to get married?" Kacey asked.

"Uh." Her eyes widened. "I'm not dating anyone, so
I can't get married."

Good save, Delta. He picked up his mug of coffee
and took a sip.

"I thought you were dating Daddy."

Garrett began to choke.

"Are you all right?" Delta smacked him on the back.
"Put your arms over your head." She grabbed his hands
and raised them in the air before he had a chance to
comply.

He continued to cough for another minute before wag-
gling his finger at Kacey. "Delta and I are just friends."

"But you bought her that gift."

"That wasn't a gift," Delta corrected. "The shoeing
stall is for work."

"And you were hugging before."

"Sometimes friends hug." Garrett scrubbed his jaw.
"Honey, I'm not dating anyone. Delta and I work together and we're good friends, but that's all." He didn't
blame his daughter for being confused. Between dinner
at Harlan's and everything else Kacey had witnessed,

even Garrett had a bit of trouble distinguishing what was and what wasn't where Delta was concerned. She fit comfortably in their lives and that reality was easily blurred while she was there. "Do you understand?"

"I guess." Kacey climbed off her chair and took her half-eaten bowl of ice cream to the sink. "Can I go try some of the notes you taught me on guitar?"

"Go right ahead." Delta's bittersweet smile helped ease the tension, but they both knew they had to be more careful.

"I've added more excursion choices to our standard winter selection." Garrett attempted to redirect the conversation back to work. "There's a dogsledding company not far from here that specializes in couples' sledding. They give lessons and send them on a romantic one-hour adventure. They gave me two dates we can book during that week."

"I'm so jealous." Delta sighed. "I have always wanted to go dogsledding."

"We should go sometime." And there went any chance of him focusing on work for the rest of the night.

Their relationship had changed without him realizing it. Ever since Delta had told him she was a cancer survivor he looked at her differently. There was a delicate vulnerability along with her strength. And that combination had awoken a part of him he thought had died with Rebecca. His heart had stirred and it had begun to beat a little brighter…for her. For a future. And that terrified him.

Chapter 9

The following day, Delta still couldn't get Kacey's comment about her and Garrett dating out of her head. She had to admit, it had begun to feel that way. And as much as she said she would never date a client, Garrett had slowly become the one exception. In her mind only. The man wasn't ready to date and who knew if he ever would be. But damned if the idea wasn't growing on her.

The morning had been relatively quiet, which she'd been thankful for. Even though she'd slept well, she was still tired. Ever since Garrett came into her life, her entire body was out of whack…beginning with her brain, which needed to be examined for even thinking about any attraction to the man.

Those kids, though…they did something to her every time she was around them. When she had offered to teach Kacey guitar, she never expected to get attached to her or her brother. But every morning since then, she'd awoken with them on her mind…along with Garrett.

He had asked her if she had ever thought about dating a man with kids, and honestly, it hadn't crossed her mind before. She'd always thought of her parenting future as a solo venture. But now…yeah, she could. She'd fallen for Bryce's cute-as-a-button charm and his melt-your-heart smile that rivaled his father's. And Kacey reminded Delta so much of herself at that age. Same love of music. Same curiosity.

On her drive home last night, she couldn't wait to see them again. She wanted to be a part of their lives and watch them grow into adults. And that was something she had no right to want. They weren't her children.

It was shortly after eleven when she left the convalescent home with Jake. She climbed in her work truck and removed her cell phone from the charger. One missed call. Garrett. She tried to ignore the double-time beat of her heart when she listened to his voice mail.

"Hi, Delta, it's Garrett. My head chef suggested we have a bakery cater some specialty pastries during Valentine's week. I have an appointment with Tiers of Joy Confectioners on Central Avenue today at twelve thirty. I don't know if you're free or take a lunch break around then, but I'd love to get your input."

The thought of tasting pastry with Garrett made her giddy. Delta wasn't a giddy girl. She should say no. But who can pass up pastry?

"How would you like to spend the afternoon at Bow-WowWowzer's?" Jake barked in recognition of the name. Delta had just enough time to drop him off at doggie daycare and change into more appropriate pastry eating attire.

She dialed Garrett's number and waited for him to answer. Instead, she got his voice mail.

"Hi, it's Delta. I'd love to meet you at twelve thirty. See you then."

Love? Why did she use that word? It was too late to do anything about it now.

An hour later, Delta parked her Jeep in front of the bakery. She scanned the street for Garrett's SUV but didn't see it. She didn't want to go in without him, although it was ridiculous not to. They might even give her an extra sample if she did. Instead, she chose to sit in her car and wait, her hands still on the steering wheel, sweating.

Why was she nervous? She was going to have her cake and eat it, too. Who didn't like that? The last time she went to a bakery for a tasting was before her wedding. Eddie had crept into her thoughts far too many times over the past couple weeks. She had successfully kept his memory at bay until Garrett appeared. The man invoked far too many feels for her to want to deal with. Yet, here she was, waiting for him.

And there he was, walking down the sidewalk toward her. She ran her palms up and down her jeans, cursing herself for not bringing her gloves. He opened the door as she reached for the handle. The perfect gentleman as always.

"Thank you for doing this with me," he said as she stepped onto the pavement. "I don't know a napoleon from cannoli. Well, I do, but—oh, you know what I mean."

Delta tried not to laugh. He was as nervous as she was and it was just dessert. They were going to eat sugar and be happy. She looked up at him, waiting for him to move. But he stood there, staring down at her.

"Um, is something wrong?" Delta examined her clothes. She'd chosen a pair of jeans and a fitted purple pullover. It wasn't fancy, but it wasn't too casual either. Nope, nothing was exposed.

"I, uh." He buried his hands in his coat pockets, only it wasn't the barn jacket he normally wore. Instead, he had on a double-breasted navy wool peacoat and it fit him beautifully. Too beautifully. She never would've chosen that cut for him, but whoever had knew what they were doing. "Never mind." He turned away and walked to the door of the bakery.

Now it was her turn not to move. Was she missing something?

"It was nothing," he said as if reading her thoughts. "I was going to ask you something. But it can wait."

Delta hated when people did that. Now she would wonder what he wanted to ask until he actually asked it.

"Hi, I'm Joy Lancaster, you must be Garrett. It's a pleasure to meet you." The woman wasn't at all what Delta had expected. She had pictured a middle-aged baker in a chef's coat, not a twentysomething stunner dressed in a black fitted flare skirt and a white short-sleeve blouse, with platinum-blond hair in glamorous '40s retro victory rolls.

"Same here. And this is Delta Grace, she's helping me decide what we'll need."

"Great. If you follow me, I have twenty different pastries for you to try in our tasting room."

Garrett looked at Delta and mouthed, *Oh my God, twenty?* Even Delta wasn't sure she could sample twenty pastries, but she was going to have fun trying. Either that or she'd explode.

They entered a small chicly decorated room located next to the kitchen. The walls were a creamy white, but the ceiling and floor were black, which gave the room a floating appearance. A white bistro table and chairs with black trim was elegantly set with fine china and real silverware. Suddenly Delta felt underdressed.

"Here, let me take your coats," Joy offered.

Garrett held out her chair, as she eyed the delectable display waiting for them.

"Let's begin with a simple macaron." Joy sat a colorful plate of delicate cookies before them. And they were anything but simple. "The lavender one is crème brûlée flavored, the orange is passion fruit with a dark chocolate center, the green is fresh mint with white chocolate and the gray is black currant."

Delta carefully sliced each macaron in half so they could each taste one. And they were exquisitely rich yet airy and light on the tongue.

"I'm already at a loss for words," Garrett said.

All Delta could do was nod. Words couldn't describe how ethereal they tasted.

"Our next selection is a cream horn." Joy set a puffed pastry covered in powdered sugar between them. "This is made with one of our flakiest pastries and is filled with apricot jam and whipped cream. We shape the horn by winding overlapping pastry strips around a cone-shaped mold."

Garrett served half the horn to Delta before sampling his half. "I don't think I've ever had dessert melt in my mouth before."

"I second that."

After tasting an éclair, palmier, galette and a slice of Linzer torte, Delta thought she had died and gone to heaven. She also didn't think she could eat another bite. Three shared slices of cake, two tarts, strudel and a chocolate profiterole later, Delta could no longer move or form sentences. She had officially reached her limit.

"Delta, you have to try this." Garrett inched his chair closer to hers as he held up a bite-size piece of Paris-Brest. The buttery choux pastry and praline-flavored cream beckoned her to open her mouth as he fed her the delicacy. The intimacy of the gesture sent her thoughts in a much different direction. She didn't know if it was the seduction of the French pastry or his closeness, but suddenly she wanted more of both.

"That's sinful and in more than one way."

"It sure is." Garrett ran his thumb over her bottom lip. "You had a little something."

She wanted more than a little something. The man was making her feel warm in places that didn't need to feel warm. At least not right now. She ached to remove her clothes and quell her increasing desire for the one man she couldn't have.

Check please! If only it were that simple. Garrett's arousal took him off guard. He was human, so an erection wasn't an unusual thing. But the desire to make love to Delta definitely was. After Rebecca, he had thought that part of his life was over. Meeting Delta had changed all that. Ever since Kacey had announced she thought he and Delta were dating, he'd started to see the potential of a future with another woman. Not just any woman. One woman. And while guilt and fear continued to creep into those thoughts, the fear of never knowing what could have been began to take control. Delta wasn't going anywhere and there was no rush, but waiting to see where their relationship went bordered on agonizing. He had already convinced her to be friends and she had unknowingly convinced him to give love a second chance, but he didn't know where to begin.

He had never really asked anyone out on a date. He and Rebecca had just happened. They had gone to school together, they had hung out together and before long, they had been boyfriend and girlfriend. He couldn't remember ever asking her to be with him. They had been a given. Dating was a foreign concept. He wanted to ask Delta out, but he didn't know how or if she would accept.

After choosing six different pastries to serve to the ranch's guests for Valentine's week, they left the bakery with one hunger sated.

Delta stopped short in front of him. "Okay, ask me."

He sidestepped her to keep from running into her. "Ask you what?"

"Whatever it was you were going to ask me before we went into Tiers of Joy. You said you would tell me later. Now is later."

"You really know how to put a guy on the spot, don't you?"

She gave him an impatient shrug. "You're stalling."

"I dreaded this tasting all day." A wave of mixed emotions surged through him. "I was afraid it would remind me of the cake tasting Rebecca and I had gone to before our wedding."

"I had the same fear. I immediately thought of my cake tasting, too. But it was different."

"Exactly." Garrett leaned against the side of her Jeep.

"It was fun and I don't think I would have enjoyed it with anyone other than you."

"I feel the same way."

"The more time I spend around you, the more chances I want to take in life."

"Okay." She folded her arms across her chest and stared at him.

Why was this so difficult? "Life is short."

"Yes, it is." She closed the distance between them and entwined her fingers in his. "It's okay to talk about her if that's what you want."

"That's not what I want." Garrett placed her hands on his chest and covered them. He looked skyward and prayed Rebecca wouldn't hate him for what he was about to do. "Um, I have never asked a woman out before."

There. He'd said it. It was out in the open.

"Oh." Her body stiffened.

Oh? That's all she had. She could have at least let him know if she was open to the idea.

Delta drew in a breath and released it before speaking. "Well?"

"Well what?" His mind whirled at her curt question.

"You can't just drop a bomb on someone like that. I get that you've never asked someone out based on what you've told me about you and Rebecca. But you haven't told me who you want to ask out."

Either Delta was blind or he was horrible at asking a woman on a date. "Delta." He gently squeezed her hands. "I'm asking you…will you go out with me?"

She let out a soft sigh of relief. "For a second there I thought you were going to ask me to help you ask someone else out."

"No, Delta. There's no one else but you." He stared at her in disbelief.

"Are you sure you're ready to date again?" Delta bit her bottom lip before looking away.

He hooked her chin with his finger and angled her face toward his. "Only if it's with you. I'm tired of this permanent sorrow weighing me down. I want to feel alive again, Delta. And I want to feel it with you."

She regarded him carefully, making him even more nervous. "But you've been extremely closed off to the idea, so please understand my hesitation."

"Last night was an eye-opener. My daughter had automatically assumed we were together and she was all right with it. When I saw you with my kids and in my house, everything clicked. It felt right. For the first time in three years, I felt good and that was because I was there with you and the kids. We were this complete package and after you left last night, I missed you."

"And the guilt?" Her voice softened.

"I'm not going to lie and say it's not there, but it's not as strong as I thought it would be. I'm beginning to see things differently. I know you have a rule about not dating customers and I'm not asking you to make any commitment past one date."

"What if it doesn't work out?" Concern etched across her face.

"Then we go back to being friends. It won't change our business relationship. I'd like to think I'm mature enough to separate that from my personal life. I would hope you'd do the same."

"What did you have in mind?"

"Oh, no you don't." Garrett shook his head. "You're not getting any details until you give me an answer. This is the last time I'm asking… Delta Grace, will you go out with me?"

Heat visibly rose to her cheeks. "Yes, I will."

"Then let me take you horseback riding this afternoon, before the ranch opens for business tomorrow. There's something special about riding when no one else is around. I know it's still chilly out, but it's warmer than it's been all week." He smiled gently. "And if we're both still comfortable with the idea afterwards, maybe we can get a drink. I'd offer you dinner but I'm not sure either one of us will be hungry tonight after eating pastries for the last hour." Delta laughed at that. "Think of it as baby steps for both of us. You're uncertain about bending your rules and I'm uncertain about opening my heart."

The more Garrett tried to convince her to say yes, the more things he wanted to share with her. Not just around the ranch. Parts of his life and his family. And for the first time, he was thinking about removing his wedding ring.

"Don't you have to work, especially with the ranch reopening tomorrow?"

"I'm the boss. They can do without me for a few hours, plus if there's an emergency I'll have my phone on me."

"I'd love to." Delta stood on her toes and kissed him softly on the cheek. And somehow that one sweet kiss meant more to him than any make-out session ever would. There was hope, happiness and the chance of a future all rolled in that one tender gesture. And already his heart felt fuller than it had in years. He could only imagine what their next kiss would bring.

Chapter 10

Delta's hands shook as she followed Garrett back to Silver Bells. Why was she so nervous? It wasn't like they had never been alone together. It just hadn't been anything beyond friendship. A date meant there was a kiss or something more intimate to come. Although Delta had always considered kissing quite intimate. And while she had initiated the peck on the cheek, she couldn't help but wonder what a full-on kiss would feel like. It wasn't the first time she'd wondered that either.

She giggled, filling the interior of her Jeep with girlish laughter. Garrett made her feel more feminine than any man ever had. And that included Eddie. Garrett had an innocent soul. His heart may be jaded, as was hers, but there was a raw pureness about him she'd never experienced before.

"Welcome to our first date," Garrett said later as he led her through the stables to Lucy's and Desi's stalls.

"We're riding the Belgians?" She squelched a tiny shriek of joy. When Garrett asked Delta to go riding with him on the ranch, she'd never expected to ride one of the Belgians. She had admired the breed her entire life, but hadn't had the opportunity to sit astride the magnificent animal. She knew their strength firsthand from working on them, but riding would be an entirely new experience.

She waited eagerly as Garrett saddled the horses. Weighing in at a ton each, they were almost double the weight of her quarter horses back in Missoula and eight inches taller.

"Would you like a leg up?" Garrett offered his hand and she appreciated the boost into the saddle. After eating all those pastries, she didn't think she'd manage to mount without it.

They rode silently across Silver Bells, until they reached the far edge of the property, a ridge overlooking the entire town. "It's stunning here." Delta reined her horse alongside Garrett. "I didn't realize the ranch had this kind of view. And there's my house!" She pointed in the distance. Although it looked more like a dot compared to the newer and larger homes being built on the land behind it.

"Come with me," Garrett said as he eased down from his saddle. He took her hand and led her over the hard-packed snow. "Once the ground thaws, we'll start building a gazebo here. Dylan designed it as a wedding present for Emma. They'll be the first of many to recite their vows and begin their lives together on this very spot."

"What a beautiful place for a wedding." Delta spun around, taking in the Swan Range and Mission Mountains off in the distance. As the sun began to dip lower in the Montana sky, she snaked both of her arms around Garrett's arm and gave it a squeeze. "Despite what you said the other day, you really are a romantic."

"I like to think I still have a few tricks up my sleeve." Garrett slid his arm out from under hers and wrapped it around her shoulders. "See, taking a ride with me wasn't so bad."

"I didn't think it would be bad, I just had to be sure this is what you wanted."

"What do you want, Delta?" His deep voice whispered against her ear, sending a delightful shiver down her spine.

She lifted her eyes to his. She had a fervent need to kiss him. To feel his mouth upon hers, but she refused to make the first move for fear he wasn't ready. The back of his fingers lightly grazed her cheek as her heart thudded in excitement, his gaze equally as soft as his caress. Her fingers ached to touch him, to hold him closer and explore what lay beneath the warm flannel of his shirt.

"You've affected me in a way I never thought possible." He lightly swept the hair away from her neck and kissed it ever so gently. Just one kiss that left her longing for more. "Is it okay that I touch you?"

"Yes." His nearness gave her comfort and made her body ache with desire at the same time.

"Is it okay if I kiss you?" His breath was hot against her cheek.

"Please," she whispered as his mouth covered hers. His lips gently caressed hers, sending spirals of desire coursing through her veins. "Garrett." Delta's voice was barely audible above her ragged breathing. "I've never been kissed like that before."

"You deserve to be kissed thoroughly every day, all day." He sighed and rested his forehead against hers. "I don't know where this will lead, but I want to find out. Are you willing to take a chance with me?"

"Yes, are you?"

"Yes." Garrett shifted, allowing the length of her body to press against his. His desire was evident both in his eyes and physically. "I want this, Delta. I want you."

She knocked his hat to the ground and buried her hands in his hair, fighting every urge to wrap her legs around his waist. She'd felt passion before, but nowhere near this intense. And never this strong. He enveloped her in strength, melting any resolve she once had.

He unzipped her jacket and slid his hands beneath her shirt, exploring the hollows of her back before settling on her waist. She yearned for them to caress every inch of her body. She arched against him, silently begging.

"I want you," he whispered against her mouth. "I want to make love to you until the sun comes up."

And she wanted him, too. She wanted to feel the length of him inside her. She wanted him to touch the very core of her soul. And as much as she didn't want to stop, she knew it was too soon. For both of them.

"Garrett, we can't. Not yet." His wounded gaze implored hers for an explanation. "When you make love to me, I want you to be a hundred percent certain. I want us both to be. Twenty-four hours ago, we both said this was impossible. I don't want to rush anything. And I don't want to ruin anything."

"Oh, I definitely plan on taking my time with you."

Delta's knees began to weaken. One arm wrapped

around her for support while his fingers continued to explore under her clothes. They seared against her flesh despite the cool air around them. As he reached the band of her bra, he searched for a clasp, pleased when he found one in the front. With a flick of his thumb, he freed her breasts. Her breath caught in her throat as he lifted her shirt, exposing her to him. The Montana breeze hovered just above freezing as it danced across her nipples, hardening them further. His rough hands claimed her breasts, covering them completely with his palms. Sliding her sweater up, he bent forward and allowed his tongue to caress them, slowly taking each one into his mouth as he teased her to the very edge of desire.

"Garrett, if you keep this up, you're going to make me—"

"I know." He returned his attention to her mouth, his lips more persuasive as his tongue parted her lips. His fingers trailed down her abdomen, seeking the button of her jeans. She knew she should stop him, but she was powerless against the anticipation. He slowly eased her zipper down. Breaking their kiss, his eyes met hers as his fingers slid between her folds. He watched her as she rode the first wave of release, exciting her further. His rhythm powerful and firm, he sent her over the edge a second time, as his eyes raked every exposed inch of her body. She felt electrified, giving herself to him so freely out in the open. "And that's just the beginning of what's to come once I do make love to you. And we will make love, Delta."

"Are you sure you can't stay for dinner?" Garrett asked as he unsaddled Lucy and Desi. "Dylan and Emma would love to have you join us."

"Thanks for the invite, but I need to pick up Jake and stop by my friend Liv's house." Delta slid the saddle blankets off the Belgians' backs and followed Garrett into the tack room. "She's expecting triplets and is having a difficult time with her pregnancy."

"Liv Scott?"

"Yes, you know her?"

"I know her and her sister Jade. Wes is good friends with Liv." He removed two polar fleece coolers from the wall and started to laugh. "He moved to Texas shortly after she announced her pregnancy. You don't think?"

"Good heavens, no." Delta grabbed a hoof pick and a curry comb from the shelf and walked back to the horses. "Liv used an anonymous sperm and egg donor. Your brother's off the hook."

"I'm relieved, but in a way, I wish we had triplets running around the ranch." Garrett draped Lucy in a cooler-coat to help wick the moisture away from her skin. "Babies liven up a place. Oh, Delta. I'm sorry. I completely forgot."

"No, it's fine. I'm fine." She began brushing the snow from both horses' legs. "Liv was in a similar position. She couldn't conceive either. Through donors, she found a way to have the children and the family she wanted without a husband or complications, for the most part. She's in the middle of her second trimester and despite the all-day nausea, she and the babies are healthy." Delta attempted to lift one of Lucy's front hooves. "Come on girl, we've been working on this for a year. Lift for me." Reluctantly the horse obliged so Delta could clean the snow out of her winter shoes, and Garrett noticed how much she leaned on her, reconfirming he'd made the right decision purchasing the Amish shoeing stall. "In two years, it will be my turn."

"Could you carry if you wanted to?" Garrett winced at his own question. "I'm sorry, that was way too personal."

"It's all right." She cleared the snow from the center of the snow pad sandwiched between the snow-tire-like shoe and the animal's hoof. "I have the same options as Liv. I can carry a donor embryo, but I've chosen not to. Plus, I can't afford it and my insurance doesn't cover it. Maybe if I was married and my husband wanted a child, then I would consider it, but it's difficult being a pregnant farrier. I know one woman who shod up until the day she delivered, but she had an apprentice handling her rasping and shaping. It's not the safest job, especially when you're dealing with the hind legs. Plus, the downtime after delivery. And that's even longer when you have a cesarean." She moved on to Desi's hooves. "If it hadn't been for the cancer and my divorce, I probably would've continued to work for my father until I had a family, then I would've branched out on my own. But life's not perfect and when I examined my available options, I decided on adoption. Now it's a waiting game. I'll get my turn. I'll have my kids."

"Hopefully you'll have someone special by your side so you don't have to raise a child alone," he said after the horses were in their stalls. "It's not easy being a single parent."

"If I find the right person, then I would love to raise a family with them."

"How will you know it's the right person?"

She regarded him for a moment before answering. "How does anyone know they're with the right person?

I thought I had married the right person. Maybe if the circumstances had been different, we would still be together, but we're not. I don't think you ever truly know. At some point, you just have to have faith."

Garrett walked her outside, not wanting to say goodbye. He wanted to know more about her and her life before Saddle Ridge. "I wish you could stay, but a pregnant friend with triplets comes before a cowboy any day. Tell Liv I said hello."

"I will, and thanks for the ride. I really enjoyed it."

"It was my pleasure." Garrett tried not to laugh at his ironic choice of words.

"No, I think it was mine. But thanks for that, too." She winked and opened the Jeep's door.

"Not so fast." Garrett braced an arm on either side of her head. "I want one more for the road." He pressed his lips gently against hers. The touch alone was a sensual sensation. One that would get him in trouble if he continued, especially in front of the ranch's stables. "Call me later?"

"I will."

Garrett checked his watch. If he didn't hurry up, he'd be late for dinner. He hopped in his truck and drove across the ranch to Dylan and Emma's. Just as he took the first step up to their front porch, he heard the sound of snow crunching behind him.

Garrett spun around and lurched in its direction.

"What the hell, man?" Dylan stumbled backward, almost falling to the ground.

Garrett laughed. "Don't give me that crap, big brother. You were going to do the exact same thing to me. I just beat you to it."

"Shut up." Dylan punched him in the arm. "I figured your head would still be in the clouds after that kiss goodbye."

Now he was the one turning red. "Didn't Mom ever tell you it's not polite to spy on people?"

"Didn't Mom ever tell you to keep the public displays of affection to a minimum?"

"Oh, you should talk. From what I heard, you practically courted Emma from the day she arrived."

"Hardly the truth. She wanted my ranch and any cordiality I had showed was because she was pregnant."

"Yeah, that the only reason?" Garrett had missed taunting his brothers while he lived in Wheatland. His life would never be the same without Rebecca, but he was realizing it was all right to enjoy what he had.

"Bet you're still slower than me." Dylan raced him up the stairs.

The front door swung wide. "Are you two going to stand out here acting like a couple of kids or are you coming in for dinner? Because if not, the four of us will eat without you."

Garrett and Dylan looked at each other and laughed. "Oh my God, I think my fiancée just channeled Mom."

"Speaking of Mom, have you heard from her lately?"

"Not since Christmas. You?" Dylan closed the door behind them as they kicked off their boots.

"It was sometime after New Year's, but not much later than that. I told her we had moved and she almost sounded disappointed that I'd come back to Saddle Ridge."

"When she left, I thought she was running from Dad's death, but it didn't take her long to sell the ranch and hook up with Artie."

"Artie is okay." Garrett shrugged off his coat. "He's

not the sharpest knife in the drawer but he genuinely cares about Mom. Mom doesn't want the memories of this place and I can't blame her."

"I keep waiting for it to go back up for sale," Dylan said.

"Why? Would you really buy that place back? Ryder killed Dad there."

"Ryder accidentally ran over Dad and he died."

"They were fighting and Ryder ran him over. However you look at it, Ryder was behind the wheel and Dad died. That's a hard thing to forgive and it's even harder to forget."

"It's in the past. And it looks like the two of us have a great future ahead."

It was looking brighter every day. The pain of losing Rebecca would never fade, but he was learning how to handle it better by allowing himself to be happy again.

Maybe Cupid wasn't so bad after all.

"It's about time you came to see me." Liv gave Delta a hug. "And hello there, Jake." She scratched the top of his head. "I'm glad you came to see me, too."

"I'm sorry. I've just been busy between work, the convalescent home, running back and forth to see my parents and—" Delta cut herself short, not sure if she was ready to talk about Garrett to Liv, or anyone for that matter. Belle was probably the one exception to that rule, but only because Belle hadn't given her much of a choice.

"Oh, no you don't." Liv eased onto the couch. "You're leaving something or someone out, and I think I know who it is."

"Yeah, okay." Delta laughed. "How are you feeling? Because you look uncomfortable."

Liv swept her long, jet-black hair up off her shoulders and held it at the nape of her neck for a second before releasing it. Her hair coupled with her feline-like emerald-green eyes was striking. "I just went to the doctor today for a checkup. We're at just over a pound each. That's three pounds of kids sitting on my bladder, kicking my ribs and poking me in places I didn't know I could be poked. This could be you someday."

"I doubt that."

"How does Garrett feel about having more kids?" Liv asked.

"We haven't tal—" Delta's mouth slammed shut. "How did you know about him?"

"You two made quite the couple ice skating the other day." Liv pulled her phone out of her shirt pocket. "I don't go anywhere without this thing anymore. I never know when I won't be able to get up. Let's see." She began swiping at the phone. "The video of you two together is on here somewhere. And it's super sexy."

"Oh, my God. Please tell me you don't have a video of us ice skating together." Delta's heart thudded to a stop.

"Fine. I don't have a video. But your reaction tells me something sexy did happen. Dish. Now."

"I will not. But he told me to tell you hello."

"Hello back. Have his boots been under your bed yet?" Liv waggled her brows.

"You are incorrigible!"

The doorbell rang and Maddie, who lived next door, walked in. "I saw your Jeep out front. Are you two having a party without me?"

Jake nudged her with his nose. "Excuse me, fuzzy butt. My mistake. Are you *three* having a party without me?"

"Since you both are here, I have something to tell you. I just finished talking with Jade about it before you came in."

"Is your sister leaving LA and moving back to town?"

Liv scoffed. "As if. Hell would have to freeze over twice for that to happen. I know I said I was going to wait, but when I was at my appointment earlier, I asked them to tell me the sex of the babies. I just couldn't wait any longer."

"You did!" Maddie bounced up and down the same way Kacey did. Only Kacey was much cuter. "What are you having?"

"Three girls." Liv beamed. "And I've already chosen their names, because I knew in my heart of hearts that they were going to be girls. How do you like Audra, Hadley and Mackenzie?"

"I love them." Delta was over the moon thrilled for Liv. She wished they were both celebrating a baby, but she was glad for her friend.

"We need to have a toast." Liv struggled to get off the couch. "I swear I'm going to have to hire a manservant just to get me up from a seated position. It wouldn't be so bad if I hadn't chosen such comfortable furniture. Everything in this house sucks you into it."

"You can't drink."

"Relax, I'm going to have apple juice and you two are having the spiced rum. I think the bottle belonged to one of you anyway. I guess we won't be having those crazy nights anymore."

As happy as Delta was for Liv, there was a touch of sadness behind those words. She had never been pregnant, but she could see why women would wax nostalgic for their former glory days.

Liv led them to the kitchen and set three rocks glasses on the counter. She added ice, then topped two off with rum and one with juice. "Here's to girl power." She raised her glass.

"To girl power." Delta and Maddie joined her and clinked glasses before sipping their drinks. "And to Delta's new boyfriend."

"Oh, you're funny." Delta took a long swallow of rum and headed back into the living room. "Garrett and I don't know what we—ow—ouch." She dropped her glass on the coffee table.

"Delta, what's wrong?"

"It's like someone's stabbing me in the shoulder and the armpit." She exhaled sharply. "Damn."

"Sit down." Maddie ushered her to the couch. "Did you do anything extraneous today?"

"No." Delta tried rubbing her shoulder. "I had one job early this morning and that was it. The rest of the day was easy."

"Here, let me." Maddie began to rub it for her. "Does it hurt when you move?"

"I don't know. I don't remember pulling it or anything." She raised her arm in the air.

"Have you lost weight?" Maddie asked as she massaged her shoulder and under her arm. "You're always thin, but you feel thin." Her friend froze.

"What's wrong?"

Maddie's fingers dug deeper into her flesh. "Delta, I feel something under your arm."

"Oh, God." Liv covered her mouth as tears filled Maddie's eyes.

Delta shook her head. "No, no, no, no. I'm sure I just pulled something. That's all."

"Give me your hand." Maddie held out hers. "You can't ignore this. Give me your hand."

Tears filled her own eyes as Maddie guided her to the middle of her armpit and pressed her fingers into her skin. Her stomach dropped as she felt it, too. Her lymph nodes were swollen. She had lost a couple pounds but she'd figured it was from working too much. That was also why she assumed she'd been tired lately. But the alcohol intolerance pain. She'd never had the symptom originally, but she was aware it existed.

"How can this be happening? My scans were clear four months ago. I can't have Hodgkin's again. I just can't."

Chapter 11

Delta had left for Missoula sometime after Garrett saw her Wednesday and he still hadn't heard from her two days later. She had sent him a text message in the middle of the night stating she had a family emergency and would call when she was able to. He had been awake when the message came in, but when he immediately called her back, it went straight to voice mail.

Normally that wouldn't have concerned him. It was her outgoing message that didn't sit right. She stated she'd be out of town for a few days and she provided the name and number of another farrier. That part was straightforward. Her shakiness toward the end of the message and the hitch in her voice when she said goodbye concerned him. And when he ran into Liv Scott in the supermarket yesterday and had asked if she'd heard from Delta, the woman couldn't get away from him fast enough. Something was wrong and Garrett believed it went way beyond a family emergency.

He'd even gone as far as asking Harlan to check all the emergency rooms in Missoula County. He found nothing. Garrett stopped short of tracking down her family. She deserved to have privacy, but that didn't mean it wasn't driving him crazy.

People had family emergencies all the time. Barring a natural disaster or inclement weather, they usually got messages to people. Garrett had left several for Delta and she hadn't returned a single one. Radio silence usually meant the person didn't want to talk.

Garrett surveyed the lodge's great room. Silver Bells had officially reopened yesterday and was bustling with guests. A Montana romance writers' group, to be exact. They seemed pleasant enough. They had taken over the great room and dining areas with their laptops but had been relatively tame. So far.

"Not a bad group from the looks of it." Dylan slapped him on the back.

"Just wait until tonight," Garrett warned. "I think you'll have your hands full."

"Nah, these women will probably pack it in early. They've been working all day."

Dylan didn't give their clientele much credit. "They are definitely looking to play later. A few of them have already asked me about the nightlife here in Saddle Ridge."

"Saddle Ridge doesn't have any nightlife, unless you count the Iron Horse."

"Exactly, I told them about a few places in Kalispell, but I still think they'll end up here, asking you to entertain them."

"You mean asking us," Dylan reminded. "We're partners now. Everything is fifty-fifty, including the entertainment."

"Well my fifty percent will be home watching three kids. I guess you forgot it's my turn to take the kids for the weekend so Belle and Harlan can have their own romantic time alone. Once the baby comes they won't have a moment's peace."

"Unless they have an angel like Holly. She hardly ever cries," Dylan mused. "I don't remember every other weekend off being a part of our partnership agreement. It's not fair to leave me to fend for myself."

"Hey, Belle and Harlan are leaving me to fend for myself."

"Yeah." Dylan scratched his chin. "You have a point there. I don't know which one of us has it worse."

"I had hoped Delta would be joining me for part of the night."

"Doesn't she usually visit her parents on the weekend?"

"Most of the time, not always." And it wasn't as if he'd even mentioned the weekend to her yet. He hadn't had the chance before she'd left with whoever she left with. He'd driven by her house. Twice. And both of her vehicles were parked around back. "Like I said, I had hoped she would join me."

"Still no word?"

Garrett shook his head.

"I won't tell you not to worry about it because we know firsthand how tragedy can strike at any minute. From the little I do know about her, she's from a very strong family and Buck Grace has always been about his kids."

"You know Delta's father?"

Dylan nodded. "It's been probably ten years, if not more. I doubt the man would recognize me. He was in town to see Henry when he shod Dad's horses. I met him on our ranch."

Garrett had no idea Delta's father had met their father, let alone on the family homestead. Not that it mattered, which just proved how small Montana really was despite its size.

According to the clock in the lobby, it was almost time to pick up Bryce and Kacey from their respective schools. Even with Emma's volunteering, he felt the inexplicable need to keep his children close.

"Good luck tonight, I need to go pick up my kids so your future wife can have a long overdue break. Watch out for some of those women. Especially the authors of some of the steamier works. I wish I could be here to watch you sing around the fire later."

"Bring the kids, that'll keep everything tame."

"Nah, man. You're on your own."

He already knew the first question out of his daughter's mouth would be about Delta. And he didn't have any answers. He had already noticed Kacey's demeanor backsliding. Delta hadn't spoken to her since Tuesday night. She never dropped off the guitar either, which Garrett was fine with, but Kacey was struggling to understand Delta's absence wasn't about her, and that they had to pray everything would be okay.

It had to be.

"Okay, Delta." Dr. Lassiter sat behind his desk Friday afternoon at the Montana Cancer Center in Missoula.

"We have the results of all your scans and the fine needle aspiration we took this morning."

Delta's parents sat on either side of her, squeezing her hands tightly, while her two brothers stood behind her for support. She already knew what he was going to say. She'd seen that look on Dr. Lassiter's face before.

"How bad?"

"Delta, don't assume the worst." Her mother attempted to comfort her.

"Stage Ia favorable. Meaning it's not bulky or in several different lymph node areas like it was the last time. Based on your scan and blood test results, I feel your fatigue and slight weight loss has been environmental and not medical. We caught this early. But—"

"Oh, God. It hurts me to hear this. It's never good when you say *but*." Her mother started fanning herself.

"Erma Jean, give the man a chance to speak." Her father turned to Trevor. "Keep her calm, will you."

"As I was saying." Her oncologist cleared his throat. "You have classic Hodgkin's lymphoma and it is highly curable because we caught it so early. You'll receive two cycles of ABVD chemotherapy, which is four treatments over the course of eight weeks, followed by ISRT, or involved site radiation therapy. You should experience fewer side effects with this course of treatment. But, Delta, I cannot stress enough that this is nothing like the last time. It's going to be difficult at times, but we will get you through this."

She wanted to cry foul. She wanted to scream. She wanted to punch something. It was bad enough to go through it once, but twice made her want to throw up her hands, look skyward and say, "What gives?" She'd never been the *why me* type of person. But twice?

And she knew—she knew other people battled far worse many more times than she had. They would be envious of her diagnosis. It was treatable. That alone made her feel guilty. She was entitled to the anger. If she held on to it, she wouldn't cry.

She wanted her pre-cancer life back. She wanted her home and her husband and the kids they had planned to have. Cancer had robbed her of that future and it had robbed Garrett of his. He was right. Cancer was selfish. How could she have even thought about getting involved with Garrett and his children. They all deserved better. It was hard enough battling cancer for yourself. It was harder when your loved ones watched you suffer through it, and you saw their pain every time they looked at you. She loved her mother, but it was easier when her mother wasn't by her side. Erma Jean wasn't strong enough. And Delta was tired of being strong for everybody else.

Trevor gently squeezed her shoulders from behind. She took a deep breath and exhaled slowly. The initial shock was out of her system. She wouldn't complain, no matter how much that pained her. Cancer sucked.

"When do I start chemotherapy?"

"Considering your history, tomorrow. Unlike last time, you will not have to return the following day to receive a chemo shot. We're using an on-body injector that will adhere to your skin and automatically administer the shot the following day so you can go home, go about your routine as much as you can. Your side effects may not be as great this time. They may be completely different."

"Will she lose her hair again?" her mother asked.

"It varies from person to person. This is lower-dose chemotherapy, so she may not lose all of it."

"That will be attractive." Delta attempted some levity.

This time she wouldn't allow cancer to take her hair. She would take it. This time she would wield the power. It was on her terms. She rubbed her forehead. She needed to hire help, an apprentice at least to help her on the days she couldn't do her job. She couldn't run a business throwing up every five minutes. She hoped the doctor was right and the side effects were less, but she had to prepare for the worst.

She also had to keep this to herself. She trusted Maddie and Liv, along with her family. If her customers found out she had cancer, she'd lose their business. Some of them already treated her differently because she was a woman. She couldn't afford any more losses. And she couldn't lose her biggest client. Knowing Garrett, he would coddle her and insist on hiring another farrier. No. Cancer would not take her life away again.

"Okay. So, uh, I guess I'll be here tomorrow to uh, do this one more time."

Delta rose from her chair, willing her legs to support her. She held out her hand to her doctor. "At least I have one of the best on my team. Thank you, Dr. Lassiter."

He covered her hand with both of his. "We will beat this, Delta."

She swallowed back the tears threatening to break free. She didn't want to cry in front of her mother and she couldn't cry in front of her father for fear they would start crying, too. She wanted to go home. To her dog. She just wanted to put this day behind her and start over tomorrow. And Dr. Lassiter was right, she would beat this. She would kick its ass all the way to the moon.

A few hours later, Delta lay on her old bed with Jake's head on her chest. She felt like a teenager waiting to be grounded. She didn't want to sit upstairs in the bedroom. She wanted to do something to get her mind off what was about to happen. But she was stuck. When she'd called her parents Wednesday night and told them about the pain and the lump, her brothers drove up from Missoula to get her. Her family was afraid she would be too upset to drive, and in hindsight, she had been. She wanted to at least go downstairs and watch television but she couldn't stand the way her parents looked at her. The pity, the sadness—everything she didn't need right now. She didn't want to wallow. She wanted to take control. She was thirty years old and stuck in her childhood bedroom.

She grabbed her phone from the night table and texted her brothers.

GET ME OUT OF HERE!

She knew they would come. She didn't care what they did or where they went. As long as they treated her normally. She hated winters in Montana. It was too cold to do anything. If it had at least been spring, she could've clipped a leash on Jake and gone for a walk into town or let Jake run in their horse pastures. She would have loved to take one of her own horses for a ride, but her mother would probably track her down and start following her five minutes later. Still, at least she would've gotten out of the house. She knew her parents meant well, it was just a little overwhelming at times.

Her phone rang and she answered it without even looking at the display. "Hello?"

"Delta, thank God. I've been trying to reach you for two days."

Delta buried her face in the pillow and screamed. She finally had a shot with a nice guy and she had to walk away. At least until she was cancer free.

"I didn't mean to worry you." She truly hadn't. In the back of her mind, she had hoped he would walk away from her and make things easier on them both. "I'm just dealing with some private family matters. I should be back to work on Monday, barring any further complications."

"I don't care about work." She sensed the annoyance in his voice. "What complications? Are you okay? Is your family okay?"

"Everything will be fine. I just needed to get home. Please tell Kacey I'm sorry for missing her guitar lessons. Is Lightning Bug still doing okay or have you had to call in the other farrier for anything?"

"Kacey will survive, she's asked about you. Everyone has asked about you. The horses are fine. And no, we haven't had to call anyone else. Why are both of your vehicles at your house? How did you get to Missoula?"

"You were at my house?" Delta wasn't sure how she felt about that. Part of her was mad that he had encroached on her personal space, the other part was touched at the amount of concern he had for her.

"My brothers picked me up."

"And that's it?"

"That's it, Garrett."

"Did something happen between us? I thought we were headed in a positive direction but I'm sensing… I don't know what I'm sensing from you but it almost sounds like you're having second thoughts."

Delta closed her eyes. She didn't want to hurt him. She didn't want to turn him away. Out of all the people in the world, she'd love nothing more than to curl up with him and hear him say everything would be all right. But she couldn't ask that of him. Not after what he had been through. She wouldn't be that selfish.

"You told me the other day that if this didn't work out, we could go back to just being friends." She pinched the bridge of her nose, not wanting to say what had to come next. "I thought about it and I'm just not comfortable with us dating. I think we're much better as friends. I have no problem helping you with the Valentine's event and I'll continue to be there for Kacey, but what happened the other day between us can't happen again."

"And here I had always been told absence made the heart grow fonder."

"I'm sorry, Garrett. I know this isn't what you want to hear. I just don't see it working out between us. We don't really know each other anyway. Maybe down the road things will be different."

"Did you seriously just give me the 'let's just be friends' speech and then hint we might have a chance later on? What am I supposed to do, wait for you?"

Yes. "I would never ask you to do that. I'm just not ready for a relationship. I thought I was, but I'm not."

There was a soft knock at her bedroom door. "Delta, it's Cooper."

"I'm sorry, Garrett, I have to go. My brother just arrived."

"Yeah, sure. Goodbye, Delta."

His words pierced her heart more painfully than any arrow ever could.

"The door's open."

Cooper strode in and flopped on the bed beside her just as he had when they were kids. Her brother was one year older than her and every bit as much a cowboy as he was a deputy sheriff. Harlan reminded her of him in many ways. Under different circumstances, the two of them would probably get along famously. But she didn't want anyone from Garrett's family involved with hers. She needed that separation.

"What's going on, chickadee?" He reached down and squeezed her hand. "Mom and Dad getting to you?"

"Everything's getting to me." Her brothers were the only people she could rely on to keep her sane. And she could trust them like no tomorrow. Jake may be her rock, but they were her foundation.

"Why don't you get your things and come stay with Trevor and me at the apartment tonight. I know Mom and Dad will want to take you to chemo tomorrow, but that's your decision. If it's too difficult having them there, then I'll say something so you won't have to."

"I don't know. I don't want to hurt Mom's feelings and tell her she can't go, but I don't want her stressed out for hours either. She'll look at people sicker than I am and think the worst is going to happen to me." Delta shook her head. "It was one thing when we went through this the first time. I'm not as sick, but they still have to pump poison through my body, which is the real reason why I called you over here. I need you to do me a favor. And I need it tonight."

Chapter 12

"Are you sure you want to do this?" Cooper stood behind her in his apartment bathroom on the other side of town from their parents' house. "The doctor said you may not lose all of it."

"What am I supposed to do? Go around looking like a patchwork quilt or buy some of that spray-on hair?" In the mirror, she saw the anguish in his eyes at what she had asked him to do. "It's okay. This isn't my first rodeo. The last time I went through chemo I bawled every time it fell out in clumps. I'm not going through that again. This is a good thing." She attempted a smile. "I still have my old wig. Shit, that thing cost almost five thousand dollars. And it's real hair. No one is going to know except our immediate family. I want to walk into that cancer center tomorrow and spit in cancer's face."

"I love you, sis."

"I love you, too."

Cooper gathered her hair in a low ponytail and tied it with an elastic band. She handed him the scissors from the bathroom vanity and nodded, reassuring him it was okay. In three swift cuts, what was left of her hair fell forward and framed her face. She continued to stare at her reflection. Part one…done. He handed her the ponytail. She took a deep breath before wrapping her finger around what used to be her hair.

They had downloaded the form from *Locks of Love* and would send in her hair along with a donation so they could create a hairpiece for a child suffering from medical hair loss. This way she didn't lose her hair to chemo. She willingly gave it to someone in need.

Take that, cancer!

"Are you sure you don't want to leave it like this?" Cooper asked. "I can take you somewhere and you can get a pixie cut. It will look cute."

Delta lifted her chin. "Do it, Cooper."

Her brother switched on the hair clippers and wiped away a lone tear before making the first pass across her scalp. She watched as he shaved every hair from her head, leaving her completely bald. Part two…done.

Screw you, cancer!

Her mom wept when Cooper and Trevor brought her home after her first three-hour chemo treatment. She probably should have warned her about the hair.

"Do you want to lay down?" her father asked.

"Not yet. The anti-nausea drugs they gave me seem to be working okay."

"Do you want something to eat?" her mother asked.

"I'm good, Mom." Now food was a trigger. She inhaled sharply. The thought alone made her feel queasy. "Let's not talk about food."

"Mom, Dad." Trevor guided her to the couch as if she had broken a leg or some other body part. "Just leave her alone and let her rest."

"Yo, bro." Delta looked up at him. "You can let go of my arm now. I'm not going to fall apart. I got this. But if you don't mind, could you grab me a bucket just in case and that bag of sour hard candies I left in the car."

ABVD chemo consisted of a noxious cocktail of four different drugs. Adriamycin, Bleomycin, Vinblastine and Dacarbazine. Adriamycin, also known as The Red Devil, attacked the cancer the hardest. It also turned urine frighteningly red and tasted like the devil's butt crack. Hard candy helped mask the taste, the stronger the better. Not much was stronger than kid's sour candy. It was vile on a good day, but a lifesaver during and after chemo.

"Are you sure you don't need anything?" Mom hovered nearby with a dish towel in one hand and a glass of water in the other.

"Mom, what are you doing?" She shook her head. "If it will make *you* feel better, give me the towel and the water."

Delta tucked the towel into the front of her sweatshirt and held the glass of water in her lap. Cooper had returned from the kitchen with chipmunk cheeks full of food. He was trying his best not to eat in front of her, but she knew he was hungry.

"Why are you wearing a towel?" he asked.

"It makes Mom feel better."

"What exactly is that doing for you?"

"Nothing, but I figured if I start drooling, I'm covered."

He sat down next to her on the couch and wrapped his arm around her shoulders as he turned on the television. "Comedy or horror?"

"Horror." She flipped up her hoodie and rested her head against him, relishing his warmth. It was one thing to be bald in the South, it was an entirely different animal being bald in northwestern Montana, in the middle of winter. "Horror means they won't try to slip a romance in there."

The last thing Delta remembered was the sound of a chain saw.

It had been six days since Garrett had last seen Delta. As much as he had tried to erase her from his thoughts, he couldn't. It didn't help that Kacey had continued to ask about her. Their breakup, or whatever she wanted to call it, still didn't make sense to him. Neither did her absence.

Garrett crested the hill in front of the stables on his four-wheeler on Tuesday as Delta entered Silver Bells' main gate. A part of him wanted to ride over and see how she was doing, but the other part told him to keep his distance. He could see her clearly enough from where he was. He didn't need to get any closer. Providing she had all her limbs intact, that was all that mattered. Whatever her emergency was, she didn't want to talk about it and he didn't need to know.

Another truck he hadn't seen before braked next to hers. No one parked at the stables unless they had business there and he had never seen the man who stepped out of the vehicle. But Delta had. Even from a distance, he could tell they knew each other well. Maybe a little too well. Was that why she'd ended things with him? Was it because of someone else?

He pushed the thumb throttle forward and rolled down the hill toward them. The stables were his business and he had a right to know who was entering them. He idled to a stop in front of them and cut the engine.

"Good afternoon, Delta." He tipped his hat to her and climbed off the four-wheeler before holding his hand out to the man who appeared much younger in person than he had from a distance. He couldn't be more than twenty years old, if that. "I don't believe we've met."

"I'm Evan, Delta's apprentice."

"Apprentice?" Garrett hadn't realized Delta had become busy enough to hire someone else. He also didn't remember her looking so pale or her hair being that particular shade of brown. It was a pretty color, but Delta didn't have that much mahogany in hers. Something was off.

Delta shifted uncomfortably under his gaze, quickly averting her eyes. "It was time for me to hire someone. It's the perfect time of year to get him up to speed while we're a little bit slower. Come spring, we'll be ready to shift into high gear and take on more clients."

Now Garrett felt like a complete fool for thinking the man was anything other than a legitimate employee. Delta wouldn't bring a man she was dating on the job. And he could tell himself he was over her all he wanted. He could tell himself they'd never had anything to begin with, but that would be a lie, too. And he could tell himself he didn't care anymore when the truth was he cared enough to know something was wrong.

"I'm available to give Kacey a guitar lesson later, if it's still okay."

"She would be thrilled if you're sure it's not a problem."

"I can't guarantee a schedule, if that's what you're getting at, but I'm pretty sure I can fit her in once, if not twice a week. I brought my travel guitar with me. I'm sorry our lesson plans got interrupted, but life happened."

"I'm leaving in a few to pick her and Bryce up. How long do you plan on sticking around?"

"I'm just showing Evan the ranch today. We're not working, so I can wait until you get home. I have nothing after this."

"Okay, I won't be long. Meet me at the house?"

Delta nodded before returning her attention to Evan.

Garrett had a sinking feeling when he walked away from her. It wasn't just the hair and her complexion. That special spark she'd always had in her eyes was missing. And maybe it was because of what happened between them, but instinct and experience told him it was much more.

Less than a half hour later, his SUV had barely stopped in front of the house before Kacey was yanking off her seat belt and attempting to open the door to jump out.

"Delta!" She dropped her backpack in the snow and ran into her open arms. "I missed you."

"I missed you, too. I'm sorry I wasn't around, I had to take care of something back home."

"I thought this was home."

"I have two homes, sweetheart. One here and one with my parents. I go back and forth between the two."

"Your hair looks pretty," Kacey said. His daughter had just confirmed his suspicions.

"Thank you." Delta ran her hand over the back of it. "I had it done when I was visiting my family."

Garrett furrowed his brow. Could he possibly be reading too much into her absence? It wasn't unusual for a woman to get a cut and color. And he hadn't been around her long enough to know what her usual style was.

"Did you bring the guitar?" Kacey attempted to look behind Delta.

"Yes I did. I know you were expecting it last week, but I had to leave for a few days."

"Can I see it?"

"Why don't we all go inside first?" Garrett held Bryce's hand as his son climbed the stairs.

He unlocked the door so the kids could go in ahead of them. "Delta." He reached for her arm before she entered the house. "I know it's none of my business, but are you okay?"

"Everything is fine, Garrett."

"I'm not asking you about everything. I'm asking about you." The closer he got to her, the more he was almost positive she was wearing a wig. The average person wouldn't have noticed it. But he'd had his hands in her hair before. He knew what it looked like. He knew what it smelled like. He knew how it fell across her shoulders. He knew the way she wore it parted. Everything he knew wasn't what he was seeing. "Despite what did or didn't happen between us, I'm still your friend. I made you that promise and I won't break it. If you want to talk, I'm here."

"I appreciate it, but it's not necessary. Thank you anyway."

"Delta! Are you coming?"

She looked to him for permission. "The question is, are you still okay with me spending time with your kids?"

"As long as you don't break their hearts."

"I wouldn't think of it."

"Just so you know, Dylan had tried teaching her to play and it didn't go so well."

"Why not?"

"He wasn't you."

"Kacey, what do you say to Delta?" Garrett asked after her lesson.

"Thank you. I will take very good care of it until I get my own guitar." Kacey looked up at him with her big doe eyes. "I will get one, won't I?"

"Maybe Santa Claus will bring you one."

"Santa? Christmas is a long way away."

"You don't want to wait that long? Hmm." Garrett tapped his temple. "I wonder what kind of occasion would call for a gift like a guitar."

"Kacey's birff-day!" Bryce shouted from the kitchen table. "Right, Kacey?"

"I don't know what he's talking about." Kacey feigned innocence. "But maybe that's a good idea."

"We'll see. You have to be a good girl in the meantime."

Delta closed the guitar case and stood it against the fireplace before grabbing her tote bag. "I hate to cut out on you already, but Jake and I have to get to a birthday party at the convalescent home."

"Can I go with you?" Kacey asked.

"If it's okay with your father." Delta looked over his daughter's head at him.

"Thanks for putting me on the spot." He narrowed his eyes. "I think there's too much sadness there."

"Daddy, have you been there before?" Kacey asked. "How is a birthday party sad?"

Delta crossed the room to him. "It might be good for her to see that not all sick people die," she whispered.

"Yeah, sometimes they just struggle silently without realizing there are people around them who truly care," he bit out in return.

Delta's body physically stiffened at his remark.

"Kacey, honey." Garrett refused to break eye contact with Delta. "Go clean up if you're going to a party."

"Yay, I'm going to a party! I'm going to a party!" Kacey sang as she ran out of the room. "I'm going with you, Jake."

"You can take her with you." Garrett leaned closer to her. "But if I lower my guard for you, then I expect you to do the same. You can hide your secret from everyone else…not me. I know. And I'll wait patiently for you to tell me the entire story. I'll wait."

"You don't know a thing about it."

"I know everything about it. I know the devastation. I know the pain. I know the sickness. And I know you need support now more than ever."

"I washed my hands and face, Daddy."

"Did you brush your teeth?" he asked. Bryce climbed off his chair and ran into the bathroom.

"I'm going to the potty," he mimicked his sister and slammed the door.

"Bryce, let your sister in there. She needs to go." Garrett chased after him and jiggled the doorknob. It was locked.

"I'm going to the potty," Bryce continued to sing

from the other side of the door, followed by the sound of trickling water and a flush. He heard the wooden step in front of the toilet scrape across the floor, and then the basin faucet turn on.

"Apparently I have one going to a party and the other going to the potty." Garrett leaned against the doorjamb waiting for his son to emerge.

The knob jiggled and then the door opened. "I went to the potty." Bryce shuffled past the three of them in stocking feet and climbed back into the chair.

Garrett clapped his hands loudly. "Good job, buddy, but stop locking the door. Kacey, teeth, now. Delta, we're talking later when you return."

"Fine."

"Fine."

Delta felt physically sick during their drive into town, but it wasn't from the chemo. Cooper had driven her home Sunday morning and had stayed until early Monday before heading straight to work. Out of the three of them, her older brother was the most even-keeled and self-disciplined. As a former marine, he didn't back down from a fight. His *oorah* battle cry had carried her through her last trip to hell and back and she welcomed it again this time. She needed to call on that battle cry tonight to get through her talk with Garrett later. She was a fool to think she could hide her diagnosis from someone who had lived with the scars it left behind.

Sensing her anxiety, Jake rested his head in her lap the entire way there. They pulled into a full parking lot and circled twice before finding a spot large enough for her work truck. She wished she'd had a chance to go home and change first, but she'd only worked on one horse earlier. Evan had done the rest under her supervision.

The bone pain that accompanied the after-chemo injection made working almost unbearable. When her father's connections had led Evan to her door Monday morning, she welcomed his assistance. He was just what the doctor ordered. Literally.

Delta clipped a leash on Jake and held the hand loop open for Kacey. "Slip this over your wrist and hold on to him tight. You wait for me while I get my stuff."

Guitar in one hand, bag over her shoulder, kid with dog in the other hand. How did parents do it when there were other children added to the mix? She was out of arms and so was her assistant kid. She couldn't even fathom how Liv would manage three infants at the same time. But her friend was making sure she was prepared for every possible scenario. If there was a class, video or book about multiples, she had it.

The party was in full swing when they entered the home's dining area. Parties usually occurred on the weekend, but today was Ralph's hundred-and-second birthday. He refused to have it on the weekend for fear he wouldn't live long enough to make the celebration. Every year, he threw himself a party, invited all the residents and staff, and footed the catering bill.

"Happy birthday, Ralph." She gave the man a hug as she walked in the room.

"My precious Delta." He held her face in his hands. "I'm so happy you joined us tonight." He bent forward and petted Jake before smiling at Kacey. "Who is this beautiful princess?"

"I'm Kacey." She hugged the man. "Happy birthday."

"Thank you." Ralph hugged her in return. "Oh, to be young again."

Kacey talked to everyone. It didn't matter if they acknowledged her or not. She smiled and introduced herself around the room with Jake close by her side. Delta wanted to believe Kacey was babysitting her dog, but the way Jake constantly kept her eyes in his line of vision told her he was the primary caretaker.

Delta had her guitar out when Kacey rejoined them carrying two paper plates full of food. "Mr. Ralph gave these to me. He's a hundred and two. How many times older is he than me?"

"Almost thirteen, I think." Delta helped her set both plates on the table.

"Wow."

Wow was right. Hopefully they'd all live to be that age and still be happy. "Thank you for bringing me dinner, sweetheart. You're a terrific little helper."

"I thought Jake was gonna eat it before I got to the table. Who is that man?" Kacey looked toward the sunroom entrance. "He keeps looking at you and smiling."

"That's Joe. He's one of the permanent residents here. Funny as the day is long. He'll have you rolling on the floor laughing at his stories." Delta lowered her voice and leaned closer to Kacey. "He thinks he's God's gift to women, though."

"Isn't he a little old for you?" Kacey wrinkled her nose.

"In his mind, he'll always be in his twenties. He's harmless." Delta took a bite of her chicken-and-grape-salad croissant. Her appetite had returned yesterday, but her taste buds were still a little off.

"He walks like Aunt Belle's rooster."

Delta almost choked on a grape. "That he does."

"Daddy's been really sad without you around. He misses you."

"I was only gone for a little while."

"Almost a whole week." She pouted. "He had to work on that Valentine's Day thingy by himself."

With all the cancer crap going on, she had completely forgotten about the couples-only retreat. She'd given him all the information she'd had, but it was a huge undertaking for one person. The event started in four days and she hoped he'd used all her contacts.

"I'll see if I can help him when we get to the house." If he still wanted her help after the way she'd treated him.

"I'll help, too." Kacey nodded her head matter-of-factly. "You and Daddy need all the help you can get."

If that wasn't the truth, Delta didn't know what was.

"Thank you for coming over." Garrett greeted Dylan on the front porch two hours after Delta had dropped off Kacey. "They are already in bed. I'll be back before they ever realize I'm gone."

"Take your time and don't race over there and get yourself killed along the way." Dylan didn't ask why he needed a sudden babysitter, but he had rightfully assumed it was because of Delta. "Emma and Holly are already asleep, too, so it's not like anyone's missing me. And if you don't come back tonight, I'll just tell the kids you had an early errand and I'll drive them to school."

"That's not going to happen." Garrett clapped his brother on the back. "But thanks for the offer."

He descended the porch steps two at a time, almost slipping on the last one.

"I hope you're planning on driving better than you

walk," Dylan called after him. "You have two kids counting on you to return in one piece."

Garrett hesitated before getting in his SUV. Was going over to see Delta the right thing to do? She had refused to talk to him with the kids in earshot and had promised to discuss it later. He couldn't wait for later. He needed to know what she was hiding, although in his heart he already knew her cancer had returned.

Fifteen minutes later he idled to a stop alongside her Jeep in front of her house. The dashboard clock glowed quarter after ten. Okay, so it was late, but not exactly super late. The lights were on inside her house, and if he saw movement, then he'd knock on the door. If he didn't, then he would head home.

His phone rang loudly in the darkness of the truck, almost causing him to jump out of his seat. It was Delta's number.

"Hello."

"Are you just going to sit out there all night, or are you going to come in?"

"I guess you heard me pull up." Garrett's gaze moved from one window to the next, expecting to see her watching him.

"It's a quiet ranch in the middle of the night and your truck has an exhaust leak," she ground out through what sounded like clenched teeth.

"It does not."

Delta sighed. "Are you going to argue with me or are you going to come in?"

"I'll be right there."

Garrett's hand rested on the door handle as he braced himself for whatever she had to tell him. No matter how bad it was, he could handle it.

Delta wordlessly opened the door as he reached the top step and Jake ran out to happily greet him.

"I'm sorry for coming over here so late."

She patted her thigh and Jake immediately returned to her side. "No you're not, but if it makes you feel better to say that, then so be it."

"Wow, okay. You don't mince words, do you?" Why was he the one getting attitude? She was the one who'd disappeared and then ended things abruptly. Not him.

"No, I don't. I have cancer again."

Garrett grabbed the door frame to steady himself from the onslaught of her words. He hadn't even made it all the way into the house. "I thought so." His legs felt like they were weighted down with cement as he finished stepping over the threshold and closed the door behind him. "How bad?" His heart thumped so loud in his ears he doubted he'd hear her response.

"Nowhere near last time." She turned and trudged into the living room, motioning for him to follow her.

For the next hour, Delta painstakingly described the events of the previous week. When she finished she waited in silence while he processed the information.

Hearing the words come out of her mouth made it all that much more real. It bothered him that she had thought he was so damaged from Rebecca's death that she had to hide the truth from him. He respected her reasons for not wanting to tell anybody else. While he would never deem her less capable of doing her job, he could see where others might.

He wanted to ask how this could happen again, but he already knew the answer. He wanted to ask how she was feeling, but he already knew that answer, too. Despite the defiant tilt of her chin, her delicate features screamed loneliness and fear.

"I wish you had trusted me enough to tell me sooner instead of trying to hide it from me."

"I didn't want you to go through this again."

"Sweetheart, it's not the same thing. You don't have pancreatic cancer. You have a ninety-five percent survival rate. It's going to be okay." He drew her into his arms and held her close. "Everything's going to be okay."

Instead of leaving like she had expected him to, Garrett had lit a fire and they watched the flames dance in the darkness while they snuggled together beneath a tangled mass of blankets from the couch. Jake stretched out on the floor beside them, lifting his head only when he heard the rustle of the snack-chip bags they had dug out of the kitchen pantry an hour ago.

Somewhere between channel surfing and mischievous childhood stories, they had settled into the most passionate make-out session of her life. Which Garrett had abruptly ended fifteen minutes ago. He had checked the time on his phone no less than ten times since then.

His body became more rigid with each passing second, making her more nervous. "Okay, cowboy." She flipped the blankets off them and stood in front of him. "It's time to call it a night. And don't argue with me. I know you need to get home to relieve Dylan."

"I don't want to go." He tugged at the hem of her flannel shirt. "My brother's okay with watching the kids all night. He said so before I left. But I should at least text him and let him know I'm staying. Unless you want me to go."

"You're sure he doesn't mind?" Delta couldn't deny

wanting him to stay. Now that she had told him the truth, she felt a thousand times freer. She had suspected Garrett would be understanding, she just hadn't wanted to put him through the agony of watching another woman fight for her life.

"Absolutely."

"So why don't you send him that text, then."

Delta began slowly unbuttoning her shirt as he typed out his message.

"What are you doing?" His eyes grew wide in the firelight as he watched her.

"I'm waiting for you to hit Send and put your phone away." She slid the shirt from her shoulders, leaving her wearing only a pink satin bra and black thermal leggings. "Do you want me with or without?"

"With or without what?" He perched on the edge of the couch.

"Choose one and you'll find out."

"Without."

Delta reached behind her and unfastened her bra, allowing it to fall to the floor. His gaze upon her bare breasts empowered her to continue her seduction. He reached for her hand, but she took a step backward.

"Now, now." She waggled a finger at him. "Patience is a virtue. With or without."

"Please, without." He groaned, reclining against the back of the couch once again.

She hooked her thumbs in the waistband of her leggings and eased them past her hips. Reveling in the warmth of the fire against her bare skin. She stepped out of her pants and stood before him, with only a slip of lace shielding his view from the rest of her.

"With or without?"

"Without." His voice was barely a whisper.

She swung her hips as the lace slid down her hips and onto her thighs, before releasing and allowing it to fall the rest of the way. She stood naked in front of him, allowing him to see every inch, every scar, every imperfection.

His piercing gaze met hers. "You still have one more to go."

Delta laughed. "I can't get more naked than this." She knelt in front of him. "Unless you mean this." She reached for his belt and began to unfasten it. His hand covered hers, stilling it.

"Ask me again."

She could play this game all night. "With or without?"

Garrett rose before her, guiding her to her feet as his eyes roamed the entire length of her body once again. He held her face in his hands and kissed her mouth lightly before whispering, "I want you without." His fingers slid toward her scalp and under the edge of her wig, releasing the band.

"Garrett!" She tried to pull away from him but his arm wound around her waist and tugged her to him. "Don't do this."

"Without." His voice was as firm as his body against hers. She stilled in his arms. "I want you, every inch of you, naked, raw, bare. I want to see you. Not the pretense of you. It's just hair, Delta. It offers no protection, at least not from me. I want you without."

Delta sucked in a breath and closed her eyes as he continued to remove her final covering.

"You're so beautiful, Delta Grace. Embrace that beauty when you're around me."

Delta ran a hand over what used to be her hair. "I

asked Cooper to do it. And I'll ask him again this weekend since it's starting to grow back. It's going to fall out and I refuse to let that happen. I took control." Once she'd arrived home last week, she'd shaved the rest of her body, with the exception of her eyebrows. She hadn't lost them completely the last time and she hoped she could fill them in with pencil again if need be.

"I love you bare." Garrett cupped the back of her head and claimed her mouth as his tongue sought hers.

"Garrett." He tilted her head back, exposing her throat. He trailed kisses down the hollow of her neck until he reached her breasts. He ran his tongue over one nipple, then blew across, causing them to harden further. "Garrett, please."

"By the time I'm finished, you'll be saying those words over and over again."

Chapter 13

Garrett listened to Delta's soft breaths in the darkness of her bedroom. And he hated it. He found himself counting the seconds after each exhale and then tensing when her next inhale didn't come as quickly as the last few. He'd done the same thing when Rebecca had slept next to him.

He lifted a sweaty hand to the side of his neck and checked his heart rate with two fingers against his watch. It was a steady hundred beats a minute and that was when he knew he'd made the mistake of staying.

He didn't know how to support Delta and keep her diagnosis a secret from Bryce and Kacey. They would know. They would pick up on the signs. They would ask questions and they would be afraid of losing someone else they loved. He couldn't put them through that again. He wouldn't.

Garrett bolted upright. He had to get out of there. The walls felt as if they were closing in on him. He glanced down at Delta and saw Rebecca instead.

"No, this can't be happening." He forced himself to stand.

"Garrett?" Delta rolled over and clicked on the light.

"Oh, God." It was Rebecca. She pushed aside the covers and stood. "It can't be."

"Garrett, what's wrong?" She turned to face him. "You're drenched!"

"Delta." He sighed in relief and dropped to his knees when he realized he was having a flashback. It had to be the hair, or the lack thereof. Rebecca had been as platinum as they came. There would have been no mistaking the two, even in the dark, if they had hair. "Delta… we shouldn't have done this…"

"Excuse me?" Delta grabbed a robe from the back of a chair and tied it tightly around her. "Please tell me you did not just say that."

"Delta, I'm sorry. I can't do this. I didn't realize—"

"Get the hell out of my house!" she shouted. Jake jumped on the bed and began barking wildly at him.

"Delta, please let me explain."

"Why did you even come here?" Delta stormed out of the room only to return less than a minute later with his clothes. She threw them at him, nearly taking his eye out with his belt buckle. "Get dressed," she ordered. "I gave you an out. This was exactly why I had pushed you away. But no, you had to come over here. You had to force the issue. I didn't want you around to see this. I was doing just fine on my own. You had me snowed."

Garrett tugged on his boxer briefs and jeans as Jake continued to bark. "I can't do this to my kids."

"Don't you dare use them as an excuse." She reached across the bed for Jake's collar to quiet him before continuing. "You told me they didn't have to know. We agreed that I would keep my distance on the bad days. You can't even admit that this is about you. You're the one who can't do this. You're a coward. Now leave and don't ever come back."

Delta slammed the front door so hard it cracked a pane of glass.

Shit!

She plastered her back against the wall and held her breath as she listened for the sound of his SUV. Why hadn't he driven away? She refused to look. She refused to give him the satisfaction because Lord knew he had his fill of satisfaction tonight. At her expense.

Jake jumped on the back of the couch and pushed his face through the curtains. His tail stood straight out and vibrated with tension. Garrett still had to be on the porch if Jake was able to see him. The cars were parked off to the side and the front door light didn't shine that far.

She heard what sounded like a door close and then the start of his engine. Within seconds, it had faded in the distance. Her body went limp as she slid down the wall to the floor…and cried. Another man had walked away from her because she had cancer. At least she had a perfect record.

Jake jumped off the couch and ran to her side. He nudged her face repeatedly with his until she met his gaze. "I'm okay, boy." She dug her fingers into his thick coat and hugged him to her. "At least I will be." Jake rested his head on her shoulders, content to remain in that one position.

She wanted to go for a run but knew her body didn't have the stamina. She wanted to hit something but didn't want to scare Jake. She wanted to scream but didn't want to frighten her landlords across the way. She wanted to throw something, but that would only make her angrier when she had to clean it up. She wanted to not have to hold it together for once. She needed a release.

Jake pressed his body closer to hers. His nose was inches from her ear allowing her to match his breathing pattern until she calmed down. It amazed her that an animal knew what she needed when the man who'd just made love to her didn't have a clue.

Even Eddie at his worst had never left her feeling used. Just unwanted. Now she had the unfortunate knowledge of both. She released Jake and pulled herself up. She needed to strip the bed and scrub any traces of him from her body. He was the one man outside of her family she thought had understood her. The one man she thought she had a future with. The man she thought she loved. If she ever saw him again it would be too soon.

An hour had passed since Delta had thrown him out and he'd returned home. Dylan had been concerned when Garrett walked in but didn't ask questions. Which was good because he didn't have any answers. He also wasn't willing to betray Delta's trust by broadcasting her illness around either. Although, he didn't think he could betray her trust any more than he had tonight. He had never meant to hurt her, especially not that way. And he was still trying to rationalize the situation.

He stood at the kitchen window and looked into the darkness. The sun would rise in less than an hour and there was no way he'd get any sleep now. Even if he wanted to, his guilt wouldn't let him.

He knew the facts. Delta's cancer was ninety-five-percent curable. Hodgkin's lymphoma was nothing like pancreatic cancer. Delta had started treatment immediately. Rebecca's cancer had already advanced before it had been detected. And it had spread by the time she began chemotherapy. The two situations were entirely different. Then why did it feel like his heart was being torn out of his chest once again?

Garrett tugged on his boots and stepped into the frigid early-morning air. Not bothering to put on a coat or gloves he made his way to the shed attached to the back of the house and unlocked it. With a flick of the switch, he flooded the backyard with light. The yard was a mess and he was low on firewood. He gathered the branches that had fallen during the last snowfall, snapped them into smaller pieces and tossed them in the kindling box on the porch. He grabbed the ax from the shed wall, stood a slab of wood on the tree stump and started swinging.

The steel head split the wood with a resounding crack. He stood another piece upright and swung again and again until his back and shoulders couldn't take it anymore. Then he gathered the wood in his arms and stacked it alongside the house.

His body ached, his hands were cold and his ears stung, but it wasn't enough to drive the anger out of his head. He was mad at Rebecca for dying. He was mad that pancreatic cancer was linked to a hereditary gene and his children had an increased chance of getting it. He was mad Delta had cancer again and he was mad for not being strong enough to support the woman he loved. The realization hit him like a Mack truck. He was in love with Delta and he had just destroyed any chance he'd ever had with her.

"Daddy?" Kacey called to him. "What are you doing out here?"

He spun around to see her silhouetted in the back-porch doorway. "Go back inside, honey. It's too cold out here. I'm just chopping some firewood before the sun comes up. I'll be in shortly."

"The sun's up and so is Bryce," she said. "I'll feed him and get him ready for school."

Garrett looked skyward. The sun hadn't quite risen above the horizon, but it was close enough. "No, baby. You will not get Bryce dressed and ready for school. That's my job." He crossed the yard and locked the ax in the shed before joining her in the doorway. "Didn't I tell you to get inside? You're letting all the heat out of the house."

After the way he'd treated her, he doubted Delta would keep Silver Bells as a customer. How could he tell his kids they would never see Delta again? Kacey had already grown attached to her and that was his fault. He should have limited contact between them, yet she'd been good for his daughter. Bryce would miss her, but he would roll with it like he rolled with everything else. Garrett didn't think he'd survive another round of Kacey retreating into her shell. She'd just begun to come into her own and be a child, and he was going to throw another wrench in her little life.

"Why aren't you wearing a coat?"

"Because Daddy's an idiot." He pulled out a kitchen chair and patted it for her to sit on. "I want to talk to you."

He sat in the chair across from her and reached for

her hands. "Daddy, don't." She backed away from him. "Your hands are cold."

"I'm sorry, baby." He rubbed them against his jeans. "I need you to let me take care of your baby brother from now on. I know you're good at it, but I want to be good at it, too, and the only way I can learn is if you let me do things for him. But you may have to show me how sometimes."

"I'd be your teacher?" Her face lit up at the idea.

"Exactly." He wanted to hug her but he knew he wasn't warm enough yet. "And since I'll be learning your job, you'll have more time to play with your friends."

"And learn guitar." She slid from the chair and ran into the living room to open her guitar case. "I can't wait until my next lesson."

"About that." Garrett followed and perched on the edge of the coffee table. "I think it's best if Dylan teaches you instead of Delta."

"But I want Delta." She deadpanned him.

"Well, honey." He had planned to have this conversation later, not before school. "That's not going to be possible."

"What did you do?"

"Me?" The accusation surprised him, although it wasn't off base. "Delta has to go back and forth to visit her family more often and she won't be able to teach you anymore."

"Doesn't she want to see me?"

"Of course she does." The last thing he wanted was for his daughter to feel unwanted and unloved. "This has absolutely nothing to do with you."

He hated lying to his kid, but he refused to allow one more person to hurt her. And while he was confident Delta would never purposely hurt Kacey, the truth would devastate her.

Kacey relatched the case and pushed it away. "It's okay. I don't want to play anymore. I'm going to get dressed for school. You need to get Bryce ready."

And her walls were up once again. An eight-year-old shouldn't even know how to turn their emotions off like that. Nor should she have to tell him how to care for his son, even though she was right. The time had slipped away from him this morning and he didn't want them to be late.

Kacey disappeared down the hall to her bedroom. Today would pass and they'd get through it together. He reminded himself that he didn't need anything more than to see his kids healthy and happy. Despite the heartache of this morning, he had done the right thing by protecting them from Delta's cancer. Then why did the right thing leave him so cold and empty?

Delta barely had the strength to drag her body out of bed Saturday morning. If she'd had her way, she would have slept until noon. But Jake's bladder and empty belly would have none of that. It had been four days since she'd kicked Garrett out of her life and she was still waiting for him to stop invading her every waking thought.

She checked her text messages and voice mail, relieved when there weren't any. Hiring an apprentice had worked out better than she had thought it would. He'd been able to handle half of her jobs and was available in case Silver Bells had a call. They hadn't and a part of her wondered if she even had them as a customer anymore. She'd like to say she didn't care, but she did. After all, they were her largest account.

She fixed a bowl of food for Jake and sat it on the floor. "Here you go, boy."

Her back ached as she stood, along with every muscle in her body. She didn't have a temperature and was chalking the pain up to chemo side effects. So much for this time being easier than the last.

She fixed a cup of coffee and had just gotten comfortable on the couch when Jake began to circle by the back door. "Are you kidding me?" she asked him. He barked a response forcing her to get back up and let him out again. "I really wish you could do all your business at the same time."

She barely had the door open before he took off down the stairs and ran across the pastures toward her landlords' house, where he'd most likely beg for his second breakfast of the day. Typical male…never satisfied.

Delta made her way back to the couch and clicked on the TV. Every channel was engrossed in one Valentine's Day activity or another. She'd always hated cupid, but now she despised the little bugger.

Today was the tenth, the first day of the Silver Bells couples-only Valentine's Day retreat and she couldn't help but wonder how her ideas had worked out. She'd put much more of her time and heart into the project than she had intended to, but she'd secretly enjoyed it. Too bad she couldn't see the final result. As curious as she was, she wasn't curious enough to risk running into Garrett.

Jake's distant barking followed by a child's laughter drew her to the window. She peered through the curtains to see Kacey and her dog running and jumping in the pasture next to the house. She reached for the doorknob and then realized she wasn't wearing her wig. That was the last thing Kacey needed to see.

She ran to her bedroom and lifted the wig from the stand. If Kacey was out there, Garrett had to be close by. But she hadn't heard his truck. That was odd. She looked in the mirror and adjusted her hair quickly before running back through the house. The action left her breathless by the time she reached the door. She swung it wide and stepped into the cold.

Jake had a ball in his mouth and offered it to Kacey, who happily threw it for him. Delta glanced around the property, but there was no sign of Garrett.

"Kacey!" Delta called to her, causing both her and Jake to turn in her direction. "Come on inside where it's warm."

Delta's teeth chattered as she waited for them. Jake could outrun anyone, but kept pace beside Kacey. They both reached the porch panting and sweaty.

"Delta!" Kacey scampered up the steps, threw her body against Delta and hugged her. The force almost knocked her back through the door. "I've missed you so much."

"I've missed you, too." More than she had ever imagined. "Let's get inside." She broke the embrace and ushered them both into the warmth. "Where's your father?"

Kacey shrugged. "I saw Jake running from the window of my friend's house so I came out to play with him."

"Where does your friend live?"

"Over there." Kacey pointed out the window to the new housing development on the other side of the ranch.

"Does anyone know you're here?"

She shrugged again and knelt on the floor beside Jake. "I've missed you, too."

"We need to call your father and tell him where you

are." Delta grabbed her phone from the living room and pulled up Garrett's contact. Her finger hesitated over the call button while she gathered her thoughts. She wanted their conversation to be as concise as possible. The less time they spoke, the better.

He answered on the first ring. "Delta, I'm so glad you called."

"Kacey is at my house."

"What? She's supposed to be at Darlene's house with Ivy. They had a sleepover party last night."

"Does Darlene live in the housing development behind mine?"

Garrett sighed into the phone. "Yes, she does."

"She said she saw Jake playing in the pastures and she decided to join him. I don't even know if anyone realizes she's missing."

Garrett swore under his breath. "Is it okay if she stays there until I get there? I can leave now."

"That's fine." Delta hit the end button before Garrett could say another word. She'd heard enough from the man to last a lifetime. Although there was a teeny tiny part of her brain that understood and might even be able to sympathize with his reaction. She'd seen enough PTSD while working with Jake to recognize he'd had a panic attack, probably stemming from the trauma of losing Rebecca and the guilt he felt for sleeping with her. And maybe if he had called her the next day to discuss it, she would have been able to forgive him. But to not own up to it…no, she couldn't accept that.

"Your daddy is on the way over to get you." Delta handed her the phone. "Why don't you call your friend and let her parents know where you are."

"I don't know the number."

"Okay." Delta tucked the phone into the pocket of her robe, which had become increasingly suffocating over the last few minutes. "Then come in the living room and watch some TV with me while we wait."

"Are you okay?" Kacey followed her to the couch and climbed on it beside her.

"I'm overly tired today. I didn't get much sleep last night."

"You look white like Mommy."

She turned to see Kacey studying her intently. Delta grabbed the remote off the table and handed it to Kacey. "I'm fine, honey, really."

Delta glanced at the clock on the DVR. It had only been five minutes since she'd called Garrett. She picked up her phone and fired off a text to Maddie: Need your help. Can you stop over? She received a reply almost instantly: On the way.

Whoever arrived first would have to take Kacey because now she was beginning to feel like she had a fever. And the damn wig...it was so much hotter than actual hair, even during a Montana winter.

"You stay here with Jake. I'll be right back."

"Okay." Kacey changed the channel to cartoons.

Delta grabbed a cold bottle of water from the fridge before heading into the bedroom. She just needed to cool off for a minute. She twisted the cap off the bottle and took a long swig of water. She set it on the dresser, then she pulled the blinds up and lifted the window sash. The cool air felt good, but not good enough. Making sure she had closed the door behind her, Delta removed her wig and laid it on the bed. "Oh, that's so much better."

Kacey's scream from the bedroom doorway nearly

shattered her eardrums. Jake began barking and circling her protectively as Delta grabbed for her wig.

"You're sick," Kacey cried. "I knew it. I knew it. Just like Mommy, you're just like Mommy and you'll leave and never come back."

Delta reached for the little girl as Kacey pulled away from her. "No!"

Garrett bounded into the room. "What is going on?" He looked from Delta to Kacey and the wig. "Oh, baby. It's not like that. It's not like Mommy. Delta's not dying, I promise."

"You knew?" Tears streamed down her cheeks as she stared up at him. "You knew she was sick. How could you give her to us when she's going away."

Garrett knelt on the floor. "She's not going away."

Delta held tight to Jake's collar. This couldn't be happening. This was exactly what she had wanted to avoid. She didn't want to scare his kids. She didn't want this to affect them.

"Delta's going to die."

"No, honey." Delta released the dog, ran across the room. "I am not dying. What I have is very curable. It's called Hodgkin's lymphoma. See, it doesn't even have cancer in the name."

"You don't have cancer?" Kacey's sobs quieted.

"I—I do, but not that kind of cancer." Delta reached out for the bed. Jake ran to her side and began barking again. When did the room begin to spin? She bent forward and almost fell to the floor. "Garrett."

"Daddy, what's happening?"

Delta struggled to open her eyes. There was something in her nose and around her ears. *Open your eyes!*

She silently screamed. *Blink.* White. *Blink.* Bright. Ceiling. She needed to turn her head. Her brain wasn't cooperating with her body. *Come on! Fight harder!* She felt her head move slightly. *Blink.* Machines. *Shit!* She was in the hospital.

"Delta?" Maddie's voice pierced the darkness. "Delta, can you hear me?"

Delta nodded, at least she thought she did.

"Garrett?"

"I'm sorry, sweetie. He's not here."

"How?"

"You're running a fever, you have an infection and you passed out at home. He called an ambulance. There's no easy way to tell you this, but I think your secret is out."

"Where's Jake and Kacey?"

"Jake's still at your house. I'm going back there after I leave to get his food and treats. I'll take him home with me and watch him until you're released. And Kacey is with Garrett."

Maddie sighed. "I don't know how much you remember, but she saw you pass out."

Delta wanted to cry, but once again her body betrayed her and wouldn't listen.

Maddie pulled an envelope out of her bag. "Garrett asked me to give this to you. You can read it later or I can read it to you now."

"No." It didn't matter what it said. The result was the same. They were over. "Destroy it."

"You don't want me to do that."

"Destroy. Now." Delta reached for the bedrails and pressed the button.

"What are you trying to do? Sit up?" Maddie pressed

the button embedded on the rail and the head of the bed began to rise.

"Stop," Delta ordered.

"How are we doing?" A nurse entered the room. "You buzzed for me."

"Please leave." Delta looked at Maddie. "Give her the letter."

"Delta, are you throwing me out?"

Delta nodded. "Please."

"Yeah, sure." She handed the letter to the nurse and slung her bag over her shoulder. "Oh, and I called your parents. They're on the way. I'll check in on you tomorrow."

"Do you want me to read this to you?" the nurse asked.

"Burn it," Delta said.

"I can't do that, but I can run it through the paper shredder if that's what you want."

"Please destroy it."

"Okay. Here, let me lower this for you so you can sleep." The bed reclined once again and Delta managed to roll over and face the wall.

She'd rather be alone than go through the pain of the last twenty-four hours. If only chemo could mend a broken heart.

Chapter 14

Two days had passed since the day Delta collapsed in front of Kacey. Leaving her had been the second hardest thing of his life. The first had been burying his wife. Delta's body had taken quite a beating from the infection she'd picked up after her first round of chemo. They had released her from the hospital the following day but he didn't know any further details. After her friends and family had realized why he had ended their relationship, they refused to talk to him. And he couldn't blame them. He'd wronged her in the worst possible way. He just hoped she'd read the letter he'd written explaining why he'd done what he did and how it had been the biggest mistake of his life. He had wanted to tell her in person, but the hospital had strict orders to keep him out of her room.

Once Kacey had gotten over her initial shock at Delta's diagnosis, she began asking about her again. So had Bryce, although he was still too young to fully understand. They wanted him to call her, but he didn't want to push her further away. If she had read his letter and didn't call, he had his answer. If she hadn't read it, that was still a clear answer.

Garrett led one of the horses out of the main stables and into the middle one. They had a roof leak and needed to get in that stall. He was surprised to see Delta's truck parked in front of the building with the back open and the forge blazing. At least that was a good sign she was feeling better and they might be able to salvage some part of their relationship. He turned the corner and almost smacked into Buck Grace's chest. He was much more imposing in person than he was in his online seminars.

He grunted a greeting. An actual grunt. That wasn't a good sign.

"Mr. Grace."

"Weasel."

"Excuse me?"

"You heard me." Buck strode past him and fired a shoe. Blazing red-hot, he held it up in front of him—or maybe he was holding it up in front of Garrett as a warning—he then examined it before lowering it to the anvil and striking it with a rounding hammer. He checked it again before thrusting it back into the forge. "I'm only here because Delta has a business reputation to protect. And since you went around telling the whole damn county she has cancer, she started losing customers."

"But I didn't tell—"

"It's not your turn to talk," Buck warned. He removed the shoe from the forge with large tongs, strode to the horse, lifted the foot and set the shoe. Steam rose off the hoof, creating a smooth surface between the two. Buck finished nailing the shoe before returning his attention to Garrett. "It takes a little man to do what you've done."

"I explained everything in my letter in hopes we could sit down and discuss it when the dust settled."

"She never read your letter."

"Why not?"

Buck spun on him. "Because she told the nurse to shred it. You abandoned her in her hour of need and then you were going to hit her with a double whammy by defending yourself in a letter. Is that the gist of it?"

"It was more complicated than that. I lost my wife to cancer. I watched the woman I loved die. I felt like I was watching it again and it tore me in half. But I made a mistake. My letter was an apology, too."

Buck wiped his forehead with the back of his hand. "I'm really sorry about your wife and what you went through. But son, if you're not strong enough for Delta now, you never will be. This can come back again. What will you do if you two are together and it does? Walk away? You did what that weasel ex-husband of hers did. You left when she needed you most."

Garrett collapsed against the stall. "How could I have forgotten about him?" He'd been so wrapped up in his past colliding with the present, he'd completely disregarded her past. No wonder she'd shredded the letter. "I need to talk to her. Better yet, I need to see her. I need to do this in person."

"Not if you're going to break her heart again." Buck shook his head.

"I don't want to break it. I want to win it." Garrett held his ground. Something he should have done last week. "I regret what I did to Delta. I thought I was doing the right thing by protecting my kids from getting hurt again, but they're more hurt without her. They love Delta. And so do I. I just wish I had realized it sooner. I don't even know how she's doing because no one will tell me."

"She's much better. She wanted to work today but I told her to take it easy at home for another day or two. I'm going to stay with her for the next week, just to make sure she's okay."

Garrett wiped away a tear at the news. "I'm glad she's feeling better. Do you think I could see her?"

Buck tugged at the collar of his shirt. "It's going to take a lot more than an apology to get her attention. You need to come up with something big to win her back, because, son, you devastated her."

Something big…he knew just what to do and who to call. Come tomorrow afternoon, he'd change her mind. He refused to believe this was the end for them. He had to try or else he'd live the rest of his life in regret.

"Sir, I have an idea, but I'll need your help to pull it off."

"Where are you taking me?" Delta fidgeted. She preferred being the one in control, the one making the decisions. "I don't make a good passenger. I'm used to driving everywhere."

"You're going to have to get over that real quick." Her father chuckled.

"What's that supposed to mean?"

He laughed as they turned off the main road. "Today you're going to sit down, shut up and hang on."

"Dad! That's kind of rude, don't you th—" She

squealed when she saw the sign. "We're going dog-sledding?"

"You're going dogsledding. I'm heading back to work."

Delta saw Garrett's SUV parked near the entrance. "Dad, what is this all about?"

"Give the man a chance to explain. He arranged this whole thing for you yesterday because he knew you've always wanted to do this. Hear him out, enjoy the ride and if at the end of the day you want me to come get you, I will. What do you say?"

Delta reached over the armrest and hugged him. "I love you, Daddy."

"I love you, too, pumpkin." Buck kissed her on the forehead. "Now, go have some fun and don't hesitate to leave Garrett in the woods if he ticks you off."

"Believe me, there won't be any hesitation." Delta swung open the passenger door and hopped onto the hard-packed snow.

"I wasn't sure if you'd come." Garrett smiled as she approached.

"If I had known you would be here, I wouldn't have. I had no idea what my dad was up to, but kudos for getting him involved. He went from wanting to castrate you to driving me to see you. I'd say that's progress."

"I'm glad you're here. There's so much I want to tell you."

"Yeah, I don't know, Garrett." Delta turned back to the parking lot but her father had already left. "I'm here. You're here. And I've always wanted to do this. So, okay."

"Really?" Garrett smiled. "Thank you, Delta."

She followed him inside the small log cabin office.

"Welcome to Musher's Dog Sled Adventures," a woman greeted them. "Do you have a reservation?"

"Garrett Slade."

"Mr. Slade, I'm the one you spoke with yesterday." She slid two clipboards with forms attached to the front of them across the counter. "If you'll fill those out for me, we'll have you out and sledding shortly. It's the perfect day for it."

Delta's hand shook with excitement as she began writing her name. If she had a bucket list, this would be pretty close to the top. She knew Garrett had planned this trip for the lodge guests, but she never expected to have the opportunity to go.

A man approached them after they'd handed in the forms. "My name is Oki and I'm your musher today. Follow me to the dog yard and meet your pack." He led them out the back door. "We offer a unique sledding experience to our guests. Most places have single person sleds, meaning the musher steers while the guest rides in the sled bed. Here all our hand-made sleds are built for three. One of you will ride up front in the bed and the other will stand on the runners behind me. Whoever's standing will experience what it's like to drive the team since you'll be helping me steer through the twists and turns of the trail."

"I'm riding in the bed." She peeked inside the nylon wrapped enclosure. Fleecy blankets lined the interior, inviting her to sink into its depths. While Oki explained how to drive and steer the sled to Garrett, she admired the team of eight dogs. She'd always assumed sled dogs were huskies or malamutes. But they had Samoyeds and Newfoundlands, among some other breeds she didn't recognize.

"Are we ready to ride?"

"Oh, yeah." Delta rubbed her hands together in excitement. "Let's do this."

Oki strapped her safely into the sled bed as she nestled into the cocoon of warmth. "Everyone should have one of these in their house. I could fall asleep here."

"Mush!" Oki called as the sled began to move down the trail. The ride was a little bumpy at first, but once the dogs began to run, it smoothed out.

They crested a small hill and gained even more speed. Delta lifted her arms as if she were riding on a roller coaster. "Yay!" This was living. This would get her through chemotherapy this upcoming weekend. Nothing would take her down.

"How are you doing?" An hour later they were sipping hot chocolate and eating cookies while they watched Oki unhook the first team of dogs and connect the next one.

"I feel like I just ran a marathon and back. That was one of the most exhilarating things I've ever experienced."

"I'm glad you had a good time."

"Good time?" She threw her head back and laughed. "That was one of the best times of my life. This is going to sound strange, but even though I was wrapped tight in that sled bed, there was a sense of freedom, of allowing the dogs to lead us. And I know Oki was doing the driving, but from my vantage point, it was all dogs. Outside of work, I haven't had an outdoor adventure in…" She blew out a breath. "At least a year. I've been busy ever since I moved to Saddle Ridge. This was special. This meant something. I'm so glad I got to experience this. Thank you."

Garrett understood how much freedom meant to a cancer patient regardless of their prognosis. He'd met many survivors during Rebecca's chemo treatments. Some had resigned to the disease and were tired of fighting, while others sought that freedom as if it were the last drop of water on earth. Delta was a fighter. He realized that more and more every day. Not just in her will to beat cancer, but in her fearless demeanor. He saw a renewed fire in her. When she had first come back from Missoula, it hadn't been there. That had scared him and had probably contributed to his panic over the situation.

The third anniversary of Rebecca's death had come and gone without any fanfare, mostly due to the launch of the Valentine's retreat. He had been aware of the day from the moment he opened his eyes that morning, but though it still hurt to remember her, this year the weight that had sat on his chest was no longer there. It had also given him the strength and courage to remove his wedding ring. It had been time.

"I read your letter."

"What?" Garrett's gaze met hers. "I thought you asked a nurse to destroy it."

"I did, but she slipped it in my bag and I found it last night. I guess she didn't have the heart to do it."

"Delta, I love you and I never should have reacted that way." Garrett reached for her hand only for her to pull away.

"Believe it or not, I love you, too." The pain reflecting in her eyes betrayed the sweet smile that graced her lips. "And despite my anger, I understood why you did it. After reading your letter I understand it even more. It doesn't make it hurt any less. A part of me forgives you. You lived through a terrible tragedy and our night together triggered horrible memories. I get all of that. But I'm sorry, Garrett. I can't risk those memories returning every time we share a tender moment or you see me without my hair. My body can't handle that stress right now."

Garrett's heart froze midbeat. He wanted to shout from the top of a mountain that she loved him. Those three words meant the world to him. But it wasn't enough for her to take him back. That ache was so deep and so raw he couldn't see the other side. Delta was a once-in-a-lifetime chance. And it was over. It was truly over.

Delta allowed Garrett to drive her home and then she spent the next four hours curled up with a tissue box in one hand and Jake in the other. Her father was still working, allowing her the time to grieve for the relationship she hadn't thought she wanted.

Garrett had told her he loved her. It was the most magical phrase on earth and he'd said it to her...*her*! As light as it made her feel, she was terrified to trust her heart to him again. But she wanted to. She wanted to be the strong woman that he deserved...that the kids deserved. She just didn't know how.

Her phone rang and she was grateful for the distraction from her thoughts. The number was unfamiliar.

"Hello?"

"Hi, Delta. It's Emma. I hope I'm not calling at a bad time."

Delta forced a laugh. "Your timing couldn't be more perfect."

"I never had the opportunity to thank you for all the work you did on the Valentine's retreat."

"You're welcome. I wish I could have done more. I got a little sidelined."

"I heard. That's one of the reasons why I'm calling."

"One of?" A part of her wished she was calling on Garrett's behalf because if he asked her to give him a second chance again, she might be tempted to say yes.

"I'm calling for several reasons. To thank you and to tell you that regardless of how things end up between you and Garrett, if you ever need anything, please don't hesitate to call me. I know you have Dylan's number, but I wanted you to have mine. I know how difficult it is living away from family."

"Thank you. That's very sweet of you." Delta sniffled. "I wish things had been different."

"Maybe sometime down the road you two can try again."

"Maybe." Delta choked back a sob.

"Before I almost forget, we have a full crew coming in tonight around midnight to help us set up for Valentine's Day tomorrow. I know it's a late hour, but I wondered if you'd want to stop in and see what all your hard work looks like. Unless you want to come over now and see half of it. At midnight, you'll actually get to sample some of the food."

"Um." Delta chewed on her bottom lip. She was curious to see if her ideas looked as beautiful in person as they had on paper. And maybe she would run into Garrett and they could talk again. "I'd like that. I'll see you at midnight."

"Great, I'll see you then."

Delta dried her eyes and hopped off the couch. Midnight was only six hours away and she needed to de-snot and de-puff herself by then.

* * *

Delta pulled in front of the Silver Bells Lodge at five minutes to twelve. She had expected to see trucks or more cars in the parking lot, but instead she was shrouded in silence. Then again, maybe the crews had parked around back closer to the kitchen. It made more sense.

She pushed open the doors and stepped onto a red runner strewn with white rose petals. The two-story entrance glistened in delicate twinkling lights, giving it an ethereal, fairy-tale feeling.

"Hello?" she called out, careful not to wake the guests. Guests she expected to be milling around. It was midnight and this was a couples-only retreat. She figured they would be partying into the early hours of the morning. Where was everyone?

She followed the red runner toward the great room, stopping to admire the floral arrangements she had chosen along the way. She wondered whose idea the runner had been, because it was very romantic and wedding chapel-like.

And that was when she saw them, standing at the end of the runner. Garrett, Kacey and Bryce, each holding a white long-stem rose. Tears sprang to her eyes as she quickly walked toward them. She had never been happier to see anyone in her life. This was what she wanted. They were what she wanted. She'd been a fool for ever denying herself that love.

"Did you do all this?" she asked Garrett.

"I had a little help from, well, quite a few people." He nervously laughed.

"There aren't any crews coming in tonight, are there?"

"Nope." He shook his head. "And Dylan took all the

guests on a midnight snowcat tour, giving us the place to ourselves for a little while. I needed to get your attention somehow."

"You definitely have it."

"We brought you flowers." Kacey handed Delta her rose.

"Thank you, sweetie." She ran the back of her hand over Kacey's cheek. "You look so beautiful in your red dress." She turned to Bryce and accepted his rose. "And you are so handsome, little man."

"Delta?" Kacey began. "Will you ever forgive me for what happened at your house the other day?"

Delta knelt on the floor and pulled the girl into her embrace. "There is nothing to forgive, sweetheart. I know you were scared."

Garrett offered her his hand and helped her stand. "Delta, I love you. The three of us love you. Our lives are happier and fuller with you in them. We'd like to know if—"

"You'll marry us." Bryce squeezed between Kacey and Delta.

"What?" Delta looked to Garrett for confirmation.

"I was supposed to ask that question, but yes, Delta, will you marry us?"

"Please say yes." Kacey clasped her hands in front of her. "It's my birthday next week and having you for my mommy would be the best gift ever."

"How could I possibly say no to an offer like that?" Delta enveloped the girl in a hug. "I would love to be your mommy." She lifted her gaze to Garrett's. "And I would love to be your wife."

* * * * *

SPECIAL EXCERPT FROM

*A K-9 cop must keep his childhood friend alive
when she finds herself in the crosshairs of a
drug-smuggling operation.*

Read on for a sneak preview of
Act of Valor *by Dana Mentink,*
the next exciting installment in the
True Blue K-9 Unit *miniseries, available in May 2019*
from Love Inspired Suspense.

Officer Zach Jameson surveyed the throng of people
congregated around the ticket counter at LaGuardia
Airport. Most ignored Zach and K-9 partner, Eddie,
and that suited him just fine. Two months earlier he
would have greeted people with a smile, or at least a
polite nod while he and Eddie did their work of scanning
for potential drug smugglers. These days he struggled
to keep his mind on his duty while the ever-present
darkness nibbled at the edges of his soul.

Eddie plopped himself on Zach's boot. He stroked
the dog's ears, trying to clear away the fog that had
descended the moment he heard of his brother's death.

Zach hadn't had so much as a whiff of suspicion that
his brother was in danger. His brain knew he should talk
to somebody, somebody like Violet Griffin, his friend
from childhood who'd reached out so many times, but
his heart would not let him pass through the dark curtain.

"Just get to work," he muttered to himself as his phone rang. He checked the number.

Violet.

He considered ignoring it, but Violet didn't ever call unless she needed help, and she rarely needed anyone. Strong enough to run a ticket counter at LaGuardia and have enough energy left over to help out at Griffin's, her family's diner. She could handle belligerent customers in both arenas and bake the best apple pie he'd ever had the privilege to chow down.

It almost made him smile as he accepted the call.

"Someone's after me, Zach."

Panic rippled through their connection. Panic, from a woman who was tough as they came. "Who? Where are you?"

Her breath was shallow as if she was running.

"I'm trying to get to the break room. I can lock myself in, but I don't... I can't..." There was a clatter.

"Violet?" he shouted.

But there was no answer.

Don't miss
Act of Valor *by Dana Mentink,*
available May 2019 wherever
Love Inspired® Suspense *books and ebooks are sold.*

www.LoveInspired.com

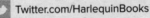

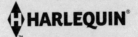

Love Harlequin romance?

DISCOVER.

Be the first to find out about promotions, news and exclusive content!

Facebook.com/HarlequinBooks

Twitter.com/HarlequinBooks

Instagram.com/HarlequinBooks

Pinterest.com/HarlequinBooks

ReaderService.com

EXPLORE.

Sign up for the Harlequin e-newsletter and download a free book from any series at **TryHarlequin.com.**

CONNECT.

Join our Harlequin community to share your thoughts and connect with other romance readers!
Facebook.com/groups/HarlequinConnection

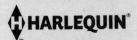

ROMANCE WHEN YOU NEED IT